Shepherds of Our Hearts

canine champions among
pioneer service dogs

Julie Nye

Shepherds of Our Hearts: canine champions among pioneer service dogs

Copyright 2025 by Julie Nye. All rights reserved.

Published by Voelker Books, Hessel, MI. *voelkerbooks.com*

No Large Language Modules (LLMs) or computer-generated art are used in publications from Voelker Books or Fieldstone Hill Press.

Author: Julie Nye

Cover photos are used with permission of the models pictured and identified according to their preferences on pages 405-406

Notice: This book is a work of fiction. Names, characters, businesses, places, events, locales, and incidents are either products of the author's imagination or used in a fictitious manner. Any resemblance to actual persons, living or dead, or actual events is purely coincidental. All information, discussion, and suggestions in this book are intended only for entertainment, and not as advice or professional input. Opinions expressed in this book are those of the author and do not necessarily reflect the official policy or position of the publisher.

ISBN: 978-0-9767762-9-1

Printed in the United States of America
10 9 8 7 6 5 4 3 2 1

Chapter 1

It reminds me, I thought, of the autumn I met Morris.

From this tiny pull-off beside a twisting mountain road, an entire world of fall brilliance unfolded below. From horizon to horizon, flamboyant orange, bright red, and winking gold wove among variegated greens, marching ever downward through rippling hills. Colors jostled for primacy, alternating endless, irregular patterns dotted with shadows from scattered clouds. Against all odds, this October had found me once again wandering the Blue Ridge Mountains.

Memories would not be denied, superimposing a recollection on the scene below: a golden dog prancing through sunlight and color, leaves swirling almost as fast as his tail thrashed. Morris learned a nearly perfect, life-changing partnership right there on those barely visible streets below.

Only the smallest corner of the city could be seen from this towering perch. But I knew it was there. I knew every road, every neighborhood, and many of the people where those foothills smoothed out to homes and farms. Those outskirts. Those last hills and valleys. For so long, they were my home, my work, my life. Was it easier or harder to see it from this vast distance? All these years later, did I feel more regret or more pride? I still wasn't sure

I'd known the emotional peril of stopping, but the overlook drew me like a living force. Sensing the conflicted emotions, A German Shepherd pressed his graying muzzle against my leg. I rested my hand on his silky head. "You don't understand," I told him. "But your great-grandma was born down there."

He wriggled against me with a tongue-out grin. As long as I wasn't distressed, he didn't care about landscape details.

Except I was distressed–and I wasn't–in ways hard to define. Long I stared, transfixed by the sight, wondering how many years had passed since the view brought more joy than bittersweet memory. Was that the emotional wrench that made me think of Morris? When he graduated, he was half of the most remarkable service dog team I'd ever yet been involved with training. That's something you never unsee and the Autumn of Morris had created its own emotional pinnacle. I'd been thrilled enough to *feel* blood rushing through my veins. I'd been old enough to understand the potential, but not experienced enough to see the overview. Young enough still to feel undiluted achievement, but too young to understand where success would lead. Standing now among the silently watching mountains, I yearned for the era when these glorious hues were harbingers of pure hope.

When I first encountered Morris, I was a newcomer in the world of service dogs–though *I* certainly didn't think so. With the ultimate confidence of a 20-something, I was certain I had the world by its non-canine tail. My boss, Nori, knew better and seemed to have telepathic radar for hints I might be in over my head. But I had nothing but confidence when I answered the phone that day. In fact, it sounded promising to an unusual degree.

This might be a real one, I thought, settling back in the desk chair with a 1980s desktop phone receiver lodged at my shoulder. Successful first inquiries about service dogs were less common than an outsider might think. Of every 10 calls, probably only one or two made it to the interview stage.

What was the first signal for that elusive "real" call? Hard to pinpoint, the cues grew from intangibles. It might have been the slight hesitation built into questions. Hesitation born of many disappointments. Hesitation born of fear to hope. Hesitation while a determined human spirit picks its way around a dozen mental roadblocks. Whatever the exact source of the scarcely definable essence, I'd started interpreting cautious deliberation as a promising signpost.

"Is it," the faint female voice asked, interspersed with long pauses, "is it…. possible… to train a dog to bring a telephone to a person?"

Unthinkable as it might be in current society, a whole world existed prior to smart phones, and yes, even before most un-smart cell phones. When the Americans with Disabilities Act first passed congress in 1990, cellular phones were mostly still tethered to car consoles. Most of our clients couldn't afford them anyway. When the average human referred to a portable phone, that meant a cordless handset that could be carried around the house by a human–or a dog.

"Yes, we can." My enthusiasm was genuine. I loved specific questions. They held so much information. It wasn't just that the question itself existed, but that it had made it through the thinking process into the action of a phone call.

"You can?" A touch of incredulity now. "Are you sure?"

"Very sure." For this question, my almost-overconfidence was justified. "It takes work, not only from us, but from you. But it's very doable." I began jotting notes in the ever-present potential client notebook. *Sounds elderly? Weak voice. Strong interest in phone retrieval.*

"Well." The lady paused. "That's surely good news." Longer pause. Rather than interject questions at this critical point, I'd learned to wait.

"How would I...." The voice trailed off again. "Rather, how would a person totally new to dogs learn more?"

"Let's start with where you're located." My fingers and pen hovered over the notebook. "We have to be able to get to you, or you to us, since we have to train you, also. We'd need to spend some time talking first to figure out exactly what needs to happen."

"I am in southern Alabama," the voice said slowly. "But I'm inquiring on behalf of my sister."

My pen stopped halfway through the state abbreviation. "Has your sister asked you to call?" Not much halted our screening process faster than learning a relative, rather than the actual client, was driving the discovery process.

"No," she said. "I wish to do some research before perhaps raising false hopes. All I'm looking for today is a general idea of cost and procedure, including whether this is a good idea for a lady already past 70 years old."

I leaned forward in my chair again, rested my head on my

hand, and began my thinking fidget: bopping myself in the mouth with the pen. I barely knew I did it. Nori, our training director and my boss, was far more observant. Spotting the gesture from across the room, she approached, made the classic open-palmed shrug and pointed to herself—always quick to wonder if I needed rescuing. I shook my head and focused back on the caller.

Be very careful, very precise, I reminded myself. I'd quickly learned how often people in such situations heard what they wanted to hear, rather than what you actually say. Use her own words back as much as you can. I was repeating my own training back to myself.

"The costs are a little high." I referenced our average figure. "Veterinary care is a big piece of that. Equipment has to be purchased. And the dog requires many, many hours of training." I, too, left frequent pauses, waiting for an objection to surface. None did. "But thanks to our donors and sponsors, cost isn't as hard as the procedure. The first step is to make sure everybody is thinking about the same goals and how to make them happen. If we all agree, and if the client decides to go ahead, then we start looking for a suitable dog, screening it for good health, and teaching it how to work. That takes several months. Once the dog knows his job, we have to train the person who's going to use the dog. That part usually takes longer than training the dog."

"Where does the training happen?" The voice sounded fainter to me. Tired. Maybe more overwhelmed than tired. "Here or there?"

"Usually both," I answered. "Your sister would probably have to be able and willing to make at least two trips here, the second one lasting at least a couple of weeks."

Silence.

"Ma'am?" This was a pivotal point, and I needed clarity.

"Yes, of course." The voice came back. "I understand.
That may present certain.... challenges. My sister has
need, however, of greater independence and mobility. I
will need to do some thinking before I discuss this with
her."

"Is there any other question I can answer now? Or would
you like for me to call you back in a few days when
you've had a chance to make a list of questions?"

"No. No, thank you." The formal voice was still faint, but
more decisive now. "It's better if I do the calling. Thank
you very much for your time."

This was a pointedly unsatisfactory ending to a promising
beginning. I made the best notes I could in the log book
about date, time, and details. Then it was time to finish
working my canine trainees. I considered it unlikely we'd
hear from her again. The majority of calls, whether with
promising beginnings or not, went nowhere.

But the next time we heard from southern Alabama, all
hesitancy and reserve had vanished. Approximately nine
syllables confirmed this was the sister, and she was all
about getting herself a service dog. Millie Tyler bounced
into our lives with the ebullience she must have shown
fifty years earlier as a southern debutante. Everything in
Ms. Millie's life exuded cheer, energy, and refusal to
accept limitations. After a lifetime of activity and
independence, Ms. Millie had lost her husband in the
same car crash that robbed her of both her legs above the
knee. Losing a quarter or so of your body weight off the
lower end can cause strange balance issues and scary

consequences. Repeated falls had landed her in the hospital several times. The most recent resulted in an overnight stint lying unattended on the floor.

I wondered aloud at the lack of help from her family. About potential costs. About what might be most practical. Very often, potential clients are better off with an easier, less expensive way to meet their needs than a dog who requires enormous amounts of attention, care, and supplies. Many clients started out clueless about how much plain old work is involved in using a service dog.

"Help is not the issue, darling," she gushed over the phone. "I have plenty of people available to help. The problem is that I do not want their help. I want to be able to do things on my own. Your program motto does still have that line about "increasing independence," does it not?"

Nobody could argue that. But not until the full battery of staff and family descended on the training center did I realize how skillfully Ms. Millie had left her daughter out of the discussion. A few days later approximately 30 feet of gleaming limousine slid up to our front door and began discharging people and equipment. Nori strode away from her class in the next room, glared out the window, then gave me a baleful side-eye. "What have you done?" she demanded. "What can that woman possibly want done that she can't hire?"

That was, indeed, the exact question I was frantically scribbling at the top of my interview list, right after confirming name and address.

"Didn't you tell me not to assume?" I threw my own challenge back at Nori, and she stalked away. I was out of time. The lobby filled with people. I had trouble sorting out family from staff, and various folks scurried in different directions with wheelchair, packs, notebooks, and bags. I relocated this circus as quickly as possible from the lobby to the suddenly-far-too-small conference room. Ms. Millie's daughter, Sophia, seized both agenda and control. Regardless of the question, she answered before her mother could make a sound. Sophia bulldozed over everyone, expounding on expectations she'd have for the program, me, the dog, the process. I was debating a fast stop to the entire interview when I noticed that, while Sophia's eyes bored into mine, Ms. Millie was surreptitiously checking her watch. A faint smile crossed the older lady's face when her daughter's pager cut through the voices.

Sophia consulted the screen and glanced around the room. "Is there a phone in here?"

Rearranging a few papers in front of me, I slid my chair ever so slightly left–between Sophia's gaze and the phone now sitting on the floor to create space. "Sorry," I said, "You're welcome to use the one in the lobby."

A huge martyr's sigh. Sophia exited, apparently bound for the privacy of the limousine rather than the non-privacy of the open lobby. The door had hardly shut behind her when Ms. Millie's voice turned businesslike. "Excuse us, please." She coolly met the gazes of her remaining assistants. They hesitated. "Immediately!" The lady's eyes now glinted steel, clarifying the origins of her daughter's command presence. "I wish to speak to Julie alone."

The response was swift. And the flow of real information began. "You are undoubtedly wondering why I would ever need a dog to do tasks." Ms. Millie's eyes were now every bit as intense as her daughter's had been. The sweet, aging belle was gone, replaced with an agile maneuvering force.

"Well, yes." I answered with considerable discomfort. This was tricky territory.

"How much do you know about elder law?" Ms. Millie ruffled through papers, apparently looking for something.

"Hardly anything," I said. I was not yet 30. My parents still in their 50s.

"That's an oversight you may wish to correct, considering your line of work." Ms. Millie held out a sheaf of papers. "Here, take these and put these somewhere out of sight. You can read through them later."

"As you know, I was not expected to survive after the accident," Ms. Millie continued with hardly a breath. "I love my daughter dearly, but she is stuck somewhere between overprotectiveness, which is probably genuine, and greed for control of my late husband's assets, which is equally genuine. It would simplify her dilemma if she could have herself declared my guardian, rather than just my caretaker. I may be physically limited, but there is nothing wrong with my brain, and it will be some time before I am ready to have anyone else making my decisions for me."

"A dog can't make your decisions for you." I didn't quite understand where this was leading, and yes, I was still rather naïve.

"Dear child." Ms. Millie's impatience reared its head. "You can't make phone calls if you can't get to the phone without major risk of falling on your head. You can't be sure of attending critical meetings with doctors or lawyers if you are relying on the person who does not wish you have those private conversations, now, can you?"

"But...." My voice trailed off. "Everyone is entitled to private legal counsel."

A lovely, rather angelic smile took over Ms. Millie's face. "Of course, child. But with a constantly changing equation, why limit your options and have to rely on anyone at all? And why opt for conflict when there are easier, and far more enjoyable, methods? I could also choose to live alone, but how often would I get to see my grandbabies?"

I began to understand and began to think our biggest challenge here would be Sophia. Except it wasn't. I was still learning to appreciate the value of our biggest asset: Nori. Brusque as she might be with us trainers, the chilling logic of an engineer-turned-dog-trainer made quick hash out of troublesome people. Nearly all difficult or technical subjects were child's play for her. In less than an hour, Nori had Sophia painted neatly into a practical corner. A complicated family group was processed, wrapped up, and out the door before the second day's reviews were complete.

The search for a dog didn't last long either. Already far progressed in his training, "Morris" had not yet been assigned. We'd been getting concerned that he'd be too "soft," too sensitive for any of our clients.

Morris had come to us with a royal doggie peerage from one of the finest Labrador kennels in the country. Purchased for an obscene sum by a gentlemen hunter, Morris had flunked out of duck school before his first birthday. He despised birds. He was horrified at the possibility of entering cold ponds or brambles. He did, however, bring his owner a handsome tax deduction and took up residence on Trainee Row at 11 months of age. His name wasn't Morris, of course, but we could barely pronounce his registered name. Some of the terms his owner used simply wouldn't do in public. Besides, he had more than a slight resemblance to the famous orange cat, both in appearance and expression. Morris it was.

At the point of Ms. Millie's appearance on our scene, Morris had become something of a canine hot potato among our staff. In my profoundly novice opinion, the light-footed, soft-mouthed dog was aggravating to work. Let's suppose, for instance, you forgot yourself for a moment during training, and had a passing thought instead about the credit card bill you were struggling to pay. Your frown would make Morris falter and slow, if not sink to the ground in a near faint. Considerable reviving was required, and the lesson would suffer anyway. I loved his beauty, and he was infinitely fun to pet and love. Training was another matter. Soon most of us were carrying around actual fried liver and learning huge lessons about how to extend our patience. Myself, I yearned to flunk him out. I dreaded working him, and I suppose he knew it. Fortunately for Ms. Millie, I was not in charge.

I lagged so far behind Nori in experience that he'd have been the last dog I'd have considered for this scenario. How in the world could she ever insist on a behavior he didn't want to do? But Nori swiftly sized up the older lady's dramatic, cheery voice, the sweeping hand gestures, and the large celebrations of all things positive. She paired up Ms. Millie and Morris without a moment's hesitation, and it turned out to be the proverbial match made in heaven.

In an almost unseemly short amount of time, the Tyler entourage returned to the training center. The first few days of client-dog orientation are exhausting for everyone. Morris had long-since learned to anticipate the signs we planned to ask him to work with yet another new person. His eyes grew more sorrowful, the sighs longer. I promise you, his ears lengthened. On the first day with Ms. Millie, his Eeyore routine lasted until she first praised him for a correct sit. Morris perked his ears to the elaborate oration, ran out his tongue, and fixed his golden eyes on the lady in the wheelchair. His tail started wagging and didn't stop for the rest of the week.

Try as we might—even via Nori's 1,001 tried and proven techniques—we could not induce Ms. Millie to be brisk and concise with her commands. The word "fetch" seemed to be about as easy for this genteel lady as shrieking profanities on a public sidewalk. She'd fumble her wallet or book to the floor for practice, clasp her hands, and exclaim, "Morris! Would you please get that for me?"

Of course, his training was advanced enough by now that, fortunately for all concerned, he hardly needed a command. Anything that fell called for an automatic retrieve. He would put the item back in her lap; she would expound with approximately 300 syllables explaining how wonderful he was.

Very few dogs who dragged fallen skiers out of avalanches ever heard the level of praise Morris received over every recovered article. Just during the first day, the golden dog's entire posture expanded by about an inch in every direction. Ms. Millie never stopped smiling. And rarely stopped talking. The two were instantly inseparable. They learned about each other and developed their own rhythm. We learned to shut up.

Yet the greatest breakthrough was still to come... the mighty advent of wheelchair pulling. Electric wheelchairs were not common in those days. Massive expense aside, most were designed for those with extremely limited motion. Where regular, or "manual" chairs were concerned, I hadn't yet come close to understanding the myriad of dilemmas of matching clients to equipment and position. Harness, brace, leash, and medical protocol all played roles. Enormous demands could be made on the otherwise very limited strength of wheelchair occupants.

On the up side, the typically lightweight wheelchairs our clients used weighed a fraction of the bulky, heavier ones we used in training, so that helped. Eventually, the day does come when a relentless physical therapist approves the process. Getting that far with Ms. Millie wore us all to a frazzle.

But then the joy! Several days of practice helped her realize that her physical immobility was dropping away. Graduation hovered close on the day we first took the training team to a large mall. Vast, gleaming expanses loomed ahead. But acres of polished floor weren't half the size of the gleam in Ms. Millie's eye.

Without even looking down–I think she was riveted on the "Big Sale" sign at the far end of the building–she grasped Morris's harness and chirped, "Morris!! Let's go *shopping*!" He pranced away. And that was the end of life as Sophia knew it.

When I caught up with her somewhere near the entrance to the Belk's anchor store, Ms. Millie was laughing out loud. "I can go faster than anyone else," she exclaimed. "Morris, you are wonderful!"

He knew it. I watched him carefully checking his eight-o'clock as the two of them took off into the store. I relaxed. He was aware of his job and adjusting to the details, not just tearing off with blind exuberance, as some young retrievers were prone to do.

Two hours later, a sweaty and traumatized daughter, a medium-tired dog, and a thoroughly blissful client faced me in a semi-circle. Morris peered up at me through the mass of shopping bags hanging from the wheelchair. *I've got this,* his eyes told me.

I know, I did my best to answer.

Three days later, Nori and I stood quietly with several other trainers, watching Ms. Millie and Morris maneuver adeptly through the heavy downtown traffic and disappear into a restaurant. An independent obedience trial judge busily scribbled on his notepad while he tried to keep up. This was what we lived for. This was food for the soul, and validation of all we'd sworn to do. Nobody wanted to ruin the moment by talking about it. We just watched.

One of the most common questions we all fielded: "How can you ever give up the dogs you train?" No trainer I know has ever found a way to express fully the satisfaction of such a success. After endless hours of labor, frustration, study, repetition, and setbacks, you see a dog restore huge portions of a life. All the varied factors merge in a chorus of functional harmony that seizes your very core. To we who stand quietly watching, reveling… the question is not "how could you give him up," but "how could you not?"

Ms. Millie and Morris departed for the grandchildren and garden parties of southern Alabama. Barely a week passed when an imperious message assaulted our voicemail. "This is an impossible situation!" Sophia's voice made the cheap machine buzz with overload. "Momma will not stay home. She will not keep me posted on what she is doing. The dog refuses to listen to me in any circumstance at all. Matters are out of control. You must call me at once."

"You mean they're out of your control," I muttered, jotting the message down on Nori's list. Sometimes it was terribly cool not to be the boss. "I think matters are exactly under control."

Morris gave Ms. Millie her life back. They cruised the streets, called on their friends, did as they pleased, and no one ever did have much success in telling her how to spend her final years. The exuberant southern belle and the golden dog gracefully grew old together. It was sad, yet appropriate, to see their excursions shorten by mutual agreement. Their annual re-certifications had to be moved to Alabama when Morris, especially, was no longer strong enough to travel. Our program team and his veterinarian watched him with the most careful scrutiny possible. Our great collective fear was how–or if–we could find a successor for Morris. Or how our beloved Ms. Millie could possibly cope without him. He couldn't tour the mall anymore, but neither could she. He could still retrieve the items she needed. He could still help her balance. And he could still sleep beside her and summon help with his definitive bark.

As with so many life events we obsess about dreading, it

never happened. We had it backwards. Ms. Millie
departed from us first, abruptly, sadly, and without
warning. Morris waited only three days before following.
He died in his sleep, curled up on her side of the bed, his
head where hers had so long rested. I don't believe there
was anything in particular wrong with him. But wherever
she had gone, he planned to be there too. Decades later, I
still think of them any time I see bright sunshine hit a
golden dog in a certain way. Wherever they are, I feel
very sure they are together, and still on the move.

Chapter 2

'Any fool can know. The point is to understand.'
—Albert Einstein

The dog was doing a great job, but a core problem still loomed. I lay sprawled on the carpet that warm spring evening watching Ben, an enthusiastic Golden Retriever, assist our client in moving from her large electric wheelchair to the sofa. All training between this upcoming graduate and his determined owner was going very well. But we still had a problem.

I scowled fiercely at that wheelchair, giving the woman-dog team at the sofa a few extra moments to enjoy their success. Behind me, a warm breeze swirled through the patio screen door, heavy with the perfume of South Carolina spring honeysuckle. The setting was calm, quiet, idyllic. The client-dog team worked flawlessly, which meant the pertinent problem was my own to solve. To me, that spring breeze meant one thing: a southern summer loomed ahead with an ocean of blistering asphalt between this lady's home and the bus stop she used to get to work. We had to get Ben from one place to the other without injuring his feet on hot pavement—yet hopefully without compelling his handler to rely on human help. Ben was somewhere around my 30th trainee, and a full appreciation of the challenges was much better developed in my mind.

I rolled over to face the happy team more directly. "Send him back to get your purse," I prompted.

Ben's owner, Joyce, a recent quadriplegic from a boating accident, pointed him back to the chair. "Ben, fetch my purse!"

The dog sprang to work on the task, which had been built from several different commands. It needed variation, depending on whether Joyce was in the chair or out of it, but Ben had already shown us he understood his objective either way. No trainer alive could deny the pure pleasure of his fluency. The dog's fringed hair blew in the breeze while he positioned himself carefully. Pulling two tug straps in different directions, he loosened the purse from its secure latch. Then he shifted his grip to the bag itself, at the same time stepping up to put his feet higher on the back of the chair. Only with the added height would the purse swung free for delivery.

I watched while he worked. Since I was still lying on the floor, I was now looking almost straight up at him. All 60 wagging pounds focused on his job. Soft wind still pushed Ben's ears and ruff in several directions, spreading the reddish-gold wisps into the glow from the setting sun. His tongue lolled out with pure enjoyment in his work. It was all good. Very good. Except for that one little thing that was not, in fact, either very little or very good. How were we going to get this team to and from work?

Joyce had severely limited dexterity and very little finger grip. Getting protective dog boots on and off, even once, let alone multiple times per day, was beyond challenging, nearly impossible. What Ben really needed was a set of Sparing Single-Pull footgear. Unfortunately, they hadn't been created yet and their availability was roughly a decade in the future. For the non-involved, it might seem a simple matter to have someone else put boots on the dog. Maybe. We might have to. But we desperately wanted Joyce to have full schedule reliability and flexibility on her own. Her goal was to return to her regular job in computer tech. To make that happen, Joyce needed the ability to come and go without relying on anyone else. Her type of work and irregular hours would not fall neatly into a pattern that blended well with someone else's. She might take any of a dozen buses on different schedules. There had to be a way. I knew it and I didn't know it until perhaps the wind itself gave the solution. Watching Ben's hair waving in the breeze made me remember a long-ago dog sporting the same ripple: a big, fluffy, black German Shepherd from my childhood "driving" a jeep along the beaches of Lake Huron.

These days, YouTube is rife with video of driving dogs. The next dog/vehicle commercial is usually not far away. But in 1968 you had to do your practical jokes live. That long-ago dog, Bear, adored riding. Any vehicle, any time, any behavior gladly offered for a cruise. Several prank-loving family members had taught him to balance in the driver's seat of an ancient, stripped-down jeep while the human facilitator lay on the floor, head out the door-less side, maneuvering by who knows what combo of contortions. I'd been too young to participate, but I remembered how responses from by passers and tourists rarely failed to reinforce the human clowns. Bear whizzed about, balancing front paws on the steering wheel, leaning into the turns, and sporting girl-watcher shades to protect his eyes. He was incredibly athletic, but more to the point, he did this nonsense with sheer joy because he loved the ride.

Would Ben enjoy it? Could he do it?

He could and he would.

Even as I lay on the floor that night, watching this light-footed, cooperative dog, I knew it could work, but only if Ben agreed. I sat up, thought hard, and began inspecting the enormous battery pack on the rear of the electric chair. Was it big enough? Strong enough? Safe enough? It took us a couple of weeks of fiddling, and not a small amount of extra training for an emergency–meaning a crash stop, a fall, or anything else we could think of. In the end, Ben and Joyce's routine was one of great fluency. Their often-superimposed heads rolling into the bus stop were true traffic stoppers. Ben sat rigidly upright with his paws braced on the seatback right beside Joyce's shoulders–yes, ears flapping in the wind. He adored the ride; this was his favorite part of any day. My biggest concern had been that he might get hung up if he fell. Joyce lacked the dexterity to free him. So Ben's leash had to come off for the ride, and we replaced the buckles on Ben's vest with Velcro closures that would yield to such pressure. But over almost three years, he never fell once. Never so much as scraped a toenail. They would glide swiftly into the bus station with easy aplomb. Ben leapt easily to the ground, spun like a cutting horse, and put his feet up on the chair, sticking his head back into the leash Joyce held out. Onto the bus and off to work without help from another living soul. Back home again the same way, totally self-powered, subject to no one else's schedule.

The graduate team's bus-stop solution made the TV news. Early on, an entranced reporter took their routine to the entire region, bringing Joyce scores of letters and enough donations to see her and Ben through many months of expenses. Eventually Joyce was able to purchase her own vehicle with an appropriate lift and hand controls, and the bus stop became a thing of the past.

The entire episode still stands out to me as one of those challenges for which there should have been better answers. In later years, better technology and better equipment usually did give better options. Yet sometimes even today, many people with disabilities still face circumstances with no truly good answers. In 1989, I was only beginning to understand such limitations, only beginning to learn about the complexities people with disabilities face every day. I was learning to see how often they worked with what they had, not with what they should have had or wished they had. All too often what they had was a society who mostly just ignored them, resulting in a crummy set of options. So if I was going to train dogs to assist, I also was going to have to learn to work with the least crummy, most effective option.

As the stream of client-dog teams increased, the Ben/Joyce scenario became a mental talisman for me. During sleepless midnight moments, I often took it out, analyzed, and relived the joy of that final fix. I used it to remind myself that very few solutions or ideas were truly new. Most functions that humans do with dogs have been in place for centuries, whether to find food, earn a living, guard resources, or–as with Bear–just for fun. In moments of job stress, I found it soothing to re-focus my thoughts by knowing an answer was almost surely already present. I didn't have to invent it. I just had to find it.

Years passed before I recognized Joyce and Ben as my first tiny lesson about paying attention to dog behavior and capability outside of command/response training. To think about what dogs do naturally, about what they enjoy, and about what motivates them with only minimum training. No matter that uncountable humans had known such principles for thousands of years; I was very young and just starting to gain perspective. At the immediate level, I understood what had happened, yet hadn't a clue I'd put my finger on the pulse of our school's future. The ultimate key to one woman's full independence grew from two big-hearted dogs' enthusiasm for riding. We'd built a solution from *outside* the normal list of options and from *inside* a dog's own personality. It seemed so simple then—and it was—but I couldn't know I'd started a learning curve that would last a lifetime.

Chapter 3

"If I can stop one heart from breaking, I shall not live in vain."
—*Emily Dickinson*

"I'm looking at the ramp from hell." The flat voice coming through the phone was barely audible over the mayhem of background noise. Shouts, laughter, bangs, whistles, and unidentifiable rattles made the microphone squeal.

"Where are you?" I knew I was talking to Trent, the youngest of my fellow trainers, but that was all I could be sure of.

"I'm at the Colliers School."

Aha. Now I knew. He was checking out the logistics for the dog we were training for a student there. "Okay....at least I think okay. What's the problem?"

"No kid can do this ramp, Julie. Probably no dog can do this ramp."

"But it's supposed to be ADA accessible. How bad can it be? Do you have a camera with you?" We were all still trying to figure out both details and implications of the new Americans with Disabilities Act, passed not long before.

"It might be ADA compliant. I don't have the numbers memorized and can't remember if they allow ramps to be a half mile long. Of course I have the camera; don't be an idiot. Maybe we can train her a small horse instead."

Our first-ever digital camera–a chunky box about eight inches square–had set us back over $1,000. But hey, we were trainers of the new 90s! That day we were quite glad we had it. Some hours later, we stood in a forlorn group around the computer monitor, gazing at the ramp. The long, narrow specter rose from the pavement at an impossible distance from the elevated entry door. It ran steeply up for what really did look like Trent's suggested half a mile. Then it made a sharp turn about eight feet before the heavy security door.

"So I hate to ask stupid questions." Trent was consulting his notes. "But how does she get up it now?" Our ninth-grade client definitely lacked the biceps to wrestle a manual chair up this monstrosity. So did probably any of us young, healthy trainers.

"She says she has friends help her," Barb was paging through interview notes. "And I do recall that she used the term in plural."

"No big mystery about that," I said. "The ramp alone is ridiculous. But that turn! How could she ever navigate that turn? That thing cannot possibly be ADA compliant"

"I measured," Trent said. "It's 87 feet, bottom to top, including the turn. And no it can't be compliant. Forget the length. The slope is twice anything you'd find at a mall."

"Can we make them replace it?" Barb dropped into a chair, looking worn out. She'd spent most of the day doing field trips with the dog who was supposed to perform at this school.

"What, replace it in this decade or the next one?" Nori spoke for the first time. She leaned on the wall near the computer monitor, arms folded, staring at the screen with her usual intensity. "Forget it. We promised that girl a dog for this year. Even if the school could be forced to replace the ramp, it won't happen by August. Let's get cracking on a solution."

We didn't normally stay so adamant about deadlines. But this was an unusual case. More than a year ago, the guidance counselor from a local middle school called us. She had "a situation," she explained. A struggling young student with spina bifida, a bright academic future, dismal home support, and red flags starting to show up in her school setting. The student talked endlessly about wanting a service dog. She desperately needed the help, desperately needed the self-reliance and focus such a project could give. Was there any way we could help her?

I turned this over to Nori within the first three minutes of the call. Placements with teenage clients could be extremely tricky. Placements with kids who have unsupportive parents are solidly impossible. This situation called for greater experience than mine.

A long series of tribunals ensued. Nori was magnificent, both with difficult family members and with worried, trodden-on kids. It took a while, but a deal was struck. The young student, Asheton, agreed to her part: no more missed school days, no more cut classes, no more detentions. Her small allowance would be mostly saved for dog food and expenses. And we needed a letter from each of her teachers by the end of this semester telling us whether they thought she could handle the discipline of training.

Asheton's parents also had their assignments. Weekly
meetings for the rest of the school year with a
professional family therapist selected by the school
guidance counselor. Agreement to the terms imposed on
Asheton. A solid promise that someone would assist
Asheton to the bus stop each school day, without fail, for
the rest of the semester.

I scanned the list of conditions, shook my head, and
walked away. Nori adored working with troubled kids,
but this was a fantasy. I couldn't imagine the mental
gymnastics just to get them all to agree to try. Actually
doing it? Not a happening thing, I thought.

How wrong I was. Asheton's grades leapt up. Her
attendance and attitude leveled off. The teachers smiled.
The parents attended therapy. We all eyed Nori with
suspicion. I heard chit-chat in the break room about
frisking her for voodoo paraphernalia.

At the end of the first semester of Asheton's eighth grade
year, we threw a Christmas party for her and started
looking for her dog. A local SERTOMA club gladly
volunteered to cover the expenses. We were on a
mission. Exactly how we missed the ramp, nobody was
sure. We'd come in from the front visitors' entrance, the
one with a long stretch of steps. At that point, we didn't
even realize our own lack of experience. The Americans
with Disabilities Act wasn't even two years old. It was an
era that bred misunderstandings, misconceptions, and
surprises. Lots and lots of surprises.

But we found Asheton a dog. Fortunately, we'd chosen
one at the top of the possible size range. We figured
she'd need a lot of tough, physical help. Boy-howdy, we
had that part right. We found Casey in a shelter during

the holidays. I'd never met a sweeter dog, or one more eager to please or anxious to learn what we wanted. During spring break of the second semester, we introduced him to Asheton, who hugged him for half an hour and left him at least six new toys. Casey grinned blissfully. By the end of the school year, they were training together. By the end of June, we saw the ramp.

The ramp from hell didn't turn out to be insurmountable. Almost, but not quite. We had a special harness made for Casey that allowed him to pull not only forward, but to set his weight backwards against pressure. In some circumstances, dogs can exert far more oomph moving backward than forward–often easily demonstrated with a game of tug. Carol, as our smallest trainer, became the test pilot. We walked, drove, rode, and tugged up and down that ramp hundreds of times. School officials lurked, apologized, and claimed budget trouble prevented them from getting better ramps. We didn't know if it was true. We just knew what we had to work with and it wasn't very good. No doubt an electric chair would have been a far better option. But neither Asheton's family nor any state waivers for which she qualified had that many dollars.

Ten days before school opened, a determined young teen proved her case to a dozen observers. We'd had the brakes on her chair refitted and the handle extended. Asheton showed great skill, flipping brakes on and off at the exact right moments. With her hands on the wheels of the chair, and Casey expertly yanking backwards up the ramp (an extra tug strap in his mouth to provide balance), they reached the turn at the top in record time. Casey backed into the far corner. Asheton slid the catch on the new harness from one side of a rigid tab to the other.

Casey reversed directions, and they entered the door
triumphantly forward.

The Asheton/Casey team passed certification with flying
colors; it was an omen of things to come. Ninth grade
was a banner year. She had perfect attendance and made
the dean's list. She started college prep courses. Casey
did his job with flair, snoozing away the rest of the days
beside her chair. We praised, bragged, marveled. We
used them for demonstrations to other clients and to
sponsors. Casey remained in perfect physical condition,
always well groomed, always willing. It would have been
hard to ask for a better ending to what I had judged a
thoroughly impossible situation.

"Well," I told myself, "That's why you're not in charge."

Another summer arrived. Asheton would change schools
in the fall. No more horrible ramps. The academic course
ahead included several more college prep classes. The
future looked bright. But midway through the stifling
heat of summer, the original dragon of home trouble once
again reared its ugly head.

We had no warning at all. Merely one phone call from
Asheton's mother. One brief message: "Come and get
this dog or we are taking him to the pound." No response
to return calls. Of course, two of us rushed across town
immediately, walking into the chaos of a family at each
other's throats. We never learned the exact events, but as
best we could piece it together, all of them had left home,
in different directions, for more than a week because of
building tension between the parents. Asheton was not
allowed to take Casey. They left him home with a dog
sitter in charge. It would seem the dog sitter had never–or
rarely–shown up. Over time, with growing desperation

for food and anxiety at abandonment, Casey had done a whole lot of damage to the home's interior.

The mother was hysterical, and the father was absent. Several miscellaneous aunts and neighbors rushed around the house trying to clean up torn furniture, shredded drywall, and unidentifiable debris. Asheton was in her room, forbidden to come out. In the gaps of the mother's tirade, I could hear her crying and calling out both to me and to Casey. We were ordered to leave, and had no choice but to obey. Asheton's cries turned to screams as the mother slammed the door behind us. We loaded up Casey and left, feeling sure, in our great naiveté, that matters would calm in a day or two and we would have a chance for damage control. It's probably just as well we didn't know we'd never see Asheton again. That Asheton would never be allowed to see Casey again.

When the client is 15, and the parent is hurling ultimatums, you have no options. We managed to get Asheton's mom to sign a release–she scrawled her name without a glance at the text. She did not care. She just wanted the dog gone, and expressly forbid us to contact her daughter again. I tried anyway. Nori tried. We contacted the guidance counselor from the previous school. We contacted the family therapist. We wrote, called, and tried to visit. And we earned ourselves a formal restraining order forbidding contact with any of them, along with a directive to cease discussing the family with school officials. After six weeks of trying to find a solution, it was over. We finally acknowledged failure one afternoon at a very gloomy staff meeting. And we all agreed it was unacceptable for Casey to sit in the kennel any longer, depressed and jobless. I'd tried taking him home with me for babying and attitude adjustment, but it wasn't working. He was not eating well and often gave us concerts of low moaning howls, no matter if in the kennel or at home.

Casey was a healthy three-year-old service dog with hundreds of hours of training sponsored by thousands of donated dollars. The only answer was to pair him with another client. Nothing else would be fair to the dog or fair to his sponsors. Casey was a sad and thoughtful boy for all his weeks of brush-up work and pairing with a new client. He was assigned to a young man, James, who had a lifelong mobility impairment and used both chair and crutches. Only very gradually did Casey's spirits pick up when he left the kennel setting and went to stay with his new person at a hotel for extended training. For many months, he would remain anxious about any separation, but his confidence slowly returned. We'd been careful to choose a client who seldom had to be away from his dog.

With true Labrador earnestness, Casey did every task exactly as asked, with his best effort, and a compliant wave of his tail. The new team grew comfortable together, passing their certification test with a minimum of stress. Arrangements were made for them to travel back to James' home on the west coast. Casey had a trainer assigned for in-home follow-up, but in this situation, it wouldn't be me, and my final goodbye to Casey loomed. On the day of departure, I drove the pair to the airport and escorted them to their gate.

Such moments are both the crowning glory and the deepest sorrow of those who produce service dogs. It contains everything you work for and everything you dread all in one gut-ripping moment. This dog who has been a huge, integral, daily part of your life for months or years is a full success, but he is leaving. Permanently. Often, in such cases, you are saying goodbye knowing that, barring disaster, you will never see this beloved creature again. Such was the case that night for me and Casey as we traipsed the long concourse to the correct gate. I could not tear my eyes away from this almost-perfect dog. Despite the disruption of the year before, he was as close to the ideal service dog as we ever hoped to see. Most definitely, he was a rarity that would have been worth trying to clone, if only that had been a more advanced, affordable science.

Casey timed his pace to exact perfection with James' limited stride and crutches. The dog's attention was riveted on this person for whom he was now responsible, ignoring the inevitable calls, whistles, and chirps from well-meaning by-passers. I was incredibly proud of him—and already felt rather teary. Suck it up, I told myself. You can do this. Swallowing the lump in my throat, I tried to do as good of a job as the dog I was watching.

We were almost at the correct gate when I saw the falter. Passing us in the opposite direction was a very young girl, perhaps 12 or 13, struggling with a manual wheelchair. Even as we noticed, an airline steward stepped in to help her. But Casey hesitated. His head turned. He stopped walking for just a moment. Just a stop, not a move. Just long enough for James to notice and wonder why. In a brief moment of confusion, while I stood thunderstruck, James scanned his ticket stub, checking it against the nearest counter. So he didn't see Casey's anguished look, or the shudder that passed from nose to tail of the glossy black body. The dog's gaze followed the wheelchair down the concourse. I heard the whine. Saw the tail droop, then pick back up. He looked up again at James and stilled for a long moment. Then Casey realigned himself to the correct position beside his new friend, and marched steadfastly forward. There was only the briefest last glance back over his shoulder.

I held together. Stayed professional until they boarded. When the jet-way door closed behind them, I stopped fighting the tears. I sank into a nearby window seat and cried my heart out, watching the sleek airliner wheel away into the darkness. I knew Casey would be fine, and the years ahead would prove that true. But on that dismal night, all I could feel was overwhelming grief and the disappointment of bitter failure. All I could see was the hopeful, earnest face of a young lady who had worked so hard and loved so intensely and lost so much. The only words in my heart as the aircraft's flashing lights faded from view were over and over and over, Oh, Asheton. I am so sorry. *So* sorry! I am so very, very sorry.

Chapter 4

"Right now I'm having amnesia and déjà vu at the same time. I think I've forgotten this before." —Steven Wright

Morris taught me small miracles could happen. Casey taught me to about the heartache of failure. But no trainer could survive this job by expecting all graduates to be either extreme. More often, results fell somewhere in between. As my experience grew, I began to understand a third category: distinct doses of very, very humble pie.

"You have an unrealistic view of a dog's capability." I listened silently to the dry professional voice at the other end of the phone. "Maybe of your client's ability too."

I listened politely, as I had to, since I was the novice upstart asking a revered public figure for input. Our idealistic crew of Johnny-come-lately zealots was already cutting way back on the number of times we sought advice from the known training gurus. Too often, youthful zest collided with hard rebuttal from better recognized colleagues. Most of them considered us way off the doggie reservation. Beyond that, it remained an ongoing mystery to me exactly how I'd landed in this position. Certainly I'd never gone looking for any kind of work among dogs.

Somewhere toward the end of graduate school, my entire adventure among service dogs had started with a sociology class assignment: volunteer for a non-profit of our choice. I couldn't locate a group close enough for my first love–horses–so something with dogs was next. Fast forward five years and a sideline hobby had flown past contract work and was rapidly growing into a full-time obsession. When congress passed the Americans with Disabilities Act in 1990, the official sanction was manna from heaven for the early (and perpetually struggling) reality of service dog training.

Guide dog groups were already decades ahead of us and well established. But for non-guides, things were different. Very different. The work of training dogs to work with other physical impairments was as widely varied as the disabilities involved. Our little band of trainers (perhaps certifiably crazy though we were) gloated and grinned at the passing of the ADA. None of us had much interest in training guides, and no doubt, the guide schools had even less interest in us. By their well-developed standards, I felt sure they considered most of us loose cannons. The lure of the new and unconventional consumed our young, admittedly idealistic gang.

Just the challenges of a single disability could move the basics of personal care into stress territory beyond most folks' understanding. Many think about service dogs in terms of picking up a dropped item. A sock lands on the floor, so the dog picks it up. But it's far harder for a dog to pull that sock on or off the human.

It's pretty common to see a service dog help open or close a door. But what about fetching half a dozen items by name, just to get dressed? Or about being the tension on the other end of a gripper to secure a colostomy bag? The daily list of commands can get very long, though the vast majority had to do with grasping, pulling, retrieving, or carrying.

We regularly encountered circumstances new to us and to
dog training. Yet in a fairly short time, our ranks of part-
timers had grown to include a variety of professionals
who combined to create a decent think tank, including
two teachers, two physical therapists, one RN, a police
officer, and a flight attendant. Even though we frequently
ran into complex dilemmas, we were often—maybe even
usually—able to find solutions. Again and again, we found
group enthusiasm carrying us ahead when the
acknowledged experts of our day told us to bug off. I
think it's fair to say nobody had any delusions about the
accuracy of *Lassie* or *RinTinTin* movies, but we
continually looked for the limits of possibility: exactly
how far out there were these limits, anyway? We ignored
the droning voices on the other end of those phone calls
and crashed ahead.

Ah, the blissful ignorance of youth. What we had yet to
learn was that most of the limits were a maximum of six
feet away, right at the other end of the leash. Today I'd
rammed my head hard into such a limitation and had to
explain the disaster to my boss.

"I think I messed up pretty bad," I said to Nori as I sat in
her office, watching a white-chested mixed breed, Jake,
squirm around on his back between us. He thrashed like a
beached gator, delighted to see us both. Me? Not so
much.

"It happens," Nori said thoughtfully. She, too, was
watching Jake. He'd come bouncing in the door, tail
waving madly, whining with excitement. He'd even
required two or three corrections for trying to drag me by
the leash—totally unacceptable in a graduate dog.

I agreed, knowing any of our trainers would see it

quickly. Most often, when we had to bring a graduate in for re-training or replacement, flat-spirited canine depression made a big obstacle. Service dogs were selected for sweet attitudes and eagerness to please. After they built a strong relationship with a client, they were typically not thrilled about returning to being one dog in a kennel lineup. By now we'd established a decent process for easing them through this stage, getting them interested and fixed up–and back out working again–as quickly as possible. But today we should be seeing a dog who really wanted to be with his human, not here with us. Except Jake couldn't have been more thrilled.

Nori's attention stayed on the ecstatic dog. "The list of options is short for why he's so happy," she said. "Bored, lack of bond, or both. So spit it out. What gives?"

I felt a little vindicated as I launched into my story. Barely three months had elapsed since Jake's graduation with a paraplegic. The elation of watching a successful team finish always put us on the top of the world. It was normal to get a call or two afterward with questions. It was also normal for a trainer to need to go out on a few brush-up visits.

Not this time. Jake's human partner, Tom, had called the day before, saying he needed to see a trainer because Jake wasn't doing so well. I pressed for details, but Tom was evasive. "How soon can you come out?" he asked over and over. A quick consultation with Nori, a few changes to the schedule, and I set out the next day on a two-hour trek to see Jake. Arriving at the client's home quickly clarified much.

"He had all Jake's things packed up before I even got to the door," I told Nori now. "Crate folded up. Duffle bag with all his stuff zipped up tight, leash on top."

"He knew he was going to send him back when he called." Nori made it a statement, not a question.

"Yep." Despite everything, I still felt like the guilty one. We didn't have a good term for "buyer's remorse" about service dogs. In our line of work, the term didn't cut it, because we were almost always spending a third party's money. That invariably changed a poor decision from the regular universal kind to something much worse. It also ballooned options for which flavor of guilt you could carry around.

"We wasted serious funding," I admitted. "I haven't had the guts yet to check the training log for a total number of hours."

Nori rubbed the back of her neck. I could feel the tension headache tormenting her, because mine was identical. Training a person to use a dog usually took more hours than training the dog.

"I went through every tactic I could think of, Nori," I confessed. "I redid the entire frigging application right there on the spot. We went over all the reasons, all the potential. His previous agreement. It made no difference at all."

"Let me guess," Nori said dryly. "A corresponding new problem for every solution."

"Pretty much," I said. I went on, mimicking the man's voice. "He barks at cars when I'm trying to sleep. He plays with stuff he's supposed to retrieve. My arm is sore from him pulling the wheelchair. He sheds so much!"

I didn't need to tell Nori that, of course, all this had been discussed in minute detail long before we ever started training Tom with Jake. She knew. In fact, some of those conversations would have been her own.

"No matter what I suggested, he had a reason it wouldn't work. And the more I talked, the more irritated he seemed to get." Eventually I had just stopped. Waited. Tried to think about what else I could do to salvage the situation.

"I finally just told him what he wouldn't tell me," I said. "I know I'm not supposed to do that. But we were wasting time. He was obviously done and had already decided. I just said, "So it's more work than you thought, and less effective than you want, right? This isn't any specific problem, or set of them. I think it's that you just don't want the dog?"

"Which is exactly what you are not supposed to ask." Nori dropped her head on her hand. "You forgot the part about "no leading questions.""

"I wasn't leading anybody anywhere. He wouldn't even look at me." I thought back to watching Tom roll his chair over to the table to pick up an insulated cup of water. He took a long swallow. I'd seen Jake following his movements closely and couldn't help wondering. I stepped toward the dog's water dish, visible beside the kitchen counter. Sure enough. Empty. Whatever else Tom was, he wasn't stupid. He watched me, watched my face, and his own flushed with embarrassment.

"Jake didn't have any water," I recounted the rest of the tale to Nori. "I filled his bowl and he tanked like a camel. He stinks. His nails are too long. And he could not wait to get in the car with me."

"Did you get a release?" Nori asked.

"Yes." I fished the paper out of my bag.

"Yes. He got defensive and pissy when I gave Jake water. I waited because I was too mad to say anything. Finally, he starts in with an explanation. He says, "I know you people said the dogs were a lot of work. But when you're struggling with every task, every day…" and yes, I am quoting "…and you read all these wonderful stories about service dogs." He says, "I did hear what you said, but I still somehow thought it would be just fine. That it wouldn't be as hard as it is.""

I reached down to pet Jake a little before continuing. "Then he starts in telling me about his new girlfriend and how she didn't like dogs. So I really figured that was that."

Nori kept quiet for so long I was hard pressed not to start worrying again. But I'd learned most of this trade from Nori herself, and well before I'd left Jeff's house, I'd had no doubt what she would have told me to do, though she remained unconvinced about the girlfriend.

"I think that might have been just an excuse," she said. "You say he was neglecting the dog." She tapped her pencil thoughtfully on the desk. "I'm not so sure that's it. I think he wasn't using Jake for any work either way. I had him in the training room for barely 15 minutes and if I didn't know better, I'd say he didn't know a basic retrieve. He was as rough as any fresh trainee. I'd bet he hasn't done much actual work since graduation."

"I don't understand why he bothered," I objected. "That's a lot of work–meaning his work–and a lot of sponsor money out the window."

"He's not the first, as you well know," Nori pointed out. "And he won't be the last."

"Tell me about it," I groused.

"But you also know it's the minority," Nori said, shuffling papers on her desk. "You'll never solve all the problems of human nature, so don't tie yourself up in knots trying. I don't think there's anything wrong with the dog, so let's focus on that part and find him a partner who actually wants his help. Screw-ups like this are still way in the minority. Don't ruin the good obsessing about the bad."

Nori stood up and started packing papers into her briefcase. "I have to run over to the middle school for a demo. Could you put him up for me?"

"Sure," I said, gathering up Jake's leash and starting for the door.

"Oh, hey, Julie," Nori said as she headed out. "Did you find the new distributor for those multi-purpose leashes? We are almost out. Get some ordered today, if possible."

I sighed. "Can I use your computer to do that before I leave?" I was still working half time here and full time at my other job. "Last time I did a web search from my office for "multi-function leather leash" and "stainless steel dog collars" I got a special visit from IT and HR. My boss is now randomly checking over my shoulder to see if he should call the cops."

Nori laughed over her shoulder. "Sounds like projection to me. Help yourself."

Putting Jake into an exercise yard, I settled in to find the needed leashes, but had a hard time tearing my thoughts away from Tom. I'd had only a few big failures so far, but this was the first one in which I wasn't sure if it was my fault or not. I was only a few years past my apprenticeship.

I worked through the leash order, but kept counting up how many problems had arisen from all our graduate dogs I could think of, compared to how many problems had come from the clients. "Humph," I muttered. I was totally at sea until I started a little spreadsheet with names and specifics. "Humans are definitely winning this contest."

The idea followed me around for days, and I realized I was becoming gun-shy. We'd had three busted client-dog teams this calendar year. Were we missing obvious cues? Were we failing to do enough education? For several days, I reviewed in my head how we approached first conversations with prospective clients. Were we discussing too much detail? Not telling enough stories? Maybe this episode with Jake would work well as a teaching example? As an interview screening tool? How should we approach this with new clients?

I started writing down the most caution-inducing stories from clients that I could think of. And the ones that caused clients the most work. Mud, mess, dog hair, illness, schedule obligations? How much is too much to tell a prospective client? Maybe I could print a booklet full of specific examples, and make them read and initial each one? Hah, I thought. Nori would probably shoot me first.

Still in brainstorm mode, I sent out a quick email to our entire group, asking everyone to send me a description of their worst "learning moment." Yikes. Results could have shut down our entire client base forever.

From Carol: *I've had three clients since spring whose dogs have thrown up at critical moments. Last one was at a job interview. Does that count?*

From Barb: *So it's bad enough to have a dog have an accident in public. But if a dog ate a washcloth, then the dog takes exactly half of a dump in public and you have to get on the bus to get to the vet's office with a crappy rag hanging out the butt of a super-stressed dog? Protect your sanity; guard your washcloths. I'm typing this for a friend, right? It never happened to me, I swear.*

From Doug: *Tell them about Terri, who kept thinking it was cute to let Casper pick up random objects, even when he hadn't been told. I kept after her. "Don't let him do that." And "it's not okay for him to carry something around unless you told him." And "it's not funny if he grabs random stuff in the store." Okay, last week she goes out for a nice dinner with a possible client her firm is trying to win over. Halfway through dinner, she goes to the restroom. All's okay until she's almost back to the table, when she realizes most of the restaurant has gone silent. Then she sees Casper is carrying a gory trophy from the trash can in the ladies' bathroom. They definitely did not get the client.*

Nori's contribution: *Get an insurance estimate from the people who thought it was wrong to confine Toby to his crate that first week of training. I think the rented violin he ate ran them around $8,000.*

From Trent: *What about a pending psych eval for Levi? A co-worker gave him a ride home one day, but they stopped at a grocery store on the way. Everyone was impressed with BJ retrieving stuff off the shelves, but the co-worker didn't get that Levi was cuing which item with a laser-pointer. Levi decides it's funny to tell the dog, "Hey BJ, go get me some unsalted crackers." The dog does. The co-worker flips. Levi laughed at him so hard the co-worker got offended and has been undercutting him to HR and his boss, claiming aberrant behavior and lack of empathy. He's not sure if he still has a job–jury still out.*

Conversation at the next staff meeting was lively. "Right, you guys," I said. "Thanks a lot, but this is not exactly what I had in mind. I don't want to scare them senseless or convince them of psychosis risk. I'm just trying to figure how we can make them understand the huge amount of work involved in keeping a dog.

"Huh," Trent said in a gruff response. "Take them to see Amy and Bridgette. Anything after that will look better."

I stilled in my chair. "Trent," I said, "Despite yourself, sometimes you are absolutely brilliant."

Trent twisted around and patted himself on the back. "Aww shucks."

But we did just that. Actually, the other way around, coaxing Amy into volunteer involvement for first interviews. As a service dog user, not a trainer, and more in the role of a bystander, she had the luxury of more bluntness than we did. In time, it evolved into something like a good-cop/bad-cop routine. She'd work on scaring them silly with horror stories, and the trainers could focus on proposed solutions and on how much effort each would take. It wasn't foolproof, but it helped.

The value of Amy's particular viewpoint was not

instantly apparent. You had to talk with them for a while. Amy was, for sure, one of the biggest practical turnaround clients we'd ever had. It had started with a classic line during her first phone call: "Can you get me a dog that doesn't shed?" We had learned not to mince words on this topic. The short answer: NO! All dogs shed. If it's not their hair, it's their dander, their crap, their urine, or their vomit. If you want your adaptive equipment to be sterile, we suggest you stick with stainless steel.

But Amy was an interesting case study. I took a demo dog to her home for the first time during an all-day downpour. The perfectly groomed woman radiated distaste as she surveyed the array of paw prints on her glistening kitchen floor. "What am I supposed to do about the mud?"

This was not an auspicious beginning. We'd barely made it in the door, and we'd almost had to swim through the storm to get that far. It was always fun to anticipate a client's excitement over meeting a service dog for the first time, even if it might not be her own service dog. Almost all of them thought this first dog meetup was big fun. Not here. Prospective housekeeping concerns seemed far greater.

"The dogs know how to "wait." I said hastily. "Can you hand me a towel? I'll wipe her off."

"Will I have to do that every time she goes outside?" Amy was not impressed. "Won't that be several times a day? Can't she learn to wipe her feet?"

Stifling a sigh, I suggested we delay the housecleaning agenda and talk about more basic concepts for now. In those first few minutes with Amy, I'd convinced myself it would never work, but she'd proven me wrong. I had underestimated both her dedication and her degree of adaptation. She learned to wipe dog feet with a damp towel. She learned about the best brands of doormats to slurp up excess water. She learned about dry shampoo and good dog brushes. Progress was slow, but steady. Amy received a dog and their relationship became functional. Exactly how much it would grow took a while to learn.

Six months after graduation, it was time to do a follow-up visit. Bracing myself for the normal dissection of hygiene and décor techniques, I took a deep breath and rang the doorbell. After the patter of trotting paws, Bridgette pulled the door lever to let me in. I was glad to see her, otherwise I might have thought I was in the wrong house.

Wasn't this floor white? I thought in amazement. No longer. A uniform coating of red clay was spread throughout the kitchen. Floor. Cupboards. Refrigerator. Walls. Applying a brick-colored chair rail at 32 inches would have been appropriate.

"Hi!" The enthusiastic response came from the hallway. Amy couldn't even wait to get all the way into the room before beginning her recitation of Bridgette's virtues. "Did I tell you we went to the opera last week? I was so afraid she would whine or howl about the music, but she was just perfect!"

Finally, I could actually see the owner of the voice as she wheeled into the kitchen.

"And she got her picture on the staff directory board at

work. My boss says she deserves recognition as much as anyone else who works there."

Much later, when there was enough pause to start a training discussion, I asked how the towels-versus-mud campaign was progressing. The answer came with a completely blank look.

"Towels?" Amy asked? "What for? Oh! You mean because of the mud?" She waved her hand dismissively. "I got tired of towels. Now I just let her in the kitchen and close the door until she's dried off. I park the car in front and when we go out we leave by the front door and stay on the sidewalk."

"Very good. Great," I said. "Do you need any help getting her to go to the bathroom on leash? That might help with the mud. Or, ummm… anything I could do to simplify the drying-off process… or…." My professional trainer monologue ground to a halt. I didn't want to comment on the obvious to this woman who'd always maintained her own version of House Beautiful. What was this dog doing? I wondered? Going out and diving in a six-foot mud hole?

"Not really," Amy responded. "She likes to play outside, so I'd rather do it this way. I couldn't stand to take her wading pool away from her. She enjoys that so much. And of course, this time of year it rains nearly every day. I'd rather just let her dry off in here. She's easier to clean up when she's dry."

There was nothing more for me to say. The dog was functional and safe. The owner was thrilled. Never mind that the amount of mud in the kitchen was something I'd never seen or heard of. It was none of my business. How much more so came home to me about a year later when I approached the same kitchen door. A small, cross-stitched sign now hung on the exterior–a slight variation of a knick-knack I'd seen for sale before: *This house is maintained for the comfort and safety of my dog. If you don't like that, please go away.*

Chapter 5

"Would it save you a lot of time if I just gave up and went mad now?" —Douglas Adams, "The Hitchhiker's Guide to the Galaxy"

"Tag, I can't believe you did that." I leaned wearily against the exterior wall of the church where I worked. The yellow Labrador beside me grinned. He was unrepentant. I'd had to rush him out of a service and the backlash might not be pretty. For quite a while now I'd had the option to bring a trainee to an office job and to services, but this might cook my future options.

Tag was pretty new to the training process. He was young and highly energetic. I'd had concern about how he'd adjust to different, unexpected stimuli around him. Church had seemed like a good plan. I was thinking about music, big instruments, movement, children, and shuffling crowds. I was not thinking about… offering plates. Tag was doing well, holding his down-stay and staying quiet, until he saw a dozen men rush up all the different aisles carrying shiny, curved plates that to an eager young dog looked pretty much like his supper dish. He bounded up with a yowl, landing at the end of his leash and almost right in the lap of an elderly gentleman. My commands for quiet and down were entirely ignored, and I ended up bodily dragging him from the auditorium while on the receiving end of plenty of scathing stares. I didn't know whether to laugh or cry, and the mental conflict wasn't a new feeling.

Despite any amount of head knowledge about our overall

success, I kept feeling an emotional drag that I tried to blame on the Jake and Casey episodes. The two cases happened close together, and both were spectacular failures. Certainly I'd had other less than perfect results, whether from failed dogs, poor judgement, or errors in training. But a nagging sense of overwhelmed disillusionment refused to leave me alone.

I was now eight years deep into something I'd started merely as a hobby. For our adventurous little tribe of trainers, true appreciation was building not just for thrills of success, but for stressors of failure. We'd grown, then grown more. We'd suffered setbacks, regrouped, and surged again. Talented trainers arrived for one set of reasons and left for others. Triumph and heartbreak were both very real. I'd been frustrated and dismissive of trainers who'd given up, but this summer I thought I was beginning to understand.

My dispirited attitude was interfering with work, both the dog job and the non-dog job. I'd been debating with myself for months about merits and consequences of quitting the non-dog job, knowing that either I or the employer had changed too much to suit anyone. But it wasn't that simple, either. Away from that office and into the kennel, the quality of my trainees was slipping, and everybody noticed. I continued to try to tell myself the problem was one accumulated strain from failed placements, but increasing errors and general mayhem seemed to follow me around. Large errors, small mishaps, lapsed judgement.

One day in the stifling heat of late summer, I committed the unpardonable crime of allowing a spooked trainee to get loose in a crowded mall. A 90-pound dog recklessly racing scared in public is any trainer's nightmare. He scared the socks off a dozen people while bolting straight to the quietest place he could see–dead center of the huge, elaborate fountain. He considered the water and spray jets a fine retreat and refused to come out. There was nothing for it but to go in after him, full skirt, high heels and all. By passers gawked. Mall security guards collapsed against walls laughing. Owners of the complex weren't nearly as amused. By the time I got soaked me and now-happy trainee home, Nori had fielded three phone complaints about the incident. The next day I was called on the carpet, but she had a far broader agenda in mind than one wet dog.

"Do you need some personal time off?" Nori was never one for much subtlety. "You look horrible, and every one of your dogs is behind where they should be. Yesterday's clown-fest was a symptom, but hardly the entire issue."

I tried to find an answer, fishing for any available rationale that wouldn't sound more lame than a sullen fifth grader. "I don't think time off is really the answer." I shifted uneasily, realizing that even Tracer, the golden on a down beside my chair, was giving me odd looks. "I may need to make some changes in my other job."

Certainly that was not a new thought, but it had lots of implications. My employer was a large, rigidly conservative church with no tolerance for divided loyalties. My mental fog was not improving anyone's outlook toward me as a favored staffer. That culture and a similar marriage were both rapidly growing more antagonistic about the time I spent training service dogs. I knew there was no way I'd give it up, so the multi-directional pressure was strangling me. But I couldn't tell Nori *that*, could I?

"I can't address the other job, Julie," Nori fixed me with her most baleful managerial stare. "That's for you to sort out. But you need to clean up the problems in this one. That's for me to sort out."

I nodded silently, twisting Tracer's leash into a crumpled wad.

"You're too good of a trainer to lose," Nori closed the notebook she'd been scanning. "We've lost three others this year already. I'm not too stupid to miss how high the pressure is getting." She paused long, searching my face "We're past the honeymoon phase with this school and it's showing. Do you realize that of the programs starting up around the time we did, two-thirds have closed?"

"No, I didn't know that." I looked up at her. That was disturbing news. "Like who, and do you know why?"

She reeled off half a dozen names of other groups we'd had contact with. "I don't know most of the reasons," Nori said thoughtfully. "I think, just like we are, lots of them hit a tipping point when their first generation of graduates aged out. Demand and obligation instantly doubles. We're already seeing how that works, especially with the rescues, when we don't know their exact age starting out. Any of the schools who've given me reasons are mostly citing burnout and lack of funding." Nori swiveled in her chair, gathered some papers, and waved them at me. "We're working on the funding part. I'll help with the burnout part if you'll tell me how."

I just shook my head. I simply didn't know where or how to start explaining. And she couldn't fix it. Only I could do that.

"Are you getting your meds adjusted okay?" Nori pressed

ahead. She knew, as did most others, that I'd recently been diagnosed with rheumatoid arthritis, and last winter had brought me my first serious flare.

"Yes, it's going pretty well." This, at least, was full openness. In the earliest years of that illness, it was mostly–if not always–a minor inconvenience that could be well controlled by good medication.

"What are you doing for R&R these days?" Nori was relentless. "Maybe it's time to get yourself another horse?"

I shook my head again. "There's no way. Not right now." I kept my stare focused on Tracer. Nori knew of my lifelong love affair with horses, because we'd first met at the facility where we both kept our horses. And she knew I'd re-homed my last one from sheer time frustration and guilt that I was neglecting him.

R&R? I thought. Be real. Service dog training had started for me as just that: a fun, distracting hobby alongside my own dogs, who I trained for competitive obedience. Now here I was making a big additional mess out of what was supposed to be the fun part.

When I left the training center that day, the savage August sun burned the parking lot, me, my car, the dogs… everything. The relentless, stifling heat mimicked the pressure that felt omnipresent for me, crushing over and into every part of life, everything I touched. As true for all young idealists, ignoring realities of your personal life, even for a fascinating part-hobby obsession, will catch up with you. I faced a watershed, and the knowledge pressed on me as relentlessly as the boiling sun.

I'd lived here on the southern border of the Blue Ridge Mountains for several years now, but the staggering intensity of summer heat had never stopped shocking me. Even bits of exposure to western deserts had done nothing to prepare me for this heavy suffocation. I marveled at humidity persistent and strong enough to grow mildew on red clay right out in the open. I learned to protect dogs from heatstroke. I learned to worship the science of air conditioning and remain thankful I was born after its creation.

I sat in my car, cranking the AC to high and considering Nori's admonitions. I decided to bear down–hard–against my performance sag, much as I did to cope with the heat. I could do this… couldn't I? I knew how. I know how to do both these jobs, I told myself that day. I just need to suck it up and get myself together. Stop being such a wuss! I continued the silent self-lecture.

Hindsight is always so flawless. Even as young as I was, I should have known better. I was trying to work one full-time, high-pressure job that I was growing to hate and another almost full time that, while I loved it, wasn't exactly relaxing either. Prioritizing both over self, sanity, or relationships kept me maniacally busy and also created excellent excuses to ignore reality. Extended sleep deprivation added to the mix.

But I was strong! I was smart. I could be practical! I could make it work!

I was an idiot.

Chapter 6

"Yesterday I was clever, so I wanted to change the world. Today I am wise, so I am changing myself." —Rumi

After overwhelming summers, autumn arrives in the southeast much as spring does in northern latitudes. The first stirring of cool air gives the sense of long-locked doors swinging open. Fresh air brings a sense of release, making breathing easy again. Walking outdoors ceases to be an endurance feat. Spirits rise. Possibilities expand. No amount of air conditioning can equal the sweetness of the first breath of cool air from the mountain peaks just west of us. For me, fall in the Carolinas will forever be about fresh breeze scented faintly of wood smoke and forest spice, about a return to breathing deeply, turning your face to the wind, and cherishing the freshness until well after darkness falls.

That summer's infinitesimal creep towards autumn felt especially slow. For a short time after the meeting with Nori, I rallied. I managed to pick up the pace and mend a few bridges. But sheer willpower carries you only so far, and I was already sagging again. Badly. I'd stopped in the middle of training more than once to consider Nori's words. What had I done in the past for fun? What was there in life now that was mentally relaxing? So many factors from my life had gone by the wayside. High on the list was exactly what she'd asked me about: my lifelong love-affair with horses. They'd always been my passion, my relaxation, and a huge personal focus. Over

and over, the idea surfaced. Over and over I told myself
the current schedule, constantly pressured from all sides,
held no time for horses. Fortunately, a chance encounter
would shortly prove me wrong. As with so many other
factors in my life, once again, dogs led me along the path
to change.

A gigantic piece of the solution landed in my world the
same way I'd met scores of other people: a referral from
someone who knew someone else who wanted a German
Shepherd, my breed of choice since childhood. From
details of the referral, I made several bad assumptions. I
didn't think this lady would be a good prospect for the
type of dog she'd inquired about. The description of this
woman from my friend made me wary: a very rural
setting, someone living in a single-wide while building a
house, a big collection of animals, no experience with
shepherds. In my limited experience, this led me to think
"redneck novice," few clues, limited understanding of
concerns I'd have before recommending her to my usual
sources of dogs. But basic courtesy to the friend who'd
asked dictated that I at least make a call. At the other end
of the phone, my new contact made similar but opposite
assumptions: she'd been referred to a clueless, prissy
city-slicker who couldn't possibly understand what she
wanted. Fate does have a wonderful sense of humor.

That first phone call with Sherry radically transformed
both opinions. Rather than the total waste of time I'd
expected, I reluctantly tore myself off the phone over an
hour later, halting a fast-paced exchange from two lives
with lots of dogs and far more horses. I promised to
check some shepherd options for her and circle back. But
as so often happened, intense time pressure got in the
way and pushed the conversation off my radar. Weeks

later, when I tore the previous month's sheet off my desk calendar scratch-pad, I noticed Sherry's phone number written in the top corner, surrounded by extensive doodles made during the call.

Ah, yes, her! I looked down at the number, many times circled and starred. I should probably call her again? Or was she supposed to call me? I couldn't remember, but I remembered how much I'd enjoyed the conversation. On that basis alone, I followed up, quickly discovering our camaraderie hadn't been a fluke. Another hour-plus into the second call, I happily accepted an invitation to her newly purchased farm to ride. It was the first step to turning my world right-side-up.

Horses weren't the only thing missing in my world, but they'd been my most intense preoccupation since I first learned to talk. Until I was back with them, I hadn't even realized how much I missed the joy and relaxation. The sheer ecstasy of my first canter through a towering hardwood forest easily showed me how wrong I'd been— and how right Nori had been. I needed their presence. I needed the quiet. I needed the mental shift of gears. I needed the total lack of pressure found in this place.

A life-altering friendship took root in that glorious autumn, a season that seemed to mark the passing of my southern years better than any official calendar. After the toughest summer of my life, Sherry's new friendship and her immense analytical candor were forever marked in my mind by fresh breezes and golden leaves. She brought me back to horses, which had been the core of my spirit since childhood. And her horses turned me loose into the magic of a silent autumn woodland. The pure relaxation and beauty were like nothing I could remember.

The new friendship gave me the most frankness, least criticism, and largest intellectual challenge I'd ever experienced. We could talk for hours, and we did just that while we roamed the maze of trails in the mountains. No subject was taboo. All perspectives appreciated. The enormity of the resulting calm was completely new to me.

I learned how to watch for copperheads and timber rattlers. Sherry learned about an old-fashioned kind of German Shepherd that looked nothing like show dogs. I learned about the soft, fast, arthritis-friendly gaits of unshod Tennessee Walking Horses. We were both surprised by the number of parallels between our families and childhoods, and we became acquainted with each other's siblings. We discovered a mutual fascination with the endless variables of human behavior–hers as a bona fide mental health professional, mine merely a strong interest now much increased by difficult client scenarios.

Despite my renewed delight with the horses, I was still in no position to get one of my own right then. But Sherry had as many as I'd once wrangled at different summer jobs in college, so she welcomed my help.

"Some people have drug habits. I have an animal habit," she told me on the first evening we worked far beyond dark to get her barn set up for an approaching tropical storm. Even a change of pace like that did me tremendous good.

We usually did long trail rides a couple of times per week, and in time the German Shepherd I'd helped her purchase loped happily alongside us with a few of my own. As weeks rolled into months, a friendship solidified that was win-win for both of us.

"You didn't warn me how bossy they are," Sherry commented one day, glancing down at Athos, her new dog, while he followed her every step around the barn. "He knows my schedule now and there's no more sleeping in. When it's time to go to the barn in the morning, he just drags the blankets off the bed, then the pillows, then me."

I laughed. I couldn't help it, though she was only partly amused. Her dogs of choice in the past had been mostly Airedales and Irish Terriers. These big—and yes, bossy—shepherds were the other side of the universe. But she rapidly figured out the basics, and step by small step, we became well-adjusted not only to each other, but to our rather large blend of animals.

Weeks rolled into months while I wondered if the corresponding mental relief would be enough to offset the other pressures that often still weighed me down. I thought they might, but I was still not facing facts. The snag? Profound relaxation—true, full mental peace—is a genie that, once discovered, can't be easily be stuffed back into a bottle. Other dilemmas in my life marched relentlessly into focus, whether or not I wanted to see them clearly. By contrast alone, endless demands and constant critique from the culture controlling so much of my world became ever-more objectionable.

One November day, I sat on one of Sherry's horses, alone this time in a silent forest of brilliant gold and orange. I stayed long in one beautiful place that had become my favorite, mesmerized by a tumble of whitewater in the river far below the trail. The quiet here always crept through my very soul like a healing balm. I yearned for more of my life to happen this way. Less rigidity, more choices. Fewer arbitrary rules, more time for deliberate thought.

In the vast silence of a brightly colored woodland, I finally faced the truth. I knew what I had to do. Only cowardice was stopping me. All my foot-dragging and head-in-the-sand reluctance was not just bad for myself—it was intensely unfair to others. How much better for all if I stopped expecting everybody else to cope with my disgruntled, resentful presence? Because absent the rationalizing, that's exactly what I'd been doing. Growing up, I thought, can be a pain in the rear.

Absently, I stroked the bright red mane of the mare I rode. She turned her head and snorted at me, rolling a quizzical eye and shifting restlessly. It was not normal to sit still for so long.

"Vision, I got myself into it," I told her. "How do I get myself out of it? What do you think I should do?"

She blew another snort, stamped her foot, and—unusually for her—hopped into a canter with no cue from me. I had to laugh as I let her rock me along the forest trail. The sun-dapples around me seemed to wink in agreement. She was right. It was time to go.

Except knowing what to do and knowing how to do it were widely separate matters. I didn't have long to muddle around with figuring out a plan. Even those with no confidence in fate could hardly have missed the significance of a *For Sale* sign that appeared a short time later on empty property directly across the road from Sherry's barn. I had no further hesitation and thus began a highly complex year. When I made my move, a marriage, a job, all my insurance, most of my income, a decade of references, and at least 80% of those I'd believed friends were left behind. It was an enormous leap with even larger consequences, both terrifying and exhilarating. But the arrival of my next autumn Personal New Year found me still riding a meandering network of trails on the lower rim of the Blue Ridge. This time, the horse I rode was my own. The air was fresh and sharp, smelling vaguely of something close to cinnamon. My favorite spot remained the astonishing beauty of that overhang where I'd finally come to terms with myself. A steep slope fell away on one side to the jagged crevice of a frothing river. On the other side, forests of giant oak and hickory marched up and down the hills, leaves dancing and swaying, projecting an orange-golden prism of shifting light. Smells rotated on the cool breeze: leather, horse, old leaves, fresh water, broken wood. I often took breaks there, both alone and with friends, marveling at how long it had taken me to gather the courage to act on my own thoughts and motivations instead of permitting others to dictate.

Returning to the equine world had also restored or strengthened other friendships. Often, three or four of us rode along in symphony, emphasizing a calm companionship that I was only beginning to realize greatly increased my effectiveness as a trainer. The relaxed exchanges of what we now called the Hay Bale Conference Room were teaching me a great deal more about true mental ease than I'd ever known, and, by extension, teaching me far more effective ways to approach human relationships of any flavor, including my clients.

Those two processes–my own maturing and my overall improved approach to training–happened together, solidifying as one in a way I can never separate. Neither would have happened quite the same way if I hadn't discovered the true freedom of life "in the open," minus the restrictions under which I'd always lived. So many of the artificial boundaries were gone. It was both geographical and mental, but I started to recognize how much excessive compulsion short-circuits extrapolation of true learning in any species. Yes, I often thought. So totally different. Such immense significance.

Well, yes. Significant it was. Smooth it wasn't.

Chapter 7

My new home was a 20-acre dome with the approximate
shape of a horse-shoe, most of the boundary defined by a
winding county road. Just beyond that road, Sherry's
barns and her partner's garage stood in a neat blue row.
Both of our properties were once part of a post-
depression dairy operation. Now my twenty acres of
farmland-gone-feral was a wild tumble of hardwood
timber and former pasture. Giant trees wrestled in combat
with an overgrown jungle of vines, thorns, snakes,
skunks, erosion gullies, and waving grass. Ancient,
barbed-wire cattle fence had collapsed quietly into defeat
30 years earlier. The huge central hill formed a lovely
building site. Everything else dipped away from the top
in pastures, ravines, and forest, hiding a multitude of
secrets, including a profusion of wildlife and the former
farmer's junkyard. The tumultuous river from Sherry's
farm smoothed out here for a more sedate bypass on the
east boundary, wooing one to complacency right before it
surged to rip out new driveways during heavy rainfall.

But I loved it. On the first night I moved in, my
electricity wasn't even hooked up yet. Still, I sat on the
top of my hill that night until long after dark, my own
dogs and several additional service dogs surrounding me.
Far below, an occasional car swept beyond the curve and

disappeared. A last faint light winked off in Sherry's barn. A full moon sailed overhead amidst more stars than I'd ever been able to see in the city that was now quite a few miles away. The now-familiar calm settled over me: relaxed muscles, buoyed joy, cleared logic.

I looked at the dogs around me and wondered at their unusual stillness. Were they cueing from me to be this still? Or did the atmosphere relax them also? I wasn't sure, but I started wondering about it. How much of the learning processes I knew, people or dog, had to do with relaxation? About deliberate choice grounded in time to think?

Considering my fascination with service dog training, inevitably, my newfound mania for relaxation and quiet would bleed over. I began comparing my own learning curve to a dog's. It was hardly a sophisticated rationale, but merely a nudge of curiosity. I knew I wanted to see the property become a livable space for myself. No dog training agenda directed me, but a relish for the sense of freedom I'd learned to love. I wanted open spaces. Easy movements. Lack of restraints. Easy transitions. I was determined my new living quarters would reflect my thoughts about the process that brought me here. For the first time in my life, I had autonomy to try what made sense to me, not only for myself, but for the animals around me.

I did my best to set up functional spaces that were as unrestricted as possible to move around in. I wanted large outdoor areas, ease of transition, and minimal headaches for the everyday chores. I wanted multiple dogs to be able to follow me around–or not–as either I or they chose, depending on what was going on. I planned, spent absurd quantities of money, and began implementing. At that point, it was just about me and my own animals. But shortly afterwards, the stakes shot upwards.

As is so common with nonprofits, growth cycles and success rapidly outstrip the original funding and support structure. Some of those growing pains had been, of course, part of the stress I'd already been trying to cope with–much as Nori had pointed out to me now almost two years earlier. More and more of the plethora of service dog schools started around the onset of the 1990 ADA were closing their doors. Except as the knowledge of service dog potential grew, demand grew right alongside. Large changes rolled over our group. So it happens to most who excel in a craft, nonprofit or not, and so it happened to our once-tiny school.

Our training ranks swelled, but the clamor for more and more dogs beat on our doors like a tide that refused to ebb. Around the time I moved to the farm, several trainers were having to step into functions beyond direct training. We needed to teach other trainers, locate more dogs, increase public relations and fundraising, and as many as the school could afford converted from part time to full time. This was not, of course, entirely bad news for me. Since I'd just bailed out of my more conventional job, a larger role in program growth made practical sense.

Nori's genius for public speaking and general brilliance in the spotlight took her toward the board of directors and program representation to the public. Barb found herself with a new focus on acquiring dogs through travel, evaluations, and cultivation of new relationships. I, the one with greatly increased physical space, naturally drew the straw not only to train more dogs but to increase our training internship program. My number of trainees shot up from three or four to 15 or 20. A new kennel building took shape. Apprentice trainers were being interviewed.

Meanwhile, in the best traditions of nearly all brash young trainers, I was quite convinced I had it all figured out. Hadn't I trained and graduated scores of service dogs now? I'd learned a complex system of initiating and requiring long strings of behaviors. I knew how to build a reliable canine repertoire of commands that our clients could manage with little more than effusive praise and insistence on attention.

But then, I hadn't met Maggie. Ah, yes… Maggie.

Maggie arrived on the farm as a service dog candidate Barb had found in a Georgia shelter. The endless hunt both for rescues and purpose-bred dogs never slowed. One of the hardest to supply was for dogs with the correct structure to help clients who could walk… kind of… but needed help balancing and bracing. Such a job called for muscular dogs with a square build and relatively straight shoulder. They needed to be, among other things, calm, phlegmatic, and naturally slow moving.

 Maggie seemed like a good start. She appeared predominantly retriever, but she was far larger. She also had a squarishness about her massive head that suggested Rottweiler or Mastiff. That was certainly no cause for automatic elimination, but we needed to proceed with caution until we knew more about her.

So I began with all the cheer I could muster and a pocket full of the highest quality treats we had. But I might have saved myself the bother. Maggie's response was new to me: she simply did nothing. At all. No aggression, no cooperation, no wagging and begging for treats or affection. She watched us, and if ever a dog actually laughed at humans, it was probably Maggie. We knew nothing about her background. Maggie had been picked up by animal control. Unclaimed, unmarked, unwanted, she arrived with only the briefest of resumes, primarily that she didn't show any aggression, seemed to be in the right age bracket, and was fully vetted for health. Diving in with my typical approach, I was rapidly humbled. I could not make any impression on Maggie at all. Not good, negative, or anything recognizable in between.

With the perspective of time, I'm sure Maggie's issues arose mostly from never having learned to learn. She showed no sign of abuse other than general neglect. Or maybe she'd been semi-feral all her short life, yet still lived near enough to humans not to fear them. We didn't know. But she did not want to do anything for me. I couldn't even figure out what she wanted to do for herself. We had almost no basis for communication.

Initial training is almost always about careful behavior shaping—or at least I thought I knew what "careful" was about. Lure with cookies. Praise with great enthusiasm. Draw into games with fun results. Control all the variables and bribe the dog with desirable results to initiate the wanted behaviors. Except Maggie was oblivious. She usually ate her kibble, but not always. And she didn't have substantial interest in food–most certainly not if it came with my agenda attached. She was mildly interested in other dogs. She had no idea what a toy was or why she should care.

After one tentative push on her hindquarters to induce a "sit" that I could reward, I saw the futility there. I was pretty strong for a medium-height woman, but I might as well have tried to push my barn roof down. That wasn't the right place to start, anyway. Enough people and tools can always apply enough negative pressure to get results. And in my view, though corrections and insistence would always have a place in service dog training, startup was not that place. If you wanted a team, wanted eventual group think and really good problem solving, this was where it had to begin.

When starting out with Maggie, caution about her potential aggression–an unknown dog that appeared to have guarding-breed origin–prevented me from using anything more restrictive than a flat martingale collar. And it was totally useless. When Maggie wanted to go somewhere, she just went. The insignificant human would flap along behind, willing or not. Her strength was amazing. She arrived at my farm just before the new apprentice trainers did, so I had no help or extra sets of hands. In those first few months at the new property, I was on my own, and besides that, there were a dozen other dogs to work. I could not spend all day and night with Maggie, trying to figure out what she might like enough to induce cooperation.

It would make a better commentary on me as a trainer if I could say I reasoned out a solution. Except I didn't. I stumbled over it totally by accident. Even just a potty break to the kennel yard was a vast undertaking with Maggie. She would walk outside willingly enough. But this new network of dog yards I'd been so thrilled to set up (we need room to move and roam, right?!) had become expansive. Even the smallest yard meant she had a quarter of an acre to roam… and to avoid being recaptured. I could leave her on a long line, sure. But she was too strong for me and we both knew it. Why reinforce that idea? I could go to a more severe physical restraint, but anyone who has worked alone with an unresponsive, 110-pound dog of dubious origins will appreciate why I was cautious starting down that road.

In the end, I just let her loose in the smallest yard. I kept thinking surely she could be had for fried liver or a raw soup bone or some doggie delicacy. Mostly she couldn't. Maggie would roam until she was good and ready to return, allowing me to close gates and doors behind her. The time factor was entirely unpredictable and making hash of my ability to schedule other trainees. Within a few days, I was enormously frustrated, ready to call Barb to come and get her. Was I right? Wrong? What was I missing?

In my new and much-loved farm atmosphere, I did what I always did to solve a problem. I went outside to sit and think about it. Under the broad, thick canopies of giant hardwoods, I would stop, relax, and soak in the quiet. Up the hill, fleecy clouds scudded about against a bright blue sky. Down the hill, the canopy retreated to the thickets along the river. Dappled sunshine covered the dog yards in endless winks and nods. I reveled in the fact that there was no human voice or form, no other house but my own, and very few other sounds in my immediate universe. Once again, the quiet soothed my frustrations, and I felt a calm steal over me. I flopped full-length to the grass, staring up absently and wondering what I could do to motivate this dog.

Then I realized Maggie had come to inquire. Exactly about what, I wasn't sure, but the quizzical expression on her face was clear enough. She wasn't used to humans sprawled on the ground. "Hi, Maggie." I extended a hand partway to her without getting up. "What's up, girl?" She actually took a few steps on her own to close the distance. I patted her chest absently, and by sheer blind luck found The Magical Itchy Spot. She groaned and twitched. With a sideways stagger, she leaned into my hand and started to help with her own back foot.

Struck with inspiration, I rolled over twice, moving away from her, still without getting up. Relaxing her helpful back foot, she cocked her head at me. "Hi, Maggie," I said again, extending my hand back out. And in she came. A tiny first step, but it was an actual first! I rolled all the way to the kennel door, giving intermittent chest scratches along the way. When I finally stood and walked inside, she followed without hesitation. I sat on a bucket in her kennel and scratched her from chest to hip for a good 10 minutes.

The following day, I ignored even the flat collar, simply opening her kennel door and walking to the yard. To my delight, she followed with interest. We repeated much of the previous day's routine. The next morning, I began hand-feeding her outside, instead of giving a normal breakfast in a dish. Adding small steps each day, we built a routine around a relaxed dog who had plenty of time to think through what she wanted to do, for reasons that she told me, not vice versa.

I'd taken my first steps into an unconventional type of shaping that, much later, I started calling Hands-Off training because I didn't know a better term. As the years rolled on, I heard a variety of other terms for similar technique–most of whom claimed to have invented it. Maybe in their circumstances, they did. I surely didn't invent my approach. I tripped over it, recognizing the value mostly because it had recently played such a big role in my own training to become a better human.

Three weeks later, Maggie hadn't yet had any collar, leash, or other equipment put back on her. She was doing well with most basic obedience, beginning a standing-brace, and picking up multiple objects for me when asked. No doubt, we were only starting. But we had built a foundation where I'd feared there would never be one.

My phone rang one day with Nori on the other end. She needed a demo dog for an event. After scanning the training logs, she liked the look of Maggie's progress.

My face flamed up, even though I was alone. "Well, ummm… I'm not sure she's quite ready yet."

"Problems in a group? Or what?" Nori asked briskly. "There won't be any other dogs there."

"Not really." I couldn't think of any way to cushion it. "I would need to get her used to a leash first." The conversation went rather downhill from there. Breaking the conventional training sequence was about the least of my sins. But I was unrepentant. I had already started a second dog in a similar way, albeit not a potential service dog. I'd taken in a skittish rescue with nowhere to go. In his case, definitely an abused dog with major trust issues. It was nearly a month before I ever put a hand on him, and only after he definitely asked me to. By then, he was fully responsive to every part of a daily routine and a dozen different words—even if it wouldn't be fair to call them "commands" just yet. But we were working in that direction.

Over time, I refined this approach to where every dog I kept and handled went through some version of the same. Did they all eventually have to learn that certain behaviors were required? Of course. Were they all given the time to think things through, make their own decisions about willingness and motivations? You better believe it. None of it would have happened as it did without the expansive quiet of the farm, without large fenced areas and channels from one area to another that allowed freedom of movement without duress. In those first few months, Maggie and I both needed time to think and to develop patterns of interaction that helped everyone.

Maggie continued to a working career of over a decade and never wore any collar but that flat martingale. I continued on to thousands more dogs. From then forward, my preference about initial training stayed weighted in favor of the most possible Hands-Free, the way Maggie and I taught each other. I found it especially difficult to articulate to incoming trainers, as nothing about this idea involved either clickers or corrections. It was not about knowledge. It was not about the details. It was not even about rewards or consequences. It was about relaxation of approach and deliberate choices. Often it didn't even involve words. And I found scant support among my peers, either, because this system of cause-and-effect teaching didn't originate from dog training logic at all. It bubbled to my mental surface entirely because of my experience of learning–for the first time in my life–how to relax fully while considering choices, motivations, and consequences.

Surely, I thought, it would be potent imprinting and also a far more reliable tool than a forced assessment about what kind of work a dog actually wanted to do? I knew that had to be true, though I was still a few years away from discovering the full power of that truth.

I don't know when or how such realizations come to

others, even while recognizing it happened relatively late in my growing-up process. But I do know I found the substance of it, for myself and then for my dogs, while prowling remote trails through hardwood hills and enjoying my first-ever full freedom of thought and spirit.

Chapter 8

"Confidence is ignorance. If you're feeling cocky, it's because there's something you don't know." —Eoin Colfer, "Artemis Fowl"

Something was off about this interview. I just couldn't tell exactly what. This was my second time trying to talk this woman through the logistics of what a service dog could and couldn't do. Glancing down at the dogs around our feet, I tried to re-frame my question to the lady who sat nearby, her crutches leaning across her lap. Two years before, she'd barely dodged paraplegic status after a terrible car crash. Now fortunate to be walking again, she had many months of intense physical therapy behind her, but still clearly needed assistance with balance and help reaching things or carrying them. Whether a dog was the best answer for her... I wasn't so sure.

Much of her motivation was still a puzzle. Of course, we always did basic checks to determine if an applicant had, for instance, any outstanding arrest warrants, wasn't being sued for anything too obnoxious, and wasn't in the sex offender database. With this latest woman, we'd stumbled onto the fact that she'd applied to at least three other service dog schools. But today when I asked her to tell us about it, she was vague and dismissive. She had no plans to explain.

Long, rambling speeches about her home life had odd rhythms. She hastened from one sentence to another, yet left long pauses in between key phrases. The only other place I'd ever heard this done was in political speech when someone didn't want to be cut off by a reporter. Yet, when we asked her a direct question, her typical response was a lonely word or two. Nothing more. We were all puzzled. Nobody could fault anything specific, but the multiple applications and reluctance to explain made us concerned.

I decided I was going to have to have some outside help. Exactly how much help I needed would take a while to realize.

In the mid-90s, the entire service dog "industry" still lacked much in the way of professional best practices, anyway. Beyond that, the entire national realm of dog training was half submerged by trainers leaping happily into the fray with greater confidence than most should have had. For the right price, a client could have nearly any promise made, breed chosen, or time schedule met. The corresponding pressure from our sponsors was huge. Joe Q Trainer says he can finish these dogs in six weeks for $1,800. Why can't you?

Far worse was the occasional board member who would descend on us with an offer from three or four "excellent trainers" with whom s/he just happened to be acquainted. Why couldn't we use them to help us hurry? And on and on. We found ourselves in a perpetual scramble to meet expectations, both the valid ones and the totally unrealistic.

Except the more we scrambled, the more mistakes we made. We were having way too many repeats of the Jake scenario, or at least parallel ones. By now we'd created enough glaring errors to make all of us unacceptably jumpy. Interviews like this latest one made it hard to sort out if I was being correctly cautious or just plain paranoid.

We were extremely anxious to avoid repeating our errors, but repeat them we did. The worst challenges didn't come from the dogs. While we considered it part of our job description (not to mention our fun) to keep each other humble, we also knew that with almost a decade under our belts, we were better than ever with the dogs. Our biggest problems nearly always came from the other end of the leash. And how, exactly, could we get better at addressing that?

In my world, I knew of exactly one highly credible source of such perspective. I thought the operative question would be how to borrow Sherry's people expertise without imposing on a friendship or asking her to disrupt professional boundaries. Yet, surely (I thought with all the wisdom of my 31 years) there was a way we could learn. There would be some way trainers could do better. We were already deep into a program of training trainers, right? Surely we could expand our skills, right? Well, as things turned out, I was not right at all. In fact, I was all wrong.

I warily approached the issue with Sherry during a day-long trail ride at a state park. We were clopping along under hundred foot pines, two or three hours down a mountain path, before I thought I'd found the right moment. And I wanted to start by asking for information, not for her help in a professional capacity. Oops. Wrong again.

I waited until the trail was broad enough that I could move up beside her. "Is there any reliable indicator in an initial interview that will give you a clue about a person's honesty? Just any kind of a flag, a cue about whether they're concealing something?"

"That's pretty broad." Sherry flicked a deceptively casual glance my way. "Why do I have a nasty suspicion there's more lurking in the context here than you want me to know?"

"Because you're a born cynic."

Silence.

"Huh. My context or the client's?" I finally shrugged to emphasize my confusion. "My own, probably. Or maybe neither. It's just that I have suspicions I can't defend, can't explain." We covered another half mile before I could find the right words to continue.

Sherry rarely bailed me out of these rambles. If I wanted to know something, I had to figure out how to ask.

"I'm 90% sure there's something significant she doesn't want us to know, but I have no idea what it is. The whole situation started out very straightforward. She says she needs a dog to do maybe eight or ten different functions. They're all direct command/response, very easy. All physical assistance tasks. But she makes me nervous and I can't tell you why. And I can't even promise it's not my own paranoia. We've had to pull dogs back out of client homes so often this year that we really can't afford any more screw-ups."

This bought me half a mile of silence. "Who is assessing this stuff for you now?" Sherry was studying the tall pines above us.

"Well. Us. The trainers. Who else? What do you mean?"

Stopping her horse, Sherry abruptly swung around to face me. "Say what?" Her voice had gone soft. I knew her well enough by now to translate that look: "Have you lost your mind?" But the vocal softness wore off as she continued. "Family therapist? Social worker? Counselor? Surely you're getting some professional input from somewhere before spending five figures of other people's money?"

I felt a bad flush rising up my neck. "Well, Nori has pulled in a family counselor before when we had a specific goal or when the client said they needed that kind of help."

"How about the specific goal of covering your own butts from lawsuits? Would that be enough to warrant some input?" Sherry started her horse moving again, easing into a slow canter up a grassy hillside.

I moved to keep up, as I had no plans to let the conversation drop. "We're talking about needing someone who knows disabilities, families, and dog training. I haven't noticed that section yet in the Therapists-R-Us listings."

"Maybe you need to start one."

Though it's a massive oversimplification, that's exactly what we did. The process didn't come without bumps and jolts, but overall I couldn't believe we hadn't done it sooner. Ultimately, we learned more thoroughly than ever how behavior is just behavior. Whether motivations and consequences are about human or canine minds, there are an awful lot of parallels.

I'd been hesitant to bring it up. Very hesitant. But I'd also been ridiculously slow to figure out that Sherry had been merely biding her time, waiting for the chance. She was both perishing to be asked and concerned about pushing in uninvited. But she wanted in. All the way in. She dove into the new endeavor with her normal high-IQ analysis. She'd been turning that intense mental spotlight on individual humans for a long time now. The knowledge translated rapidly into more effective learning for all of us.

First off, she did two interviews with the lady who was causing me all the concern: one meeting alone, and one meeting in which she required the rest of the family to attend along with all three assigned trainers. A very short time later, our little group sat in the conference room in what seemed to me like another stalemate that wouldn't be long-lived. We trainers tried to be quiet, observe, and learn. An impatient husband huffed and sighed. One sullen teenage girl and a very wide-eyed little boy rounded out the mix. Sherry kept tight control. Word wizard that she was, she artfully removed all excuses and insisted on a direct answer about the other applications.

But now every member of the family was silent. No one answered. There was no feedback at all. Then, rather abruptly, Sherry dismissed everyone from the room but the prospective client herself. Thirty minutes later, she was initiating calls to a substance abuse program and making arrangements for her enrollment. We—the illustrious, professional trainers—were dumfounded.

When the family had departed, several of us, Nori included, crowded back into the conference room. We all stood, arms folded, demanding further information.

"How did you know?"

"What tipped you off?"

"She had at least three physical signs," Sherry said easily, barely looking up from the notes she was still writing. "But I can't make deductions based on physical signs unless I'm a doctor, which I'm not. I wasn't sure until I saw the family interactions. You want to know how to decipher that? Enroll yourself in a grad course for social work."

I exchanged chastened glances with my co-workers and we rapidly exited back to our jobs. Barely a month into our experiment, Sherry was hooked, lock, stock, barrel, and leash. And she wanted to upgrade her perspectives in other ways. She enrolled in the regular program for apprentice training, battling her way through the same eighteen-month process we used to teach all our staff. In doing so, she set an entirely new standard in my mind.

No doubt, we should have understood the issue and started something similar years sooner than we did. But this was truly a case of better late than never. Absolutely nobody could argue with the results. The increased quality of help to clients was earthshaking for our school. Even Nori was sufficiently astonished by the turnaround that, by the end of the calendar year, she started deferring all final client approvals to Sherry. The number of drop-outs and cooperation problems fell dramatically. Assessment time was cut in half. Quality and speed of orientation improved.

It was more complex than I'd even known how to consider. Usually, our clients faced such a vast array of practical challenges that complex dog handling was the least of their worries. The addition of a licensed Master Social Worker brought an influx of new solutions that didn't always have a thing to do with dogs. Suddenly, we had access to more physical therapists, vocational rehab, state funding sources, and a dozen different types of experts we hadn't even known existed. Sherry not only found them, she lit a fire under them on behalf of our clients.

Beyond the assessments and practical help, she taught our trainers what to look for in home visits that could signal physical or emotional trouble. Taught us how to give help without condescension. Taught us to assess our own and clients' dominant learning method and adjust training protocol accordingly. The benefits were extreme. Yet as we were about to learn, no such extreme benefit arrives without a certain amount of shock value.

Chapter 9

"Do the best you can until you know better. Then when you know better, do better." —Maya Angelou

A first meeting with a new client usually involves several trainers. With our new setup, that group now always involved our new Behavioral Health Advisor. And so it would work for today's meeting. Sherry, Trent, and I, along with four service dogs in training, arrived at a mall for a meet and greet. "Demo dogs" helped us rapidly see the entire family's reaction. It was the fastest way to spot fear, distaste, allergies, inaccurate assumptions, or another potential trouble without having to ask questions that could sometimes appear pretty pushy for a first meeting.

Today's family consisted of a couple somewhere in their 30s and two children. I hadn't been with them more than 20 minutes before I was ready to rubber-stamp the application. I was accustomed to basing much of my impression about an adult's "training" potential by how much influence they had on their children. These kids were a boy around 11 or 12 and a tiny girl who looked too young for kindergarten. Both kids charmed me completely. The boy stayed close to his mom, very attentive as she maneuvered her crutches and wheelchair. He was quick to hand her what she needed, move her chair for her, and sit back down close by. He seemed oblivious to the thousand or so nearby attractions designed for pre-teens.

The little girl was enthralled with the dogs. She carefully asked permission to approach and pet. I watched her make eye contact and wait for the go-ahead.

"I love doggies," she told me, using nearly perfect diction on each word. "I've always wanted a doggie. Can he sleep in my bed?"

"Maybe," Trent told her, kneeling down and guiding his big retriever up to her. "We will have to see what your mom needs a dog to do before we decide."

"All right." The little girl agreed promptly. "But I can pet him now?" Her broad grin stayed put.

The boy didn't have as much to say. He gave us his name. When Sherry asked him which dog he liked best, he shrugged, then pointed to the big Labrador his sister was sitting beside. His smile was much more tentative than his sister's. To me, he seemed a little insecure, but I wasn't sure exactly why. Most likely just typical adolescent social jitters, I thought.

Dad had little to say. He sat quietly nearby, letting his wife answer the questions. Once he reached out to touch his daughter's shoulder when she was squealing and jumping. She immediately stilled and sat back on the floor to resume stroking the closest dog.

Mom was enthusiastic about the training. She readily agreed to any suggestion we made, though she was not as far along with her list of desired tasks as we liked a client to be. We usually asked them to come to the first interview knowing their five most important concerns with which they thought a dog could help. Denise said she needed help to balance when she used her crutches. She wondered aloud if a dog could be taught to bark for help if she fell or got into trouble requiring a human's help. But that was about as far as her list went.

I took this to be a lack of experience and information, not necessarily anything else. Not every service dog had to have dozens of tasks—or even a half dozen. Plenty of people needed a dog to perform just a few critical functions. But at this stage, we wanted to know the client's thought process, not our own, so the blank spaces here were the only sticky points I could see. Several times Denise came back around to asking, "Well, what would you suggest? What are their normal jobs?"

Many schools did more standardized training. And we weren't necessarily averse to that. A little later in the process, we'd be happy to answer with a list. But not at this moment. We considered ourselves more of a custom-dog, custom-training specialty group. We'd often train dogs for jobs that other schools wouldn't consider. But here, today, we had a primary goal of learning how much thought a client had already put on this part. Before asking any sponsor to commit to that number of dollars, we wanted the idea completely, thoroughly thought out by the whole family. So we tried hard not to make suggestions. Later, sure. But not right now.

About the third time we deflected the task question back, we got the one and only response from the husband. "Surely there is a list you can give us to help us understand what's possible?" Mr. Vince asked. I noticed that, when he spoke, his gaze was on his wife, not us. Her fast response came before any of us could speak.

"Oh, that's okay," she said hastily. "I can put together a

better list. I just thought I'd ask."

"We want to get the clearest possible idea of your goals," Sherry said. I noticed that, as always, her speech in these sessions was distinctly slower than usual. Nobody who didn't already know her would realize, but I had learned by imitation to slow down and talk with much greater deliberation. I'd been surprised at how much it cut down on misunderstandings.

I also noticed that while Sherry was speaking to the wife, her eyes kept going back to the husband. "Denise," she began a new topic. "Do you have a strong preference about what kind of dog you want? We can't ever promise a particular breed. Several trainers would give input on the best selection for you, and a lot depends on what we have available." Now her gaze was moving repeatedly back and forth between the husband and wife. "Still," she said, "depending on the options, if we had several to try, we would want to know your first choice."

"Oh, I would love to have the shepherd!" Denise's response was instant. Clearly she'd thought about this much, at least. She motioned to the big black and tan girl, Tasha, lying near her feet. "Is there any chance I could have that one? Any chance at all?"

"It's too early to know," Sherry answered carefully. "Tasha has been in training only a few weeks. We don't know yet what kind of job would be best for her."

Sherry held out her hand to Trent for the Labrador's leash. "Coal is more typical of what we train."

Trent handed him over, trading for the mixed breed Sherry had been holding. She then drew Coal toward Denise.

"When a dog's job involves a lot retrieving, pushing, and pulling, retrievers usually do best," she explained. "Not always, but usually. Mouth-oriented tasks come very naturally to them, and they are usually less body-sensitive than herding breeds."

"I just really love the shepherds. We used to have Rottweilers when I was a kid. Do you ever train those?"

"We have once or twice," Sherry told her. "But not very often."

"I'd be willing to help fundraise for a shepherd, if that would help?" Denise was still fixated on the dog near her feet. She had barely glanced at Coal, but my heart swelled in her favor when I noticed tears in her eyes while she stroked Tasha's head. This lady really craved a dog. Her effusive manner spilled over with running commentary to each member of the family and to each of us. "She is so wonderful! Just look at those eyes, and how well she behaves, and how she's just watching for a signal about what to do next! Have you ever seen anything so pretty–"

"We will have to see how things go," Sherry responded, gently inserting herself into Denise's flow of praise for Tasha. "It's way too early to know. Let's take a walk and you can see some of the things the dogs are learning."

Our whole group spent another half an hour touring the mall. All of us trainers took turns using a demo chair to show how the dogs rotated positions for different tasks, how they would tuck themselves into the small area below the chair in a restaurant, and how they would retrieve a dropped item almost automatically.

The family still had far fewer questions than normal. But I was enthralled with the children's close attention and lack of distraction. This, I thought, was rare and wonderful. Or so I thought until the dogs were back in the van and the trainer/dog entourage were driving away.

"Nope." Sherry stated flatly. "Nope, nope, NO."

Trent and I nearly fell out of our seats. "You're kidding," he blurted out. "Why not?"

Open-mouthed, I narrowly avoided hitting a parking stanchion, and pulled the van to a stop again. I was unable even to find words to respond. In my mind, I was already three months down the road, contemplating advanced training and who would do best with it.

"Because," Sherry sighed and leaned her head back on the seat behind her. She closed her eyes. "What she wants is a protection dog, not a service dog."

I found my voice. "What? Why?" I had to challenge this. "Why would you say that? I'm not following."

"That family situation is a pressure cooker of domestic abuse," she said with finality. "No way are we putting a dog into their home. We can see about trying to get her some help, but no dog. No way. Not on my watch."

"You cannot possibly know that," I objected strenuously. "That's not fair at all. Those kids had perfect manners. They minded beautifully. Nobody interrupted anybody. Everybody cooperated."

"Perfect, for sure." She answered, giving me a withering side-eye, then propped her head on her hand. "They were perfect because they were 'perfectly' terrified of that man. Every piece of body language from the wife and the kids was rigidly controlled. Every sentence of their conversation underscores the body language. He was totally detached from our whole discussion and stared down every speaker the entire time anyone's mouth was open. Denise has bruises on the back of her neck, on her upper arms, a cut near her eye, and she freezes every time he moves. The boy is favoring his left leg and stiffens every other step because he's trying not to limp. The girl constantly adjusts her position to keep something between her and her dad: another person, a dog, the chair, anything. And that's just the outward part."

The argument was long and intense. I had noticed the healing scab by Denise's eye, but I wasn't buying. Neither was Trent. Sherry would not budge, and Nori backed her.

"We chose this route for your expertise, Sherry," Nori said, fixing her strongest evil eye on me. "We said we would give you veto power, and we're going to stand by that."

And just like that, the decision was out of my hands. I was glad I didn't have to write the determination letter to the applicant, and I was angry, unbelieving. Ultimately, Nori told them only that we didn't think we had a dog well suited for them at this time, and perhaps they should check back with us next year. That was sufficiently open-ended to avoid offense, without making any commitments either way.

Sherry further rocked our little boats when she told us she'd reported the family to the state Child Protective Services for suspected physical abuse. She told us that much only because each of us who'd had contact with the family had to be interviewed. I don't think any of the rest of us were especially cooperative. If any other action was taken, I never heard about it. I was not privy to Sherry's conversation with CPS, of course, but I thought she was way far out on a long, shaky limb.

Safely out of the training center and back on the farm, we had a huge argument about it. I blew up in frustration, waved my superior training experience around, and objected on every level, especially about her calling CPS. "You cannot possibly have known that from an hour's meeting," I objected, tossing a hay bale into my truck with unnecessary vigor.

Sherry tossed on another bale and slammed the tailgate with equal vigor. "I had a strong suspicion, and could see physical evidence, Julie," she shot back. "In my profession, that leaves me no choice. That's called mandated reporting. Could I prove it? Of course not. But that's not my job. Reporting strong suspicion is my job. If you want me never to do that, then we're going to have a problem."

I dropped it. We would never agree, and my resentment at the outcome lingered long.

Several months later, I arrived at the training center to find a sheet torn from the morning newspaper draped over my desk. Red marker circled a headline: "Family of four dead in apparent murder-suicide."

The floor below me seemed to spin and drop away. Every part of my body went hot and cold at the same time. I saw that beautiful little girl squatting on the floor next to Coal. I saw the quiet, alert eyes of the boy. The pleading ones of the mother. And that still, still, quiet of the father. In that hard moment, I knew I'd never view any interview exactly the same way ever again.

I scanned the article, feeling prickles in my scalp and

sweat on my face. Jonathan and Denise Vince, and their children Taylor and Jessica.... previously reported domestic disturbance calls.... previous child protection services investigation.... lack of evidence.... funeral arrangements would be....

I dropped the clipping and rushed from the room, making it to the bathroom just in time. Vicious nausea wracked me for some endless period. I was sitting on the floor mopping my face with wet paper towels when Nori entered.

"You okay?" She asked.

"No," I answered, barely able to push out the words. "I might never be okay again."

"You couldn't have stopped it," she said flatly, showing her typical cold logic. "Best thing that can be said from this building is that he didn't kill one of our dogs, too."

"That's sure not much to brag about." I wasn't in a mood to be placated. "Who does it help?"

"The dog. The sponsor," she said, "And whoever else needed the dog."

That was, indeed, a darned small positive to grasp, but it seemed like it was all we were going to get.

"Next time, don't argue." Nori said, walking out the door. "You started the whole idea of professional assessments. Let it work. She knows people like we know dogs. And get yourself past the idea that you can fix the whole world. We did what we could."

This was the logical approach, the administrative approach. Vintage Nori. But for me it was absolutely no comfort. I'd had a brutal lesson in not making assumptions.

But a longer-term effect took root that day: the horrid episode went a long way toward cementing my trust in a professional's competence. I'd had a bone-deep shock to prove to myself that I didn't know every fact in the world. I was, finally and fully, disabused of the notion that nearly every client at every interview could magically be restored to full living capacity by a service dog. It was the end of my rose-tinted glasses, and it was none too soon.

None too soon because back then, in our relative innocence of the late 90s, our training group was largely ignorant about a tidal wave rising to overwhelm families everywhere. Mostly unrecognized, mostly unknown to us, the incredible proliferation of autism had begun its advance.

When the flood finally broke over our school, we were grateful for the years we'd already had of learning to work with specialists in human behavior and not just in dogs' behavior. We were clueless about how complex the new need would be, but we'd had some powerful lessons. We now had a solid group understanding about assessing, adjusting, and blending human and canine behaviors. We'd grown to trust true professional evaluation. Except for that, what came next would never have happened the same way. Autism was swelling from coast to coast. Exactly like throngs of affected families, we had absolutely no idea how profoundly it would change everything.

Chapter 10

'I was gratified to be able to answer promptly, and I did. I said I didn't know.' —Mark Twain

"Tell me about autism." I wasn't sure how else to ask what I wanted to know. Sherry and I were sprawled in our usual post-work-day slump, half on, half off bales of hay in the side wing of her barn. It was a years-long tradition now to linger here as often and long as time allowed, watching the sun lower over the rolling pastures where our horses grazed.

"Tell you what about autism?" she asked back. "That's kind of a broad question. My gut reaction is that I don't know much."

I swirled the wine in my barn mug. "I'm not sure I know how to be more specific." The echoes of several phone calls from the last week jumbled together in my thoughts. "Seems like there are an awful lot of upset parents calling lately. I mean, I did my grad work mostly about exceptional students and I barely remember more than a mention of autism. Lately, it seems like somebody calls at least once a week asking for us to train a dog."

"Train him to do what?" Sherry's voice sharpened with curiosity. "Are they thinking therapy dog? Or actually task trained?"

I stretched, leaning back on the hay bales. That was a tough perspective to give. "I'm not sure most of them know what they want. Or, like me, don't know how to ask. The usual approach starts out that they want a dog to calm their kid down. Or they want the dog to be a friend because the child doesn't have any other friends."

"Not service dog work, then." Draining her own cup, Sherry started to get up. "You need to get a good list of referrals together to use, then. Come on, let's get the horses–"

"Wait a minute." I shook my head. "No, that's not what I mean. And you still haven't answered the first question. What can you tell me about the condition?"

Settling back on her bale, Sherry propped her chin on her hands. "Well, it's classified as a mental disorder, but most research that I know about leans toward a neurological basis." A frown crossed her face. "Now that you mention it, seems like I've seen quite a few articles lately about increased prevalence. But is that because of more diagnosis or more actual occurrence? I wonder if anybody knows."

"But what's the gist of it?" I felt very much out of my depth, unable to articulate what I wanted to know. I couldn't possibly have understood then how much of my own confusion was almost exactly the same as what many parents faced when their worlds were rocked with a new diagnosis. "I don't get how it's different from other developmental disorders. How do you even approach the question of whether or not a dog could assist? Specific tasks, I mean."

A long silence ensued while we watched blue shadows lengthen over the darkening grass. I waited. I knew Sherry was thinking, not ignoring. Neither of us was bothered by long lapses in the conversation. This was all part and parcel of how we'd learned to extend each other's thinking.

"Well, so far as I know, and again my disclaimer is that I don't know much, I think it's more of a developmental delay than a defined limitation. How much and when any kid can overcome a given delay depends a lot both on the degree of affectation, and after that, how much really good therapy they get. There seems to be a lot of distorted sensory issues to go along with that. Hearing or vision. Maybe tactile. Any one or a combo either way higher or way lower than average."

Sherry started picking wisps of hay out of her bale and lining them up in her fingers. "Autism is called a "spectrum" for a reason. One of the main issues with standardizing therapy is how much each kid's needs vary."

Sherry continued lining up her hay wisps, and I began to worry for real. This sounded to me like she knew an awful lot, but if she considered her point of view to be limited, it was going to be hopeless for me. But she was still talking.

"Maybe one kid who is old enough to start elementary school has the approximate language and social development of a toddler. But he absolutely can't stand bright lights or tight clothing. The next kid can do advanced computer coding at six years old, but he can't handle the racket of noise in school. One student is nonverbal; the next can't shut up. That last one is toddler stuff again, but from a different angle, see? A regular "disorder" might have just one or two factors, then you have to look for what level of intensity. Autism is extremely multi-faceted. It can come in a hundred forms, with thousands of variables. Neurology is like that, right?"

I understood the pieces she was describing. Kind of. But had already convinced myself I'd be way out of my depth with the actual disability. "So how are we supposed to answer parents?"

"A family dog could maybe help build bonding. Provide distraction. Yes, have some emotional calming effect, if the kid likes the dog. But task-trained jobs? I don't see it. What could the child even tell the dog to do? More to the point, why would he be interested in trying?"

All of which goes to show that neither of us had much of a clue. Perhaps we really should have connected some dots sooner, but autism was just beginning to appear on our radar and we already had our hands more than full. Several more months passed before we received the first request with enough specifics to take action.

We thought it odd that the client wasn't interested in an actual service dog. A psychotherapist approached our school with a definitive plan for her daughter, who was entering adolescence. Autism factors aside, most pre-teens have an absolutely normal amount of distaste for continuous interference from a parent. In this case, one of the child's greatest hindrances to academic progress was incessant "stim" behavior–which can be nearly any repetitive movement for a person that has become overly habitual. A stim might be a stress relief or point of focus in over-excitement. Hand-flapping, rocking, nail biting, head banging… anything at all. Not usually harmful in and of itself, a boundary was crossed when a stim interfered with safety or necessary learning.

Our new client had a moderate amount of dog experience piled on top of her people-training experience, definitely enough to wonder if their own grinning and easy-going family Golden could be trained to help. The wise parent wondered if it would provoke less frustration from the girl than if she, herself, provided the interruption. We didn't know. Neither did the mom. Nor did any of us have any context to know if it was a good, medium, or horrible idea. But this astute professional lady's brain blended with Sherry's like mashed potatoes and good gravy. It was soon apparent we'd be finding out.

This project was not remotely service-dog-ish. It was a straight single-case experiment and happened only because the parent was a friend of a board member and paid directly for the training. We didn't even know how to name this project correctly. I wasn't directly involved, but watched with interest. With the help of an excellent behavior-shaping trainer who had a pretty good flair for drama, Lindy, the goofy Golden, became convinced certain human behaviors indicated excellent food was available somewhere on the human's person. All the dog had to do was nudge, push, lick, or otherwise interfere until said human produced the treat. Lindy's trainer turned the daughter's most common interfering or dangerous stims into doggie cues to come get treats. Before long, they separated the reward into a reinforcement that would come from a second person.

The project consumed a lot of time, but did get where the mom wanted it to go. Lindy learned to be extremely persistent with mostly gentle nose-nudging and shoulder-pushing. We'd all been pretty sure we could make that part happen, as it was just basic dog training: a specific action from a human gets a specific response from the dog. However, both cues and task departed any norm we'd ever used. Nobody had huge confidence in the project, but then we didn't really understand the rationale, either.

None of us thought we had enough expertise either to praise or criticize the mom's plan. She knew what she wanted. Everybody was safe. The dog was functional and content. I watched with interest but skepticism, not sure how or why this would make much difference to anything that mattered. But we taught the process, taught the mom to manage the process, sent them home, and in the normal schedule crush, the project gradually faded off our radar.

Hindsight being so flawless, doing better follow-up might have provided a shortcut to some solutions that would take us long years to find again. But for us, this sideline interest wasn't more than a slight curve in the road. And had more to do with correctly answering a steady stream of calls from parents than with anything we had the power to influence. Or so we thought. Besides, I told myself, one day when I noticed a young boy with stims in a grocery store. Now it was much more interesting to me because I understood what I was seeing. But, still, I reminded myself, for one thing, that doesn't require help. For another, you don't have any time anyway. Forget it!

Spread thin? Yes. I loved my farm, had no regrets about moving, but the basic truth remained: it was more than a full-time job for several people. Only beginning to realize how over-mounted I was, I tried to carve out some time for a return to freelance writing work again. That was overly optimistic, considering my lack of discretionary time. But for me it was also a desperate bid for survival

funding, since trainers' salaries were so low. It worked—
sort of, keeping me afloat, but adding layers of
complication and time pressure. Nowhere in this mix
were there many extra moments for contemplation of
concepts like autism that were still very abstract to me.

Intense schedules persistently tried to interfere with my
newfound peace of mind from the farm, but Sherry and I
both fought to guard the aspects of the rural setting we
loved. Each of us having the other immediately nearby to
backstop horse care and various farm tasks made it
possible for us to protect our time in a way that probably
wouldn't have worked if either of us had been totally on
our own. That year was the first, however, in which I
noticed a new trend: we weren't the only ones drawn to
the quiet beauty of this hilly woodland.

Sherry stopped by one evening while I was still talking to
several trainers who lingered well past the end of their
work hours. All I had yet for a house was the most basic
beginnings of utilities and foundation, but the yard beside
it was frequently full of trainers and young interns
lounging here and there, talking among themselves and
soaking in the surroundings. This was a trend I wasn't
exactly sure what to do about. On one hand, it was
obvious the beautiful views and soft silence gave them
the same stress antidote it did me. That alone had lots of
value. On the other hand, their presence pushed against
the boundaries of my introverted nature. It cut into the
very essence of this property's function for me and made
it difficult to get away from work.

Sherry eyed the group while she approached. "Hey, Julie,
can I have your help for a little while over at my barn?"

"Of course." I stood up, not at all reluctant. There hadn't

been any polite way to tell this group I was done playing hostess for tonight, but I was ready to get on with my evening.

All of them rather reluctantly abandoned the yard, drifting to their vehicles. I climbed into the passenger side of Sherry's truck. "What's up?"

"Nothing," she said absently, handing me over a travel cup of gin and tonic. "But I think the work day is over."

"And hallelujah to that," I said, taking a long sip. "Where are we going? Nothing is wrong?"

"Nope." Sherry had driven exactly 100 yards to the front of my half-finished barn. "I think our business tonight is to decide whether to do a walk or a ride."

"Cool beans," I responded, hopping out of the truck. "Some of that group wanted to stay the whole evening, I think. I mean, I get it, but—"

"Nah." Sherry interrupted me. "They're good kids. Maybe should start some regular social time here. Something more specific. Whatever we can come up with."

We both entered the tack room and started pulling down saddles while Sherry continued. "But meanwhile, I think we need to start ranking our weeks on a scale of 1-10, depending on how many of them want to move in and stay."

Chapter 11

"An inferiority complex would be a blessing, if only the right people had it." —Alan Reed

Even while the complexities grew from a burgeoning service dog school, more and more often I keenly felt the impact of my move to my newish acreage. The Great Farm Relocation project brought its own levels of complexity. The farm, space, setup, and variety added both bonus and complication to all dog training. The school and the farm became my personal edition of the-chicken-versus-the-egg debate. Did my involvement with the school grow because of the farm? Or did the farm happen because of my involvement with the school? Yes.

No doubt, I continued to learn about both training and evaluating dogs in new and better ways than would ever have happened in a more structured setting. I'd quickly realized even taking dogs on field trips to farms didn't give the same information as watching a young dog live 24/7 in that same environment, having to adjust behavior to a wide mix of critters, people, and spaces. How they learned, if they learned, and what they learned was playing a larger role than ever for most of our program trainees. But, then, how could I be surprised when the humans were experiencing the same learning curves? The move to the farm was a major adjustment all by itself just for me–a young woman so naïve on the practical level that I'd never operated so much as a battery-powered screwdriver.

Sherry's dog-training internship had begun shortly
thereafter, which was another really large change of
footing for both of us. Program growth continued in
geometric multiples. It seemed we had a new and
unheard of need for a specialized service dog
approximately every other day. When all the changes
combined, I knew I had to get better at
compartmentalizing, and that was definitely not one of
my better-known skills.

In her role as Master Social Worker doing our school's
client evaluations, I answered to Sherry. In my role as her
internship instructor, Sherry answered to me. We were
good friends who became immediate neighbors and
promptly started sharing horse care, errands, and many
life logistics... nearly every aspect of our daily lives now
overlapped, creating constant new dilemmas where
nobody answered to anybody.

Rushed, conflicted thoughts ground to a halt multiple
times a day. Any recipient of parent training or business
coaching has been taught about "time out" to relieve
pressure or allow thinking time. We soon developed our
own version. Over and over we had conversational
sequences that went sometime like this. One person
would yell, "Wait! Give me a minute to think!" followed
by the other one: "We're out of time for thinking!"
Followed by "Just ten seconds! Shut up!" And so on and
so on. After much trial and error (heavy on the error) we
eventually distilled this down to someone shouting
"TEN!" During any given discussion, as our evolving
strategies went, shouting "ten!" was a safe-word. We
swore blood oaths to honor it with a few moments of
silence for frantic thought, head-clutching, and
reclassification of exactly what might be going on.

Gone were the days of casual, sideline, part-time employment, training few dogs at a time. What our school needed was a dozen new full-time trainers, and we needed them yesterday. Since we didn't have them, we had to get intensely creative about maximizing time with the ones we did have. All who were teaching apprentice trainers tried to make every session, every outing teach not only dogs but also trainers. It's fair to say that some days we did better than others.

By the time Sherry picked up her first leash as an apprentice trainer, she was already about 10 times as effective at teaching humans as I would ever be. Yet, while endlessly devoted to the clients, her patience with the general population and a legendary temper sometimes needed a little work. She was used to having absolute control of the setting when she applied her skills. One of the roughest parts of training service dogs is that you usually just... don't.

Teaching the dogs specific responses to commands was almost always quick and easy. Teaching the same dogs to generalize those responses well enough for novice handlers to stake their lives on was way harder. For starters, no service dog school owns its entire city and the dogs have to learn to work in widely varied circumstances. So you get to work the dogs–trying for intense focus and critical, split-second timing of reinforcements–amidst a constant parade of fascinated by-passers. Fellow lovers of dogs, wanna-be trainers, and self-appointed experts created a lot of trainer frustration. However, the same flow of humanity also brought us fosters, apprentice trainers, clients, and occasional funding. With such a dichotomy always looming, we didn't have the luxury of telling them to bug off.

Not to say that all by-passers were interested–or sympathetic. Worse than fascination was oblivion. Some people would ignore the dog entirely, bumping into him, stepping on toes or tail, or stopping at elbow distance to have a long, loud conversation right next to a trainer trying to ease a dog through a difficult task.

I'd taken Sherry out in public with a group of dogs maybe four or five times before I decided I was brave enough to introduce the full sequence of door-opening. Today's task: introducing a pair of retrievers to this complex skill. About two months of prep came before today's part. Teaching the entire task meant chaining eight or nine commands into one process. It wasn't a frequently needed task, it was a critically important for true client independence.

Prior to the age of "accessible" doors that popped open from a button, wheelchair users far more commonly faced tough obstacles entering and exiting a weighted door. Moving it, holding it, maneuvering a chair through, and getting clear before it fell closed (perhaps on a vulnerable body part or expensive wheelchair control) created a laborious task for many. Impossible for some.

Once the dogs worked through the basics at the training center, it was time to venture out in public to work with a wider variety of doors: different handles, different weights, different directions, different surroundings. And of course, the major difference: lots and lots of humans we shall call unique.

Today we'd been working our two retrievers, Chip and Baxter, barely 20 minutes when Sherry blew up, breaking professional decorum with a streak of profanity. "What is wrong with these people? Can't they take two steps to

use another door instead of charging through this one?"
Her complaint was not quiet, carrying easily to anyone
within earshot. Plenty heard.

I developed an abrupt itch near my left shoulder, directly
under the logo patch from our training school. A dozen
pair of unfriendly eyes honed in on us. I could already
imagine the complaining phone calls to Nori. Yet we had
no choice but to keep working. One of the dogs now
learning this task was for a college student who'd been
treated for frostbite the previous winter. Her small
college in Minnesota had no automated doors. Not far
into her first semester, a skiff of ice on the sidewalk had
erased her ability to open any door to any building. She'd
been left sitting helplessly on the sidewalk, in frigid
temperatures and high winds, until someone had
happened along. With safety at stake, until spring she'd
had to rely on other students—and their varying
schedules—for help.

Following her approval over Christmas break, we were
now teaching Chip, a stocky, strong retriever mix, to
handle those heavy doors for her. It was almost May. The
team-training of dog and client together needed to start
shortly if she was to make it back to school in August
with a fluent dog. The time pressure was on. Not only to
train the dog, but to work around the mall shoppers.

I couldn't deny agreeing with Sherry in principle. We
worked in tiny increments to increase the amount of heft
the dogs learned to apply. We added tiny increments to
get them steady and confident while the handler moved a
greater distance away. In a polished process, the dog had
to hold the door fully extended while the handler rolled
the chair through the opening, turned around, and used
the chair to block it from closing before signaling the dog

to release and return. That translated to about 10 feet of separation between dog and handler, some of which kept them out of the direct line of sight. The entire process might take anywhere from one minute to three minutes, depending on the weight of the door, the handler's dexterity with the wheelchair, and…. let's say… "interruptions."

Interruptions happened when a by-passer decided that this beautiful dog needed to be petted and cooed over. Or when the next interrupter decided the horrible trainers were abusing the beautiful dog by making him work instead of accepting their offered chunks of hotdog or French fries. Or, by far, the most common? A small herd of people swarming past with nary a glance at the dog, chair, or trainer. Groups of chatting teenagers would hustle through with shrieks and squeals, whacking the poor dog in the head with an oversize shopping bag. Arguing couples elbowed each other back and forth, bumping into the door the dog was holding, turning their backs on the protesting trainer. The single shopper with a cell phone glued to an ear was always a safe bet. Making a beeline for the easiest passage–the open or partly open door–he'd brush through with total indifference to our presence, let alone the process.

Ultimately, of course, service dogs had to work with and through all these distractions. But this early on, while they just barely understood what we were asking, the disruptions built a tough work environment. We had exactly two weighted doors at the training school. Identical except for direction of swing, both were in the main room where the dog had worked every day for months. A dog could learn the basics, but not much more, and working consistently in every set of circumstances takes a lot of time to develop. The goal was, of course, to build both the dog's confidence in the process and tolerance to distraction.

When time and schedules allowed, we trained in small herds: half a dozen trainers, eight or ten dogs. Usually an unbroken half-circle, human and canine, would catch attention from even the most distracted. But with our still-limited hodge-podge of part-timers, substantial groups weren't often realistic. More often, with our limited numbers of that time, we had to work in pairs and make the best of it.

Today, we were starting again after two aborted attempts to get Chip to hold the door long enough for the chair to move. Twice now we'd had to reposition him when hurrying shoppers cut between us, pushed on the door to "help," or stopped between us and the dog to ask what we were doing. We re-established Chip's attention, praised him lavishly for holding his sit, and started over. He took the leather strap in his mouth and eased back carefully, slowly, as he'd been taught. As the door achieved 90 degrees, Sherry told him to wait and hold. So far, so good. Sherry rolled the chair backwards inside the mall, bracing the footrest against the door itself.

We'd set up at the farthest door at the extreme end of the entire complex, but today it wasn't enough. We were no sooner in position than a trio of chattering ladies rounded the corner.

"A dog!" One squealed. "Oh, look, it's a dog!"

Apparently, a lot of mall shoppers had never seen a dog before. Or maybe just not one close enough to pet? I tried in vain to wave them off as they headed straight in.

Attempts to intervene almost got me run over. One lady crouched in front of Chip with her hands on either side of his face. "Oh aren't you a beautiful boy!" she crooned. Chip tightened his grip on the strap, held his sit, and rolled his eyes at me. He couldn't see Sherry, and she was the one who'd told him to sit. He thought it might be a setup. I snatched up his leash, told him to release, and turned him away from the group. He followed me with great relief.

But I hadn't counted on Sherry. She shot out of the wheelchair and landed in front of the woman who tried to follow Chip and resume petting. Reaching well upwards to this lady who had about six inches on her height, Sherry put her hands on both sides of the woman's face, squeezed her cheeks together, and imitated her croon. "Aren't you just an amazingly stupid fool!"

The group went silent. I felt my heart not so much skip a beat as stop completely.

The woman jerked away. "I was just petting him. There's nothing wrong with that. Keep your hands off me."

"There's everything wrong with it," Sherry spouted. "He's not your dog, so keep your hands off him."

"Let's go talk to security," one of the other women said. "Come on, Marge."

Sherry rounded as if to follow them until I grabbed her arm and literally dragged her away. "Get a grip!" I hissed at her in a whisper. "What do you think you're doing!?" I saw her temper recede and her logic plug back in. At least a little.

"I have had it with these people. We can't even train!"

She yanked the wheelchair out of the door and dragged it to the shade.

I ignored her and focused on the agitated dog, who was now certain all this angst was directed at him. After giving him several simple commands that I could praise lavishly, I offered him a drink and put him on a down-stay in the shade of a potted plant. I slowly returned to Sherry, who was now sitting in the wheelchair with her forehead propped on her hands.

Thinking it might be safe to talk now, I started the standard train-the-trainer response. "It doesn't matter what kind of fools they are. You can't lose your temper with them any more than you can with the dogs. There are a dozen reasons for that. If you don't care about the humans, care about the dog who now thinks you're mad at him."

That brought her thinking around faster than any number of appeals about the general public. Sherry's head came up, and I saw regret, but frustration, too. She glanced at Chip before answering. "I really thought this would be more fun."

"Some of it is. You know that."

"I know." Sherry's accompanying sigh was huge and deep. "I love the highs. And I can handle the big lows. Well, mostly, I can. But I had no idea the average daily grind was quite this strange."

"The people will always be strange," I said. "How can you, of all our trainers, not know that? You have to work around it. From here on, you stay focused on the dog and let me deal with the people. Tomorrow we'll come earlier, before it's this busy."

We returned to the problem of the moment: wrestling 30 minutes of training from a two-hour marathon of interruptions and inference. Sherry was right about one thing: the entire process was incredibly draining. Two hours here left everyone, human and canine, more exhausted than a 12-hour workday.

"Sherry?" I dared to pick the conversation back up as we headed for the van again. Both of us were riding wheelchairs, encouraging the dogs to pull us a little, but also assisting the chairs along by walking with our feet. This training phase was about working to smooth the dogs' different tasks into one blended process, but it was important not to exhaust them either mentally or physically, and today everyone, human and canine, was already wiped almost flat.

"Yeah?" Her voice sounded even more tired than I expected.

"You're going to have to make yourself cool it." I was weighing every syllable, knowing that over-explaining would do more harm than good. She must have at least 10 IQ points on me, and she already understood the dilemma.

"That's really hard to do," she said with surprising candor.

"You do it with your clients, in your office sessions, all the time. You do it when you're assessing our program clients. This is no different."

"Yes, it is different. It's not the same at all," came the more subdued answer.

"Then we disagree. It's close enough. The main

difference is that you don't have a public audience when you're counseling or interviewing. When you're training dogs, sometimes you do. If the board hears what happened today, Nori will murder both of us. And she'd start with me."

Silence held until we were all the way back to the van. I knew she was thinking, and I knew enough to wait.

"I guess," she finally ventured, "that I'll probably have to look at all this as an extension of counseling, not a break from it. Which isn't nearly as much fun."

"Pretty much correct." I considered my next words with great care. "It's more than that, though. We are so incredibly dependent on volunteers. A whole lot of our volunteers come from people we run into when we're out and about. For better or worse, word of mouth travels fast. We have to keep that in mind every minute."

"Yeah," she finally answered. "Okay."

We had reached the van. First step was always to get the dogs loaded, off the hot pavement and out of the reach of any traffic. Second was to fold up our training wheelchairs and get them stashed in the back. One dog, two dogs. One chair, two chairs. Sherry began filling the dogs' water pails. I dug out my keys and slid under the wheel, eager to get moving for home. But today apparently we weren't quite finished with curious people.

"Excuse me," a voice came from behind us.

We both turned in our seats to see a pair of dewy-eyed women staring at the dogs with familiar adoration. I tensed a little. Everybody appreciated people who loved dogs, but today… enough was enough. We just wanted to go home. I stepped back out of the driver's seat, plastered on a smile, and eased myself in between Sherry and the newcomers. "Can I help you?"

"I'm sorry to interrupt," the lady said, slightly breathless. "But I watched you coming all the way from the door. That dog is so beautiful! Is he your guide dog?"

I stared at her, clenching the keys in my fist, considering the driver's door standing open behind me. Sherry muttered something unintelligible and departed for the passenger side. I gritted my teeth and strained to find a friendly answer, marveling that this lady probably both reproduced and voted. The rest of the conversation wasn't worth recounting.

Five minutes later we were in the car, rolling away.

"Hey, Julie?" Sherry's leaned her head back against her headrest, eyes closed.

"What?" I half gasped. I was halfway down a cold bottle of water and already wanted at least three more. I could hear dogs snoring in the back.

"If that last woman volunteers with us, I quit."

Chapter 12

"A learning experience is one of those things that says, 'You know that thing you just did? Don't do that." —Douglas Adam

The cross-entanglements of property development and program growth seemed poised to stay forever entwined. With the passing of the ADA now almost a decade in the rearview mirror, few service dog schools had yet mastered the logistics of coping with the tidal wave of increased demand. But at least we had a professional core. We knew our business. We had each other for consults. With property development? Not so much. By any yardstick, I was wholly unprepared for the personal drama of living in the middle of an old farm gone feral... and trying to reclaim it.

This agricultural comedy of errors started abruptly and ran indefinitely. I found myself the owner of a piece of raw property on very short notice. We unexpectedly saw surveyors on the property next to Sherry's. Within the day, I'd hunted up the owner and had a contract on the tract before they had a chance to post a for-sale sign. I was too excited to pay much attention to friends–friends with acreage and far more experience–who gave me penetrating stares over their reading glasses. I couldn't be bothered with their wry perspective: "You have no idea what you've started."

Truly, I did not. I adored my wide open spaces. I joked about my future memoirs: "All the Things I Never Knew and Never Knew I Didn't Know." Yet I saw only possibilities, not the parallel implications. In the beginning, most of the early learning curve felt like pure fun and unbounded opportunity. Until, of course, it didn't.

It's just that some lessons carry a little more impact than others.

I had arrived at my new abode with a hatchback sedan, an aging RV, one gas-powered weed-eater, a medium-sized basic tool set gifted from my father, a dozen dogs, and an abundance of rash confidence. Probably in one sense, even my cluelessness served a purpose, as anyone with any sense would have dropped the deed and run. But I did, truly, love the space. I loved the quiet, loved the autonomy. As first seen with Maggie, inevitably, the vast changes in daily circumstances would make themselves known in my dog training. Both the available space and my proximity to Sherry added new options and possibilities to the program—as well as additional layers of complexity! What I hadn't quite realized just yet was the leverage for epic screw-ups grew right along with the size of the acreage.

Of course, everybody knows the basic concept of "stop and think!" We all know in a rather absent way that you need to look for long views and disconnected possibilities. Not doing so is a definite disease of youth. For me, on this rural adventure, I was so thrilled with the situation, so excited about proceeding, that it may be a tribute to an apparently merciful God that I survived my first year at all. But for most of the young and brash who live to maturity, if basic concern for safety won't plug in, sometimes general public humiliation can turn the trick. One fateful afternoon, fate—that fickle schoolmaster—

taught me more about cautious thought in about two hours than I'd learned in the previous 10 years.

The vet list was growing long that week. One German Shepherd with a lingering urinary tract infection. A Golden Retriever undergoing periodic re-checks for a large wound. A Labrador mix who needed annual vaccinations and another going for joint x-rays. Two recently trapped feral cats needed spay stitches out. A rooster was getting sold. One young goat, recently dehorned, needed a verdict on whether bandages could come off his little stubs. The apprentice trainer group was out and about with Trent today, so with little additional thought, I loaded the whole menagerie into my car and took off for the clinic. Had to get-er-dun, didn't I? Only the rooster and the cats were in carriers.

Ten minutes later, the lady ahead of me braked her SUV for a left turn. My brake pedal went flat to the floor with no response, and my middle-aged vehicle made immediate and jarring contact with the SUV's tow bar. It was a low-speed event; no humans or critters were injured. But the impact was just enough to set off an airbag. The SUV's tow bar went front to back through my car's radiator, sending a cloud of steam sizzling skyward. Animals lurched off seats and against windows. A bystander noted a cloud of what he thought was smoke. He called 911, and the show was on. The incident happened just a block or two from a firehouse, so first responders were there in moments, far faster than I could extricate myself and get hold of various animals.

Aside from the dissipating veil of steam, all anyone outside could see was a white goat in a purple turban hanging out a half-open window, screaming insults at all humanity. Goats are loud. He almost—but not quite—

drowned out the insulted screeching of the cats whose carriers were upside down on the floor. The rooster's crate door had come unlatched, and he was halfway free, shrieking and flapping. Both retrievers showed pack spirit and joyfully yowled along with the commotion. The shepherd was quite sure everyone and everything in the vehicle needed protection. She bounced from window to window, raging at the strangely dressed men racing toward my car. From the outside, I seriously doubt anyone could see or hear any evidence of a human.

The first responders, logically suspecting fire, rushed the car, yanked doors open, and discharged the entire zoo onto the sidewalk. By-passers gawked. Pure pandemonium ensued. Nearly every imaginable event that could logically be assumed to follow this mess did, indeed, happen. The miracle was that all animals returned home safe and sound, despite my idiocy.

I recall how long it took for my hands to stop shaking. I remember how long my friends laughed at me and reminded me I was, yes, an absolute fool. I definitely remember chasing a goat several blocks on a four-lane road and carrying him back, staggering under his thrashing, 70-lb weight. We made the local paper, purple turban and all. *Fender Bender on North Cedar Really Got Her Goat.*

Somewhere in the melee, I'd found my phone and called Sherry for help, since she wasn't far away. She arrived in a few short minutes. I was thrilled to see her, but slightly less thrilled with her response. Barely glancing my way, Sherry snatched up all the dogs and promptly abandoned me to my legal penalties without a backward glance. It turned out to be a very long afternoon.

Standing in my bathroom that evening, stripping off ruined, torn, soaked clothing, I stared at myself in the mirror. It would be a while before my black eye and cheekbone faded. The backs of goats' heads are remarkably hard. I touched the swelling gently, cussed myself silently, and wondered aloud, "*What* were you thinking??" The only plausible answer, of course, was that I hadn't been thinking at all. It had simply never occurred to me to wonder what would happen in case of an accident. Basic? Yes. Honestly overlooked? Also yes.

I thought of the phone calls I needed to make and shut my eyes in dread of having to explain this mess–and my need for temporary use of a program van–to Nori. All in all, I think it was the first moment in my life, albeit far overdue, that instilled in me adequate respect for unknowns.

I really had thought of myself as a cautious trainer. Yet where in today's episode could I claim any respect for caution whatsoever? I closed my eyes, breathing a sigh of thanks that it hadn't turned out worse, then mentally thrashing myself again for such poor judgement. As I stood admiring my black eye that night, a barrage of guilty memories saw the tackle and piled on.

I thought about my very first service dog client who'd used one of those bulky electric wheelchairs. Unlike many paraplegics I'd worked with before, this lady actually traveled around on her own. A lot. We had a smashing success with a great dog for her until her first solo trip in public. She called me from a restaurant one night. "When I'm alone and have to use a bathroom stall, where does the dog go? He doesn't fit." Cue a long moment of strained silence from the trainer. Oops. I had no idea. It had never occurred to me.

I thought about another one of my earliest trainees: a dog
for someone who had extensive third-degree burns. He
was ecstatic. There was no budget in his life for a vehicle
he could manage, but the dog gave him his mobility back.
All was fine until I got the call one afternoon to hustle to
an emergency room two hours away. Someone needed to
take charge of the dog. The client was barely conscious
and being treated for heatstroke. Too much time outside
in the sun. People with extensive burns often lack
sufficient sweat glands to cool themselves. "What kind of
time limitations did you give him?" An angry nurse with
a rigid face scribbled notes without looking at me. Well,
none, of course. I hadn't considered burn protocol to be
my part of the equation and it never occurred to me. I
learned from that, I protested to myself, still staring in the
mirror at my eye swollen half-closed. I never let it
happen again.

For all the good any amount of forethought had done me
today.

That day's sharp fear for the animals, alongside the
profound embarrassment, lingered long in my mind. I
think I can say honestly that despite many future errors,
few ever again came from failure to consider. I went
forward with near paranoia to scan every setup of
humans, animals, and/or equipment to wonder what my
worst-case scenario could possibly be. Ten years later,
one of my training interns threatened to quit, telling me
in no uncertain terms that I was the most suspicious,
pessimistic cynic she'd ever had to work for. She was
truly perplexed when I grinned and said, "Thank you!"

But that evening, I simply wondered if I'd ever again
take a single step anywhere, with any animal, before
considering what horrid eventualities would stalk me.

"Congratulations," Sherry responded to my concern when she settled herself in my tiny RV living room a short while later. "Isn't that the sign of a true professional? Someone who has made every possible error in a very narrow field."

I sighed and sunk deeper into the sofa. "I like the one better about the expert being the one who's talking about his trade at least 200 miles from home. Because nobody around here is ever going to let me forget today."

"Well, at least it's something you can use." Sherry swung her legs over the arm of the chair and we settled in to dissect the situation thoroughly. "Did I ever tell you about the alcoholic I released from treatment, because I was so sure he was fully sober? Except I entirely missed the little problem that he'd started on opioids. My insurance went up a whole lot after that."

Chapter 13

"What's the good of living if you don't try a few things?"
Charles M. Schulz

I found Sherry up near the top of the hill. She was sitting in her truck, staring across the road at her own barn. Even when I walked up beside her open window, she didn't look at me. "What are you doing?" I asked, puzzled by her concentration.

"Watching karma happen." She responded without turning. Then she pointed. "Look."

I followed her gesture to the broad pasture beyond her barn. Two bright red trucks were parked inside the pasture. I couldn't read their logos from this distance, but I didn't need to. They were contractors for the water system whose eminent domain access cut across the corner of her property. I frowned. "That's not on their right of way."

"Nope, it's not. They like to use my gate because they're too lazy to go around to their own."

"Aren't you going to kick them out of there?" This was odd, I thought. Sherry was rarely so passive.

"The goats are handling it. Watch."

I looked, but couldn't see anything until I stepped up on her truck's running board to raise my eye level. Aha! Several of the goats she kept in the pasture for weed control were cavorting around just beyond the trucks. As I watched, one sprang up to a truck hood, rapidly followed by several more. In a hooved game of follow the leader, they bounced cheerfully from hood to roof, leaped across to the next truck for a few pirouettes, then circled back for another lap. I winced, imagining what 16 hooves were doing to the surfaces. "Are you going over there?"

"Wasn't planning on it." Sherry finally turned to look at me, wearing an expression of intense satisfaction. "That's their fourth pass, and I hope they do ten more before those guys notice. What's that, anyway?" She noticed the box under my arm.

"I don't know." I handed it up to her. "It just got here, and it's addressed to you."

"That" was a box with half a dozen videos sent by the mother of the young autistic girl for whom we'd trained the family dog the previous year. She'd promised us some video of her daughter and Lindy. We'd all but forgotten about it. We departed the hilltop for the nearest VHS player, curious, but only mildly so, expecting to see some fun, cute video of a kid and her loyal dog.

Far past midnight, we'd not yet torn ourselves away from the bombshell tapes. Lindy's performance was as goofy as ever, but the sequence of events captivated us, body and soul. We re-ran some sections over and over for hours. The info inside that box surpassed anything we ever thought we knew about blending dog-human interactions.

We watched the child repeatedly begin to hit herself in the face with a book (one of the problematic stims), which cued the dog's interruption. The girl didn't notice the mom's surreptitious reward to the dog, but she did respond to her mom's praise for putting the book down. Teaching resumed. In the space of a half an hour, we watched that one stim go from multiple repetitions in a single minute, to less than one per minute, to one every five minutes, and finally, amazingly, a self-check and refocus from the child before the dog could intervene. The mom's handwritten note told us that after several similar sessions of less than 30 minutes, that one unsafe stim, which had been one of their most persistent barriers to learning, had faded entirely and was seen no more. My primary thought: thirty minutes?!?!

Sherry and I exchanged frequent glances, and she started scribbling notes. I chewed the eraser right off my pencil. This was to us what the first rustle of leaves is to a big-game hunter. All the previous year's attempts to analyze what dogs could or couldn't do to help with autism came roaring back. Our brains ran to overload as we re-considered details of all the calls from overwhelmed parents. What else could we pull out of a child's behavior to create cues?

From the standpoint of dog training, developing cues from human behavior was unremarkable. All dog training does exactly that–it just so happens that the cues usually have a different, more deliberate origin. How much of this behavior would extrapolate? Could this work more like our process of training a dog to respond to a seizure and hope the response someday morphs to an alert? For both of us, an intense fascination sprinted off down a road we'd never considered. Our extended conversation continued for days, weeks.

"The possible applications go way beyond therapy,"

Sherry mused the following afternoon when we were
back in our hay-bale conference room. "Any kid, most
kids, resent corrections. So, okay, a lot of the stims
happen when the child is already stressed or triggered. So
from a kid's point of view, interrupting a stim is doubly
negative. And it's already a point of confusion for a
parent, therapist, or teacher. I mean, what justifies
interrupting a stim? It's not supposed to be only because
the stim annoys someone else."

Sherry would automatically fall into teacher-therapist
mode herself during these discussions, which was
fortunate for me, since I was usually far, far behind.

"Hypothetically, if a person actually could 'force' a kid
to give up a stim, then the next question is whether that's
a good thing or not. Or if you're producing a bigger
problem than you're solving. The behavior is likely to
resurface in some other way that might be worse.

"So the knowledgeable standard seems to be that it's
justified to interrupt stims that are self-injurious or
otherwise dangerous," she continued, "or else if the stim
is blocking progress to learning a critical skill. No doubt
that in those videos, the dog's interruptions gave them
both a subtle, but really important, shift they could build
on. It looks to me like it happened without adding
stress—or at least her mom thought so. What I'm
wondering is how this plays with other behaviors."

I was so lost. "I don't get it. Like what?"

"Well, like bolting. Almost all kids have a try, sometime,
at running from their parents at least when they're little,
like a toddler thing. They probably don't recognize
danger. Autism could turn bolting into something you

find in an older kid who can outrun Mom."

"Hmm. Like the woman who asked us last week if we could teach a dog to knock her son down in a parking lot?"

"Yeah, exactly."

"Exactly what? We'd be in business maybe five more minutes if we ever did something like that. I mean, yes, I do get her point–that he's better off on the pavement bleeding than in traffic dead." I stretched back on the hay and rubbed my eyes. "But authorities would take a dim view. What are you suggesting?"

"I'm still trying to figure out what the dog could do. But nobody can watch that tape and argue against successful redirects. I'm suggesting something other than knocking the kid down."

"All of it would be limited by the parents. How typical do you think Lindy's family is, either in therapy experience or available time? Should we even say this out loud anywhere?"

"I have no idea at all," Sherry admitted. "Probably not very typical. But "how many" is more than zero. Lindy's family proves that much. But one dog dealing with one child? I don't know. We used only five specific behaviors, with an extraordinarily competent parent. I'm not sure we could teach the average family to manage it with enough consistency to get similar results."

Several catastrophic training memories sprinted through my mind. She made a fair point.

Brains still churning, we sat in silence, watching the sun sink behind the Blue Ridge peaks. We knew we were onto something, but sheer variability overwhelmed the potential. I felt actual butterflies in my stomach, but could not tell if they came from excitement or worry.

The barn's analysis center stayed busy for weeks as we dissected the equation needed. Sherry spent as much time on the phone with Lindy's owner as the beleaguered lady was willing to give us. Her therapy experience gave us our first useful yardstick. "Your criteria would have to be very strict and very specific. I'd recommend working only with families who've already established a behaviorally-based program. If you don't have that, you'd have no starting point at all."

That comment alone set us back months while we tried to self-educate. But every question answered gave rise to several more. Meanwhile, the number of calls from distraught parents increased.

A full year passed before we tried to train another dog for another family with an autistic child. This time, it was just the two of us. Almost as a whole, the rest of the trainers said we were speculating way too far. Nobody else wanted to be involved. But we finally obtained clearance from the board, and from Nori, as long as we were spending our own time and resources, not the school's. The one retired teacher on our board told us it was a huge waste of time. Neither of us was sure she was wrong. Yet we couldn't unsee the videos.

We'd seen the mechanics of a frustrated child-to-parent relationship greatly altered by a dog. There had to be a way to extend it. But we were still struggling to verbalize a solution, let alone know how to train for it. Had we really appreciated the magnitude or complexity, I doubt we'd have dared try.

Years later, one father gave us the best summary ever: "Before we had our dog, our interactions with our daughter were mostly about 'don't, don't, don't.' She had such limited freedom, and every unwelcome boundary came in parental form. Don't touch that. Don't walk there. Don't chew your fingers. Don't eat that. Don't pick that up. We were the Don't Police. For her, it never stopped. Most of 'don'ts' were about safety, so we had little choice. When the time came that the dog provided the 'don'ts,' we were freed to focus on positives in a way we'd never been able to before. It changed everything. It changed the entire dynamic."

But that was far in the future. Here, in this earliest part of the learning curve, the path ahead was steep. Though we understood the idea of behavioral intervention, we had only the vaguest understanding of how to apply it. Many months passed from the arrival of those videos to the placement of the next dog. At first, we considered our second placement 100% successful in an unconscionably short time. And we couldn't have been more wrong. In truth, the project was a fine example of novice short-sightedness.

The young autistic fellow in question was five years old and had had a fascination with power outlets. Who knows why. His worst problem behavior was to seek them out, insert fingers, toys, forks, or anything else he could put his hands on. His mother, Jackie, was ready to return to oil lanterns and wood heat. She spent most of her day blocking him from outlets. By the time she could move the sofa and get him away from one outlet, he was upstairs behind the bed, intent on another. "I can board them over, keep the breakers off until I need to turn on a lamp, or I can put him in leg irons," the mother told us.

"So far as I can tell, those are my only options."

No, she had other options. It was not that hard to teach a dog to react to a child near power outlets. Somewhere in this process, I even learned that dogs can detect current in a power outlet. Scent or sound, I didn't know, but Trudy, the young mixed breed we taught to intervene, didn't bother to respond to unpowered outlets. But she never missed interference if one was live.

A few months later, we were feeling quite smug. We had a dog in the home who would not let the child near a power outlet! With obnoxious licking, nudging, and pushing, Trudy put the problem behavior to rest in less than two weeks. Sherry and I spent most of a day drowning ourselves in celebratory wine. Jackie was ecstatic. Fabulous success, right? Truly, not so much.

That quandary about some squashed behaviors reasserting themselves in other ways returned to haunt us. With youth's infinite creativity, Jackie's son soon refocused on a different disruptive behavior. He turned his focus to windows. He liked to open windows. He like to break windows. He liked to throw things out of windows. He liked to crawl out windows onto the roof. None of us were sure exactly where to draw the line between normal obnoxious child behavior and autism-fueled dangerous fixations. It was in there somewhere. Even Jackie referred to their responses as 'The Mom and Dad Show.' And she was keenly aware that some portion of the fixation (true to form for any bright kid) fed off their scrambled responses. But how could they fail to respond? Their home therapy program for skills acquisition was having very limited success, safety be hanged.

Meanwhile, Trudy prowled the house, watching alertly for any child going near a power outlet.

In the end, the dogs taught us the missing piece from their very natures. Sherry and I hung up from the conference call and walked the hills and pastures for hours that afternoon. A dozen dogs followed us with glee. We watched them rather absently while we drifted closer and closer to a conclusion that what we dreamed about couldn't be made to happen.

"We're back to using direct cues from the parent, aren't we?" Sherry's frustration was evident in her voice.

"I think so." Discouragement made even short answers hard. "Maybe they can get faster at it, but how do we teach the parents to teach the dogs about new behaviors? They can barely keep up with their kids. They don't have enough hours in their lives as is, and that makes it possible in theory, but completely unrealistic in actual life. Especially if the behaviors are going to change once a month."

"Even if the parents could learn that much dog training, it messes up a big chunk of the logic," Sherry answered. "What we're after is something that eases demands, not makes things worse. And that kind of training is way too hard for most—even if it was a quick process, which it's not." Sherry stopped in the middle of the field, pressing fingers to her temples in an attempt to concentrate. "No, we need something that increases their odds… just something…. there's something there. I know it. We have all the pieces. It's just not…. quite…. I'm missing something…."

Half a dozen retrievers charged back to see why we'd stopped. I noted, as usual, Sherry's favorite dog, Athos, the enormous German Shepherd I'd helped her buy years ago, circling to stay between her and the rambunctious crew. A faint idea stirred, but it drifted away again.

"Did you teach him to do that?" I asked. "I don't remember."

"Do what?" Sherry opened her eyes to see Athos guarding her legs. "Oh, that. No, I think he started doing that during all the times when we were down by the river with a bunch of dogs. I'd throw a fit and try to keep clear because all of them were soaked and muddy."

The idea circled again, paused, and retreated, just out of my mental grasp. "How? How do you think he picked it up? Did you call him? Encourage him to stand between?"

"Well, no." Sherry stared at me, nonplussed. "I guess he figured it out by my reaction. Big, fussy response. Me shrieking at getting wet and trying to shove the dogs away."

And there it was. Build a cue from handler response, not from the specific action. Essentially, basic imitation? The boss is concerned, so the bonded dog is also concerned?

I left the path, striding to the top of the steep river bank. Pulling several dog toys from my pockets, I hurled them all into the water far below. A small army of dogs went off the bank like a herd of lemming. All but Athos. He dropped to a half crouch and positioned himself between the incoming wet dogs and Sherry's knees.

Looking down at the canine surge around my feet, I looked next at Abby, my shepherd and my current competition dog. I remembered her response to a new kitten who'd been very difficult to teach not to scratch furniture. That had been years ago, and I no longer had house cats. But I remembered my frustration at hearing a long ripping tear from somewhere nearby. I would leap up and rush to stop the cat's behavior. Then young Abby started charging along with me. I remembered laughing and celebrating when I realized she would rush off to stop the kitten's scratching without me. She never harmed him, but she learned it from me, not from the scratching or a direct cue.

I stood there on the riverbank, looking from Abby to Athos and back again. Just as in the long-ago dilemma of Joyce and Ben, I remembered the dogs of my childhood: German Shepherds with farm jobs who'd dragged me away from the creek on my grandfather's farm, kept me away from the sawmill, away from the road. I stared down at Athos, who was still on-guard around Sherry's knees, trying to clarify a rush of new thoughts. It wasn't command-response. The realization solidified: it comes from the bond and from the dog's value of the human's concern. A specific action, a specific response, but the cue isn't about the action. It's relationship-based and built from the handler's reaction.

How hard could it be for parents to portray their worry in an exaggerated way that the dog would respond to? They were already responding–they wouldn't dare *not* respond. It was those half-zillion responses that were eating up their entire functional lives. If they could up the ante? Oh yeah, and have the exact right kind of dog.

With that one shift of focus, we had a new starting point. This was more about the inner workings of a dog's brain than about training. More control-freak, less direct cue. More basic tendency, less taught behavior. In short, we needed dogs with as much hyper-compulsion as the young clients they served, but who focused on the parents' concerns, not the child's.

But how were we supposed to find more of Abby and Athos? Most of their genetic "family" of German Shepherds also had a far higher degree of protectiveness than was acceptable for service dogs working in public. Yet the breed's fixation on their own humans, and their origins in containment herding played a role here. This breed had been developed to do livestock boundary patrol rather than "fetch and gather" more common to Border Collies. We needed dogs with a very specific set of personality traits and a very narrow range of acceptable temperaments.

But where were such dogs? Athos and Abby had the necessary behaviors, but neither of them would be able to work in unrestricted public settings. They were far too protective and suspicious of strangers. What else would work? We had no idea, and we had no idea that first we had to learn what wouldn't work.

Chapter 14

"Wishes father thought, but they don't breed evidence."
— *John Galsworthy*

Sherry and I began searching for our ideal "autism dogs" during a curious time in my life. The farm continued to chase me along the path to being a more astute and deliberate human. I'd learned much more about the true origin of "live and learn." I became fully convinced this old truism wasn't a matter of getting smarter from lots of lessons as you age. Not even close. The "live" part was because the last stupid thing you did hadn't (quite) killed you. So you get to "live" a little longer and therefore not do the stupid thing again.

I'd learned far higher stakes for reliable dog training than I'd ever encountered in the city. Jammed-up downtown sidewalks caused fewer dogs to break their stays when dogs learned stays alongside frolicking goat kids. Squirrels and pigeons in city parks stopped being an issue when my trainees learned around flocks of free-ranging chickens. Traffic sensitivity? Forget it. Let me show you bulldozer insensitivity. Dog nervous about commuter trains? Fine, we'll proof that issue right next to the freight track that ran beside Sherry's farm.

Yet property development forced me to expand other capabilities, mental and emotional as well as physical. To make progress here, I had to grow my brain, to push limits, in ways I'd never before had to. Lots of people get a school-of-hard-knocks education in different ways. Mine came at least partially couched in the unforgiving atmosphere of the old-fashioned, rural south who'd never completely given up on the idea that no woman should do what I was doing.

Truly, it was excellent human training for other events soon to come, and without that rather rocky path, I doubt the rest would have happened the way it did.

By now, my house was taking shape. The barn was all the way finished. We had a small but functional kennel and plans for a covered training arena. Those first two years, I fumed at the burly southern men who patted me on the shoulder and called me "little lady." I began to resent the ones who peered hopefully past me through the forest of dog tails and asked if my husband might be home. I paid a personal stupidity tax over and over and *over* before I learned not to take anyone at face value or trust what they told me about a project without a ream of research and a detailed contract signed in blood.

The incorrectly sloped floor of the kennel initially refused to drain. I'd had to have it broken up twice, once at my expense, once at the contractor's, until I learned to stand overtop of the workers and not assume they would follow my instructions. I was just a woman; what did I know?

I paid for three driveways before it dawned on me that for approximately 20% of the cost–no matter if it involved five times the hours–I could rent equipment and do the grading myself. Sherry had learned to drive a tractor early in her property-buying experiment. Together we came up with a new idea one day while we ranted and raved at the almost immediate washout on the steep hill of my main entrance.

"Didn't you tell him about the river surge…" Sherry started in.

"Yes!" I almost yelled back at her. "I told him until my eyes crossed. They do not listen!"

"Where were you while they were working?" Her response was chilly. "Surely you know by now that you have to be breathing down their necks every second?"

I knew. But I'd still screwed it up. Yet somewhere during that intense discussion of The Third Failure of Steep Driveways, we decided if we could sew tailored seams or play the piano, plus drive a horse trailer with six equine passengers, we could probably learn to drive a skid-steer.

We could. And we did. And the driveways got right. It took time, but eventually, the roads and approaches evolved into something that stood up to the gully-washer storms.

Starting the first day we bought home our very own New Holland 735, we started a week-long argument on which color to paint it. I wanted pink. Sherry preferred purple. We compromised on hot pink with bright purple flowers scattered everywhere. Every place we asked refused to paint a skid-steer pink, so we did it ourselves. Showroom quality it wasn't, but we loved it. Despite the distinctly feminine appearance, we named him "Bob." For bobcat.

Then started the endless jokes from by-passers who asked us some version of "What are you doing with *that*?" Or else just the scornful raised eyebrow and headshake. Initially, I did a lot of cringing. I'd spent most my life overly concerned about how others viewed me, and the habit was hard to break. But now I was getting intense Farm Re-Training.

One day, I miscalculated and ran a tooth on the bucket into the wall of my barn. Horrified, I scrambled off the seat to inspect the damage, wondering how I'd explain. What would it cost to repair? Everybody would see it!

The small hole at knee-height had damaged nothing but the sheet metal. I stood for a while staring at it, then scolded myself. Get a grip. It's your barn, your skid-steer, and your project. Resolutely, I climbed back into Bob's cab. I paused an extra moment, looking down the long driveway, looking up behind me at the many fences surrounding the various buildings. My little kingdom, I thought, with a grim smile.

With great satisfaction, I drove the point of the bucket into the wall a second time. My hands might have been busy on the controls, but inwardly, I was doing a classic overhead fist-pump. It's my barn! If I want to, I'll perforate it all the way around! This was total nonsense and beyond childish... but oddly liberating.

Not long after, I painted yellow flowers around the scars, with the holes forming flowers' eyes. They were definitely eye-catching, and I was quite proud of them. The little display became something of a barometer I used to gauge newcomers, whether friends, contractors, or clients. Even better, one day they greatly bolstered my confidence in a new relationship I'd dared to attempt.

"What's that about?" Scott, the hapless, unsuspecting soul, pointed to the floral display as I was giving him his first farm tour. The cartoonish daisies gleamed in the afternoon sun. "Are you going to paint the whole barn?"

"That?" Shrugging, hands in pockets, I kicked a little gravel off the driveway. "No, no more. Just those two. They're my reminder to myself that I get to do things any way I want here."

Scott eyed me cautiously. "This requires reminders?"

"Sometimes, yes." I shrugged again. "It took me a while to learn."

I saw his gaze flick from the bright flowers to pink and purple Bob parked nearby. "All right, then." He rubbed his mustache thoughtfully. "They look pretty good to me. Nice touch with the paint."

It was worth another inward fist pump. This, I thought, could go somewhere.

Sherry had far fewer hang-ups about others' opinions. And far better ripostes. One day, we had a group of program volunteers swarming the kennel area. Projects of the day were to set up new dog yards and paint an addition to the building. One of our more, err… knowledgeable… volunteers happened to be the new treasurer of our board. As a brand new CPA, he had a five-point critique of almost everything he saw on either farm. Too expensive. Too impractical. Too cheap. Too big. Too small. Everything he noticed was too something, including us.

Late in the afternoon, Sherry showed up with Bob to scrape away brush that had been cut for a new fence line. She'd invested in a pair of purple jeans and a pink jacket to assure full color coordination. Our treasurer was right on hand to criticize how she'd churned up the ground as she pushed the brush away.

"Look at that!" He called to her over the loud diesel engine, pointing to a small hillock of new red clay. "Look what you left! Do you know how to smooth that out so the fence panels can go up?"

Sherry cut the engine, leaned forward, and smiled sweetly at him, maintaining steady eye contact. "I didn't leave that today. That's where I buried our last treasurer. Want to take a ride with me?"

As best I remember, the treasurer quit soon thereafter. Whether one considers that a triumph or tragedy, we found his departure fairly typical. In those years and in our area, we found remarkably low tolerance for women who refused to stay in their time-honored lanes.

Fortunately, those farm endeavors were toughening my skin. All the rural-life training arrived just barely in time to save us from capitulating to the critics. More and more often, I found myself drawing comparisons from the property pain to the searches for the kinds of dogs we thought would be most useful in helping families with autistic kids. In short, most humans we encountered thought we were nuts. Professionals in a dozen fields told us to get a clue. The handful of other dog trainers we found who were working with autism in ways very different from our goals told us we were looking for the wrong kind of dog.

As for sources of high quality German Shepherds? About fifty percent of those we spoke with, throughout the country and internationally, too, announced we were dangerous idiots and would we please go away. The other fifty percent, without exception, assured us their genetic family would be perfect for the job. One hundred percent of them were wrong.

After some seriously expensive trial and error, we began to understand it was impossible to buy what we needed. The dogs might exist, but finding them would exceed our collective remaining years to live. All there was for it was to develop our own. That was a project of staggering proportions, but we were–fortunately or unfortunately, depending on one's point of view–too intent on our immediate goal to appreciate the overall scope of the problem.

By now we'd located a vast count of three—count them, *three!*—German Shepherd females we thought merited use in developing future litters. With one litter of pups on the ground and another due in a month, we were going to considerable length to shield the whole experiment from everyone else's view. For one thing, we were weary of trying to explain. Every one of our contacts inside the service dog world considered us candidates for the looney bin. For another, we thought there would be hell to pay in certain quarters over the idea of raising puppies at all; there was already a backlash building against "breeding" anything as opposed to sticking with rescues. Besides all that, we weren't sure enough, anyway, even between ourselves, how well this was going to work. Before we made any more attempts to present our case, we wanted more evidence, less theory.

Yet other events from our own school were building up to create a scenario we hadn't expected. Our far-fetched autism plans had one kind of dog-supply issue. But our group as a whole was also developing some dog supply issues. Different, but parallel. Autism aside, we'd long relied on sources of trainees that were becoming very impractical. Huge changes loomed.

Chapter 15

"If at first you don't succeed, try, try again. Then quit. No use being a damn fool about it." —W.C. Fields

If the problem with training service dogs for autism was about innovation, much of the corresponding problem with the mobility service dogs was simply about scale. We faced so much, so fast.

Better public education about the ADA was bringing not only more sponsorship, but an enormous increase in applications. We'd successfully boosted our trainer count, but each trainer needed dogs to teach or it was time and money wasted. The endless searching for more candidates seemed to get more difficult every year–every month.

From our onset in the 80s, we'd kept an option open to consider a potential client's own dog. It didn't happen frequently, but occasionally, if an applicant already owned a suitable dog, we did our best to consider it. For lack of a better term, we called them "pre-owned" dogs. It sounded too much like a used car lot, but we didn't have time to debate grammatical fine points. Following the passing of the ADA, the avalanche of applications meant most routes to a decent training prospect seemed like good ones. A decade later? Harsh experience pushed most well-established trainers into big reservations, at the very least.

Yet within our school, we had lingered. Our rationale

was at least partly about potential clients with a lot of dog experience. In such situations, especially with a newly acquired disability from trauma or illness, using that "pre-owned" dog could be a far faster fix. Especially if said client was paying his own expenses.

Matters became far trickier, however, with a relative newcomer to the dog world. Maybe the dog was not-quite-so-suitable, or maybe it was just hard to tell from a relatively brief evaluation. Even with a dog of the correct age dog in perfect health, often the only way to be sure was to try it out and see what happened. Even then, an owner's control of and previous bond with a dog could cloud objectivity. Habitual behavior is *the* cornerstone of effective training, and established habits between the client and the dog often haunted us long after we thought we were finished. Worse yet, failing out an unsuitable "pre-owned" dog could provoke disagreement and resentment.

Our staff was becoming quite polarized on the question. Nori still tried to capitalize on the very diversity among our members that had made us strong. Our unity endured where other schools had failed, but this divisive issue was becoming a big one. Sharp arguments sprang up. Disagreements lingered. Episode by frustrating episode, most of us were inching to conclusions that the entire process wasted more time and money than could be justified. But the entire topic of using "pre-owned dogs" was still a touchy subject when we arrived at the saga of Luke.

Luke was owned by someone who fell somewhere in between those divisions of experienced and relatively novice owners. Jenny had always had dogs. In fact, still had two when she received a Parkinson's diagnosis.

Jenny was only just beginning to debate the merits of a service dog when she picked up Luke on the highway one day. He was starving, sick, and suffering from major, infected wounds. Luke was a big boy of no particular heritage. Best guess is that he had a dozen breeds in his lineage. In the beginning, Jenny's sole focus was only on saving his life. Her vet had told her the injuries could have been from being hit by a car, from abuse, or from a dogfight. At his stage of advanced necrosis and infection, it was impossible to know.

Jenny teamed up with a rescue group who helped her cover expenses and get him healthy again. No owner could be found, so over time, her bond with the big dog grew strong. Even as she developed the habit of placing her hand down on his huge shoulders to help steady herself around the house, Jenny's thoughts returned to service dogs. We were one of the few groups in the entire southeast who'd even consider using a client's own dog. Jenny lived very near one of our trainers, so it was pretty much a given she'd find her way to our door.

Luke's health was perfect if you didn't count the scars around his shoulder, neck, and abdomen. His multi-colored, somewhat curly coat was always highlighted by a wagging tail, his attitude strong to please. Luke was friendly, surprisingly outgoing and showed us no sign of concern about cars–a double relief, considering his background on the street. It wasn't possible to know his age, except the vet guessed from his teeth that he was probably not more than three. Older than we liked, yes, but for an owner paying her own bills, that much of the equation was her choice, not ours.

In line with our rapidly growing concerns, we held several meetings with Jenny, in small groups and one-on-

one, emphasizing the uncertainty of the next steps. We might be able to try. We were thinking about it. But we showed her, multiple times, the list of similar dogs we'd started with in recent years. Not quite 30% had made it all the way through the program. Despite his health and willingness, we really preferred to start with a younger dog about which we knew more.

Jenny was adamant. She loved Luke and wanted to go ahead. All other factors aside, she wasn't sure she could afford a third dog, and wasn't going to give up either of her current two. Conversation at that week's trainers' meeting was rowdy.

Trent, who had overseen the last two failures with pre-owned dogs, was vociferously opposed. "I thought we were going to avoid doing this again," he pounced on the topic before I'd finished passing out the vet's report. "I can't even figure out where we'd put another dog on the schedule right now, let alone one with a bunch of potential problems."

"What problems?" Carol objected. She had volunteered as primary trainer. Jenny lived near her house, and the logistics for her to be in charge seemed to be the easiest choice. "Specifically what problems? Nobody can see any problems with the person or the dog."

"That's my whole point," Trent shot back. "We couldn't see any problems with three quarters of the last dozen, either. But they were all disasters. Haven't we proven how much higher the risk is? At the very least, to start with this dog would mean one less candidate that we could start from a more reliable background."

"You can't know everything about any dog." Barb still

tended to favor using rescues and had an even bigger soft spot for them than most.

"No," Trent agreed, "But we know a lot more about some than we do about Luke. Add in the issue of an owner who doesn't want to give us sole control of the dog during training."

"That's my biggest concern," Doug said. "I think where we've often gone wrong is not requiring the clients' own dogs to do the kennel portion of training just like the others."

"Jenny doesn't want to have him kenneled," Carol said. "I don't think she can afford it. If she didn't live so close to me, the project might not be possible. But I can make it work."

"I don't agree," Doug responded stubbornly. "It's not the same as having the dog here where we control all the factors and all of us can work with him. That makes for more objectivity and better generalization."

"Almost every time we try this, it turns into a money pit and a time pit," Trent cut back in, folding his arms. "Doug's right. The generalization is enough of a problem all by itself. Look, it took us a couple years each to learn to be consistent enough that we don't undercut each other when we rotate trainees. We're shooting ourselves in the feet to set up a training curve where someone without that fluency messes up progress."

"She has the right to train her own dog!" Barb shot back. "We follow the laws, yes? She has the funds to cover expenses, doesn't she?"

"Don't confuse law with practicality," said Doug, our former cop. "We're already completely overrun with all we can handle. She has the right to train, but no law says we have to be the one to do the training."

"We've done it for plenty of others," Carol objected.

"And we've had to flunk three for every one we finished." Trent wasn't giving up. "It's a bad drain on our time, and we're already drowning in time pressure. I'm way against it. Are any of you even considering that she's still working a full-time job, without the help of a service dog? How does this possibly rate high priority with us? What about the people on our waiting list who are still trying to get out of bed on their own?"

Silence held around the table for over a minute. Several pens scratched in notebooks. Almost no eyes met. Nori waited it out, then spoke. "Sherry, how are you feeling about it? See any exclusions looming?"

Sherry sighed. We'd been talking about this a lot lately, and I knew she felt very on the spot. "I think she'll try to do the work. That's a separate question from the dog's suitability. But I think it's also an almost separate question from how effectively she'll do the work. Her physical timing isn't that good, even aside from the illness. The trouble is that she doesn't understand she has lousy timing. There's an average lapse of almost a full second from behavior to her reinforcement. What I can't find anyone to assess is how much is her own nature and how much is because of the disease. It might get worse instead of better. She could learn her part way more easily on a finished dog than having her involved in the training process. I don't like the idea of her helping to train, but it's not justified to disqualify her for any dog."

"Carol," Nori continued, "have you had our attorney take a good look at the contract and have you asked Jenny to go over it with her own attorney?"

"Yes," Carol answered quickly and firmly. "We've gone through it line by line. She says she is willing to take the risk in favor of getting whatever training she can get for Luke."

"You're still a contract trainer, not staff," Nori riffled paper and checked some lists. "Are you willing to take this on as additional commitment without slowing training for any of your other assignments?"

"Yes, I am."

"All right, then," Nori made some notes on the ring binder in front of her. "I want one more meeting with her, with at least two of you present, clarifying that the initial 30 days is to be termed a trial. And after that, we can still fail him out on our sole discretion. Document the meeting, and send her a copy of the documentation."

Snorts and sighs went around the table from different viewpoints, and the meeting adjourned. For quite a while, nobody mentioned Luke again unless absolutely necessary. I carefully kept out of the way. It didn't really involve me, yet logic was drawing me to Trent's side. Every one of us was at absolute capacity. We were all working more dogs every day than could be sustained much longer. The kennel at the school was full. My smaller kennel at the farm was full. Every trainer was keeping an advanced dog with him nearly 24/7 for final polish. Yet the pile of applications continued to grow. I suspected most of our group wanted to prioritize the most severe needs, but that was a decision for the board of directors, not for a staff opinion contest.

More and more, I began to understand how some larger schools had progressed into standardized training and away from customization. Yet in scarcely more than a decade, our training unit had meshed into a strong, competent team. We could put together intricate details for certain clients when the same service just wasn't available elsewhere. The time involved, though, was extreme, and without a major staff increase, we needed a better process to sort priorities.

No miracle of consensus happened. We were still divided about 30/70% against when the decision from Nori and the board came back in Luke's favor. We were going to try.

Chapter 16

"The single biggest problem in communication is the illusion that it has taken place." —George Bernard Shaw

Away from the staff meetings and back on the farm, Sherry and I had a ton to discuss. This entire subject of where to find which dogs was a tense one on many levels. We were now halfway through our second year of trying to rear German Shepherd puppies suitable for assisting families with autistic children. Even with several young prospects shaping up well enough to thrill us, it wasn't hard to see the handwriting on the wall. Assuming we succeeded, we would have to come to address these same decisions before long. I wanted it to be simpler, but I didn't know how to make it that way.

"Some of these days," I complained to Sherry late one afternoon, "we're spending more time arguing about policies and dog choices than we're spending on training. Nobody wants to go to boiler-plate training, but we have to have better definition for what we will and won't take on." Boiler plate was our term for the idea of training all dogs to do a certain set of tasks, nothing more, and letting the clients take it or leave it.

"You want a set of rules," Sherry responded. We stood along our favorite riding trail in the woods and watched nine shepherds frolicking in the river below us. Two of our own. Seven adolescent trainees. "You want some formula to go by that absolves you of responsibility for making tough judgement calls."

I flung a few more float toys back down the bank with more energy than normal. "That's not fair. What's wrong with having some guidelines?"

"Guidelines are good. Rigidity isn't." Sherry strolled along the bank, one eye on the dogs, the other on the horses grazing between the trees. "I stood right here a few years ago and heard you promise you'd never let a set of "stupid rules" make your decisions for you anymore. What happened to that?"

"Nothing happened to it." I caught up my gelding's reins and climbed back into the saddle. "I just don't think it's any excuse for no policy at all, either. I'm pretty much in Trent's camp. This is hard enough when we start with a nearly perfect dog." I gestured at the furry crew around us. "Look what we had to do to get these, and we're still darned unsure. Starting with big unknowns? How long can keep up this pace—forget adding anything—before we have to pick and choose what we can do?"

Neither of us had a good answer, and we both knew it. We had trainers, experienced, competent trainers, who were still convinced using dogs like Luke was possible. And sometimes it had worked. Yet even without extra complexities from autism, others with more objectivity were getting quite critical of our training routines just for mobility assistance dogs. Case in point: Gretchen.

Over the last year, I'd struck up a friendship with Gretchen. She worked for a large guide dog school and was frequently on the road between the main training school of her employer and the satellite station where she worked. It became a habit for Gretchen to break her travel at the farm and relax as long as her schedule allowed. Sherry and I had both been pleased to get to know her, savoring the same tendency for blunt, in-depth analysis that had originally had drawn the two of us together.

To our mutual sorrow, Sherry and I had learned that by contrast, the bulk of dog trainers, professional or amateur, rarely shared our thrill with dissecting the extensive minutia of training theory or dog psychology. Taught by rough lessons ("I'm sick of you constantly second-guessing my training." Or, "Take your skepticism somewhere else, will ya?") we'd learned to value those who understood that we craved to look at every dog action, every human-dog interaction, with the highest-powered microscope we could think of. When we found our own mindset among other professional trainers, we loved it. So I loved Gretchen.

Except when I hated her.

Gretchen had stopped by the previous weekend on her way home from a Florida obedience trial. She had looked a long, silent time at the full kennels, the stack of notebooks by the door, and the four-foot whiteboard jammed with trainee names and notes. She said not a word, but her heavy concern was a palpable weight. I'd told her about Luke. Still, she had nothing to say.

Several glasses of wine later, she finally raised her point. "Do you know how many dogs are in my training string?"

I didn't. And I wasn't sure I wanted to know. "I feel sure you're about to tell me," I finally answered.

"Yep. Six," Gretchen said, toasting me with her glass. "I

get a seventh when I'm within two weeks of somebody else graduating. That's considered full-time employment. When I'm done for the day, they kick me out and I go home."

"And your dogs cost, on average, more than twice what ours do."

"It's sponsor money, not yours. Why do you insist on being such a friggin martyr?" Gretchen had enough alcohol in her now to get direct.

"It's not your money, either!" Maybe I'd had a bit too much wine myself. "You people have zillion dollar endowments. You *compete* with other schools for clients just to justify your seven-figure operating budget. We compete for funding, not clients. We scramble for every dollar and every non-guide school I know has stacks of applications they'll never be able to fill."

"And that's exactly my point!" Gretchen was getting seriously irritated with me now. "You'll never be able to fill them all. You can't change that. Why don't you admit you can't and stop killing yourself over it?"

"Yeah," I grumbled. "I think you just re-made our entire point of the last week."

We both dropped it. Like my continual debate with Sherry, there simply wasn't any good answer aside from big seven figures of income that we simply didn't have. Our school didn't have huge endowments or the giant infrastructure. Maybe once upon a time the big schools had been where we are now. I didn't know, and knowing wouldn't have made a shred of difference to our current dilemmas. We still had to sort through options one at a time and keep choosing where to spend limited resources.

I'd quietly concluded to myself that I thought the whole pre-owned dog concept needed to go by the wayside. Luke, however, appeared as though he would prove me wrong. His training had sailed ahead under Carol's expert instruction. Jenny had navigated the basics, passed her first field test, and inside about six weeks was working him in public settings. Which is where we hit the first snag.

"He's spooking at something," Carol reported in the break room one day. "I can't figure out what. It's happened on the sidewalk, in the parking lot to Jenny's office, and even near her desk. I don't even know if it's a noise or a sight or what." She was busily making detailed lists of every scenario from the past week. Everyone present peered over her shoulder, analyzing the lists for common factors.

"Problem is," Carol spoke almost absently, "It's not just something he looks at and decides he doesn't like. It's more like a startle reflex. I think it has to be noise."

"How often has it happened?" Trent's poured himself a cup of coffee, not looking at Carol when he spoke.

The room went silent. Carol was slow to answer. "Only once last week. Again on the weekend. Then three days this week so far."

Trent took a long swallow. "Fail him, Carol. Do it right now before we waste any more time."

"I can desensitize him if we can isolate what it is!" Carol objected strongly and wasn't about to be pushed.

"Well, count me out." Trent took another sip and headed out of the room. "He's not on my training list and I'm not wasting another minute on a project we shouldn't be doing."

Silently, I stepped backward into the kennel and resumed my own work. I didn't want to be pulled into the discussion if I could avoid it. Nobody agreed, and I couldn't change any minds or any circumstances.

But the ultimate answer for Luke wasn't far away. Our experiment with rural-style potluck and bonfires had become a regular thing, much expected among the staff. With fall weather rapidly cooling, it was time for another. About a week after the tension in the break room, the troops were gathering on the grassy slope below my almost-finished house. These events were usually restricted to our staff and volunteers, but Carol had pleaded with me to include Jenny in this invitation, so tonight we had our own version of a Plus One.

Doug tuned up his guitar. Others set up folding tables. As dusk gathered, a hodgepodge of trainers, fosters, and dogs surrounded our fire pit. All was idyllic as Sherry touched a match to the old cardboard stacked under the pile of brush. Smoke curled upwards between the branches, pushing the scent of burning leaves through the group and making everyone want to grab the nearest marshmallow.

Luke did not share our delight. He shot backward to the limit of his leash, bucking, crying, and trying to bolt. In vain, Jenny tried to calm him and unwrap the tangled leash from her knees. But the dog was beside himself, completely panicked. After a single shocked second, Doug leaped from his chair to assist. Jenny crashed to the ground. Luke took off across the pasture as hard as he could run. I was never happier that the entire acreage was fenced. Luke was well beyond panicked. Four trainers finally combined efforts to talk him to a halt, check him over, and hustle him inside my house, where he continued to shake and salivate. He had urinated on himself and blown his anal glands.

The rest of us stood motionless, drinks, hot dogs, and roasting sticks limp in our hands.

"It's the fire," Barb said tonelessly.

"No," Carol corrected. "It's the smoke. He's spooking anywhere he smells smoke, even from cigarettes." Her eyes were closed, fists clenched, as she concentrated to recall the variety of circumstances.

Nobody else had much to say as we all thought it through. A glance around the circle showed me that every trainer was considering the likely origin of those horrible scars around Luke's neck and shoulders. Accident? Purposeful torture from some sick person? We would never know.

Carol still thought she could bring him around, but Nori called a halt after barely another week. Luke's phobia wasn't getting better. The bonfire seemed to have formed a catalyst; Luke's fear was getting worse. Consensus was now 100% that we could not get him to a graduation-quality performance. Nori and Carol went to Jenny's house to go over the conclusion with her, but were unprepared for the explosive rage.

"You're just afraid you're not good enough to fix it! How dare you not give him a decent chance! You think he's going to make you look bad!" They could not reason with her. She asked them to leave.

Eight days later, our board of directors was served with a lawsuit for negligence, failure to meet terms of a contract, failure to seek adequate expert opinion, emotional pain and suffering, time lost, and punitive damages such as the court might see fit. Not one trainer had a single comment when Nori posted the text of the lawsuit on the bulletin board. We stood silently and read every word. We knew this was indescribably wrong. We'd met–no we'd exceeded–that contract in every detail, and we'd undertaken the entire project expressly to prevent her from emotional pain.

No canine training group on our side of the nation had more collective experience than stood in this room. But we couldn't do the impossible. Nobody was ever going to make Luke fully forget what enormous pain fire and smoke had brought him. The memory would follow him for a lifetime, creating unsafe situations not just for the client but for him, too. Even if he could be safe, he would never be happy thrust into circumstances of constantly facing what he dreaded most. How could anyone justify pushing a thoroughly traumatized animal forward into confronting his worst fear on a daily basis?

The same day our school was served, Jenny sent a copy of the lawsuit to a local newspaper. Of course, we were not allowed to comment, but the paper published the story anyway and the phones started ringing off their hooks. Two major donors were among the callers, announcing their withdrawal. We all gritted our teeth and bore down, trying to focus solidly on our training lists. The more sensitive, emotionally astute dogs in our groups made little progress.

Beside the text of the posted pages on the bulletin board appeared a copy of one of the news articles, topped with a post-it note with Nori's terse instructions: "Come to Monday's staff meeting prepared to discuss."

That weekend Sherry and I wandered the farm trails with morose spirits. "After this year," I said, "there's zero doubt my biggest dread will forever be what I don't know that I don't know."

"Yeah," she answered lackadaisically. I hadn't heard Sherry utter a dozen unnecessary words since viewing the lawsuit.

I could also tell she was very tired. Beyond tired. Exhausted in body and mind. So was I. Neither of us had been directly involved with Luke, aside from Sherry's best effort at an initial assessment. But the intertwining was there just the same. All the dogs were part of all the effort from every trainer. This result was far more than a single person's over-reaction. It spoke to the core of why we did what we did, and how we were judged for it. And it wounded the soul, sucking the very spirit from us, to make such strenuous effort to do the most we could, yet have someone–many someones–assume the worst possible motives.

"I guess the question answered itself," Sherry said, her low voice reflecting her state of mind. "None of us can take this kind of drain on our time when we're missing such big pieces of information. It might be different if using peoples' own dogs was the only way. But it's not the only way."

"That's the entire story of my life now," I said, looking absently around at the yawning expanse of farm acreage that was returning to civilization with only the greatest reluctance. "Everywhere I look are more things than it's realistic to do, so all I can manage is choose whichever ones I know I have the highest chance of finishing."

On Monday, I think every trainer showed up with muscles literally sore from tension, tossing, and turning. Nori didn't even pretend that the staff meeting held any other topics, but she led in with further bad news. Our insurance underwriter had announced they were going to settle the claim rather than fight. In the space of her single sentence, our collective discouragement turned to resentment.

"That's not right!" Carol exploded first. "We bent over backwards to accommodate her!"

"Tell that to a jury who will listen to the "experts" bemoaning the poor, misunderstood dog." Barb answered, never taking her eyes off her feet.

Doug's viewpoint was more practical. "It's going to kill our insurance rates, isn't it?"

Nori nodded silently. It was rare for her to be short on words.

"Can we negotiate the policy increase if we are never going to train any more privately owned dogs?" Trent sat with arms folded once again, but no anger now. He, too, was always one for the practical outlook.

"Money spent is money spent," Doug objected. "When it comes to insurance, you're already guilty until proven innocent. After a big claim, forget it."

"I don't know," Nori said, the discouragement heavy in her voice as well. "I'm sure we'll check into the possibilities. But there's a more immediate question. We have to stop trying to work with such situations, no matter how hard it is to say no. We can't be everything to everyone. Just the decision-making process alone has turned into too major of a drag on our time. It's hurt us in a big way, and even aside from that, I'm absolutely sure Luke himself would have been better off if we'd never started."

There were no objections.

Just for the record, Nori called for an anonymous paper ballot. We all scribbled a single word on a tiny slip of paper, tossing them into an empty water pail in the center of the table. Nori shuffled them. Counted. Then stacked them together and passed the verdict around for inspection. It was unanimous at 33-0. We were out of the business of training privately owned dogs.

We ignored anything else that should have been discussed that day. Nobody had the spirit to continue. We adjourned, filing silently out of the room, returning to our dogs and our low-paying jobs for the greater good of mankind. I headed home for the solace of the forest as soon as possible. Especially today, I was quite sure my animals and the quietness of the farm acreage could soothe my spirits faster than people.

Chapter 17

Our decision to stop training privately owned dogs had us all glancing cautiously at the next step in that staircase: training rescues. Already we'd become almighty cautious about taking on dogs from completely unknown backgrounds–any kind, from any source. Extrapolation of the Luke rationale raised ever-higher concern about how much time we were wasting. None of us were ready to take such a step. Finding enough dogs from any source at all was already so hard we simply couldn't afford to ignore any serious possibility. But we had no idea that next decision was already being made for us.

A last event of any kind, in any life, can be wonderful or horrible. A last repetition of a dreaded job. A last hug from a loved one. Sometimes anticipated. Sometimes a shocking loss. And sometimes the loss is a gradually fading distinction you don't understand until long after. Kelly, our last shelter dog, was such an experience for me: the end of an era I'd never wanted to stop.

The ongoing work with the young German Shepherds was, so far, only adding to my own confusion on this complex issue of rescues. Despite all our initial enthusiasm, less than half of the dogs we'd considered so promising were, as young adults, showing us the definitive behaviors Sherry and I wanted to see for the work we imagined. Those odds weren't much better than the pre-owned dogs. Did that mean we could do better with future generations? Or should we give up on the massive drain of time and money... go back to looking for dogs to purchase? We weren't sure yet, but we spent many a long hour splitting hairs over it.

But other program demands marched ever forward. One of the biggest logistical hurdles for finding new trainees would always be teaching new trainers to understand exactly what qualified. I thought about that dilemma, now sitting quietly, listening to Nori talk to the group of new apprentices.

"You're going to get big emotional highs," she told them. "But even while you're celebrating, you have to prepare yourself for some of the toughest challenges you've ever faced."

With our current staff mix of full- and part-timers at 33, This latest group of seven was smaller than the last, a size chosen more by budget constraints than by preference. But we all felt cautiously optimistic. Our teaching experience was increasing. And Sherry's perspective from having completed the process herself added a lot. We really did think we were getting a better handle on things.

Like nearly all non-profit jobs, we faced the major hurdle of simply not owning enough dollars to hire the specialized skills we needed for full-time staff. The only fix for that was to rely on contract trainers who were already professionals in some of the needed fields. This new group held a new physical therapist and a bi-lingual Spanish instructor, both sorely needed, but both would work just one dog at a time as a side job. It wasn't ideal, but "ideal" didn't play much of a role. We were doing the best we could with the options we happened to have—much the same way we hunted up our dogs.

This group also held one other first for us: two young college grads we'd secured grant funding to hire full time. If they were as good as we hoped, if they could stick it out, we could turn them into competent trainers in about a year and a half. But the entire issue of screening rescues was one of the tougher tests looming. Might as well get it over with.

Nori explained what the afternoon would hold. "Today, all of you are coming with us on an initial visit to three county animal shelters to check for training prospects." Nori stopped her typical pacing in front of the class and started using a great deal of direct eye contact. "I'm not going to lie to you that it will be easy. But you have to learn how to apply distinct filters for the kind of dog that will succeed in this work. Sympathy, pity for all the dogs can't influence you."

Nori paused and turned to her whiteboard. "Okay, time for brainstorming. Tell me what you think would have to be true in a new training candidate."

Hands shot up. Comments began. No aggression. Gentle. Cooperative. Natural retrieve. They were all good answers. But they were all doing exactly what most newbies did—miss the more obvious starting points. The most significant filter was hard numbers: age, health, and size. SuperMan couldn't train SuperDog to brace, pull a wheelchair, or get items on or off a shelf if the dog wasn't tall enough or strong enough. The job, not our preferences, dictated those terms.

Age made the next formidable barrier. Any prospective trainee had to be at least seven or eight months old before we could even ask a vet even for a preliminary analysis. Considering the average dog's relatively brief life–at least compared to a human's–it was critical to get the team graduated and working in early adulthood. Starting with a three or four-year-old trainee could severely shorten a graduate's working lifespan, which was not acceptable either to sponsors or clients. As a result, the age window of appropriate trainees was very narrow, and that's assuming you could even know an age. Call the window around eight months to eighteen months, maximum. And of the prospective dogs we found in that range, at least half of them would fail the health screening. These factors alone combined to create a daunting black hole into which we poured a nonstop stream of time and funds. And it all had to happen before we knew the first thing about how well the dog did or didn't do in training.

As with Luke, unknown backgrounds often ultimately overshadowed both physical traits and age. Like other schools, we had plenty of stunning success stories about rescues performing incredibly well as service dogs. But the percentage of failures remained a constant problem. The more our numbers grew, the more backlash we felt from the board about dogs on whom we'd spent lots of money, but who failed before graduation–or far worse, had to be removed from their job after graduation.

Luke's example had been a strong one made far worse by the lawsuit, but he was hardly the only one. And it wasn't limited to dogs owned by clients. Any dog coming to us out of a shelter carried similar risks. Scrapping months of training steadily was a built-in part of the process that grew right along with the overall size of our school. Even more than funding, the drag on our limited time was worse. We ranged ever farther to find suitable dogs, but found ever fewer. More and more often we were turning to purchasing pups from other schools or known breeders. In the end it was usually the more economical choice, but despite rationale, not always that well received in the public eye. And we lived or died by public opinion–and the corresponding donations.

"How can you dare not use all rescues?" During a fundraiser the previous weekend, one lady had stood by our display booth, fussing at us for the better part of an hour. "There are so many dogs out there who could have a chance for a better life. So many dogs who need homes."

I was running out of patience with her. "Ma'am, our primary obligation is to our clients, not any particular group of dogs."

To her credit, Nori hadn't actually knocked me unconscious, but she did more or less shove me behind the booth, taking over the discussion with the woman and trying to ease her into an understanding of the practical challenges. I really wasn't sure it was worth it, but at that point my public relations skills hadn't grown much past the handling inquisitive by-passers at the mall. And then, of course, the obvious: we *were* still using rescues. At least some.

Almost all our incoming "rescues" now were dogs that some reputable breeder took back in for some reason or another. I was no longer sure if that should be called "rescue" or "repurpose." The classic concept of a traumatized, abandoned dog scooped off a street and restored to life on the end of a service dog leash? That was becoming rarer by the year. As we departed that day, interns in tow, I was hopeful, but not optimistic. We needed to locate a couple of extremely easy-going dogs with high tendencies to fetch and carry.

One of those needs, especially, I could blame on Sherry, as her social-worker skills and adept maneuvering of state funds brought us an ever-increasing number of complicated scenarios. Coping with a single disability presents enough challenges. Coping with two unrelated disabilities can cause more routine challenges than there are minutes in the day. We had recently approved an application from just such a new client.

Stephanie had been born with cerebral palsy, so she was no stranger to finding creative solutions. A refusal to take "no" for an answer had seen her through high school, college, the successful start of a home business, and the birth of her daughter.

At 34 years old, Stephanie's life changed again when she was diagnosed with multiple sclerosis. Prognoses were grim. Doctors were un-encouraging. By the time Sherry finished sorting through a long list of varied tasks, one critical need stood out above all the rest: Stephanie needed a dog to be extremely fluent in fetching objects by name, especially a phone.

Needs were clear. Funding was in place. A contract was signed. Off we went to see what we could find. I didn't know it that day, but we were making one of our last-ever trips to shelters for prospects. After a dozen people spent an entire day scouring potential adoptees, we came home with exactly one dog: a beautiful, plush-coated, cream-colored Golden Retriever. We named him Kelly, and the training race was on. A client was waiting.

He was sheer ease to train. The process could best (and most blissfully) be described as uneventful. We were perhaps a month away from starting his in-home training with Stephanie when I took him home from the kennel for some intensive schooling on the matter of the emergency phone retrieve. Home-based training was always the best route for this task, since it might have to happen at any hour of the day or night. Even just getting the dog out of the kennel for a session was, by definition, an advance cue, and we needed to establish performance in any set of circumstances, at any time.

Hard as it might be for our current generation to understand, even in the early years of our new millennium, cell phones were not yet ubiquitous. "Phone safety" for a client did not mean then what it does today. Today a dog might need to learn to search for and retrieve a cell phone by scent or sight, to learn the name for the object, to learn typical places it might have been left. But at this point in our school's history, most people still had landlines. Even wearable emergency call buttons were still uncommon. The surest safety option for most of our clients was to have a designated "dog phone," a cordless unit with a specific shape to accommodate the dog's retrieve. Nobody else was ever to use that phone. It was only for emergencies, and it was a cheap fix. A $20 phone, a known location, and a well-trained dog made a reliable backup plan that lasted many years.

One day Kelly and I were working on my front porch when Sherry pulled in. She headed for the door, walked past me, then did enough visual rewind to realize I was upside down in the porch corner, mostly concealed behind the cushioned glider.

"Are you drunk or sick or meditating?" Sherry directed her skeptical question to my feet–all that was visible.

"None of the above. I'm trying to figure out how Stephanie would land if she fell over furniture."

"Don't you think you're focused on the wrong thing?" Sherry didn't seem all that impressed by the training fake.

I rolled to a sitting position and looked up at her. "What do you mean?"

"It's all well and good to proof him for you, and all these related gyrations," Sherry sighed the words out as she sat down to pet Kelly. "But she can't do any of that. Not safely. How are you going to transfer the task?"

I squinted at her carefully. "This is your first phone retrieve, isn't it?" I asked.

"Yes, unless you count Payton, who wore the phone on her harness. What's that got to do with it?"

"Let's put it this way," I answered. "If the dog is sufficiently generalized, then we can transfer the behavior without exact replication. So it's more a question of whether or not Stephanie will do the hours. Will she?"

"I think so." Sherry stroked Kelly absently. "We've sketched out a practice schedule in as much detail as we can. I broke my crystal ball last week, but I don't get any indications she'll quit on us. What she's had to do in the last year just to stay mobile has been at least as hard for her as what's ahead."

"Okay, then," I replied, "how about I do my job and you

do yours? I think he'll be ready for in-home training in about a month. Tomorrow we can get Nori's opinion on the timing."

When Kelly finally transferred to Stephanie's house, another gradually varied routine began all over again. But we set up a detailed practice schedule. It was tough, but the young woman persevered. She knew her safety might be at stake. As is typical in more complex placements, the in-home training lasted longer than the initial training of the dog. Sherry took over Stephanie's case entirely. The two of them spent months smoothing and perfecting. Though the phone-fetch became routine, practice continued until the process was woven into their daily life by habit.

Stephanie had a few tumbles during this time, which was unfortunately normal for her, but only once in the first few months did she use the "phone" command to call her husband for help. The other times, she was able (with Kelly's help) to get herself up again. We all took a few deep breaths of relief, and cautiously patted ourselves on the back about a new graduate team.

More than a year passed before they faced their biggest test ever.

We often think we know what "worst case" means. Except real life can surpass our largest expectations. One day the Stephanie/Kelly team faced a test of rare severity. Stephanie was moving around her kitchen fixing dinner. In attempts to hurry, she stumbled. There was no time to break her fall or otherwise protect herself. As she fell, her head struck the corner of a countertop with substantial force, plunging her into unconsciousness. As she slowly awoke, Stephanie knew she was badly injured, but wasn't sure exactly what had happened. Her vision was clouded and dark. She was having trouble making her voice work at all. Stephanie had a severe concussion, a fractured skull, and intracranial bleeding. Before the night was over, she'd undergo emergency surgery to relieve pressure on her brain.

But as she lay there, crumpled against the kitchen cupboard, her only coherent thought was to call her dog. He could bring her the phone. All the bottom-numeral speed dial keys were set to 911. As Stephanie tried to focus, tried to summon energy for the effort, she noticed a slight breeze near her arm. It was Kelly's tail fanning the air. A hard, cool object pressed against her hand. He was already there—with the phone.

I can never think of Kelly's stunning success as a service dog without the pang of knowing he'd been our last shelter dog. But for our school of limited resources, reality just was. All the wishing in the world wouldn't change it. For all the years ahead in which we bore criticism for moving in other directions, I defended it along those lines of reality. But real doesn't always reach your yearnings. Even as I ceaselessly explained, Kelly stayed in my mind—an unceasing reminder that I wished reality was different.

Chapter 18

Courtesy of an ambulance-chasing reporter, Kelly had his own news story after Stephanie's fall. Several months later, the YouTube version of the feature had six figures worth of views, and we still got calls every week asking for dogs "just like him." The group of interns who'd helped bring him home were halfway to graduation, now sometimes even working solo with clients. We'd been back to the shelters several more times, but not since Kelly had we come home with a dog who made it past health check and initial training.

Hard to find shepherds. Hard to find retrievers. Different logistics–parallel problems. We wracked our brains. We searched farther and longer. Part of our problem was something we hadn't yet caught on to. The increased growth of breed-specific rescue groups scooped more and more dogs out of shelters before anyone could adopt them directly. The coming age of "retail rescue" loomed. We weren't plugged into the pet adoption scene, so didn't have enough perspective to see it. We'd explored options for working with some of those rescue groups–most of them nonprofit like we were–but quickly learned that most required direct access to screening any dog's final home. For our situation as providers of medical/adaptive equipment, privacy laws flatly forbade such access. So much for that.

Many rescue groups were doing a fabulous job; that was apparent. Most started with a dedicated group of breeders or aficionados trying to stand between their dogs and horror ahead. It became impossible to miss, however, that a rapidly developing branch of "rescue" saw an endless pipeline of adoption fees at the far end of the new "Adopt, Don't Shop" slogan. On brief acquaintance, it could be really hard for us to tell which was which. Ultimately it often didn't matter since the results for us were the same. We repeatedly ran into overt resistance, objection to our criteria, and refusal to let us take dogs into our kennel for testing.

While we understood caution and policy–after all, we had many policies of our own–nothing changed the fact that we couldn't get what we needed and we couldn't, as various folks often suggested, sit patiently waiting for a year or so until said rescue group thought they had a match.

What weighted the equation even more was simple math. There were a lot more of the various rescue groups than us. We had one group. They had dozens. By now, their collective reach was far greater than ours, sweeping through shelter intakes with growing efficiency. Somewhere around this time, we learned about the large trucks taking off with scores of dogs from local shelters, bound for large population centers in the northeast. Whether these dogs did, indeed, find excellent adoptive homes, we didn't know.

Unfortunately for the average service dog trainer, the most stable dogs with the best-known backgrounds were also the most adoptable to private homes. Whether the remaining kennels full of independent hounds, pit-bull types with problematic dog aggression, and the few other clinging-fearful remaining dogs would ultimately make someone good pets.... we didn't know that either. What we did know was that if we were going to meet the ever-growing needs of our clients, we had to have better resources.

Continuing an uncomfortable trend, my understanding of how larger and older schools arrived at their policies kept growing. Gretchen was a never-fail source of wry perspective. She was sympathetic and helpful to many rescue causes, in fact was a substantial financial supporter of several. But she would not budge from a strong conviction that haunting shelters for training candidates was a disservice to our grant funds and to our clients. "How many do you have to fail out after months of training?" Gretchen had challenged me on this regularly for years now.

"It happens," I always had to admit. "But don't tell me you never fail a guide dog who's already started training. I know better."

"Of course we do," Gretchen agreed. "But I'll bet it's a lot fewer than you do—and I mean in terms of percentages, not just the number of dogs."

"I'm not sure," I said honestly. "I don't know what our percentage is."

"A lot of it comes back to scale," Gretchen pressed on without mercy. "It's one thing if you're all doing this in your spare time and not relying on it for income. That's how you were for a long time—none of you were dependent on the school for your primary income. Now you are. So you have to get your head out of the sand and think about the corresponding patience of those funding your grants."

Even while she lectured me, Gretchen was moving around with her lovely Labrador she was prepping for an entry into an obedience trial. She'd adopted her dog from the school for which she worked, as he'd proven to be far too high energy to pair with an unsighted person. "If it's just a dog here and there, and nothing but your personal time or funds out the window, it's one thing. But believe me, the bigger your grants get, the more accountability they're going to want. When your totals read like you're wasting an entire person's salary, you won't be getting a grant renewal."

That debate had happened months before, but it was ringing in my memory while I drove around the state with a few interns on yet another dog-scouting trip. Our group trooped into the first animal shelter to view a total of 17 dogs, three of which were even possible to consider just due to size and structure. I tried not to think about Gretchen's lectures while we checked over the three prospects–and left empty-handed. We sucked up our collective courage and pressed on.

Four hours and 150 miles later, we started back to the training center with empty crates. At the three places we worked with regularly, there was nothing at all. From sheer desperation, we took a brief detour to a fourth, a new location. They were breed specific–Labradors only– and quite wary of our interest. We spotted one nice young male, but the shelter would not allow us to take him to our vet for the required health screening before making a decision. We called Nori, who in turn called the rescue's director. He wasn't in, and the staff gave only scant hope they might hold the dog for their director's decision. Someone else was coming to see him the next day. It was a long, silent ride home.

Nori and I spent an overtime day combing through our contacts and begging for donations from breeders. Barb had driven to Georgia to see someone who might offer us a puppy. We finished with two "maybes" from folks who said they'd call us back in a week or two. Unfortunately, we needed at least eight new trainees, not just soon, but preferably yesterday. From today's work, if everything went perfectly, and nobody backed out we might have three.

"We have to do better than this," I said dispiritedly, dropping my head on my keyboard hard enough to leave random characters on the screen. "It wrecking every schedule on the staff."

"I know," Nori answered thoughtfully. "We need to start hitting up some of the breeders when their litters first arrive. I think some might be more inclined to donate pups at that age than the older ones. But it would mean coming up with volunteer fosters and all the headaches that go with raising younger dogs." Nori doodled on her legal pad that was now crammed top to bottom with notes and numbers from the afternoon's calls. "It's a lot to take on. A lot of time commitment."

I objected to that with more vehemence than I usually dared. "Nori, look at the clock!" I sat up and tossed my pen at the desk so hard it bounced against the back wall. "At the rate we're spending hours searching and not finding anything, we're already spending that time. We're just not getting anything back from it. Is anybody keeping track of how many hours we're running around to shelters looking and sitting in here begging?"

Nori stared at me thoughtfully. "That may be a valid point. But no, we haven't been keeping track."

"I'm serious," I said. I was thinking of Gretchen's remarks about grants. "We have two interns out there who are full-time staff. I think the people paying their wages would rather they spent their time learning to train than driving the roads looking for dogs."

"Depends on how you slice that argument," Nori wasn't really buying in. "If learning how to find and select the dogs is part of their training, then the time screening adult dogs is not wasted."

"And if it's the least effective method of getting trainees, what are we teaching them? Especially when we come home with no dogs." I knew I was getting onto shaky ground with Nori. It didn't usually pay to argue with her. But things were getting ridiculous. "Counting everybody who went on the road looking this week, plus you and me in here today, we just spent about 36 staff hours and 12 volunteer hours and have zilch to show for it. Forget the interns for a minute. Just counting your time and mine, that's a month's worth of classes for foster pups."

Nori hadn't yet broken eye contact with me. "Okay," she said, "go back through your calendar and see if you can total the hours since the holidays that you've spent hunting dogs. Be conservative, but put it together in a report format, along with the results. I want it by the time I go to the board meeting on Thursday."

Me and my big mouth. I left for home, wondering where this was going. At rock bottom, I had a strong sense that Gretchen was correct–that if we planned to continue growing, and focus more on training than searching, we were going to have to start home-growing a steadier supply of correct prospects. The parallels hadn't stopped surprising me about how it compared to what Sherry and I were doing with the German Shepherd puppies. The adult dogs we needed simply weren't available to us–the shepherds by specific temperament, the retrievers by simple numbers.

I thought our own board of directors might nix the whole idea on the spot, but any objections dissolved on the spot when Nori entered their next meeting with a two-month-old Lab puppy tucked under her arm. Little Nicholas was the brand new donation from Georgia. Nori had taken the trouble to outfit him in a matching leash and cape in the school's colors. The board members tripped over each other to fawn over the puppy and fantasize about public relations value.

We'd had puppy donations before, but we'd always arranged for them to be reared by one of our experienced trainers. Nicholas became our first pup to go home with a novice volunteer, despite our two new staff interns nearly coming to blows over who would have him.

"Get over it," Nori told them both briskly. "You have better uses for your time right now than a pup's night-time potty schedule. But she cornered me immediately after the board meeting. "You're on. There's a Lion's Club meeting next Tuesday, and then there's that meeting with the engineering firm the week after. Take the pup, or borrow some others. Or both. Go see if you can get funding for an entire group."

"Hey wait!" I objected, "Why me? You're the public relations lady."

"You got stage fright?" Nori asked me sarcastically. "You obviously want to try this route. Put your mouth where the money is. Take whoever you think you need. I want to see a written presentation by the first of the week."

My thoughts were extremely mixed, but this wasn't about my preference. It was time to answer the question of which method worked better, if not for the entire world, at least for us. I thought of the stoic, determined people I'd interviewed in the last few months. The dogs at the shelter weren't the only ones wishing for better chances. Our mission statement made certain promises to humans, and that was our first obligation.

Our training group had grown, but my preferred selection for this event favored those most fluent in public speaking. I begged until both Carol and Doug agreed to go. Carol had a deeper, longer training background than I did, and still worked freelance as a photographer. She could strike up conversations with anyone. Doug was our former sheriff's deputy, and I had yet to meet the group he couldn't work his way around.

"Okay," I said in our next staff meeting. "We have three people committed. How about at least three more. Barb? Stephen? Allyson? Who wants to come?"

Silence. I contemplated the wisdom of my next move. "We're taking puppies." I waved at the door, prompting Sherry's entrance, followed by two of our farm neighbors, all three carrying one of our shepherd pups tucked under each arm. Every hand in the room shot up.

Prices had to be paid. For the rest of my week, plotting occupied all my work and most of my non-work hours.

Several of us busted our personal budgets buying more matching capes. We borrowed extra people, put together gorgeous handouts, and timed speeches. We put together an extensive plan for convincing the groups. Nori tore it apart, critiqued, and modified. We finished a second version, then a third. By the night of the presentation, we knew we had a brilliantly crafted, logical presentation that would win the minds of every shrewd business person in the room.

Too bad all the prep was a total waste because no one paid the slightest bit of attention to the humans. The funding won that first night was the easiest we'd ever received. From the moment the puppies entered the room, none of the club membership saw or heard anything else. They were cooing over puppies and admiring little jackets. The impact of emotional appeal swamped any logical rationale I'd ever dreamed up. True enough, we'd requested a modest amount. Also true: this was still relatively early in the era of mobility service dogs. Such requests were still a novelty, not–as they are now–merely one request lost in a sea of similar voices.

But that first night, the puppies themselves scored a major victory. No soul alive could argue the powerful appeal of their waddling parade. Two of our board members also attended. They, also, were utterly gone. Their brains were far down the road of planning local fundraisers with puppies at the forefront.

"Fabulous," Trent grumbled about the board members' reaction before we'd even cleared the room that night. "What do they expect? Are they gonna want us to teach all the pups to schmooze with and take treats from every soul on the planet? This is going to be a disaster, Julie."

"Ummm. Hmmmm." I couldn't think of anything better to say. I was focused on the funding, and on a new and exciting chance to have a whole group of high quality dogs to teach correct habits from the start.

Nori shut Trent down in a hurry, though. "Man up, dude," she told him. "Think of it as a training discrimination exercise. Socialization and obedience proofing all in one package. We're not the first, nor the fiftieth, school to do this, so let's all get moving on the research and protocol."

Not all the trainers were thrilled. Tammy, a part-time training intern, quit just three weeks shy of her graduation. She walked out the day after we received funding for the puppy project. "I just can't see it, Nori," she'd objected in the staff meeting. "I can't believe we can't use more rescues. It seems to me like it would be a better use of funds to serve two needs with the same money."

"This isn't an either/or discussion," Nori told her, completely level as always. "We're not going to stop using rescues. But we can't let the training process grind to a stop while we look more and find less. Bottom line: this school is less about the dogs than it is about serving clients. Dogs are the tool, not the end-game."

"Then I just disagree, I guess," the young woman said. "I can't justify it. I think we have an obligation to do better. To do more."

The brief, tense pause hummed around the table with electrical force. When Nori spoke again, her voice had gained a lot of crispness. "Yes, we do disagree. Our bottom line is simple. We're a non-profit, legally bound to a specific mission statement. By law, and by any moral principle, we have to pursue that mission statement to the best of our ability. In a larger city, with closer access to more rescues, it might be different. But we're who and where we are, so for now, we're going to try both approaches and see how we do."

Tammy got up and walked out of our staff meeting, out of our training school. I had to give her credit for standing true to her convictions, but wondered if she might be better off working for an actual rescue or shelter than for a service dog school. Ultimately, Nori used her massive network of contacts to find Tammy an equivalent slot with a larger school in another state who worked exclusively with rescued dogs. That was the best we could do for all concerned, including protecting the sponsor dollars of those who'd paid her internship expenses.

But Project Puppy was off and running. We started with a group made up of Nicholas, the little Labrador, and four donated Golden Retriever pups of similar age. With mixed thoughts on the whole matter and after extensive chat with Nori, Sherry and I committed a few of the shepherd pups to the group, on conditions that we had sole control of their training protocol. But the bulk of this effort involved retrievers for mobility assistance.

As word spread, we had access to an ever-increasing number. Just a few months later, one of Barb's friends bred an entire litter of Labradors just for our school. The foster classes grew, and though they took a lot of time, our staff found much stress relief in the knowledge of the dogs' upcoming availability. Even though we expected it, the schedule relief made a pleasant surprise.

"I think one of the big draws is just that it's so much fun," Carol told me one day, "I really didn't like this idea so much at the beginning. And I don't mean to downplay how much work the fosters put in. But there is a huge sense of community and purpose in this." She was busily shuffling through a stack of photos she'd taken for a new brochure: long lines of pups in matching jackets trooping through crowded downtown sidewalks.

"Talk to me after the vet checks." Trent tossed a coffee cup in the trash and left the room. He was still very skeptical, but then he always was.

Barb was also a full convert, especially after hearing that her friend was willing to repeat the process of another litter next year. "Shoot, you guys, the public relations factor alone makes it very worthwhile. When have we ever had this many volunteers?"

Ultimately, Nori was proven correct: for our school, this would not be an either/or question. Rescues remained an option, but the stream of upcoming pups allowed us to be more relaxed and selective. Oddly enough, the combined approach increased rescue usage rather than diminishing it. The puppies themselves greatly helped in public relations, thus helping word spread about our school itself. We eventually developed a better network with individuals, most often breeders, who did rescue on their own.

The presence of our puppy pipeline relaxed pressure enough that we could take a longer view and do more extensive evaluations on "repurposed" dogs in a way that time might not otherwise have permitted. In a shelter setting alone, we might have had to bypass a dog with a potential problem. But with a growing repertoire of foster homes, we could now put that dog into a home long enough to do a fuller evaluation. That contingent of volunteers grew in number and experience, so we had more people able to take in a rescue, work with it for a few weeks, and see where we landed. Should the dog go back to the rescue/donor/breeder or come to school for a try? It worked for everyone, because even if the dog didn't ultimately make the cut as a service dog, intense socialization and training made it far more likely the rescue personnel could place the dog elsewhere with better success. For the first time, we had a win-win balance for all.

Over the next three years, our total number of graduates surged upward, and we were all astonished in the end to realize how much our number of re-purposed dogs had increased. The Laws of Unintended Consequences come in many forms.

"Use more rescues by raising more pups from breeders?" Trent remarked at a staff meeting in which Nori outlined the trend. "There's a slogan that won't get you far in the public eye."

But we were all used to Trent's grousing about things and mostly just ignored him. From any viewpoint, the combined focus seemed to be working better than we'd dared expect. But the new system brought one more impact that sneaked up on me.

Our original two groups of pups, now grown and a dozen strong, were well along in advanced training. Eight successful rescue dogs had gathered with them in the training room one day for a group photo. A group of six more donated pups had just passed their vet checks at nine months old. To add extra fun, two brand new litters of Golden Retriever puppies tottered into the lineup, almost tripping over their jackets, tails wagging furiously. Quite a few people had gathered to watch Carol struggle for the perfect Christmas card photo. In the middle of August, 30-some staff and twice as many volunteers sweltered in holiday-print sweaters, arranging their charges around a lavishly decorated fake pine tree. It was quite a show.

Once finished, I stripped off the heavy sweater, parking myself and my soaked t-shirt under the nearest ceiling fan. Leaning my head back against the wall, I closed my eyes and enjoyed the cooler air. Until I heard the tiniest of sniffs nearby.

Looking up cautiously, the only person I could see nearby was one of our newest incoming clients. She sat patiently, apparently waiting for her husband to return. When I saw her take a furtive swipe at her eyes, I realized she was the source of the sniff. I hesitated, considering my next move carefully. The line between concern and intrusion could be a delicate one. But she saved me the trouble.

"I'm Melinda," she said with a rueful smile. "Sorry to be emotional."

"That's okay," I responded. "I get that way myself plenty often. Is there anything I can do for you?"

"No, thanks," she said. "Well, you already are. All of you." Melinda wiped her eyes one more time. "Nori told me today that I'm approved to start classes with one of the older dogs next week."

"Ah, yes, the new class," I said with a smile. I already knew she'd been approved, but it was her prerogative to raise the topic for discussion if she wanted to—or didn't.

"I was just counting the dogs, you know?" Melinda ventured with considerable hesitation. "I think I see 42."

"Yes," I said. "We weren't expecting quite so many pups from one litter, but nobody is sorry. I hope they all graduate."

"Me too. I waited for more than a year, you know," Melinda was studying the controls on her wheelchair carefully.

I knew, but I didn't comment. She clearly had something more to say.

"I've come in several times to watch the classes with the puppies. Well, they aren't puppies anymore. The older ones, now, I mean." She began tracing the outline of the power buttons on the arm of her chair. "I don't really know how to tell you how much it helped. It's one thing to hear people say "oh we're doing everything we can," but it's another to see it for yourself. To know that you guys started raising the pups for us, and not for any other reason."

"Yes," I said cautiously. "Right. We were worried about finding enough dogs for our waiting list in any reasonable time frame."

"But don't you understand?" Melinda continued without looking back at me. Her gaze stayed riveted on the young trainees who were now staging a photo with several of them holding a large Merry Christmas banner in their mouths. Tails thrashed tinsel on the bottom of the August Christmas tree. Santa-Claus hats tilted precariously off a dozen Labrador heads.

I almost made the mistake of trying to answer, but stopped myself just in time. Between Sherry and Nori's endless corrections, I really was learning to wait.

"See," Melinda's voice was quiet enough that I had to strain to hear. "When you find yourself disabled like I did. Suddenly paralyzed, all thanks to some drunk driver who didn't care, it's not just "easy" to get discouraged. It's a daily battle. And I don't mean the battle to adjust to limitations. Everything is harder, sure. But it's way worse, way harder still, not to feel totally alone. It's really easy to forget that people are trying to help. A lot of my friends kind of faded away. It wasn't that they disliked me. Or even really that they didn't care. I know they did–that they do. But I don't fit their lifestyle anymore. I can't go all the places they go, or do all activities they enjoy. It's not everybody, but it's a lot. And it's almost impossible not to feel forgotten. Talk is cheap, you know?" Melinda paused for so long I wasn't sure if she would go on.

"All the therapists, the doctors, tell you it's important to be positive. To be optimistic and look ahead. Did I mention that talk is cheap? That's way easier said than done." She shifted in her chair, then turned it slightly to face me more directly. "But to see a whole group like this, these dogs, the puppies, I mean. You guys are starting up a whole new program in addition to how you were already getting dogs, well, that's not cheap talk, and it comes from those who donated the money, the ones who raise the dogs, and you guys who train them. I'm being repetitive, but the discouragement is so bad…." Her voice broke, but she steadied it and pressed on. "Here's the thing…you're home alone day after day and week after week. So tired, and so overwhelmed, and maybe all you can focus on for a few days is your physical therapy and your son's homework. Hearing all the challenges about good attitudes just doesn't work so good."

A single tear rolled down Melinda's face. She didn't even bother trying to wipe it away. "Good attitude can be cheap talk, too, when you know you're never going to get up out of this darned chair. And most of your friends are gone off who knows where. But nobody can watch this group train these pups, nobody can watch those dogs grow up and think that nobody cares about my situation. I know you guys are doing it exactly for me, and the knowing follows me around all day, every day. It's way more than the jobs the dogs will do. It's what it represents. Sometimes I just have to sit here and let it soak in."

I surveyed the maelstrom of frolicking retrievers who'd suddenly taken on new stature with these words. When Melinda and I said our goodbyes, I hustled straight to Nori's office to launch my next campaign of administrative hassle. "Hey, Nori!"

Tossing her Mrs. Claus costume onto the nearest chair, she answered me wearily. "What now? I can already see that bargaining gleam in your eye."

"Yeah, you're right. How about we put a webcam in the training room? I think it might be nice if the clients could sometimes watch the dogs from home."

Chapter 19

Tammy returned to her regular classroom yesterday. The best thing we can say is that the entire morning was uneventful. Her therapy sessions pick up after lunch, as normal. We walk her to and from each classroom with Fresco. The skills she's gained since he arrived are making all the difference. ~Ellen Jackson

I scanned the email about a recent dog placed with an autistic child. With more infrastructure and better puppy raising, Sherry and I were able to get better leverage of the promising young shepherds, and even increase our numbers. We were still doing all the advanced and in-home training of the shepherds as volunteer time, but one graduate became three, then five, then more.

It was working. A steady, alert, and seriously obsessive-compulsive dog, highly bonded to a parent could, indeed, learn to contain, alert, and redirect, cued from a parent's response to… almost anything, even if the "anything" changed frequently. Doors and gates became safe. Dangerous behaviors dialed back. Nighttime wanderings became almost non-existent. Bolting and disappearance were things of the past for all those who had the dogs.

The true value of Hands-Off training (never dreamed of in my initial thinking) proved up mightily as we learned to evaluate for the correct, naturally occurring behaviors.

Neither the process nor the results were a "miracle," as some later expounded. Not at all. It was a matter of a strong, correct bond between a certain need and a certain type of dog.

But however functional, it was an incredibly time-consuming process. The number of shaping and training hours was staggering. As we began to get our process defined, we also had to face reality that two people by themselves couldn't continue this indefinitely. The time had come to move this rodeo up a stage or three. We were sold. Parents were ecstatic. And all of us expected the world to rejoice with us.

Enter the next nasty jolt: incredulity, if not overt resistance, from every direction, especially from any of our normal sources of funds. Grants, corporate donations, and even most private donors have categories and criteria by which applications are sorted. The short version: nobody had a category for this. It took a resolute trainer to stand against the criticism. I became more and more grateful for my farm's intense early training: stand my ground!

"I never heard of such a thing," we were told over and over. "Where did this idea come from? That's not even possible, let alone practical. It would be dangerous to try." The day I heard the CEO of a large training school give me this lecture, I was watching silenced video of several dogs doing exactly what he said was impossible–perfect fluency, and no injuries yet. I often speculated about whether or not this was similar to the objections against the very first guide dog schools a century before. From what I'd read, it felt true.

I listened quietly, if not patiently, to the rest of the

intense scolding, absently shifting my focus to the glossy black German Shepherd sprawled by my chair. Over a year old now, this dog, Bear, who dragged his paws as a fuzzy baby, was proving up as our best-yet demo dog and tool for teaching families. Given his resemblance to the dog from my childhood, what else could I possibly have called him? We were holding him as a breeding prospect in hopes he'd pass his qualities. Besides, we needed a good, permanent demo dog to help us through the initial sessions with the families. From Bear's seven littermate siblings, we now had a group of four we felt sure were suitable for further training if we could just find some help. Past litters had given us one or two. Maybe. But we were learning not only how to see it, but how to reproduce it. The strongest proof yet lay by my feet. But getting people to listen and believe? So far we hadn't found the magic formula.

Quite a few parents were trying to help us swim against the tide and find funds. Most were told some version of: "That's irresponsible. You want a dog to do your parenting for you?"

"We find no justification among the well-recognized schools for your proposal," one foundation told us in a tersely worded refusal. "We advise against the project and encourage families with such challenges to seek remedial therapy." Sherry threw several objects at walls when she read that one.

The stonewalling, skepticism, and often thinly veiled contempt gave us our first real insight into what the parents of these children struggled with on a daily basis. Research and literature constantly urged (nearly berated) parents that the strongest chance their children would

have at a self-supporting lifestyle would happen (or not)
because of early intervention. But pre-school intervention
and therapy came at a cost often greater than their annual
salaries. At that time very few states provided much help.
Enormous costs, stacked up against the value of a single
human life? That might make an interesting fundraising
concept, but it didn't touch the true financial substance.
No, the part so often overlooked by the business analysts:
the cost of expensive, early intervention paled by
comparison to far greater costs of lifelong support,
especially if parents died or abdicated.

A time-honored controversy resurfaced between two
unappealing realities: major expense immediately versus
astronomical expense later. We watched, amazed and
appalled, as this struggle played out again and again.

We couldn't fix the therapy access issue, but we held a
piece of the equation for a few exhausted, overwhelmed
parents. And more than any type of client we'd ever
served, those parents needed every tool in the box to
meet the demands of child rearing.

We'd proven our point now with multiple placements,
but convincing even our own training group was going to
be a big undertaking. Half of them had already joined the
rest of society in thinking we were nuts, and we'd barely
begun trying to explain.

"So let me get this straight," Trent asked us one day as he
paused in the doorway between the training room and the
kennel runs. "You guys are going to take the most time-
intensive training track I've ever seen, and offer it to the
most time-challenged clients I've ever heard of." He
stood looking back at us with a retriever on each side of

him and a notebook tucked under his arm. "What am I missing?"

"You're missing one major point," I said as I filled my training bag with supplies. "We are not "offering it" yet. Not generally. Not publicly. We're thinking about it. We've done a dozen so far, no more, and we're only just now finishing those up."

Trent said nothing else, but shook his head in disapproval as he continued on to the kennel to put his trainees up.

Beside me, likewise packing up for an outing, Sherry didn't even look up. She wasn't usually in town at this hour, but she'd stopped by to pick up some mail and was seated nearby, engrossed in a few new applications. I wondered if she'd even been listening. I glanced at her, debating whether to disturb her.

"Yes, I heard," she said, folding up some papers and stuffing them back in an envelope. "I think it will be the most common response."

"And so…. what?" I turned around and starting making notes on the whiteboard about who we were taking where, and why, and when we would return. "Do you think it's realistic to scale it up? Or what?"

"I vote for what," Sherry said. "Even though I don't know what *what* is yet." She tossed the larger stack of junk mail into the trash. "There's no more doubt that it works. Whether it's realistic for more than just a handful remains to be seen. As best I can see, it's a money problem, not a training problem. That's true even for the ones we're working now, let alone adding more."

I recapped the marker and leaned on the wall. "True. But we're at the saturation point. Forget growing. We can't even keep doing what we're doing now all by ourselves."

"I know." Sherry finished packing up the mail and rose to leave. "If we're going to do any more, we have to get some leverage somehow. But it has to be tackled as a separate problem from the regular dogs, and it has to stay mostly out at home."

"Are you going to talk to Nori about it?" I wasn't looking forward to that discussion.

"I guess so."

I closed my eyes. The mere thought of this debate going to the board of directors gave me an instant stomach ache. But I couldn't think of anything to say.

"There's a fork in the road coming, Julie. You know there is."

"I know. But let's not talk about it here. I have a lot left to do before I can go home."

What I'd said to Trent went only so far. We might not be publicly offering the option of service dogs for children with autism, but more and more parents were continuing to ask anyway. Explaining that we could not was taking so much time that we'd gone to auto-responders and fax-on-demand, and it still wasn't keeping up.

Beyond that, Sherry was correct: this was a job to be tackled on the farm. At least in the beginning of the training process, the space available played a critical role. The open acreage had already proven its value as a prime location for selective breeding. Even more so for the selection of pups and early behavior shaping. The trend was definitely toward wide open rural spaces.

But Trent, with his usual talent for cutting through the extraneous, had summed up our biggest problem: the dichotomy of parents already so time-stressed by highly demanding childcare that they barely had time to brush their teeth, let alone mess with dog training for any reason. A service dog was not the right solution for many of these families. Should I say for most? I wondered as I loaded up my mobility trainees and headed out. Yet, for that small percentage who could find a way, the results far surpassed anything we'd ever imagined.

I left the kennel that day to help Sherry do a final evaluation of our most recent project. We still made a big point of not letting work demands keep us from the woodland we loved, so today, we were combining tasks.

We strolled along the river trail with a client in tow. Susan, a young, single mom was still learning to trust and prompt her daughter's service dog. She'd worked many months to achieve exacting, specific amounts of precision in the dog's responses, in her own perceptions, and learned to apply them to her child's behavior.

Now she strode confidently along the forest trail, watching her little girl race around in the first real freedom she'd ever had. Missy, the petite, sable German Shepherd seemed to bob on a string, maintaining a distance as specific as a ruler could measure, keeping the child within a designated safety sphere close to Mom.

I held my breath momentarily as the little girl reached for something on the ground. One of this child's problems was pica–endless mouthing and eating of inappropriate, dangerous things. But the mother's weeks of exaggerated role-playing had done its job. An alert dog instantly put a large, furry barrier between the child and whatever she had planned to pick up.

"Annette! Look at the flowers!" With admirable timing, the mother stopped to scoop up a gorgeous spring daffodil instead. "Come pick flowers!" Rather than fuss over the blocked behavior, the child re-centered on the bright yellow blossom and came chattering happily to her mother.

Score! I thought.

Missy's tongue ran out in a satisfied grin when Annette tossed her a treat. Another relationship was solidifying.

"It's so beautiful here," Susan told us. "You have no idea. I've never been able to go anywhere since Annette could walk. I've never been able to take her anywhere unless I never let go of her hand, which she hates. It was always such a struggle just to walk around our own back yard."

I smiled. I knew the feeling of peace and contentment available in these woods, especially to people who hadn't had much of either for a very long time. Or perhaps never.

"I shouldn't cry." Susan said, swiping the tears away.

"Happy tears are a good thing," Sherry assured her. "Don't stress. Just enjoy being out."

"I guess so. In the beginning, you know," Susan said, "I just wanted to be able to sit down sometimes. And to sleep at night. Maybe to take a shower without panicking.

You don't ever get away from wondering what could happen any minute." Susan brushed both hands against her eyes, staring up, up, up at a towering oak. The tree's crown of bright spring green swayed against a cloudless blue sky. I felt sure I could see and feel her very soul relaxing. How well I remembered.

"There was just so little help, and so little rest. Now it's like I have extra eyes and ears and legs all the time. Annette can walk around, move, explore. There's time to think."

My thoughts stretched back over the years. Like me, I knew. Like Maggie. Like so many others

Susan walked close to her daughter again and held out another flower. "Look, Annette! Here's a new one."

Annette turned to face her mother, made actual eye contact, took the flower and escorted it to Missy–holding it out for her dog's inspection. "New one!" she echoed.

Interaction. Imitation. Engagement. I could see and feel Sherry cataloging the changed family dynamic.

"You can't know," Susan repeated. "You just have no idea. When you wanted only a good night's sleep, and then…here we are…it's hard to take in."

Annette took the few remaining steps that separated her from Missy. She took firm hold of Missy's collar. Missy grinned in delight and followed her along. "My dog." Annette told Sherry, who happened to be closest. "My dog."

"Yes, she is, and she is a very pretty one!" Sherry fell into step beside her. "What's her name?"

"Issy!" The childish voice proclaimed. Autism or no autism, it can be a lot easier to chat when you have a beloved dog to discuss.

I hung back slightly to revel in the entire scene as the tiny steps of little feet–and the enormous steps of new growth–carried them along the sparkling riverbank.

Chapter 20

"You can do anything you set your mind to when you have vision, determination, and an endless supply of expendable labor"
                                                    —*Justin Sewell*

Two days later Sherry barged in my front door and flung herself on the sofa. "We're on," she said. "Do we have a goat we can sacrifice for good luck?"

"You better be careful where you say that anymore." I signaled the young pup I'd been working with back into his crate. "This place is constantly full of other people now. One of these days somebody will hear you who won't know you're joking. And what are we 'on' for? Or do I want to know?"

"I'm not sure I *am* joking. That was one seriously intense meeting with Nori. We're gonna need all the juice we can find to convince her. A little magic wouldn't hurt. She grilled me on every step of training protocol and client selection. But she's coming to watch Farley's public access test on Thursday."

I also dropped into a nearby chair, rubbing my temples and feeling her same blend of wariness and mental fatigue. I wasn't sure anymore if this process was more thrilling or more exhausting, but like adrenaline junkies and skydivers, we just couldn't quit.

Later that week, we watched Nori from a distance, trying to hide our mixed glee and terror. She stood about halfway along the block of downtown bustle while an obedience trial judge followed a daddy-child-dog threesome in and out of several shops. Nori leaned against a lamppost, never taking her eyes off the trio. Even she could not possibly fault the performance, but from 100 yards away I could still feel the skepticism coming off her in waves.

When the judge signed the forms, congratulations wrapped up, and the others departed. Nori finally gave up her vigil on the post. She sank to a nearby bench and buried her face in her hands. We waited, hardly daring to breathe.

"That's number twelve, right?" Nori's voice was muffled, but we barely had to hear her to know the question.

"Yeah." Sherry sat down beside her. "And four aborted attempts that were total disasters."

"Have you logged the hours?" Nori sat up and stared back down the block.

"We've logged them," I answered, "but we haven't totaled them up. Up to now, neither of us really wanted to know."

"Take a guess," Nori shot back. "And then tell me how many other people you've been paying out of pocket to help."

I froze. Nobody was supposed to know about that part. But this intense director of ours knew me well enough by now. She stared me down, and I finally confessed. "Around 400 hours per team," I said, following her gaze down the block where Farley and family were disappearing into the crowd. "And don't ask me about money totals. I don't know and I don't want to know."

"The main thing is that it works," Sherry said. "In the right circumstances, it works like nothing I've ever seen in 25 years of family counseling."

Silence.

"Have you had a chance to read the summaries or the notes?" Sherry was relentless, and I knew she had no plans of being told she couldn't continue these placements.

Nori leaned back and folded her arms. "You two do realize that you are the biggest pains in the rear, ever, of my entire staff."

We knew. And knew enough to stay silent.

Nori fixed Sherry with her customary side-eye. "I suppose that you have thought about what's going to happen the first time you show one of these dogs to the general public and say what's going on."

I flinched. I couldn't help it. Yes, I knew that, too. "Eight thousand people a day will want one," I answered, though she hadn't been asking me.

Nori flicked a glance at me, then back at Sherry. Clearly she knew where the driving force was. "So whether you want to do four more or four hundred more, the question is how you plan to fund it. Because both of you look horrid and are stretched as far as you can stretch."

Neither of us could argue that point. And we didn't have an answer.

"You're going to have to convince donors it's possible,

fight off the naysayers, and screen the clients before you can even start the training. That much alone strikes me as a full-time job for the next year." Nori wasn't telling us anything we didn't know, but she had a gruesome habit of summarizing in a sentence what it could take others an entire day to get said.

After this rather depressing conversation wound down, Sherry and I retired to the hay bales to continue reflection. We watched half a dozen German Shepherds trotting around us, in and out of the barn, back and forth to the truck, alert, watchful, calm, but never letting us out of their sight. We'd scoured the continental US for the genetic families that ultimately gave us these few. Our initial thoughts about natural tendency, not just trainability, had proven up many times over in the incredible judgement and dedication of these dogs. Slowly–very, very slowly–we thought we were making progress. But the costs, both in dollars and hours, were staggering. No other word would do.

"Are you sure you don't know a voodoo spell for a winning lottery number?" Sherry rubbed her eyes and stood up. It was almost midnight, and we both needed to get home. We had talked the subject threadbare and had no reasonable proposal for ourselves other than large grants or endowments. Neither of us discounted individual contributions, but short of turning this over to a massive fundraising company, individual contributions wouldn't touch what we needed. If we did turn to professional fundraisers, we could kiss grant prospects goodbye, since most of them called that "too much overhead."

We started the long slog to finding more funds, but within a few weeks, were rapidly starting to wonder if we'd shot ourselves in both feet by starting this out as a volunteer process. Over and over we encountered the rationale: "Well, you've come this far with volunteers. What's wrong with continuing that way?"

We heard this even from some of our own board, none of whom understood how much the last few years had stretched us thin—financially, practically, physically.

"Think we could find a few hundred more volunteers as crazy as we are?" I asked Sherry one night while we lounged on my front porch. We'd been quiet for a long time, listening to the wandering, melodious call of a mockingbird. We tried not to talk work constantly, but this volunteer mentality was wearing on us.

"Let's stay with obsessive-compulsive and avoid crazy," she replied. "I'm getting sensitive about that word crazy."

It was a favored term, for sure. We heard it every day now as we hunted for people who would even look at the demo dogs, let alone consider helping us. "They're so set against the evidence." I went on, intensely frustrated with the people who kept insisting what we were doing wasn't realistic or even safe. "It's new information, so it has to be suspect. Did guide dog trainers get this response eighty years ago?"

"Probably. It's the same kind of thinking—this challenges my pre-conceived notions, therefore it's bad. You have to wonder," Sherry speculated, "if the naysayers would be happier if one of the dogs failed spectacularly and let a kid get killed wandering. At least then they could feel self-righteous, I guess. I bet you're right—the guide trainers probably heard the same things."

I scuffed my toe on a loose porch plank, mentally making

a note of yet something else I wasn't getting done. "A grant committee member from the Thorton Foundation told me last week that they were considering filing a report on us with Child Protection Services."

"With what justification?" Sherry shot back.

"I don't remember the exact words. It was something like encouraging parents to abdicate responsibility. And another one of them said it was irresponsible to use *those* dogs with little kids. I don't think she likes shepherds much."

"Humph." Sherry drained her wine glass. "Let them try. CPS has bigger fish to fry."

Scott, who had manfully stuck it out, skid-steer, barn flowers, crazy women, and all, was now a frequent participant in these conversations. He'd been sitting nearby, quiet until now, but this was too much for him. "Have any of your dogs ever hurt or bitten a kid?" he asked?

Trust a lawyer to get to the heart of things.

"Not unless you count a teething puppy," Sherry remarked. "We've spent our IRAs chasing the right genetics for dogs that would be hard-wired-good with kids.

"I don't get it, then," Scott objected. "If the kids are safe and the parents are happy with the take-away, why are others so bent out of shape?"

Silence held for a few moments.

"Because there's almost always somebody who objects to

new stuff?" Sherry speculated. "I'm not all that sure."

"I'm sure," I reviewed another recent conversation with the training director of another large, long-standing school. He had called with a single purpose: talk me into stopping using the shepherds for autistic kids. "Okay, maybe I don't know all the reasons, but I know one, at least." I paused, leaning over to stroke the multi-colored sable head of the soon-to-be momma dog at my feet.

"Don't make us wait for it," Sherry said testily. "You're overdoing the dramatic pause."

"I'm not being dramatic. I'm trying to decide if I'm a flaming, egotistical ass for saying it." I straightened up and dropped back into my lounge. "I think, or they think, it makes them look bad. They've been telling people–parents of these children–for years that it's not possible. That there was no help available for them through a service dog. And yet here we are."

Scott laughed. "No wonder they hate you."

"Ah, okay, I see." Sherry pieced together the rest of the thought. "It's bad PR to hate another school, so it's much better if we're raving lunatics?"

"Pretty much," I agreed. "Except, you know, it's going to catch up with them. I've spotted two other groups online this month who are starting to offer dogs to affected children."

"Doing what?" Sherry frowned.

"Mostly deep pressure therapy, companion, and a little behavior interruption." I swirled the drink in my glass. "Beyond that, I don't know. And I'm not about to ask.

I'm just happy they're doing anything at all."

"Somebody else will figure out the rest eventually," Sherry mused. "Or more likely already has."

"Yeah, if so, they're probably hiding in the weeds like we did, afraid to say it out loud."

"Exactly." Sherry saluted me with her glass. "And sometimes, after enough of these negative Nellies, I think we should have stayed there.

"Well," I pushed myself up out of my lounge chair. "I know where we're going tomorrow, and that's back out to see Alice. She still hasn't done the Public Access Test and it's time."

Chapter 21

"Half of seeming clever is keeping your mouth shut at the right times."
　　　　　　—Patrick Rothfuss, "The Wise Man's Fear"

Alice was a typical initial contact. More than typical. Alice was a case in point, representing nearly an entire category of client. Autism is diagnosed more often in boys than girls, and the divorce rate in affected families was astronomical. By the tallies we kept, the pronounced majority of people who asked us for service dogs were single moms with young boys. They called us every week. Sometimes they called every day. A few called multiple times a day. Their stories of bleak desperation shared a common set of themes: no sleep, no respite, no resources, no help, no schools, no therapy, no safety, no social relief, and almost no hope.

Despite the commonalities, Alice still stood out to me, but it was a while before I realized why she seemed so unusual. Many parents are absolute fountains of emotions. They are stressed, frustrated, grieved, and far overloaded. Tears and various flavors of outburst happen frequently. Unlike most others, I never once saw Alice cry, and I'm not sure if that is good or bad.

The first time I met her, Jeb, her four-year-old son, was purple, black, and swollen across the entire top of his eyes and forehead. I stifled a gasp when I saw him, thinking instantly of a car crash or worse. But I soon learned it came from pounding his own head on the wall at his daycare. Nobody knew what set him off. Nobody was able to stop him. Alice had been told he could not return, since they were not equipped to deal with his challenges. As though she *was* equipped?

Alice had no family in town. We knew her husband had left her, and that Alice's full-time job paid just enough to keep them housed and fed. She had limited childcare options through state agencies, and so far not much of a plan for school next year, either.

"I've taken the week off my job," Alice told us, sitting absolutely motionless on her battered sofa. "I have five more days, including the weekend, to come up with a solution."

We watched Jeb bouncing endlessly up and down on a small trampoline standing in the corner. His battered face made a gut-clenching sight. I could not imagine how he tolerated the repetitive bouncing, but he went on and on and on, gaze fixed at some indiscernible point across the room. I struggled to understand how children could self-harm to this extent. The level of frustration and overload that would create this behavior was foreign to me. I could acknowledge it, but nothing in my experience gave me the slightest shred of understanding.

I perched on the edge of a folding chair, scribbling myself an occasional note or question, but nothing else. In these first home visits, Sherry took the lead. I answered when spoken to. On the day we first met Alice, we'd trained and placed exactly eight successful dogs. The number of training hours–for clients more than dogs–ran into the hundreds. Weeks. Months. The vast majority of that training had to happen in the clients' homes. This was the brick wall of reality dictating that we had to pursue any further placements through the school, not on our own. We didn't own enough hours or dollars to meet such needs. Yes, we'd had to hire additional help out of pocket. And as we'd told Nori, a classic case of the dime running out.

Notably, the cases in which we'd tried and failed also loomed large. We knew the success-to-disaster ratio grew directly from how many focused and disciplined hours the parent(s) could–or would–spend on the project. Therefore, this initial discussion with a prospective family was a tricky balancing act. We had to learn the truth about lots of variables without tipping our hand. Parents frantic for solutions often didn't limit themselves to hard facts. It wasn't that they set out to deceive. They might tell us what they thought we wanted to hear, fully intending to make it so, if that's what it took to get help. Maybe they could, or maybe they couldn't. It was our job to figure out the difference. Just as often, a client like Alice might hear what she yearned to hear more than what we actually said.

Armed with 20 years of psychotherapy experience, Sherry was approximately 500 times better at this than I was. I kept carefully quiet.

"It will take some time to assess whether or not we can help you with a dog," Sherry cautioned. "There is no possibility that we can put a dog with you this week."

"I understand," Alice said flatly. "It just seemed like since I had the chance to talk, that this would be the place and time to start."

"What other people would be involved with a dog project?" Sherry liked to get this one on the table quickly. For instance, well-intentioned best friends could be tricky. Often they were even harder than those who disagreed with the project. The only factor harder to cope with than not enough help was too much help from the wrong direction.

"None." Alice's voice contained no emotion at all. "I have no family in this state. My husband left over a year ago. You are the first people who have been inside this house since last summer."

"Are you divorced, then?" Sherry was careful with her question, but we had to know. "If your home is still co-owned, and depending on the custody agreement, then we will have to have certain permissions from both of you before we could proceed."

"Good luck," Alice's flat voice did not alter. "You would have to find him first. He's currently dodging child support payments. I have no idea where he is. And no, we are not divorced. That costs money I don't have."

As with so many families, fractured marriages or not, a service dog could be a powerful tool, but could not fix budgets, courts, childcare, or education dilemmas. Often a wholesale practical invention needed to be the first step. More and more often, I was feeling like we were bailing a flooding steamship with a plastic spoon. We could not fix such problems. We knew only what had to be true before a dog could help.

"All right." Sherry always sounded absolutely resolute in these situations. "Tell me about Jeb's therapy. Is he, or has he ever been, in a behavior intervention program?"

"We started one when he was two," Alice began twisting her fingers together. "He made some progress. That's where he started talking. But we couldn't keep up the cost. And when his dad left, it was impossible."

"Would you be willing to talk to some friends of ours if we could get you an appointment this week?" Sherry's spoke with slow, measured syllables. "I can't make promises. This is not our area of specialty. But I can try to find you some options."

"I'll try anything," Alice said frankly. "I don't want to be irrational or grasp at straws or do something stupid. But I'm in no position to be picky. If I can't find someone at least to keep Jeb while I work, we will lose this house because I'll lose my job."

Not until I realized that the woman's knuckles were absolutely white did I realize how hard her fingers were clenched.

Alice's voice was rambling now, and the story was painfully familiar to us. "I sit here and I know that in a month or two we could be living on the streets. There's no family, no friends where I can go and take Jeb. There is not a single house I can take him where he would be welcome. But sitting here right now, all I want is a nap. I am so tired."

Alice's voice cracked just once. She paused, took a couple deep breaths, but no tears followed.

"He doesn't sleep well. And even when *he* sleeps, *I* can't sleep, because I'm too worried about not hearing if he wakes up. I get a couple hours here and there. I've taken to locking his door from the outside so he can't wander. The room has a baby monitor, but in the morning, I usually have a mess to clean up because he will just go in his room rather than call me. If I try to sleep in the same room with him, he wakes up if I so much as turn over or cough. He has to have absolute quiet. He's my son and I love him, but I can't do this alone and I can't do this on three hours of sleep a night."

This, indeed, was possibly the number-one issue for many parents who contacted us. Nearly all of them listed sleep deprivation as a major life issue. Despite all the challenges, if other factors lined up, this was one way we knew we could help. Almost anyone who has ever been awakened by an insistent dog will rapidly understand why. From the standpoint of the average dog (who adores his humans), sleeping people are boring. People are lots more fun when awake. They talk, walk, go outside, ride in cars, feed dogs, pet dogs, and do any number of interesting things. The average dog loves to wake people up for no reason at all, let alone for fun, exciting, or important reasons.

Our growing contingent of German Shepherds, context aware, routine sensitive, and strongly bonded to a human, already has a lot of control-freak attitude. It took incredibly little behavior shaping to reward the dog into jumping on the bed, pulling off covers, licking the parent senseless, and barking until the puny, reluctant human plugs back into the land of the aware. The dog could generalize this quickly and effectively: the child is up, therefore the parent must get up. This is a bossy herding dog's dream job, no batteries required. Even if crated or locked in a different room, he'd just bark the walls down. It was as close to foolproof as anything we'd ever done.

But at that point of first interview, sitting in a prospective client's home, we dared not say so. Other issues had to be settled first. Perhaps the very first entry on this list? We needed to know if self-harm was the extent of this child's violent behavior. Would the dog be safe? How could we be reasonably sure?

Other basics included whether the family had the financial resources to care for the dog. We never charged for the dogs themselves, or for training. But where would the money come from for dog food, equipment, vet bills? Was this a situation in which we would have to find sponsors for these expenses?

The almighty time issue was right up there at the top of the list. Regardless of need or desire, did enough discretionary time even exist in this parent's life? To take part in scores of hours of training? Caring for a child with a disability is all-consuming, and by their own admission, most of these parents are severely sleep deprived. Yes, the dog can add powerful tools, but only after weeks of intensive training. Could Alice find the time?

"Are you going to make her chart her hours?" I'd asked Sherry on the drive over.

"I'm still deciding," she answered, absently tapping her fingers on the steering wheel. "I guess it depends on whether or not she looks like she has control of things now."

"Well, if I get a vote, I'm in favor," I commented crossly. Our last attempt to put a service dog in with an affected child had included three adults in the home: two parents, one grandparent. Yet they still couldn't get the training homework done. Every training visit, every checkpoint met with another excuse for why and how it couldn't happen. The dog's lack of progress eventually deteriorated into unacceptable behaviors. With no change in the adults' participation, we'd had to remove the confused and frustrated dog from the home. "I'm not up for a repeat of the Conyers situation," I reminded Sherry. "They're still busy telling anyone who will listen that we are the devils of the southeast who stole their dog and didn't give them a fair chance."

"Yeah, well," Sherry didn't much care. "Let them rant. They may be the first but they won't be the last. People will either do this or they won't. I just have to get better at figuring out who will."

"Easy for you to say," I continued to grumble. "Ranting decreases our chances for funding, you know. Please don't forget it."

"Yeah, well," Sherry said again. "That's mostly your problem, not mine, if we're going to stick to the job descriptions."

"Please make her account for the hours before we start. Please?" I really didn't think we should start another client until we were farther along with the ones already in motion. We simply could not stretch any more. The hours did not exist. Yet, as we sat listening to Alice, the impossibility of her situation pushed me forward, despite all misgivings. And then, the misgivings themselves evaporated when we brought in Bear for the next part of the assessment. Bear, of course, had come from our first seriously promising litter almost three years ago when we finally started getting some things right. He'd now matured into a stunning adult: perceptive, intuitive, extremely social. He'd learned this initial routine with speed and zest. As functional trainers went, we figured he was worth at least another 1.5 humans.

When bringing Bear into a setting like this, we never knew exactly what to expect. A child might be terrified, neutral, casually interested, or even angry at the dog's presence. So it was always a breath-stopping moment of pure suspense while we both tensed to leap in any possible direction. No worries this time. Jeb proceeded to give us the most pronounced response we'd ever seen. When the glossy black creature strode into the room, Jeb froze. The trampoline bouncing–incessant since our arrival–stopped instantly. Jeb stared long, and he stared hard. We all waited. Alice had been cautioned not to move or speak until Jeb gave a first response. I don't think anybody even breathed. Bear, long accustomed to this routine, sniffed delicately into the air in the small boy's general direction and waved his plumed tail.

Jeb stepped off the trampoline. Bear's tail sped up its wag. Seeing his paw lift to take a step forward, I waved fiercely for him to stay put. He almost did, but in some ways he was wiser than I. He turned sideways and shot a truly flirtatious glance over his shoulder at Jeb. That did it. Walking straight to the dog, Jeb dug his hands into the thick, soft fur. I heard him make a sound, but could not identify it.

"Yes, Jeb." Alice still sat rigidly on the sofa. "It's a dog! Doggie!"

"Dooo." This time the sound was more clear. Jeb dropped to his knees and buried his face in the silky coat. "Dooo."

Alice looked up, her eyes wide in total astonishment. "That's the first word he's said in weeks." Most parents would dissolve in tears at this point. I almost was. It was days before it occurred to me that Alice was not. Did not. Never did. I never saw her cry, for good or bad reasons. And I always wondered if she had seen every possible form of distress in every degree, and was simply too inured to it all. Or maybe she was just too tired.

But Jeb? Jeb didn't care about any of this. He was busy with Doo. This, I strongly suspected, we could help. I risked a glance at Sherry. She gave an almost imperceptible nod. Many factors had to line up in the proverbial row, but in that moment I knew we could not possibly walk away from this woman and her son.

Less than a month later we brought one of Bear's daughters to stay with Jeb. We were prepped for, braced for, weeks and weeks of intense effort. But this time we were in for a happy surprise. Nineteen-month-old Careen, also solid black like her daddy, took Jeb over as ruthlessly as any momma dog with new pups. She would not willingly be separated from him. Almost immediately she started reliable alerts to certain behaviors and blocked Jeb from approaching the gates in their fenced yard. As we had found true before, the reduced parent-child conflict created an enormous balm for the entire relationship.

Three mornings later Alice called us, and her voice sounded reborn.

"He slept through the night!" she exclaimed. "Careen gets in the bed with him and they just stay there...." Her voice trailed off. In the long pause that followed I thought furiously. We'd come up against that one a couple times before. Normally, having service dogs on peoples' beds is a big no-no. But in certain situations, parents and the circumstances had to take the lead, as long as it wouldn't cause trouble with the habits of the individual dog.

Alice wasn't finished, though. "He got up one time to use the bathroom. Careen came into my room and poked me with her nose, then followed Jeb. I sat up in bed and listened, waiting to see what would happen. He just...."

her voice was fading again. "He just went back to bed. And stayed there until I woke him up this morning."

However miraculous the parents thought this was, it was quite average for these placements. We thought it likely the increased activity, especially outdoors, accounted for a lot of increased sleep quality. Parents tired out faster than the average child. The dog's help in maintaining safety usually extended the playtime and physical exertion several times over, thus greatly increasing sleep readiness at the end of the day. For the kids that responded well to the tactile comfort of a dog in their bed, the double-whammy helped the entire household.

Not a few youngsters with these dogs soon discarded their weighted blankets–purchased by their parents for "deep pressure therapy"–in favor of a 70-pound dog. In Careen's case, a photo soon arrived in my email of a dog and boy tangled together in sheets, blankets, and a dozen stuffed animals. The boy was fast asleep. Careen lay quietly on her back, twisted into an impossible contortion. The only part of her face visible was one eye with a bright gleam. She'd landed the high life, and she knew it.

On the day after our downtown demo to Nori, Sherry was headed over to talk Alice through the steps to expect during her own public access test. I had an evaluation to do with Trent on the other side of town. He was driving, but I was plotting a quick visit at Alice's house on the way back. Surely, I thought, if I could just get him to see the pair?

Not really. When I asked to make a pit stop, Trent was not fooled. "Save yourself the trouble, Julie," he remarked. "Of course I'll stop so you can do whatever, but I'm not going in. I really do think you guys are in the ozone. I met that woman when she came in last winter. She looked wound tight enough to explode across five counties."

"Well, that's kind of the whole point," I said frostily. "What's your complaint if it's working?"

"I just don't see how we can add anything. We're already ridiculously overstretched."

I stifled a sigh and kept quiet. He was both right and wrong. Yet even as we pulled into Alice's yard, fate intervened.

It was late afternoon, early in the spring. Unseasonably warm weather had children out in droves, playing on the residential street. Movement, commotion, and noise were everywhere. It struck me as a whole lot of child activity for a road as busy as this one. Trent slowed considerably and tried to watch in multiple directions at once. As we stopped in the driveway, I could see Jeb outlined in the living room window, watching the goings-on. I doubted he was all that interested in the other kids, but noise and excitement would always draw his attention.

Or maybe not. Before I had even touched a door handle to exit the van, I saw the mail carrier, a large bag over his shoulder, step up on the porch and ring the bell. Then several things happened all at once. Just as Alice opened the door, several children raced down the sidewalk directly in front of the house. Jeb shot through the doorway, right under Alice's arm, hot on the trail of the running group. I heard Alice squeal. Saw the postman jolt in surprise. Saw Jeb racing for the street.

No human can move as fast as a dog. Before any of us had had more than point-zero-five seconds to gasp,

Careen was out the door, down the steps, and blocking Jeb from the street. Annoyed, he attempted to push her aside. She held her ground, shoulder turned in, moving in the perfect, training-prescribed arc to keep herself in proper position–which kept Jeb from moving any farther away from his mom or any closer to the road. Not three more seconds passed before Alice had reached him, and Jeb was returned to safety.

I felt, rather than saw, Trent's total stillness beside me.

"Holy hell," I heard him mutter.

After two seconds of quick thought, I said nary a word. I just climbed out of the van and left him sitting there. Barely halfway to the house, I struggled to suppress a smile when I heard a second vehicle door open and shut as he silently followed me inside.

In another two weeks, the Alice-Jeb-Careen team passed their final tests with flying colors–one of the fastest, most dramatic results we'd ever experienced. By the time fall arrived, along with Jeb's return to school, their entire household routine was much more under control, most of the credit going to an extremely bossy, child-obsessed, fast-footed German Shepherd.

Before the holidays, we received an email from Alice. It was sent to us, but written as a thank you to the rotary club who'd sponsored Careen's expenses. She'd asked us to share the whole note with them, along with several photos.

The email was longer than usual for Alice, detailing the changes, the new grasp on safety and routine they now enjoyed. The note closed with a fabulous paragraph: "I hadn't slept through a night since I hit the seven-month mark of pregnancy with this kid. I'd been relying on sponge baths for years, and washing my hair over the side of the tub because I couldn't risk getting in the shower where I couldn't hear my son. I couldn't sleep, work, shop, or meet Jeb's needs for exercise and activity. For the first time since his birth, we can do all those things. And now he can run and play in the yard until he's actually tired. For me, for us, this dog is life itself. She is our ability to cope, and the biggest reason we are now making progress with Jeb's therapy and my work. Thank you so much for your part in providing her to us."

You can live a long time on a note like that. Before I even replied to it, I forwarded it to Trent, then glanced out the window from my new little office on the farm. The current view in the closest pasture was worth a broad smile. Trent had organized several volunteer children to help stage training exercises for adolescent canines. Each child's parent was leaning on the fence to watch. It was hard to tell who was more excited–the half dozen elementary-age kids darting here and there, or the young dogs anxiously holding their stays until it was their turn to practice blocking the "run-aways." Even our biggest critic, our most cynical trainer, hadn't been able to resist the evidence.

Now, I thought, how do we translate that to other audiences?

Chapter 22

I raced through the doorway of the hospital emergency room, waving my trainer's ID at the desk clerk, who hastily pointed me in the correct direction. The first glimpse of our client stopped me cold in the entry of her cubicle. Karen looked worse off than any domestic violence photo I'd ever seen. Scraped and bruised face. Clothing torn off most of the right half of her body. Lower leg covered in ice packs while a medical team worked to clean and suture a gaping wound on her thigh. Halfway down her left forearm a long seam of angry stitches already loomed. The wound looked as straight as though inflicted by a knife. In fact, my first coherent thought was exactly that. A mugging? A robbery? Then I saw her wheelchair propped against the wall with a broken wheel and one armrest hanging crazily askew. Oh my, I thought. It finally happened! Somebody was hit by a car!

The phone call had come less than 20 minutes before from a local emergency room. "We need one of your trainers to come down here quickly." she said, thankfully speaking in concise, professional terms. "One of your dogs and his owner are here. Both are badly hurt."

I'd screamed for Nori to take the phone and ran out of the building, headed for the hospital. Fortunately, by the time

I'd made it halfway, Nori had convinced one of the
EMTs to grab the dog and rush for our vet. Jax, the
graduate dog, was bleeding profusely from a dozen
wounds and had a broken–almost crushed–front leg. Barb
and Nori raced for the vet. I continued to the hospital,
now needing to find out what I could.

"Karen?" I said softly. I approached her bed slowly,
squelching the urge to clutch at her and demand full
recounting. The last thing she needed was more anxiety
shoved in her face. "What can I do? How can I help?
Nori and Barb are with Jax."

Karen opened one eye. The other was swollen shut. She
turned a battered face to me. "Find the dog," she said.

I didn't understand. Then I thought perhaps she didn't
understand. Looking at her head trauma alone, Karen
could well have been unconscious for parts of this saga. I
reached out to touch her lightly on the shoulder closest to
me. "Jax is at the vet with Nori. I should get an update
soon."

"Not my dog." I realized the tremble in her voice was
fury, not trauma. "The other dog. The one that did this.
And its owner."

I felt a physical jolt from her words. "A dog did this?" I
knew my voice was raised, but it was out before I could
stop it. I took a closer look at the deep punctures that the
doctor was working on. A cold draft shot down my spine.
Yes, it was a bite. Four deep punctures on the outer
corners, with a deep rip between. The cold took me over
entirely, head to foot.

"Ma'am?" An official voice came from the curtained
doorway.

I turned to see a uniformed officer beckoning to me to come with him. "I need to get some information from you, please."

I looked at Karen again. "I am not leaving." I promised. "I'll be right outside. I will not leave until you're ready to go and until your family is here."

"She's going to get an x-ray of that ankle next," the doctor spoke without looking up. "She'll be here a while."

"I'll find out how Jax is doing," I promised her. Closing her eye, Karen nodded slightly. I followed the officer to an empty alcove. "I have so many questions," I started in. "What…"

He interrupted me. "Let's start from the other end. I'll give you the rundown, but I need a clarification first. The lady told me her dog belongs to the school who trained him. Is that right? Do you have an ID for the school?"

"Yes, that's correct," I told him. I unclipped my trainer ID from my pocket. "He stays with her permanently, but we guarantee his training and assume a lot of the costs."

He took the badge and scanned it. I was busy pulling more cards from my wallet: my own, Nori's, and the Executive Director's. I handed them all to him. "I really need to know what happened."

The officer scanned the cards, rubbed his eyes, and heaved a sigh. "They were attacked by another dog," he said wearily. "We don't know enough yet. Some officers are still at the store getting witness statements, and there are some security cameras in the store. There may be some information available from them."

"In a store?" I had to work hard to keep from shouting. "How–"

"Wait," the officer broke in again. "Just wait. Let me tell you what I know first."

I ground my teeth and bore down. Get a grip. You need to stay cool, stay cool, stay cool. I clasped my hands together tightly and vowed to keep quiet.

"The other dog was also a service dog," he said. "Everyone who saw agrees he was walking with another customer, and wearing a jacket identifying him as service dog." The officer rubbed the back of his neck and stared at the floor. "The other lady, the owner, was using one of those stretch-out leashes that pulls out and coils back, you know what I mean?"

A Flexi, I thought, with a spurt of anger. I just nodded.

"So apparently the other dog saw this one, your dog. He runs at him and jumped on him and a big fight started. The people weren't real close together, but that long leash caught around this lady's arm. You seen that cut by her elbow?"

My chills were back. I knew very well the thin cord the policeman was describing.

"Then that leash caught around the chair, I guess. All the people who watched say something a little different. But either the fight or the cord or both tipped this lady over and dragged her into a display and a bunch of stuff fell on her and her chair."

The officer's voice got very thick. "Your dog is beat up pretty bad, ma'am. It don't sound like he was doing much except trying to get away. But that lady in there," he waved toward Karen's cubicle, "was trying to pull them apart. She couldn't. Got bit more than once. So did two other guys who jumped in and helped. I think quite a few people piled on and got the dogs apart. The other guys are down there getting stitched up." He nodded toward the far end of the curtained hall.

"Where is this other dog?" I felt my own hands shaking. "And who is the person who had it?"

"Well," the officer was still doing a stare-down with a piece of floor tile. "There's where we have some trouble. While everybody was trying to help your dog and the lady here, the other one grabs her dog and takes off. We haven't found her yet."

A rage coursed through me of a sort I never remembered at any point in my life. "We are going to find that dog." A deep quiver started in my stomach and worked upward.

"Yes, ma'am," the officer said. "We got people working on that right now. Course another problem in all the hubaloo is we can't know which dog bit who. So aside from all the rest, we gotta know if the other dog had his rabies shots." The officer still didn't meet my eyes. He busied himself sticking the business cards into his notebook. Belatedly I realized his hands were trembling as badly as my own. I thought it might be from plain emotional backlash until I realized the muscles in his forearms were corded outward and twitching like live animals.

He's as angry as I am, I thought. He's just a lot better at concealing it.

The young officer spoke again, without a trace of anything but professionalism in his voice. "Don't you worry, now, okay? I think a lot of people saw the other dog. And with the store cameras, it's almost for sure we'll be able to find 'em. From the sounds of things, she was showing him off to other people. Walking back and forth and telling everybody about her service dog."

A severe nausea rose in my stomach. I stepped to the water fountain, took a sip, then splashed a little on my face. Turning back, I met the man's eyes and could see easily that his anger and contempt matched my own. "Let me know how we can help." I couldn't think of anything else useful to say. "We have staff and a decent-sized crew of volunteers. There has to be a way we can add leg power."

My phone vibrated. I glanced at the caller display. It was Nori. "I need to take this," I told the officer. "I'm not leaving, but I need to step outside and take this." He nodded. I hustled to the door.

"Hey, how is he?" I asked without preamble.

"Not good. We're at the University Specialists. Dr. Johnson redirected them enroute, which is fortunate for Jax. They got the bleeding stopped, or at least most of it. Dr. Johnson came over to meet us and help. They're all working on him. One of the bites slightly punctured an artery. Another eighth of an inch or another couple minutes getting him here and he'd be dead now. We're bringing in a bunch of the dogs from the kennel to donate blood and to restock their supply. If he stays stable another 30 minutes, they're going to do emergency surgery to try to repair the leg. Nobody's sure something inside there isn't still bleeding."

My nausea hadn't gone away. I thought of the slender

little red retriever with the always-sad eyes, and the sickness swelled up into my throat. Jax was always so dedicated to his job. So serious. So thrilled with praise. I pushed hard on my forehead, and tried to concentrate.

Nori was firing questions at me, now. "What happened? Vets say the wounds are dog bites. Where was she? Whose dog did this?"

I took a deep breath, found a nearby bench, settled down and tried to explain. For once she had less control of her temper than I did. Jax was a pup she'd raised herself, from the day he broke his birth sac. Several years, thousands of hours, untold amounts of effort and expense–to say nothing of the trauma–were savaging her views of the situation. I understood. Mine weren't much better.

By 2005, the year of Jax's massive injuries, more than a few professionals in the service dog world had developed severely mixed thoughts about certain aspects of the Americans with Disabilities Act. When it was new, it surely seemed like a telegram straight from heaven. We reveled in the far greater freedom for our clients. New programs seemingly sprouted out of the sidewalks in response to the demand following the passing of Public Law 101-336. In those first few years, I had never known anyone, nor did I know anyone who firsthand knew anyone else, who'd ever abused the statute. But times change.

I sat on the hospital bench, thinking about my first moment of unease about our new law, not terribly long after my internship. I was busily typing responses to prospective clients when it occurred to me this magnificent federal law, as much as we loved it, was a bit

broadly written. The query in front of me now had
thrown light on that problem. The writer wanted an
explanation of certification and why we required it. But
this client had added a question I hadn't seen before.
"Whatever the test is, can individuals use it to certify
their own dogs? Where do you go to try?"

My first thought was instantaneous: why would you want
to? But nothing is ever as simple as we think it should be.
The truth of the ADA, however, was that no legal
requirement for any kind of certification even existed. In
legal terms a finished service dog did not have to be
certified, registered, or verified. The only certification
that meant anything was a contractual agreement between
trainer and client.

Moving back inside the hospital, I found a hard, plastic
chair outside Karen's cubicle, still thinking about that
first breath of genuine worry from so long ago.

"Hey, Nori," I'd asked, "what's to prevent people from
passing off untrained or unsound dogs as service
animals?" I remember how my hands hovered over the
keyboard, looking for a better way to communicate the
concept.

"Depending on the degree of cluelessness, probably not
much," Nori told me dryly.

"Then what do I say to these people about certification?"
I still had nothing to type. "This guy wants to know about
the origin of the test. How do I say that the access rights
belong to the people, not the dog, without making it
sound like he doesn't have to do full training?"

"Don't say so at all." Nori turned to face me. I had just
reached the point of feeling vaguely competent as a

trainer, but dogs were way easier than people and this was a whole new concept to me.

Are you kidding? Just in time I stopped myself from saying it out loud. As a very junior trainer, I hadn't earned the credentials to question her on something like this. But perhaps my look spoke for me.

"You tell them that it's required. Not by whom. We require it. That's all they need to know. Nobody in this building is going to have any part of encouraging someone to do something they're not trained for."

I definitely knew better than to argue, but I always marked that episode as the day I felt the first nervous zing of "uh-oh." Not at Nori's words, but at their implication: there were people out there who were going to try this on their own. Maybe some could do it. But even then at that early point I knew that "some" wasn't anywhere near "most."

I shifted my attention back to the traffic around the ER. Pity the ADA wasn't written with this situation in mind. I thought about Jax. Wondered if he was in surgery. Wondered if he was alive. Wondered what to say to Karen when she returned.

A minor commotion roused me from my drifting thoughts. I looked down the hallway to see a young woman greeting her husband with tears and horror. Standing up, I started down the hallway. I was pretty sure this was one of the bystanders who'd tried to intervene and help Karen and Jax. His right hand was heavily bandaged, and he was wearing hospital scrub bottoms. He awkwardly wrapped his good arm around his sobbing wife. Words passed between them, but I was too far away to have any good idea of what was going on. Then he looked up at me over his wife's shoulder.

I stopped, considering a return to my chair. It suddenly seemed intrusive to approach. But he struggled forward with a pronounced limp. "Excuse me," he asked, stopping my retreat. "Aren't you the lady from the service dog school? I saw you talking to the cop earlier."

"Yes," I stopped and introduced myself. "I'm Julie. I'm just a trainer, but I'm here waiting to see how Karen does."

"Can I ask you something?" The man's face was white, and he moved with extreme care. Dog bites are extremely painful–something he was learning the hard way.

"Of course," I answered cautiously. "I might not know the answer, but if I don't I can try to find out for you."

The couple stopped near me, then stepped to the side of the hall to avoid traffic. "I just don't understand how a dog who is that aggressive can be allowed out in public. And that ridiculous long leash–are those things approved for service dogs?"

I sighed before I could stop myself, and it took some effort to steady my voice before answering. "Service dog training and access don't have a lot of regulation. The wording of the law says only that the dog has to be trained to do the job. There's no legal requirement for how the dog is trained, or with what." Answer what they ask, I reminded myself. Don't elaborate.

"So the dog that did this is legal?" The man's voice sharpened. "He killed that retriever, didn't he? He looked dead when they carried him out."

"The dog is still holding on. I think he's in surgery right now," I said carefully. "I can't say if the other dog was legal or not. I don't know."

"All I can say," the man reached for his wife's hand, "is if that's what's considered okay, I really don't know why every decent trainer in the country isn't screaming his head off. What could possibly justify what happened today?"

It was an excellent question for which I had no answer. "You're not the only one wondering," I had to say. "But it's extremely complicated to do anything about. That law is federal, not state, so any change would be a really big undertaking."

Once he limped out the lobby door, I returned to my hard seat, thinking about the recent chit-chat about individual states expanding access rights from the disabled user to the trainer of the service dog. I really wasn't sure anymore if I thought that was a good idea. Through most of the years I'd been training, we could not take a trainee into a public place without permission, unless the training happened in a place that already allowed pets. We had considered the permissions gathering to be a lot of hassle. Every location where we (we the able-bodied) trained service dogs had to be scouted, solicited, and approved. However, it was a rare business who didn't quickly see the light when you outlined the logic. For instance, you'd round up a list from a particular client about where he shopped, traveled, worked, etc. You'd visit each place with the dog in tow. "Okay," you'd say briskly, "we are training a mobility service dog for John Doe who regularly shops here. We'd like to train his dog in your store before we teach John how to use the dog. Once the dog is working with him, federal law requires that you allow him to be here, just like everyone else." The average business owner or manager was quick to see their store was better off when the trainer did advance homework.

I thought about poor Jax. And thought back to the first time I'd ever fielded a call that was targeted on outright deception. "Can you certify my dog as a service dog so I can have it in the apartment where I'm moving? They don't allow pets." After I took the first such call, I ranted. I raved. I shared with the other trainers. We paced the floor and gesticulated wildly. We expounded on the crassness of the call and the lack of ethics. We assured each other that nobody was going to tolerate this kind of nonsense. That this kind of inappropriate behavior, amounting to outright graft, would be stomped from the face of the earth.

Fast forward a few years. Once again we stood around sharing our collective astonishment, this time while staring dully at a headline in the *New York Times*: "Nobody knows for sure if hell has frozen over, but it's official: pigs can fly." Cue the music for a dramatic scene: a 300-pound porker showing up to board a USAir flight from Philly to Seattle. "This pig is a service animal," said the passenger. Frustrated but powerless USAir employees followed the letter of the law and boarded the pig. Tenuous control held until the landing approach when the pig panicked and ran amok in the plane, finally being trapped in the galley by a horrified flight crew.

"We are in really deep doo-doo," Barb commented delicately. "What will happen?"

Everybody had a dire prediction. Nobody would ever let

a pig fly again. The airline was correct and would be protected. The airline was wrong and would be sued. The passenger would be prosecuted. We were all wrong. Nothing at all happened, and the snowball rolled on.

Every one of us had run into more and more problems, whether it was the tiny, snarling dogs in sequined jackets riding in the grocery store carts and the owner exclaiming "Oh, he can be here. This is my service dog." Or the hulking beast straining at the leash, trying to drag his human into the face of any other dog on a city sidewalk– but the picture wouldn't be complete without the "Service Dog" jacket on the lunging dog.

At the training center, the calls increased. Over the last year or so, it had become routine.

"I want my dog to fly in the airplane cabin with me. How do I get him certified as a service dog?"

"Can I buy a vest from you for my dog? My landlord won't let me have him unless he's a service dog."

"Can I get a copy of the paperwork you use to certify a dog as a service animal? I can't afford a pet sitter, and I have to be able to bring my dog to work with me."

We grew past the shock, past the amazement, and far into disgust. And the calls kept coming. Disgust gave way to anger. We'd seen seriously sub-par dogs while out training. And we'd had reports from our clients about their dogs being challenged and harassed by "service dogs." A few had needed help when their dog grew unacceptably reactive from bad experiences. Up to now, only one situation we knew about had escalated into a physical confrontation. But nothing like this. Nothing even close.

The loud thump of a stretcher banging into a swinging door jolted me from my recollections. Two medical aides wheeled Karen out of radiology and back to her room. I followed, only to learn that they were going to admit her for observation and probable surgery tomorrow to repair the damage to her broken leg.

As often seems the case, hospital experiences swing from long periods of boredom to brief stretches of commotion. In the middle of the updates, Karen's family finally arrived from their hometown an hour away. Explanations started over. I was getting better with stock replies, but nobody in this group was any happier with them than the previous people. Very soon I left Karen with her family to get checked in and departed to see about Jax and what else might need to be done.

The plucky little retriever pulled through surgery, but already we had serious doubts he would ever be the same dog. The x-rays of his damaged leg were the stuff of nightmares, and he was fortunate just to be alive. Nori absolutely refused to leave him, telling the clinic they could put up with her or arrest her, but nothing in between. They relented, and she stayed to monitor his progress.

Most of the rest of us focused on helping the police locate the dog and owner who'd caused the injury. Sifting through the store's security video was, all by itself, a time-consuming task. It was a full day before we were all able to view some photos of a large, dark-colored dog, strong and stocky, ranging well ahead of a woman who was usually looking around at anything but her dog. A short snippet of video from the camera by the exit showed the bulky mixed breed dragging his owner outside by remnants of a long, corded leash. They

careened into the parking lot, a "Service Dog" vest
hanging askew. We pulled the best photos, printed up
hundreds of copies offering a reward for information, and
took to the streets. Social media was not quite yet much
of a life feature for us, but a full-scale blitz of fliers, a
local TV news spot, and a major effort from the entire
police department did finally locate the owner and the
dog–for all the good it did us.

The woman swore by her right to have a service dog.
When faced with the (actually legal) question of "what
work does he do for you?" she stated the dog would
guide her out of the store in the event of a disabling panic
attack. In the face of dozens of contrary witness
statements, the argumentative lady claimed Jax was the
aggressor. She vehemently refused to consider
responsibility for the medical charges. The best that can
be said is that her dog had at least been current with
rabies vaccinations. The injured people did not have to–
on top of everything else–undergo prophylactic treatment
for rabies.

We turned from her in total disgust, focused on Karen
and Jax, and left this woman to the program's attorneys.
What we suspected was proven in short order: she carried
no insurance for the dog. Had no verification of training.
And there were, at that time, no state criminal penalties
that could be applied to the situation. The attorneys filed
a lawsuit against her for medical expenses and damages,
which were easily defined and won. Except that
immediately thereafter, the plaintiff declared bankruptcy
and vanished from our state, taking her problematic dog
with her.

But even as that was months in the future, our training
group and board of directors joined forces to salvage Jax

and Karen's working relationship. Every possible medical treatment, physical therapy, behaviorist consult, long-term therapy, and anything else we could think of was poured on. And it was all in vain. No other dog on our training roster at that time was suitable for Karen. She could not live alone and attend her college classes without Jax's help, and he had months of recuperation to do. She dropped out of school for the semester, forfeited her tuition, her apartment deposit, and went home to North Carolina to help Jax recover. We had trainers in the house twice a week, along with physical therapists for both dog and human. Sherry helped Karen locate therapy for herself. Nori contracted multiple specialist behavioral consults for Jax.

But it was not to be. Jax entered his life naturally "soft" to corrections–this was the terminology we used for a dog who had a high desire to please and a low tolerance for any displeasure from his handler. For soft-spoken, gentle Karen, Jax made a perfect match. But the attack and the uproar involving dozens of people had thoroughly traumatized him. The beautiful boy was a trooper. He tried. He would follow commands. He would honor what we asked him to do. But he was utterly miserable, and every line of his body language showed it on every trip into public. Months of desensitization could not make him comfortable in going back to a regular unstructured work environment. Functional? Perhaps. Comfortable? No way. We all knew it was unfair to ask him to try. And behavior aside, odds were very high he would develop substantial arthritis in the injured leg, anyway.

Karen sobbed nonstop through the entire conversation when we finally told her our conclusion. She didn't disagree. "I knew it wasn't going to work," she said. "I wanted you to try, but I never thought it would work. He hates going out and I hate asking him to go. But I don't want to lose him."

Among the resulting problems: Karen simply could not either care for or cope with two dogs. Financially and practically, two were beyond her ability. We could get her another service dog. In fact, we had identified one for her, as a viable option, before Jax ever left the hospital. At that time, we couldn't know if Jax would ever be sound again. The new dog's training was nearly complete now. But we all agreed: if there was anything meaner than pushing Jax to work in public again, it would be to make him stay home and watch another dog take over his central place of honor and teamwork. That was unacceptable to us and to Karen. He left her house two days later, and they never saw each other again.

Jax lived out his days with a retired man who'd been diagnosed with MS. He was in the early phase of his disability, but had constant balance trouble and often needed help to get hold of hard-to-reach items around the house. Jax went through a rough adjustment, but eventually blossomed into a content home-companion dog, confident and happy in his supportive role. No doubt the man who received him was happy for the relationship. But not even he would have chosen the route by which it happened.

The last time I saw Karen, she was finished not only with college, but with graduate school; and she was moving to the west coast for her job of choice. Her successor replacement dog, a lovely Labrador, Sheila, was greying around the muzzle, but still working well. When Sheila passed away, Karen ultimately got her next dog from a

program geographically closer to her new home. But I
never forgot her words from our final meeting.

I couldn't keep my eyes from the heavy white scar on her
arm. I also knew she still had persistent pain around the
old break in her leg. She saw where I was looking. I saw
her reach out to stroke Sheila's head.

"You know," Karen said. "I really don't think I am a
violent person by nature. Not even an angry person by
nature. But no therapy ever made me stop feeling rage
toward that woman. Less about me than what she did to
Jax. He got no choice. No choice at all, and he didn't do a
thing wrong. I still dream sometimes about what
happened, and sometimes about what I would have done
if I could have reached her myself."

"You didn't do anything wrong, either," I reminded her.

"I know. But I don't think I did enough right, either.
Hardly a week goes by that I don't see another out-of-
control dog somewhere. I live ready, now." She slid a
hand discreetly into a pocket on the inside of the arm of
her wheelchair and held the pocket open slightly. I could
see the pepper spray there. We'd raised this idea as an
option for her and other clients. In every case, we wanted
them to make their own decisions, and we did our best to
fully disclose all possible complications. The decision
had to be the client's own, not ours. But we never again
wanted anyone to be as helpless as she'd been on that
terrible day.

Karen had chosen to get the spray and travel with it.
"Even the risk of getting my own face full of it, or
involving my own dog in the spray…. that's still way,
way less than what Jax had to go through," she said,

checking the Velcro closure on the top of the pocket. "He couldn't carry any pepper spray. He just had to trust me, and look how that worked out."

Karen absently rubbed her heavy scar. "Therapy can go take a jump. I don't think I will ever stop being angry. All the people who supported Jax's training and care. All the people who worked with him. All the pain he suffered. All the money and time lost." She stared straight up at me. "It took me two whole years to make up that ground."

It will take the rest of your life, I thought. Some wounds go far beyond the practical.

"I can just about cope with it for myself," Karen finished quietly. "But I wish the incredibly selfish people who fake the service dog thing would have to answer to Jax. Who makes it up to him?"

I watched her leave, Sheila dutifully alongside, and thought she was far too kind. She must be one of the strongest people I know. I had seen her flinch and stiffen at the approach of another dog. I knew how hard she was working–and would probably always work–to overcome that flinch. I knew how many thousands of dollars and how many long, painful months the disaster had set her back. In Karen's case, the immense difficulty of learning to use a service dog, the enormous expense, the hundreds of hours of training, had paved her route to independence. Without the dog, she could not do the same functions, and for me, the arguments started and stopped there. Jax wasn't the only one who deserved better. Karen also deserved better.

I watched them roll and trot away with a feeling of sick

foreboding about the overall hopelessness of practicalities and legalities. It's just as well I couldn't see the future from that day. I couldn't know that this barrage of unqualified, unsafe dogs would someday make it nearly impossible for schools like ours to obtain even the most basic general operating insurance anywhere in our state. That day I knew only that I'd seen a huge, yawning hole open under the very foundation of the service dog concept. And I knew I couldn't do anything about it.

Chapter 23

"Let's carpe the hell out of this diem."
—Alexandra Bracken, "The Darkest Minds"

"Can dogs really have autism?" The drive-through attendant looked down in puzzlement at the new program sign on my van door.

"What?" I was still writing out my deposit slip, only half hearing, and this question was not computing very well.

"Your sign." She pointed at the logo. "It says "dogs for autism." I didn't know dogs got that."

Sherry, riding next to me in the passenger seat, leaned over to look up at the confused face in the window. "It's awful," she said, deadpan. "We have the devil's time getting them into therapy."

I closed the window and hit the gas as fast as possible. "You better hope she isn't our next applicant," I said. "What if she has an autistic kid?"

Sherry rolled her eyes. "Please," she objected. "Nobody who's gone through the hell of getting a child diagnosed would be that clueless."

"Then you better hope she's not married to somebody on the next grant committee."

"Hah!" Sherry was in one of her obstinate moods. "She's probably better educated than some of the ones we've

been applying to. Did I tell you about the guy I was
trying to talk to last week? The guy who heads up the big
golf tournament over on the east side? He looks at the
sign and asked me 'who's Austin?' He didn't even know
the word autism, and no, I never got anywhere close to
getting him to understand."

However much I didn't want to hear it, these were
unfortunate truths. Our struggling little experiment was
still wobbling forward, if not exactly thriving. Since it
moved out of our personal pockets to become regular
school feature, we'd trained and placed a grand total of
nine more graduates. Each was now certified according
to Nori's exacting specifications. To say the process had
been exhausting and phenomenally time-consuming did
not begin to explain. Each funding dollar had been hard-
won from individuals. We had yet to land a single
substantial grant; no one we contacted would even listen.
One in particular for which we'd had very high hopes–
since they favored programs using German Shepherds–
told us any program that involved dogs working with
autism in any way was automatically disqualified for
funding. We could not imagine the rationale, but were
powerless to change it.

The farm now hosted a new training pavilion and a puppy
nursery with an indoor training room. At this point we
had three litters of pups between one and six months. We
knew this group could supply probably 30-35 high-value
training candidates, but couldn't decide if that was more
thrilling or terrifying. Several years had so far netted us
only about two-thirds of that number. What brand of
insanity would prompt us to add this many more all at
once?

"But it's not a question of insanity," I told Sherry one day while we sat on my porch. "If it was, then I think that ship has already sailed. This is straight numbers. Dollars and hours. That fork in the road you were talking about? We're there."

"Yeah," she said absently, "but if we're ever going to do it, this is the group of pups we need to go ahead with." We were watching a trio of fur-balls from the youngest litter waddling around our feet. We were taking the five-week old pups out a few at a time now in small enough groups to keep monitoring closely while watching behaviors.

"Except 'we' are not going to move ahead with them, Sherry," I objected impatiently. "There is no way to add anything more. I can't vouch for you, but I'm out of liquidity and starting to accumulate debt. Remember that conversation?"

She declined to answer, which was her mode of passive resistance. But we both knew we had no resources left from which to pull training funds for even one more dog, forget 30. Yet the proof was right here chewing my shoelaces. We'd come so far. *How* to make others see?

Another voice joined in. I turned to see Scott leaning on a porch post. "Have any of your families ever had a missing-kid episode after your dogs were placed? I mean like the kind you read about in the papers that require 300 people and helicopters?"

Scott had been something of an anomaly to our canine-obsessed clan. With zero background in dogs, but a keen brain for business and ample cynicism, his take on this project had been both refreshing and maddening. He was wowed by the dogs' functions, but had zero understanding of the process. I was learning, though, to borrow his perspective for a peek into the minds of potential funders

Sherry and I stared at each other blankly. It took us a few minutes to do the inventory.

"No," I said. "I don't think so."

"You're forgetting Emily and Desi," Sherry objected.

"Oh, right." I clarified for Scott. "We had one episode where the parents thought the kid was missing. She wasn't. She was hiding in their own house and the service dog found her. But they had called 911 and all that. Big mess, but if she'd asked the dog to find the kid before she called, it would have been okay."

"They're really that reliable?" Scott was still dubious.

"Pretty much." Sherry re-crossed her feet and settled back for continued explanation. "One of our very first dogs was fully cross trained for search and rescue. We assumed she'd need to do serious searching if the kid went missing. But it turned out to be wasted time because the dog never him out of her sight. None of the families who've used our dogs have ever had a kid get gone."

"You mean 100%?" Scott was obviously skeptical. "Never at all?"

"No, never, ever. Once we get far enough to—hey, watch that pup." Sherry interrupted herself and gestured wildly at Scott, pointing behind him.

He turned in curiosity. We all watched a smaller than average female fuzz-ball wandering away from the others. She approached the path Scott had been walking just a few minutes ago. The fat baby could barely manage the slope, but when she intersected the "trail," she stopped like she'd run into an invisible wall. Her head came up. Her nose waved back and forth, testing, seeking. Unerringly, she turned the direction he'd walked and followed the "hot" scent straight to him.

I almost tripped in my haste to get up and intercept her, praising, cooing, making much of her, and feeding her the tiniest shreds of fried liver. She hadn't saved a life, but I wanted her to think she had.

"I don't get it," Scott said, frowning. "Watch what?"

"She was following your scent," Sherry told him, still gesturing. "She crossed your trail where you just walked. Your scent is hanging in the air there. She noticed, picked the freshest direction, and followed it to you. That's what Julie is praising her for."

"Really?" He looked doubtful. "How can you possibly teach them to do that so young? She can barely walk."

"You can't," I said, cradling the now-exhausted pup. "When you see impulses like that in such young pups, what you're watching is genetics and nothing more. Most dogs could do it, but our question is *will* they do it, automatically, naturally, and early.

"But isn't that why you train?" Scott objected. He always wanted the process, not just a conclusion. "Lots of dogs do lots of different jobs where they smell stuff."

"Of course," Sherry answered. "It can be trained. Sometimes. But in the scenarios we train for, available hours from the family are so minimal as to be about nonexistent. So we constantly try for dogs that already do all the behaviors we want." Sherry scooped up another snoozing pup and got up. "Totally aside from the family's schedule, the more we have to train, the more hours we have to pay trainers, right?"

Scott plopped down and succumbed to the irresistible lure of petting the one pup still awake. I smothered a smile. We were making progress, for sure.

"So, then, that's the basis for raising these litters, and you're telling me–"

"No, it's part of the basis," Sherry interrupted him. "There are other reasons. Like these dogs' reliability with children is also really high. If they don't naturally respond correctly to kids, they're out of our program."

"What's correct?" Scott asked, his own yelp punctuating the question. "Not biting fingers?"

"Way more strict than that." I answered this part. "We want the pups to recognize that they need to be careful around any little kids without even being told. We're looking for the young dog that naturally dials back their body language. No bumping, pawing, grabbing food or toys. Most pups around four or five months are pretty rambunctious. When an adolescent dog gets around a toddler and starts slowing down, walking softly, being careful where they step, that's another test passed."

"That's usually a good sign, too," Sherry added, "that means a dog will have another natural urge: keeping a family group together. They are a herding breed, after all."

"Okay, fine," Scott was falling into cross-examination mode. "You have a list of criteria. These pups are meeting it. But my point is still this: none of the kids who have these dogs have ever required, for instance, a helicopter search. How much do you suppose it costs per hour to run a helicopter search? Where are the people who would pay attention to that?"

Eureka, I thought. Now there's a concept. I wondered who ran those kinds of budgets. "Probably people and groups who are about as cash-strapped as we are," I thought out loud.

"But those are terms more people would understand," Scott persisted. "Because you hear about searches like that in the news almost every week."

He was right, sort of. This was a line of thought we should pursue, if we could ever get a donor to look past the fact that we weren't serving only people in wheelchairs. Our graduates out moving around in public were, as we'd known would happen, bringing us a completely insane number of applications. We'd cautiously bred these last litters hoping to be able to increase scale. So far we were batting zero.

Reluctant to release these hard-won baby dogs to the world of pets, several trainers were each raising two or three pups at once, which was a mega-bad, mega-exhausting arrangement for all. We were also leaning on quite a few friendships for other rather reluctant puppy raisers. That scenario, also, had a really short shelf life. The dogs were great–everything we had dared to hope and more. The grant process? Not so much.

One afternoon I was deep into another application, one eye on the screen, one eye on the roaming shepherd puppy circling my feet, when Sherry barged through my front door without so much as a knock. She held a battered envelope in one hand and a somewhat crumpled piece of letterhead in the other.

"Hey, remember the Krandal Foundation?"

"How could I forget?" My heart leaped a bit at the sight of the paper, thinking of the solid week of effort we'd put into that application. The foundation emphasized its mission to "Find new and innovative ways to increase safety and quality of life for entire families affected by autism." We labored, agonized, inspected, edited, and meticulously groomed every syllable of our proposal. Their stated mission was a perfect fit. Our concept followed their exact criteria on every point and we sent it off with great hopes. It was as perfect as we could make it, including a detailed proposal for follow-up on effectiveness.

"Right, just wait." Sherry held up the piece of paper and read the scant words. "Thank you for submitting your proposal. Our foundation helps children, not dogs, so we cannot consider funding. Best of luck as you seek other options."

I didn't believe her. Until I snatched the paper and read it myself I was sure she was just tormenting me. Nope. Word for word. No joking involved. I believe at that moment, the truth of the Great American Grant Process distilled in our brains: pure, unadulterated, haphazard whim. Groups of people we did not know, could not evaluate, could not question gathered in private. They were not bound to explain their rationales, and could change any factor, for any reason, at any time. Nor were they bound even to read and comprehend what was submitted before making any decision they felt like, possibly based on which way the wind was blowing that day. Clearly either this group hadn't even read the proposal, or else they were committed to pretending they hadn't. Either verdict gave us the same result.

"This is a pure crap shoot," I said wearily, sinking back into my chair.

"Apparently." Sherry took the paper back. She smoothed it out and tucked it into a folder on my desk. "I'm keeping this one. This is too good not to have on hand to show my grandkids."

"What grandkids?"

"Oh wait, right. I don't have any children, do I? Good thing. If I did I'd have lost track of them by now for all the worrying about everybody else's."

A few weeks later a great day finally arrived. After almost two years of trying, we won our first response to an application; a grant committee wanted to meet with us for further discussion. We nearly lost what was left of our minds with excitement. The oldest of our pups had just passed six months. The next litter was barely five weeks behind them. We needed vast sums of money–soon–for medical screening before we could even be sure of continuing their training. And we didn't have it. Having totally exhausted our own bank accounts, we were now openly begging at pet stores and selling things on Craigslist to keep the dogs fed. Yet, here was hope: a grant committee who wanted to listen!

For the next two weeks, every aspect of our personal lives was blatantly neglected while we perfected the best heart-wrenching appeal we could muster. And lined up the best facts we could think of. Memorizing our speeches and answers to possible questions, we practiced the presentation while staring at ourselves in mirrors.

We pressed Scott into mimicking legal opposition, testing ourselves on all the objections he could come up with. I nearly overdid it with that one, intervening one evening scant moments before he and Sherry resorted to violence while disputing details of an equipment budget.

Fortunately for our sanity, we hadn't a clue it was almost entirely the wrong approach. We'd probably have turned all the dogs into a shelter and collectively thrown ourselves into traffic.

On a warm summer evening, we joined a group from the foundation in question, about 15 strong. They sat with unfathomable expressions while we made our pitch. Several perfectly trained dogs held their down-stays around the room while I scanned every face for the slightest nuance that might show me what to adjust, what to emphasize. Not much feedback. I reminded myself this was a group well accustomed to every kind of pleading known to mankind.

How to up the ante? I ransacked my brain, even while starting in on the demo of showing them how Bear, still our primary demo dog, could stop Sherry from walking (almost running) out the door of the room. He performed flawlessly, but all I saw was a polite smile here and there.

And then... deliverance.

"Wait a minute," a man from the back of the group stood up. He pointed back and forth from Sherry to Bear, gesturing with something close to derision. "I've trained hunting dogs all my life. I have a pretty good idea what they're capable of, and that right there is just a setup.

That's a trained trick." The man strode to the front of the room. "My brother has an eight-year-old son with autism. There's no way that dog could stop him from getting away."

The entire room went dead silent. Sherry's face flushed a deep red. I edged between her and the man speaking. My thoughts churned furiously, knowing any real hesitation would sink me. This guy was stocky, but rather short. Athletic. An idea pricked at my mind. He was dressed in perfectly pressed jeans, polo, and, shifting my position again, I was thrilled to see... tennis shoes!

Hastily, I rummaged for my wallet. Earlier today I'd pulled $500 from my own bank account to use at a mom-n-pop shop where they sold our dog food for a cash discount. In our current circumstances, $500 was a fortune. I held a violent internal debate that lasted about one third of a second. But then, this guy already knew we were strapped, didn't he?

"Mr...." I stepped forward, with the wad of cash in my hand. "I'm sorry, I met so many people on the way in here, I can't remember your name."

"Taylor," he said. "Chad Taylor."

"Mr. Taylor, I have a deal for you." I pointed out the large window to the yard of the building we were in. "See that line of trees out there?"

His glance flicked there and back to me. "Sure."

"Let's all go outside for a few minutes." I set my cash on the table closest to where we were standing. "I've got $500 right here, that says you can't make it from that front doorway to those trees without this dog stopping you."

A low mutter of voices came from somewhere in the room. I could see Sherry drifting closer. I didn't break eye contact with my target.

"I'm not planning to get bitten." He said, with a wary glance at the big dog.

"He won't bite." I smiled at him, then at the room. "But you're not allowed to hurt him, either. If the dog can't do it, you put the $500 in your fund for whomever you choose for your grant. If he can do it, then you at least have to come visit us and see the rest of what we're doing before you decide."

Only total desperation would have pushed me into this move. So much for all the admonitions not to look unstable. Maybe only Mr. Taylor's ego kept him from refusing. But it was, by Nori's lingo, a put-up-or-shut-up moment. In short order we were outside and Chad Taylor took off running for the tree line.

Doing this task as a demo was standard fare, often just for clients or trainers learning the craft. So Bear already knew what was coming. When I pointed and told him to "Go on," he needed approximately five jumps to dart around Chad from the side and push in front of the man's knees.

The man roughly shoved him aside and kept running. Bear magically reappeared in front. He dragged the big dog back by the collar, shouted, "NO," again shoving him away as he started out again. Bear ran out his tongue in a happy grin and slid back into blocking position. He loved this game.

The next time he tried holding Bear by the collar, off to the side, while he kept running. Except somehow, the big dog twisted his body around and put the opposite shoulder in front of Chad's legs turning the man sideways and off kilter. He had to let go or fall.

Chad did an impressive athletic jump straight over Bear's back, and managed two more running steps before the dog's persistent shoulder once again gave him the choice of landing on his face or stopping.

After Bear's first two successful blocks, Sherry and I began a slow, casual stroll toward the pair. We let the contest continue for perhaps three more repetitions, but everyone present could see Chad wasn't going far. The black shepherd kept his shoulder stuck to the man's knees as though magnetically held.

Stopping behind them, Sherry tapped Chad briskly on the shoulder. "Tag," she said in her sweetest southern belle tone. "You lose. I'm your mother and I've already caught you."

Several laughs came from the group behind us. We heard a smattering of applause. Chad braced his hands on his knees to catch his breath. Bear promptly threw himself on the ground in front of the silent man and rolled his tummy upward, hoping for a rub. He thrashed about like a beached gator, grinning skyward, and even defeated Chad couldn't keep from smiling at him.

When we turned back to the building, I could see at least a few faces that were no longer impassive, but quite thoughtful. I knew from pre-meeting chitchat that this group held at least two parents of autistic children. So it was no vast surprise–though an unbelievable thrill–when barely two weeks later our school was the proud owner of a new grant. The size and scope would carry us through training and placement of most of this group of young dogs.

When the check arrived, that night's farm party ran long and wild. We splurged on champagne. Nearly our entire training group gathered on my front porch, with the fire pit shooting flames into the star-filled sky. Even my long-suffering neighbors, who had helped with endless small details, were present, so nobody minded the blaring music. Trent and Scott conducted impromptu West Coast Swing classes on the grass. Several others sat by the fire, already scribbling or typing on to-do lists. Everyone was toasting the grantor foundation, each human involved, every dog we'd ever graduated, and every live animal on the place, including a few score of feral cats.

Trent seemed especially euphoric. His last act before joining us had been to wrap up a phone interview with an intern application from the west coast. "We got her, Sherry," he said with satisfaction as he flopped on the grass beside the fire. "She's waiting for you to call her back to verify tomorrow, but we've got her, 99% sure."

"Good enough," Sherry answered. "Where are the rest of the applications? We'll need at least three."

"On your desk." Trent emptied his paper cup of champagne. "Who's got a couch I can sleep on tonight? I'm not driving home."

"Use the one in my office," I said, still staring at my list and contemplating our best, quickest route forward. "I won't be touching anything in there until at least noon tomorrow. I'm headed to the vet at 7:30 with the first six pups for joint x-rays. We're still going to have to release and find homes for a few of them," I thought out loud.

"Funding for 25 isn't funding for 35."

"Ah, Julie, get your head in the game, kid." Scott dipped his fingers in his glass and flicked champagne over me. "You're initiated now, see? Nothing primes the pump like a little start-up cash. You're going to be visible now, have more to show, and just the fact that there is funding will make others more confident. Don't release those dogs. Make them your poster puppies for more money."

This was the flip-side of the advice we'd hated for so long: "don't look unstable." The phrase had irritated me to no end for years, but this is how public perception works. In the great American love/hate-affair with nonprofits, you're not judged so much on the merits of what you do, but what your budget breakdown looks like to outsiders, totally separated from any actual service to human need. Contributors liked high numbers of beneficiaries for the lowest possible budget, so our problem was all tied up with the fact that we weren't serving pizza lunches. We were providing complex benefits with a really tough cost-to-benefit ratio. Any group who proved successful–and was therefore expected to grow–faced some astonishing questions of financial "scale."

In the end Scott and I were both right and wrong. None of us sitting around that celebratory fire pit on that night could have foreseen what was just around the corner. The dilemma of scale was about to be revolutionized from a completely unexpected source: a new client.

Chapter 24

"It takes considerable knowledge just to realize the extent of your own ignorance." —Thomas Sowell

"Antecedents are what happens right before a target behavior happens. Behavior is the resulting response or lack of response to the antecedent. The consequence is what comes directly after the behavior. This is what we call the 'ABCs' of behavior analysis."

Sherry and I could not avoid shooting a quick glance at each other across a glossy dining room table covered by a forest of heavy textbooks and notepads. A dozen people gathered below a lovely chandelier listening to an intense, analytical speaker walking them through a detailed training process.

"When we focus on those ABCs and then add in strategies involving prompting, shaping, and reinforcement, we can teach meaningful skills."

We studiously avoided further eye contact with each other, not wanting to cause distraction or lose the thread of thought in any way. This was training instruction at its finest: minute detail, layered breakdown, each section categorized, prioritized, and recorded for later adjustments. One tiny little fact, however, made this session entirely new for both of us. The concepts were familiar to us—more so to Sherry than to me—but the application was in a field we'd barely even known existed. This meeting was about autistic children, and about the people learning to help them.

We had joined in to audit the sessions, by gracious invitation from a new client who was getting a dog for her son. This group was meeting in the client's home. While it wasn't the first time we'd heard of Applied Behavior Analysis, it was by far the most detailed and in-depth look we'd had. And it formed a critical gateway to the start of an entire new division at our school.

Quickly apparent to us: this particular client had different goals for her son's dog than what we were used to. For one thing, he was not an extremely young child, which was more often true of our applicants. The initial discussions took us nearly full circle to our very first dog who'd worked for the child of a psychotherapist. But not quite. Something was different here. The boy was remarkably well adjusted, not at all a flight risk, but yet profoundly affected. This mom knew exactly what she wanted to address and had a sophisticated understanding of the teaching processes. We were fascinated.

Both Sherry and I were almost always easily hooked by a complex blend of human psychology and dogs' interactions. By the time we'd completed our second conversation with this family, I could feel myself falling down yet another rabbit hole.

"It's not always about physical safety," our new client, Lisa, told us. "There's a mental, even emotional, component here that I think you're missing."

We sat in this lady's yard, gazing around at an upscale home, well maintained, outwardly under excellent direction and control. Yet the familiar undercurrents swelled and pushed. An almost non-verbal boy who frequently showed a lot of stress while trying to communicate. A mother living on her own with her children. While she was considerably more smooth than most, angst was still visible.

"Colby didn't speak at all until last year. Most people had given up that it ever would happen. I decided I wouldn't quit until he did. So now, he's giving us sounds, working on words, but it's incredibly hard for others to understand. Besides not being used to his voice, they don't have any context for what he wants to talk about. His topics are often something like 100 details on the inner workings of a Disney film. If he had the dog, liked the dog, had that interaction…" The mother's voice trailed away. "Well, all that you've told me about how badly people want to interact with the dogs, couldn't that be a springboard? Couldn't it be a tool for building his communication with others?"

I could see Sherry weighing, considering. "Probably," she said cautiously. "But would your expectation be that the dog should respond to Colby's directions? Or to yours?"

That was a critical piece of any family puzzle, as it often called for a totally different type of dog. In fact, any dog whose job was to extend a parent's legs, ears, and eyes was quite specifically *not* supposed to respond to children's commands. Just a few weeks before, we'd had to shoehorn a new expense into one dog's training budget: replacing every doorknob in a client's home with levers. The affected child had decided he was all done with this four-footed snitch. He would lure the dog into a room, close the door, and go about his business. Ooops.

New skill set for the dog: opening doors. So from the outset, it was critical to define a dog's expected scope of responsibility.

"Does it have to be one or the other?" Lisa asked us.

This question was mine. "Not necessarily," I hedged a little. "But you have to filter it through consideration of what we're training the dog to respond to. From the dog's point of view, a command doesn't have to be any particular word. They don't know the vocabulary definition of "down." They know a sound. You and Colby would both have to make similar enough of a sound that the dog accepts it as the same. Forget what humans think about it. This is a different yardstick." I paused, thought hard. "Can the dog learn a little adjustment? Sure, eventually. In the early stages, it can be hard."

Many years later I sat in this remarkable lady's house and watched the now-adult Colby polishing his intonation and phrasing to get what he wanted from countertop Alexa–something that would have been undreamed of when I first met him. Alexa was, of course, totally unforgiving in her standards, requiring a specific pronunciation before delivering the goods. But with a far younger, far less dedicated child, and a dog who was less-than-computer-perfect... how could that bar of achievement be put into a functional position? Lisa solved this riddle for me with one sentence, one idea. For most of the rest of my life, I stayed embarrassed I hadn't thought of it sooner.

"Can the dog be taught a hand signal? Something I cue when Colby makes his best effort? This is going to be a process, not an event. Autism is about development. That way I could insist on a gradual improvement of pronunciation."

That brief speech from a proactive parent grew from her years of defining progressive goals. It flung open the door to an entire new focus for our school. It was a really big door, and had looked formidable for a long time. That day in 2006, when the latch came loose, Sherry and I both heard the clang. Loudly. We froze. Considered. Stared at the dog. Stared at each other.

I nodded. Sherry took the next part. "Would you let us watch some of his therapy sessions?"

What we discovered, however, was that Lisa was already far ahead of anything we'd even dreamed of. As matters turned out, she was about eight years into the creation of another nonprofit with a much broader scope than ours. She'd teamed up with another mom, also with an autistic son, to create Project Hope Foundation. They were now providing a whole range of autism services, including therapy, a school, and the beginning of programs for adults. They built all their programs around the principles of Applied Behavior Analysis, which we learned to call ABA. It took the three of us about an hour to realize how well our approaches meshed. Behavior is behavior. Only the logistics varied.

As Colby's relationship with his soon-to-be dog took off in new and varied directions, Sherry and I learned to massively adjust our understanding of the Americans with Disabilities Act. The defining precept of the ADA? Dogs must be specifically and individually trained for tasks that attenuate the effects of a disability. Sure, right.

We knew that part. What we were being schooled to understand... there was no limitation on what *type* of attenuation.

"Autism challenges go far beyond safety," Lisa emphasized until we plugged our brains in. "These kids face immense struggles learning to communicate, to relate, to engage. That's part of autism, too. You've been focused on physical issues. That's valid. But it's not *all*. So if dogs can be trained to help with one part, why not with another? Both are valid needs."

Vast horizons opened–in our heads, at least–for the hundreds, no, thousands, of families whose schedules, finances, and logistics could not accommodate a service dog in the home. Demands had overwhelmed us for years. But until now, we had no realistic alternatives. Beyond that, it had been apparent from the beginning that many, if not most, families could not handle the training hours for full-fledged service dogs we were graduating. Those dogs made fabulous solutions for some, but definitely not the majority. What about them? Were we forever bound to tell them, "No, sorry, there's nothing we can do for you?"

Months later, now much educated by auditing the training classes for ABA therapists, we had learned. And learned. And learned more. Progress was astounding. Sleepless nights for parents were a major thing, but they were not the only thing that caused family stress and frustration.

More than a few of the typically long-winded discussions between me and Sherry had moved out of the hay room and into a local restaurant where Lisa joined us. Instead of being two, we were now three. Pens and keyboards could barely keep up with racing thoughts. We plotted, analyzed, messed up, regrouped, and plotted more. We had our own table in several locations and were on voice-recognition basis with quite a few servers. We monopolized tables for ridiculously long times, but heavy tips kept staff from tossing us out the door. Finally, we got our thinking synchronized.

"You have to understand," Lisa had first challenged us, "those of us doing ABA are in the business of removing barriers created by the disability. So many of these kids spend tremendous effort trying to communicate. But sometimes their successes are really tiny. Being able to successfully communicate something they want, and get *results* they want, is incredibly motivating, incredibly empowering."

She would sip her drink and draw diagrams, sketching flow charts of how a child progressed through language development. We watched, questioned, blundered, and kept trying. The dogs were my thing. The kids were Lisa's. Sherry was our bridge between, forcing us to learn to understand each other.

Sherry and I slunk stealthily around the halls of Project Hope, observing, taking notes, thinking furiously. We watched therapy. We watched school classes. We spent uncountable hours listening to Lisa walk her son through many exercises–language and practical–of ABA. Except now a tactile, responsive animal could occasionally replace a two or three-dimensional teaching aid.

Before long we found ourselves back in the grant world, pursuing funding for a joint project between both our groups for a totally new set of goals. And it was much easier to get approved. This ease was tied to an obvious metric. Regardless of what thought about the rationales, this concept was justifiable to grant committees through ratios alone. One trained dog could interact with dozens of children per week. What the potential funders saw was numbers: more benefits to more people.

A remarkably short time later, our school had officially begun its first partnership with another nonprofit: Hope Unleashed. It formed the first step of many. Clinical therapy dogs, now off and running, would soon skyrocket to being our largest, farthest-reaching, and most successful yet. Applications for training internships came in droves from the students at nearby universities. While clinical therapy dogs weren't the answer many parents wished for, they became a partial loaf available to families who would never be able to manage a whole one. The clinical dogs required far fewer training hours and would typically work well for multiple people— unlike the relationship-focused German Shepherds. The overall ease of implementation surprised us even more than the comparative ease with which we could find grants.

Beyond the dogs themselves, our new partnership netted other astonishing results. We'd teamed up with someone– a whole campus of someones–with professional ability to address the myriad family issues we constantly encountered. Not since Sherry's entrance to our staff had such a huge void been filled so effectively. We now had a reliable source of help for the non-dog challenges that overwhelmed so many of our clients. We carried stacks of Project Hope business cards everywhere and passed them out like candy when it came to questions or issues about autism. We both stayed astonished at Lisa's tolerance for this, but we'd definitely met the group whose dedication to autism far exceeded our own.

Soon there was even some crossover membership on our board of directors, formalizing some joint solutions to thorny client problems. Now we had a competent, fast source of professional help for those on the spectrum from toddler age to adulthood. It was the beginning, but not the end.

Chapter 25

"The simple things are also the most extraordinary things, and only the wise can see them." —Paulo Coelho, "The Alchemist"

We'd placed dogs with clinicians before, especially considering Sherry's background. But all the dogs up to now had been a matter of comfort and redirect, such as aid for trauma issues. What happened at Project Hope was entirely different. Inserting task-trained dogs into science-based education created rocket fuel. We began to realize the weight of what our first client in this field, Lindy's owner, had said: it was all about understanding behavioral motivations, whether for the two-footed or the four-footed. It's just that neither she nor we had the experience then to understand broader application. More to the point, we still didn't, but Lisa did.

The process wasn't without challenges. Sherry and I had much to learn about the nuances and logistics of ABA. It initially seemed obvious to us that therapists could be trained to handle the dogs, but Lisa's logic and knowledge of the therapy kept us from floundering. Her adamant refusal to let therapists take that role was our first big reality check.

"No way," she objected. "We can't have a therapist's attention divided between the kid and the dog."

"That's what a "place" command is for," I objected. "Or a crate."

"And what if the dog gets sick? Has to go out? Somehow

breaks training protocol? What if the kid is sick and the dog has to be left unattended?" Lisa was firm on that point. "It doesn't fly, Julie. These sessions are designed–and paid for, I might add–based on guarantee of one-to-one attention. We can't add the responsibility of a dog to a therapist's load. It's not fair to anybody."

There was no arguing with the expert. Eventually a functional team concept took shape. Designated therapist for the child. Designated handler for the dog. Both therapist and the handler needed enough cross-training to understand each other, but it became manageable. And the grants kept happening. Even our newfound optimism underestimated sponsors' thrill level with the large numbers these teams could reach.

Barely a year later, armed with two grants surpassing our entire sum of autism funding to date, our weary trio watched through an observation window at Project Hope's clinic as a skilled pair of humans and one seriously engaging dog delighted the socks off of a little boy. It was clear from watching–but underscored by numbers on the progress chart–that this child's delight with his own success pushed his motivation farther ahead than anything else had in quite a while.

The little chap's mother had told us he'd always wanted a dog. It wasn't possible in their home. But today he bounced around with greater animation than the ball he was using to entice Tucker, the flashy Golden Retriever who stood rock solid, eyeing his handler on the other side of the room. Tucker was on a stay and he was busy staying.

"Charlie, do you want to play with the dog?" the therapist was working to get the child's attention, to get everything and everyone in correct position. "What do you want him to do?"

"Ooooowwww," said Charlie.

"Then you have to tell him. Get his attention, Charlie. Is he watching you?"

Charlie moved around to face the dog and put his eyes approximately three inches from Tucker's. "Ooow."

"Where's your D sound, Charlie? Push your tongue against your teeth. D-d-d-d."

Charlie tried again and made the barest beginnings of an alveolar consonant before his "owww." The therapist made a fist–her signal to the trainer. In the same half second, the handler waved to the dog. Tucker dropped. Charlie leapt about the room in a thrill of accomplishment.

Anybody who has ever watched a very normal obedience exhibition at a trial held by the American Kennel Club would recognize this as part of the signals exercise. Slight hand waves or motions for sit, down, stand, come, heel. Very basic for a well-trained dog. Absolute nirvana to a child struggling for successful communication. Serious leverage in the hands of a judicious therapist who knows how to edge the linguistic bar upward.

The therapists learned to search out the right motivation for interested kids. Trainers learned to expand the dogs' basic vocabulary in every possible direction. Everything we could come up with morphed into another sequence that provided live, interactive learning. Every so often, Lisa, Sherry, and I reoccupied that table at our favorite restaurant to work out kinks, but the program roared ahead, rapidly spreading to other locations, not only in our state but across the country.

Closer to home, we celebrated an answer to a common parental dilemma. Autism can be extremely isolating, but add an intense fear of dogs and matters get far worse. A walk around the block, a visit to a friend, or many kinds of common interaction can be cut short if a child is terrified of the mere appearance of any dog. A noteworthy milestone happened through the partnership with Project Hope by helping define a process that helped children become more comfortable in a dog's presence, significantly expanding their social opportunities. Some even learned to have fun with the dogs.

Before then, at least in our corner of the world, the therapists alone had never had very successful answers for that one. By themselves, the dog trainers had fared even worse, since they had no realistic idea what process would actually help. But both together... it worked. And it had the component we'd long lusted for: it was reproducible in widely varied locations.

None of this was apparent that first day in the clinic. But after standing entranced on that Historic Day One until our legs and back ached, Sherry and I finally wandered to the parking lot, somehow finding the car through our general fog of euphoria. We didn't know that the near future would put some of these dogs into peer-reviewed research programs. We didn't know how immense the breadth and scope of influence would become through therapists and psychiatrists. We didn't know the growth explosion just around the corner. But we knew what we'd just seen. In all the years either of us worked with service dogs, we rarely had such a definitive moment.

"Do you think it matters that it wasn't what we started out trying to do?" Sherry's question probably wouldn't have made any sense to anyone who hadn't traveled this path with us. But I understood. We started out looking for a way to give a parent a tool–call it an axe for chopping wood. But one parent had turned around and asked us why we ignored the possibility of a wood chipper and a sawmill. And oh, by the way, this is how you build it. So here we were.

Even recognizing that vast shift, we hadn't yet considered all the impact. Almost two years later, we were tallying up evaluations for the first grant. A second grant from the same group was midway through its process. Third and fourth smaller versions were in place from other sources. Even Nori had relaxed some. Now, how could we explain these results to our original funders in a way they could understand?

We huddled in my living room one afternoon, assessing our wording and making lists. With painstaking detail, I tallied up the graduates, the clients, the dog-training certifications, the number of clinic hours, how many participated, the children's ABA progress, new equipment, and every other outcome they could imagine asking us about. With one eye on the clock, Sherry and I poured over the wording, trying to make it sound as good as we could, with no departure from the facts. "Each dog has served an average of 80 children per week for 16 months," Sherry read aloud. "Each dog has gained proficiency in working for multiple handlers. Each dog has increased initial working vocabulary to a minimum of 70 commands or signals, creating increased options for the therapists as we begin Phase Two–"

A tap on the screen door interrupted. I'd been oblivious

to the trainers on the front porch who were taking
advantage of my adult dogs sprawled here and there to
practice their puppies' obedience. But now I looked up to
see the young, earnest face of a trainer who'd moved here
to work for us at the onset of the work with Project Hope.
Renee grew up with two autistic siblings in her
Midwestern home. I'd never seen a new trainer tie into
any project with such wholesale dedication.

"Yes? Hi, Renee, what is it?"

Sherry went to the door and opened it, motioning her in.
"What's up?"

"Well," she said, stammering a little, "we've been out
there for a few minutes. I couldn't help hearing what you
were reading."

I considered this, but aside from thinking in the future I'd
better pay more attention to who was nearby, I just
nodded. "Okay," I said, "What about it?"

"Well," Renee clearly didn't have a full statement ready.
"I wanted to ask…. I mean…. well, what about us?"

"About whom?" Sherry backtracked to the couch and sat
down rather wearily.

I, too, was confused.

"Just…us." Renee made a vague circling gesture in the
air.

We were still silent. Puzzled.

"Us, the trainers," Renee pushed on. "What about us in
that report?"

"Something you want to say to them?" I frowned. "Or

you think you want a chance to help us structure the wording?"

"No!" The young trainer seemed impatient, but still resolute. "I mean… you're listing all these benefits, but you're not including us."

"Sure we are," I objected. "See, right here, you're all named, even. When we hired you, what dogs you trained, which people you worked with." I was tracing my finger across the computer screen, but Renee wasn't listening.

"That's not what I mean. I mean the benefits to us!" Her voice rose with excitement or frustration, bringing her rambunctious puppy bouncing up against her legs in a forbidden jump. Deftly the young trainer sidestepped, nudged him off, and lured him into a sit at her side, giving a correct reinforcement without even breaking the rhythm of her sentence. I had to admire her fluency, considering she'd started her first formal dog training barely 22 months past.

"You're listing benefits to all these different people, mostly the clients. Yeah, I get that. We were all part of how they got their benefits. But you're still leaving us out. We're the ones who learned to train, who learned how to help, who got the satisfaction, the skill set." Renee gave each of us a look that bordered on a glare.

We sat staring, no doubt mouths ajar, trying to absorb her intent.

"Those grants? Those grants taught five more people how to train these dogs and how to help the kids and the families. I can train the dogs, yeah, but I've got my first ABA certification now. That don't grow on trees, okay? I couldn't have learned that at home, and without that

grant, I'd still *be* at home. I have twin brothers, both on
the spectrum. You already know that. It nearly busted our
family to get them up to school age and talking and
learning. Not a lot left over, time or money, for college,
you know? So what would I be doing without that grant?
Minimum wage somewhere? If you guys all fall off the
world tomorrow, I can do a couple different real jobs
now."

Sherry and I exchanged glances.

"That's what I mean," Renee opened the door, walked
out, and flung a glance over her shoulder. "What about
us?"

I stared at the screen again, then looked at Sherry with
amazement.

She was sitting bolt upright on the sofa. "Do they have a
category for that?"

"Nope. But I think I'd better add one."

Chapter 26

"Never underestimate the power of stupid people in large groups." —George Carlin

Months melted into years, then five, then more. Clinical therapy, in all its variances, had put a long pause on our school's largest nemesis since inception: regular cash flow. Yet any business, nonprofit or otherwise, always had new challenges developing. Just like everyone else, we had to adapt or sink. The underlying problem for us? No matter how much we grew, the needs grew more.

Not only did the numbers of autistic children continue to rise, but, well… the children grew up. Adult services were a pressing need, not that we could do anything about it directly. We'd been listening to Lisa explain a lot of those challenges, watching her nonprofit struggle with the onslaught of ever-growing need the same way we were. Many of our earliest, youngest clients were becoming young adults. As their dogs aged and passed away, their needs, and their parents' needs were now very different and few of them could be met by a service dog.

The explosion of social media fueled many of challenges, both ours and Project Hope's. However useful for all of us, there were big drawbacks. Now society had readily available groups where every sub-culture known to mankind could easily congregate–and they all had a direct conduit to the rest of the world. Once upon a time, to gain traction in most trades and sciences, you had to be the best-thought-out, the most accurate, and the most effective. Now you just had to be the loudest. Or possibly just the most entertaining. The new principle applied to many areas that affected all of us. Groups who scorned service dog schools and advocated everyone train their own dogs. Other groups intensely critical of ABA therapy, which was the very cornerstone of our clinical therapy dogs' effectiveness. Perhaps most of all, the self-appointed specialists who categorized non-profit groups into levels of effectiveness based on all the wrong criteria.

One day, Sherry, Nori, Barb, and I were sitting in my little farm office brainstorming an ongoing challenge: how to get more (and younger) social workers better plugged into our training protocol. We'd been chasing this issue for a decade and still didn't have the right answer. Sherry was stretched far too thin, and even though none of us wanted to admit it, age was making itself felt. As the old saying went, nobody in this discussion was 25 anymore.

"I'd guess we have three out of the current seven who will stick," Sherry was concluding her summary of recent efforts. She started passing around several sheets of paper. "Here's a list of two things: a summary of placements, all different circumstances, that each of them need to see soon. Then, also a few training seminars they should all attend."

"Seminars?" Nori asked, scanning the list. "Are they local?"

"Not hardly." Sherry rubbed her temples. "But most within driving distance, at least. It's all specialty stuff they need to learn, need to know."

Silence held for a few moments while we all absorbed the list–and the dollar figures alongside. I stayed quiet. The professional aspects here were not mine to comment on. But I was mentally reviewing the training capabilities of the people on this list. Sherry had, indeed, neatly summarized the three with the most potential. I agreed. All three had made a great start. Their participation time varied, all having begun at different times, but each was somewhere between six and 18 months along. That was a lot to them, and not to be minimized. Quite a few we'd started in the past had quit much sooner. But I couldn't avoid a pang of anxiety while considering most still needed years of additional experience before they'd be anywhere close to ready for solo assessments in complex cases. We hadn't yet found a single one of these young professionals who were willing to–or could afford to, practically, financially, or otherwise–spend the time Sherry had during her first few years. As a result, these processes were now much slower than hers had been.

"Are they willing to attend?" Nori was still studying the list.

"All of them have to have CEUs, no matter what," Sherry answered. "That process never ends, so it's just a matter of choosing focus. The ones with serious interest in doing this long term will get it and agree. If they don't then they're not the ones we should be spending our time on anyway."

"What about–" The door banged open to break in on Barb's question.

"Sorry to interrupt." Doug's face was tight with anxiety.

"But you guys need to see this, right now." He set his phone on the table. It was open to the Facebook page of a person we'd recently turned down as a service dog applicant. I recognized him, though I could see others didn't. The reaction numbers on some post he'd made were ticking upward, even while we watched.

"That's the Salcer family," I said. "They applied for a dog for their autistic son; we said no."

"Why?" Nori asked, turning the phone toward herself. "What's this about?"

"Here." Doug hit the little "see-more" button near the top. "Read it."

Nori started with the magazine headline and read out loud. "Autistic child denied service dog. A local non-profit long supported by many area residents and groups has declined to approve an application for a service dog from a family with critical safety needs involving their young son. 'We were not given adequate reasons for the refusal,' says Michael Salcer, 'and believe it's imperative to enlist the public's help in our quest for answers'...." Nori's voice trailed away as she continued to scan the article.

"Are you kidding me?" Barb was now typing furiously on her own phone. "Was anyone planning to ask us for comment?

"You haven't even gotten to the good part," Doug added, his voice thick with tension.

"I have now." Nori started reading aloud again. "An investigation during the development of this article has revealed the organizations percentage of overhead expenses ranks higher than is considered ideal by Charity Watch." Nori put her head down on her hand, covering her eyes and pushing the phone away. Even while it still sat on the desk, we could all see the count of replies, reactions, and shares ticking upward.

"Why did we turn these people down?" Nori asked from behind splayed fingers.

"No behavior intervention plan for the son," Sherry answered. "He's nine years old, big for his age, antagonistic to the parents, starting to get physical. They have no reliable communication system with him, at all. For the most basic consideration, the dog wouldn't have been safe. For the more advanced, we can give tools, but not miracles. If they won't stick to therapy, they won't do the training, either."

"Why does it matter at this point?" Doug asked angrily. "These responses alone are going to eat us alive."

"I'm just trying to understand," Nori said tiredly. "We'll have to answer this, somehow."

"No you don't," Barb objected. "Anything you say on there now," she waved vaguely toward Doug's phone, "will just throw gas on the flames."

"Forget on there," Nori responded. Her voice was barely audible. "The board's response will be epic."

"What do they call overhead?" Christy, a brand new training intern, stood in the doorway behind Doug.

"Since you're not working directly with clients right now, overhead is your salary," Sherry said dryly. "And quite a lot of everyone else's."

"And this building, our insurance, the utilities that keep it useable, those vans outside, and on and on." Barb slumped back in her chair.

"But that doesn't make any sense," the young woman objected. "All those things are for the program!"

"From the mouth of babes...." Sherry murmured.

"Christy, go back to your work," Nori said. "We'll talk about this in staff meeting tomorrow. Please try not to spread it around, okay?"

"Yeah, okay," Christy said dubiously.

As the young trainer withdrew, Doug pulled the door shut behind her and sank into a chair. "It won't matter if she spreads it," he said. "Every one of them will see it before they're home tonight."

How correct he was. By the time we gathered in the main training room downtown for the next afternoon's staff meeting, the train wreck of fallout was apparent. Every trainer had stopped counting the nasty emails and messages. Not just to the school, but to each trainer personally from a wide variety of people who knew where they worked. Nori had reported to us that one of our board members had resigned, two more were threatening to do so, and the remaining six had called an immediate meeting. Far worse, two of the school's largest pending grantors had contacted Nori, stating a dismissal of our applications. Those two alone were almost 80% of the funding for our current class of trainees.

Nori did her best to explain to the trainers what was more a perception problem than a substantial one, and that nothing had actually changed—only how people viewed our process. Nobody had to tell this staff about the insanity of trying to place a dog with people who wouldn't do disciplined, segmented training. But criticism of our spending percentages was new to many of them.

To close out the meeting, Nori played them a video of Dan Pallotta's recent bombshell TED talk about the fallacy of "evil overhead": *The Way We Think About Charity is Dead Wrong.*

As a die-hard fan of Pallotta's book, *Uncharitable,* none of the video material was new to me. I spent my time watching the faces around the room as this word-wizard went through his razor-sharp summaries of inequitable expectations for charities. I could see that, like me, most understood, and probably all agreed. But I could also see a lot of new recognition about what we were up against. It was a silent, subdued group who left the meeting that day. We promised to keep them updated as best we could while we searched for solutions. But we knew the real problem was coming the next day.

Lisa was now a member of our advisory board in an effort to have her help educate board members, offer grant input, and assist with blending our outreaches whenever possible. A three-way phone call started mid-evening and ran to the wee hours while Sherry and I brought her up to speed and we all debated strategy.

My point of view differed slightly from theirs and was considerably more cynical. The board had unanimously approved this last year's budget (including all that evil overhead). It would be pretty tricky for the group, then, to object to what everyone had agreed on. So I was pretty sure they were going to unload on us over the grounds for the declined application. For once, I was not wrong. The board meeting started with confrontation and rapidly went downhill.

"So if the child was such a problem case," one board member challenged angrily, "isn't that exactly why we have the partnership between our groups? To prevent this kind of trouble?"

"Yes– " Sherry tried to answer, but the man cut her off again.

"Money was clearly not the issue here, since they were offering to pay all their own expenses for the dog. If the child needed therapy, then you make that part of the package. Isn't that our entire point?"

"It is the point," Lisa tried to insert herself into this exchange. "But when the parent refuses the therapy this program is based on, it doesn't give us what we need to work–"

Another interruption: "So you're saying your way is the only way? Isn't that pretty arrogant, considering our program is funded almost entirely by third parties?"

I struggling against my rising temper that the two most eminently qualified professionals on our entire board were being so flagrantly disregarded. I was the one who'd made the first move to nix the application, based on the parents' responses to the demo dogs alone. Everything else was, to me, just gravy. But my phone buzzed with a text. Glancing down, I could see what Lisa had sent… from three feet away. *Stay quiet. Let me answer.* I glanced up to see her looking steadfastly the other way, still engaged with the angry man. I took a deep breath and almost broke in anyway, but Sherry, sitting directly opposite, kicked me. Hard. I was outvoted. I stayed quiet.

"Mr. Browndale," Lisa addressed him in a new tone. The inner lawyer had arrived in this chat. She might have given up her legal career for nonprofit founding, but the *modus operandi* was still there. "ABA is the method with the most evidence behind it. That's not a matter of opinion, and it's not arrogance to make actual results the basis for measuring progress. If that weren't true, the justification for having your dogs in so many clinical therapy programs would be completely erased. And that program has, as you know, been paying the majority of your bills for years now. It's simple fact. Neither our program or yours will change that focus, because it's been proven to be the most effective. If a prospective client refuses to work with our program, we have no options because we're not moving to an inferior therapy."

There was a slight pause in which nobody spoke. Sherry again short-stopped my open mouth with a glare, then stepped into the gap. "Around 1995 when we first started fielding calls from parents, we'd read that perhaps one in 500 children was affected. By around 2000, when we started trial-placing our first dogs, the rate was estimated to be 1 in 150. By the time we were regularly graduating teams and began clinical therapy, the rate was 1 in 88."

She paused just long enough for Lisa to insert, "This year it's one in 54."

Then Sherry picked right back up. "If our school immediately grew its capacity by 500%, we couldn't reach all the families who call us for help. *All* we can do is choose who has the highest odds of using a dog correctly. Someone who refuses therapy is never going to qualify. This is probably a good time to point out that this family refused all therapy, not just what we were recommending."

I could stay quiet no longer. "That makes it an absolute certainty they would never have followed our training protocol for the dog, which could get us worse PR than public criticism about overhead spending. I don't know of any sponsors who enjoy having their funds wasted."

"Well," another glowering board member answered, "we'll never know now, will we?"

In the end, it was worse than we expected. Fully half of our executive board resigned. Some stood firm in their sharp disagreements. Some were just tired. I could see it in their postures and expressions by the time the room emptied that day. The ones hanging on looked strained. Nobody knew how we were going to make up the shortfall of lost grants, and we had no choice but to report it to the trainers.

Late that day, we called all the trainers together and updated them. It was incredibly discouraging news. Because of yesterday's meeting, they understood, but now also understood the drastic implications. There were very few comments and worried faces all around.

I wasn't surprised though, that one of the few who spoke up was Renee. Once a new intern from the very first clinical therapy grant, she was now our Program Coordinator for all the clinics in Georgia and North Carolina who used our graduates.

"I don't want to sound like some little kid screaming about things not being fair," Renee said, her voice low and discouraged. "But doesn't that kind of assessment actually penalize any program, dogs or no dogs, that succeeds and grows?" She paused a beat, pressing a hand to the top of her head. "I mean, there's only so far anybody can expand without upping general operating costs. It doesn't matter what a program is about."

I gave her some combination of a head shake and shrug, not knowing what to say. She was exactly right, yet it *was* how we were judged, and it wouldn't change anytime soon.

"We're all supposed to starve nobly and enjoy our homelessness for the sake of whatever we're doing." Stephen spoke up with a note of bitterness that worried me greatly.

By the time the training center cleared, I'd gone far beyond worry. Dusk was falling as the trainers left. I took my dogs for a walk, then retreated to the top of the hill by my barn, finding a time-honored seat on a hay bale.

Darkness fell. The moon rose, the wind picked up, and the temperature dropped. I was ignoring a score of program obligations, but didn't even realize I was waiting for Sherry until I heard her voice behind me.

"We're in trouble." She chose another bale, sat down, then stretched out full length.

It was not a highly astute conversation opener. We'd been in trouble before this day had started. We sat there in silence for a very long time, both thinking, analyzing, and getting nowhere.

"Let's start at the bottom," I finally spoke. "What are our known factors? We have so many moving pieces. I think it would help me just to separate the wish list from the reality list."

Sherry had been quiet, unmoving, for quite a while now, and I mostly hoped she hadn't fallen asleep.

"Right," she said, "here's one given. We'd have to locate an absolute minimum of ten thousand per dog for every one of the current trainees, just to finish out this calendar year."

Whatever remained of my mental fortitude sank right out of my head onto the ground. I tried to answer. "Quarter mil just for current dogs. Are you sure?"

"Based on the clients we're considering and the training support they need, yeah, I am pretty comfortable those are hard numbers."

I didn't have to think long about my answer to this. "Well, at the risk of being Captain Obvious, here's a second given. You and I don't have it. Unless we can find that kind of money, PDQ, we won't be finishing the current dogs."

"Want third given?" Sherry finally rolled over and sat up, but she was still looking out at the pasture rather than at me. "If we start releasing current trainees, the fosters, trainers, and sponsors will hate us with a purple-spotted passion that will probably murder our ability to raise three dimes in the next five years."

That brought the silence back for a while.

"I've got a number four," I said, after a little tallying. "In the last four months, I've put out at least 15 grant applications or inquiries for service dog training, not clinical. I say "at least" in case I'm forgetting one. Amounts requested were anywhere from $10,000 to $60,000 each. We've had a positive response to three. One is still pending. We got a total of $7,500 from the other two. How can it be that much worse now than it was five years ago?"

Sherry started picking pieces of grass and throwing them into the darkness. "Can I add a "given" that may or may not be related at all?"

"Sure, why not."

"I think a lot of it is internet 'influenced.' I watched two fundraising campaigns online last week that each raised around thirty grand in a day. One was for a dog that died. One was for a sanctuary for unadoptable horses."

I sighed. It was impossible to draw comparisons. "Your point?"

"I'm not sure I have one. Or not sure I have just one." Sherry's voice was as bleak as I'd ever heard it. "This whole idea of the good nonprofits being the ones with no staff on livable wages, no overhead, is what will ultimately kill us. Forget everything else. Our choices are more funds to pay our staff or way fewer dogs. There isn't anything else and we don't have long to decide. Our new group of fosters is supposed to start in less than a month. That would increase our trainee load by 12, forget the current group."

"So, we do what? Go back to what's left of the board

with the announcement that we're going to start releasing dogs? And when they kick us both out, what happens to the dogs?"

Silence.

I glanced up at the moon, which had progressed far enough over our heads to tell me it was way past midnight. Again. Another of our changing factors? We were a long, long way from being energetic 30-somethings who could pull all-nighters unscathed. "We have to get some sleep."

"Yeah," Sherry answered flatly. "We also have to do something about training morale. Like Nori said earlier today, if we don't get their confidence and spirits up, nothing worthwhile is going to happen no matter what else does."

I nodded, forgetting that she couldn't see me in the darkness.

"Got to find a plan…." Sherry's voice drifted off. She stood up and started down the hill. "These kids are working their hearts out, and so are lots of the volunteers. But they need better encouragement."

"I know," I said. "But it's hard to come up with much right now that's very encouraging."

"I know. Let's think on it." Sherry disappeared into the darkness toward her truck.

I watched her lights descend the winding driveway, cross the road, and out of sight to her own house. The darkness closed around me in complete, velvet silence. The dogs, sensing my mood, stayed still. I breathed in the chill. December on this hilltop was darned cold, and the relentless, burning aches of RA were pulling on me lately, worse than ever before. But I still lingered, listening to the yipping of coyotes down by the river. Even without daylight, it was easy to pick out a dozen farm jobs that were falling farther and farther behind. Vine clusters pulling at fences. Unmown grass. A big plastic tarp pulled hurriedly over a pallet of supplies that we had nowhere to store.

You're getting way too far behind the curve, girl. I looked down at my dogs, clustered silently near my feet, intensely aware of my mood. They'd been alone almost all day while I obsessed about everyone else's dogs. How fair was that?

As usual, it was easy to pick out my gray mare standing near the barn. She was the last of two horses for me now. We'd had to sell the rest because of simple inability– physically and financially–to keep up with them. How long had it been since I'd even taken a ride? You're being stupid, I thought, reminding myself that this whole location had been about correcting this kind of idiocy. Ignoring personal needs, beliefs, and goals would never get me anywhere good. Where and how is the magic line between dedication and crucifying yourself on an overblown sense of mission? At that moment, I had no answer.

"When is enough really enough?" I asked myself out loud. We had analyzed this question in 100 different ways for most of the years we'd known each other. Abandoning what we'd put so much into would break faith with every other person who'd helped us along. But now we faced a problem that wasn't of our own making and we had no answers. Even before this latest crises, changing factors had been pushing us toward awareness that nobody could maintain this pace indefinitely. Dizziness from extreme fatigue made me unsteady as I limped down the hill to the house, still having no idea what to do.

Chapter 27

In the end, our remaining board members put up an astonishing amount of money to cover deficits. Nori, Sherry, and I donated our entire salaries back to the school, throwing ourselves on the mercy of spouses and partners for living expenses. Most of the senior trainers volunteered a huge number of hours to finish the current graduates and start the new group of trainees. A score of experienced fosters who'd been raising pups for years now spent extraordinary amounts of time backstopping trainers with everything from kennel chores to daily training, just to reduce the work load and keep everyone staggering forward.

In the aftermath of the December disaster, we re-instituted the farm bonfire gatherings, which had come close to vanishing in the schedule pressure. After some thought, we realized we hadn't made time for one in over a year... or was it closer to two years? We weren't even sure. But we started again by hosting new ones every few weeks, instituting a no-dog policy to reduce distractions and make it feel more like a break from work–not more work. It was an instant, wildly popular tradition. When the spring class graduated in April, we turned the next bonfire gathering into a giant *We Survived* bash for all trainers and fosters.

Sherry had pushed us pretty hard to continue morale building efforts. "They're better, but they're tired. Really, really tired." She told us at our administrative meeting one day.

"We all are." Barb was almost asleep on her laptop.

"Sleep will fix most of that," Sherry said with a briskness I knew was mostly feigned. "But this gang needs several shots in the arm. Confidence, team-think... we need to give them all the help we can."

I wasn't so sure, wondering about the old saying: "if it ain't broke, don't fix it." I was far more concerned about the outcome of the upcoming grant awards. We'd submitted dozens in the last few months, and we'd be hearing verdicts soon.

Yet and still, there were all kinds of reasons that Sherry, not me, was our Behavioral Health Advisor. I knew enough not to argue, so plans developed.

The cool spring weather was ideal. But we had to set parameters. Despite a certain amount of grumbling from the trainers, especially the younger ones, we'd stuck to the no-dog rule. We intended these bonfires to stay a time of human relaxation totally apart from dogs.

We also had to restrict certain aspects of attendance. Twenty years of farm growth had long-since revealed a distinct twinge of pyromania among Sherry, me, our partners, and other neighbors as well. "I think I'll burn a little brush" could become a community password for a dozen people to linger fireside for days, watching the burn, swapping stories, roasting something edible, and dragging up more fuel. The process had been an R&R oasis many times. But the We Survived party was for program personnel only.

Sherry and I had forbidden anyone to come near until given permission, promising them adequate pyromaniac playtime when group business was finished. This had initially created a sore point with Scott, recently returned from several weeks on the road, but once he heard the rationale, even he agreed. "Text me when I can come," he said, and departed for a lone stroll by the river.

Every one of our group arrived early. Spirits and nerves were both high. As dusk fell across the fields and hills, fingers of flame crept through a giant brush pile and shot skyward. The leaping orange mixed with a brilliant sunset and added the pungency of smoke to wafts of an outdoor dinner underway.

Sherry was in her element, escorting large piles of brush to the fire with Mr. Bob, the skid steer, always looking far too small to handle such a massive machine. She was everywhere at once among the visitors. She engaged the hesitant, took the curious for rides to the woods, and let a few of the boldest drive Bob a little. We visited horses over fences, admired the flamboyant sunset as it sank behind the blueish peaks, and started in on the snacks. Add some adult beverages and the atmosphere continued to loosen.

By the time full dark settled and part of the flames lowered to coals, the group was gathered haphazardly around the blaze, far more loose and very curious about the presence of our board members. I eyed them briefly, considering that the mix of staff and volunteers was nearly 100 people strong. This was the other side of the world from the small group of intense young people initially banded together over rumors of an impending law called the ADA. I didn't think it was too arrogant to admit our current group had matured into a force to be reckoned with. That ship had sailed years ago.

No, our problems had long-since stopped being about skill. Now it was about endurance, funding, longevity. And our world had changed. Funding was no longer just a question of needing growth, but one of greatly increased competition for every sponsor dollar. Our program had made huge strides. Comparing current graduating numbers to those of five or 10 years ago, it looked pretty impressive. But if we used a different metric—calculating the number of applications we received against the number of dogs we graduated—we were losing ground, not gaining. And that wasn't even counting the disaster of the previous winter. Most of this group was sacrificing the bulk of their personal lives for a cause they believed to be important. The eternal question hovered: how long could we keep this up?

Nori called for attention and spent some time praising and thanking the group for the enormous effort that had pulled us through the winter. Gradually, cautiously, she explained more about the grants for which we were waiting on verdicts. We felt honor-bound to make sure each person in this group understood our reality. The board officers provided a much-needed sense of solidarity with their assurances.

For a while, we let everyone ask their questions and did our best to answer. Then, with immense skill honed over decades of group therapy, Sherry grabbed control at the exact point when impromptu questions began to drift. She asked each trainer to entertain us with two things. "Tell us the worst and the best moments of your training history, no matter if you've been training a week or a decade."

This idea was news to me as well as to the group, complicated by Sherry putting me on the spot: she asked me to go first. Understanding her reasons, I dove in. For me, this comparison took no debate.

"Well," I said, "you all know we have a whole lot of highs and some very significant lows." Laughter came from a now totally relaxed group. "In all the upsets and frustrations, I think it would be hard to beat one that happened a long time ago, before most of you were involved. For sheer trauma, and for making me feel like the biggest heel in the universe, I'd have to tell you about Asheton."

Being as brief as I could, trying not to let the story wallow, I outlined the basics about a young girl and our wonderful Casey, who both worked so hard, yet lost so much. I still struggled with this memory from time to time, and even through a few sentences of retelling, had to push myself to pick up the pace, move on. The silence around the fire was heavy when I finished even this abbreviated recounting. An ember popped and crackled.

I caught Sherry's intense glare and hurried on. "My most satisfying moment, I'm pretty sure, happened while I was sitting at my desk, on the phone, listening to law enforcement grill me about a missing kid." I shifted position a little so I could see more faces in the firelight. "This family hadn't had their dog very long. It was one of our earliest autism placements. The daughter got gone, and the entire world was going nuts. By the time the mother called me, there were probably a dozen cops crawling around the scene, and at least two official search and rescue dogs hunting for the kid. The mom was frantic and wanted me to talk to the deputy. All the officers were insisting she crate Desi, the service dog, so she'd be out of the way of the police search dogs. The mom wanted Desi involved. It was chaos. Everybody was talking overtop of everybody else. Finally, I got one deputy on the phone and convinced him to let the mom have two minutes with Desi loose. So everything goes quiet. I heard the mom say, "Desi, go find! Where is Emily? Go find!" Right about then...big cliff hanger because I got cut off!" The group around the fire half laughed, half gasped. "They called back inside two minutes. Desi had gone straight to the girl's room, then from there, up the stairs to the attic, and from the attic to a crawl-space behind the rafters, where they found the girl curled up and playing with her Gameboy. There was a whole lot of hoopla for the rest of that day, but it was one of my most intense moments of thrill, sitting there, listening to the deputy explain, listening to the whoops of the other officers and the mom crying. We'd had a lot of doubts and had been getting so much criticism from other trainers, other schools. But I knew right then we were vindicated. It worked. There have been other really big moments, lots of them. But that one was a watershed for me. I think I stopped doubting the dogs after that."

Silence hung around the fire for just a breath or two before Barb spoke up. "My very worst day was the first time I had to go with a client to have a retired, failing service dog euthanized. It wasn't my first time, of course, especially not with my own dogs. But that's when it really hit me how huge these dogs loom in the life of clients and how horrid the loss is for them. It was a really bad day." She barely paused before hurrying on. "But the best of the best," she said, "was watching Brady Johnson graduate law school with Baxter pulling his wheelchair. That dog was such a colossal pain as a trainee, and Brady so clueless when we started. I've never worked so hard on anything in my life, and seeing that team–four or five years later–succeeding and going strong gave me a rush I never forgot. I have a print of them at home that's almost life-sized: the two of them crossing that stage with the diploma in Baxter's mouth."

One of the younger trainers spoke up next. Jeff had been with us only about a year beyond his internship. I was surprised to hear him deal into the conversation so quickly.

"Mine might be different, since my worst and best time came from the same event. When I started here, it really wasn't very serious for me. Hate to admit I saw it more as a sideline thing I could show off later when I started my own training business. Good resume entry, right? I screwed up pretty bad and posted a picture online of a dog who was acting up with a client. I didn't have permission; I really thought it didn't matter because it was from the back and was kind of anonymous."

A little stirring passed through the group. Most people remembered this episode. I sure did.

"Well, Julie tore my head off and handed it to me in a bag. Took my trainee back and put me on probation. I was embarrassed, mad, scared…name it." Jeff was looking at the ground. He brought his eyes up and met mine for an instant before looking away again. "Then I had to meet with the client in person, with Julie and Nori. The lady was really very nice about it, but, it's hard to explain. I sat there, feeling like a fool, watching the amount of effort it took her just to get into the room and arranged at the table with the big wheelchair, all her stuff, and the dog, all to meet with me over something I had thought was funny. I guess it was the very first time I really got the importance, the significance of the job. That life is so incredibly hard for some people, that all this *work* with a dog was liberating for them, not just extra. I'm not saying it very good, but I don't think I'd ever gotten my head around their reality before." Jeff stopped, made a half-hearted gesture with both hands, then pushed on. "I was still embarrassed, for sure, but I also had like this big jolt of understanding how I could change it. It wasn't a joke or something for showing off or a blue ribbon at some show. That it was somebody's whole friggin life. And how many people ever get that on top of their paycheck? That screw-up is still embarrassing, but it changed everything for me. It's been over a year now and I still think about it every day."

If I'd had to respond right then, I'm not sure what I would have said. I remembered the awareness that Jeff got more serious about his work around then, but I'd never understood how the episode had factored for him. Because you didn't ask, I thought, chiding myself to pay better attention.

One by one, every member of the group spoke up. Some of the best/worst scenarios were predictable. Some, like Jeff's, were real surprises.

None jolted me more than Trent's. When he was done with his worst moment–reminding us of our horror over a graduate dog's death because a careless family member allowed him to get into rodent poison–he recounted the long-ago episode of watching Careen stop Jeb's bolt to the street. Sherry and I both stared at him with open fascination as he went on. "I hadn't told anybody yet, but I had decided to quit and move on. I was getting worn down by the pressure, by the grind and how everything we did seemed like such a drop in the bucket. But when I saw that dog and that kid, it really clobbered me. I could see, right there in that one dog, what kind of power the dogs held. How can you walk away from something they can't get anywhere else? I knew I wasn't quitting. I couldn't. It mattered too much."

Trent wasn't much for hyperboles, and the entire group stayed quiet for several beats after that statement. But the rest of the viewpoints continued.

Successful emergency alerts that possibly saved lives.

Seeing clients return to their jobs with the help of a good dog.

The ongoing frustration and despair of watching poorly trained or entirely fake dogs in public busily messing things up for legitimate workers.

One trainer's astonishment at realizing how readily a parent or grandparent dog's behaviors could be observed in a tiny puppy.

Stephen waited a long time to speak that evening. I had almost decided he wasn't going to, and I was still worried about him. He'd been one of my very first interns, part of the same group Sherry had enrolled in. Only the most dedicated of trainers lasted this long. But he was tired. I could see it in every line of his face and every piece of his body language. When he finally told us his worst low, it was another piece of astonishment for me, because he'd never given me a clue.

"When we first started with litters of pups instead of adult dogs, I struggled with that a lot," Stephen said thoughtfully, keeping his gaze on the flames. "One thing that drew me to this school more than any other was because we used rescues, and I was really against changing that."

I spent a few moments in frantic thought, sifting through my memories for any sign of his objections. If he'd ever said, I couldn't remember.

"It was a big, hard disappointment, but I tried to settle in to the new approach. A couple of years later, Nori asked me to keep a new litter at home for a month or so. I didn't want to—well, okay, I did. I mean who doesn't like puppies? But it was a project I didn't want to do. Really out of my comfort zone as the saying goes." Stephen picked up a stick and started poking some stray coals into place. "But I remember thinking, okay, I'm a professional. I can do this thing. And I really tried to put my heart into it. Right as I made it through, more than half my litter of pups got released just because we didn't have enough funds to put them all in training." Stephen tossed his poker stick into the fire. "I stayed angry about that for months. If I'd had another job to go to, I'm pretty sure I'd have left."

Sherry, Nori, and I had been avoiding eye contact to keep from being distractions. But this brought fixed stares among the three of us. Stephen had hidden this well. How had we never realized? He'd told us he understood, that it was fine. But clearly it had not been fine at all.

"I adjusted in time," Stephen kept going in his quiet way. "But still, it kind of led up to my very best time having a couple different parts. More than a year later, one of the homes that one of those pups had gone to had some trouble. I don't remember exactly, but there was some sickness and a scattered family. I was worried about the dog, but it turns out I wasn't the only one worried. Nori made a trip all the way to Oregon to get Brodie and bring him back here. And I know she did that out of her own pocket."

I shot Nori another look. This I remembered. So did she.

"The day she got back, she handed me the leash of this slightly-familiar-looking yellow Lab. I guess he was almost a year and half by then. She says to see if I could make a service dog out of him. Not until right then did I finally get it, really, that you guys–all of you," he gestured around to the group of administrators and board members, "were doing everything you knew how to do. About eight months later, Brodie graduated with a quadriplegic, and I never felt prouder of anything than I did that team. He helped that guy start a transport business, you know, with his custom van. Brodie helped him drag loads on and off with special hooks on his harness." Stephen finally shifted his position back from the fire a little. "He was a long way from my first graduating dog, but he was the first one after I really had full confidence in everyone here. I don't know quite how to explain. It added a lot. I always look back on that as kind of a trophy time."

The stories went on and on. And on. Sherry and I watched, listened, and gauged each other's reactions. We'd expected this to run its course in a couple of hours at most. But a late-rising moon was far overhead and starting to sink before the discussion wound down. Hours before, I'd tallied up potential damages from never having texted Scott to join us, and I was sure Sherry was doing the same with her promises to home and neighbors. But considering the profound discussion going on, the only reasonable thing we could do was stay quiet and let this play out. A group we'd fought for years to establish was building rapport while we listened, forging a greater sense of purpose within a flickering circle of orange flame.

As the fire burned low, a memory from several years before crept back to mind: Renee's relentless insistence at the start of our clinical therapy. *What about us?* She had asked over and over, explaining until it sunk in. That realization resurfaced now, despite being so easily lost in the daily crush.

Tonight's discussion highlighted the part of this work that had slipped quietly out of focus: this set of vulnerable humans, right here, those who worked and trained the dogs, the ones who held the line and fought the daily battles. I wondered how many of them I'd missed understanding that they wanted to ask the same. *What about us?* This was also a success group for our school. Possibly it was the largest one of all, considering their collective scope of influence. Most grant applications or reports didn't consider it even to be a metric, but it made the benefit no less real.

Past and present, here were lives touched, minds changed, growth realized, skills learned, progress made. Don't forget it again, I scolded myself. Don't discount them in the rush. My gaze circled the fire again, watching the light reflect in many eyes, seeing the same thoughtfulness in each that weighed on me now.

When conversation stilled, people wandered here and there. Some left for home. Others lingered. I waited for them to choose their own pace, not wanting to rush anyone away. Lying back in the damp spring grass, I listened to voices rise and fall. Far above us, the bright belt of the Milky Way glistened, smudged in varied brightness behind the brilliance of the moon. Sweetness of night blooming honeysuckle mingled with sharper wood smoke on a warm breeze. Low along the horizon, the intense speckling of stars gave way to a jagged line marking the tips of the mountains. Such nights, as always, stilled the mind, eased the spirit. I must not neglect again to share this with others who needed it as much as I did.

I considered the faces still visible nearby. We didn't know the future, but we were all absolutely sure of the value. Even more, after just this one night, we were far more sure of each other, our collective motivations, of each person's input and view. We all knew we'd all give it everything we had.

Many years have passed since that quiet, fragrant spring evening, but nearly every person there has since confirmed to me I was not alone in recognizing the melding of minds that night. The sense of cohesion bound us together and stayed for life. From honest truths, amid immense pressure, came a rare sense of purpose that we all recognized for what it was. No matter what happened from here forward, we were all convinced our time had already been well spent. Now we would wait and see what happened.

Chapter 28

"The worst part of success is trying to find someone who is happy for you." —Bette Midler

Our new resolve faced an unprecedented test sooner than we expected. That calendar year hadn't finished when Nori announced her retirement, pending her move to the southwest to greet her soon-to-be-first grandchild. The news shook the school to its very foundation. Another tribunal board meeting was called to strategize, but did little beyond highlighting a sharp division of opinion between our long-standing members and the new ones on how to proceed.

We shuffled responsibilities, reworked job descriptions, and did our best to compensate. It was utterly impossible to hire anyone even remotely close to Nori's level of experience. It would have taken three or four specialties. Discouragement ran strong, far more so among the administration than the trainers. Nori was definitely sorry to be creating such an additional obstacle, but she was adamant: her family came first, and she'd waited long enough. A decade-plus older than I, she was fully retirement age, and would not postpone it any more.

Catalysts, however, come in unexpected ways. The added stress forced the disconnect already present among the board members to a resolution, even if it wasn't a pretty one. Soon we saw a flurry of additional board member resignations, leaving an unexpectedly strong majority focused on increasing services for children with autism. The continued strength of the clinical therapy program harmed nothing. Time and time again we fell back on those dogs who were now working all across the country to bolster our numbers, keep trainers in paid jobs, and demonstrate success to sponsors.

Not long after Nori's departure, we gave up on the expensive maintenance of the training center in town. The building was sold to bolster that year's budget. All the staff's daily work and all group classes were now held at the farm, unless there was a need for them to be out and about somewhere in public. It was an excellent solution for the school's budget. For the privacy and mental peace of those who lived there… somewhat less so. By now I was a pretty tired 54, and RA difficulties were increasing to a level I'd never felt before.

So many factors were changing, and most of the reasons were totally outside our sphere of influence. At the very root, the societal trends themselves on which we'd based our services were changing. Supporters' views changed along with such societal shifts. The needs of our clients were evolving and always increasing. We ourselves were changing, aging.

Nothing was the same as it had been a decade earlier, a conclusion much reinforced to me recently by Lisa deciding that, as of the next school year, Project Hope would stop the use of clinical therapy dogs altogether. The reasons showed me yet another factor to which I hadn't paid enough attention. I'd heard her talk for years about their need for adult housing options, but hadn't yet let it fully register how pressing that need was becoming. She broke the news one night while sitting in her yard by the pool.

"I don't remember where I first read that the true art of focus isn't about saying 'no' to things you don't want to do," Lisa said, watching Colby's shadow move around inside her house while dusk fell. "It's a lot harder to say no to things you *do* want to do, but can't if you're going to be most effective. You have to pick and choose. This is just where we are."

I couldn't come up with much to say. They'd been our first, and the best, but nobody had to tell me how priorities changed, no matter what your own preferences had to say about it.

"How close are you to starting the facility?" Scott asked. He was always intrigued by new horizons.

"Not very," Lisa said quietly. "We have the space. We could manage a funding campaign to get the building up, but the real problem is with operating expenses.

"Same song, different verse," I said with a sigh. "For almost all nonprofits who excel and grow, this is the wall we hit."

"Scale alone is a big issue," she agreed. "But there are percentages in play, here, too, just like there are for you. We've started almost 25 years ago, and the growth has outstripped everything we ever imagined. But all those same kids who were toddlers at the beginning are now in their 20s. They'll be adults a lot longer than they were little kids, and their parents won't live forever. Many of them—meaning the autistic adults—will need lifelong support. That's a lot of parents losing sleep over what to do. We're going to have to pick and choose what we can do."

"Julie, you guys have, what," Scott asked the next

question, "at least 30 local handlers who could bring in a dog occasionally if it's ever needed for some situation?"

"More than that, really," I said absently, much distracted by Lisa's obvious worry about her son. "Some of those are on the Project Hope staff, so it will always be an option if they need it."

"Yes," Lisa answered, pulling her attention from the house back to us. "We can. But everyone, especially administration, is stretched so thin that we're having to be really stringent about where we focus. So much is about grants, and that gets more complicated by the year."

"There have to be grants that would at least start you an endowment fund." Scott frowned at this. "The world is full of those kinds of facilities."

"Not many designed for the needs of our group," Lisa answered wearily. "And not many that meet the criteria for accessing government money."

Not that far off, I thought, from the core differences between our school and the big guide dog programs that started before any of us sitting here were even born.

Uncharacteristically, Sherry stayed silent. Her expression told me she was running through the variables, analyzing, calculating. I could see that she also recognized Lisa's tension. We glanced at each other briefly, knowing our therapy component was now so heavily weighted by private clinicians that, however sad Lisa's announcement might be, it didn't change that much for our school. Few private clinicians depended on grant funding, so drawing comparisons was classic apples and oranges. But hearing Lisa state such a similar rationale for all that currently pressured our school so badly… it loomed huge in our thoughts. I could see Sherry was thinking about it, same as I was. In short, sometimes all the good intentions in the world just aren't enough. When you don't have enough resources for them all, well, then, you just don't.

Such thoughts made a bitter drink to swallow, as every new litter brought us closer to the ideals it had taken so long to establish. Barely a week after Lisa's announcement, we began testing the newest group.

"Look at that little beggar!" A new intern watching from outside the short puppy fence almost squealed the remark. Sherry shushed her quickly, since the pup's head came up and turned toward her voice.

I had a hard time not squealing myself. The sable pup was giving us a nearly perfect response. Well, perfect for *our* purposes, anyway. This litter was the eleventh successive generation of crisscrossed genetics, selectively chosen for ever-better inclinations, from the best dogs we'd ever found for working with autism. Back in the beginning, we'd logged thousands of miles driving around the country, and spent an amount out of our own pockets that we preferred not to discuss. In later years, we had swapped breeding stock and mixed bloodlines with several larger guide schools. Now we had two genetic "families" established, and the puppies in front of us were the first from those two families combined. For us, it was heady stuff. Each litter taught us more. Each litter made the percentage of useable pups higher and more predictable.

The strongest proof yet waddled around in front of me. Almost three weeks old, little Miss Yellow collar puppy wasn't yet named. She wasn't eating solid food yet,

either. Her only food source was still her own momma–
which was the time frame in which we'd learned we got
the very best information. Plenty of dogs could learn
certain skills, but we continued our quest for
characteristics that were matters of genetic hard-wiring.
We wanted the behaviors that not only did you not have
to teach a dog to do, but that you could mostly not
prevent him from doing.

Not that anybody minded skilled training, but the odds
were so much higher when dogs started out with strong
tendencies. The stronger the better. It saved time, grief,
and money. Beyond that, the original problem with
families struggling with autism would forever be that the
ones who needed this kind of dog most were the same
ones who had the least time to spend training a dog. The
more we could shift the balance toward relying on natural
behaviors, the higher the odds of success.

What we were watching now made itself known from the
moment Sherry placed Miss Yellow down in the little
exercise pen. The pup had given me a casual sniff as I sat
just outside the barrier. She knew me and enjoyed some
petting, but people weren't especially significant to her
life so far. She had some use of her eyes now, albeit not
much. And her ears were working enough to provide
basic feedback. But her primary senses were still scent
and touch. And as we had finally put together: routine
versus difference. What we wanted to know today was
how well she would identify and how she would respond
to factors in her environment that were not her norm.
Today, all the new things were about scent. She'd already
explored two of them. We were watching to see if her
still-developing little brain would direct her to the third.

The puppy's tiny nose came up, weaving back and forth,

seeking and questioning. I held my breath. She'd been up and moving for almost 10 minutes now. She wouldn't last much longer. At 20 days old, their activity periods were brief, and the naps that followed were long and deep. Miss Yellow took an unsteady step toward the old sock hanging on the enclosure fence. The sock had been sprinkled with anise extract. One step, two. Her nose moved right and left in a wobbly puppy imitation of a search scent cone. I clenched my hands and reminded myself not to move. Then she faced the source of the odor and unerringly toddled straight in to stick her nose on the sock. An experimental paw followed, then a nearly toothless bite. Her tail gave a few intense wags, then she turned away. Three more steps and she collapsed onto her side with an enormous sigh. In moments, her eyes were closed, and she barely twitched as we returned her to the nest to snore among her siblings.

"Three for three." Sherry was making notes in the puppy log. I let out a breath that actually hurt from holding so long.

"Three what?" A second young trainer, our newest intern, Theresa, was passing by on her way to the larger training room. She was not involved with training dogs for autism yet. So far, her strongest interest was with the mobility assistance type. "What are you guys doing?"

"Checking how well she notices new things, and what she does about it. In this case, unfamiliar scents." I pointed to the socks hung on the low fence and counted them off. "First one is scented with used motor oil. Second one, over there, has lawn-mower clippings. This third one right here, has anise extract."

"But," the young trainer looked confused. "Why would

they be interested in those? It's not food."

"No, it's not." Sherry set the notebook down and went for the next puppy. "That's the whole point. It's just new. Different. Something the pup has never been around before."

"So you're watching to see if they're afraid of it?" Theresa sat down on the edge of a chair. She looked truly perplexed, which was a very average response to what we were checking.

"Well, of course we wouldn't want the pup to be afraid," I answered, since Sherry had disappeared into the puppy room, searching for our next candidate. "But we want more than that. We're hoping for pups that automatically investigate just because it's there and it's new and different. Later it will be more than scents. It will be new items, or new people. Or a new light, maybe. Or a window open where it's never been open before."

Theresa sat quietly for a minute. I waited for the next comment and was not disappointed. "I don't understand. What does this have to do with service work?"

"It has everything to do with which puppy is obsessed with anything new or out of place. Which is what's needed from a dog we want to alert parents to disruptions or changes in the home environment. Those are the dogs most likely to let a parent know about something out of order. It could be anything from a kid out of bed at the wrong time of night, to a kid in the basement experimenting with matches while his mom is on the phone. It's different. It's unusual. The dog who has an enormous amount of natural curiosity for the new or different is the best bet for that kind of job."

"Of course," Sherry added as she came back with the next pup. "That's on top of all the regular things, as you said, like not being afraid. Not being aggressive to people. We also have to have normal and correct in the usual puppy-testing ways." Sherry set the puppy down in the middle of the pen. "Now, be quiet and sit still, or leave. He'll be too easily distracted by your voice."

Theresa cast a final disbelieving glance over her shoulder as she quickly exited. Sherry and I exchanged glances and shrugged. We were pretty used to such responses by now, and no longer bothered to try to change them. Either Theresa would become more receptive or she wouldn't. Scores of pups and clients had shown us the reliability of this approach. We'd lost count of how often we'd tried to explain to those who were simply not interested in hearing. You want pups who will alert to new, creative behaviors from a child who has no recognition of danger? Fine. Pick a puppy who cannot ignore anything new or out of context in his environment.

We fully understood that insatiable curiosity and a strong desire to meddle were the exact opposite of what many schools were looking for in a pup. Guide dog prospects, for instance, needed working canines who could ignore pretty much everything and focus straight ahead on the exact path his handler needed to travel. Different dogs for different jobs.

We watched Mr. Green collar puppy wake up, stretch, wet on the floor, and waddle off to explore a little bit.

Choose pups based on responses to breaks in routine? And at this age? I'd heard from a dozen recognized experts now that we were making much ado about nothing. I'd stopped listening. Nobody could tell me we weren't seeing what we were seeing. Not until we'd spent copious, utterly ridiculous amounts of time watching these litters of very young pups did we see the proper connection. The world had so many sets of puppy tests competing for recognition that it was hard to hear much of substance through the noise: buy this book! This video! We have the perfect selection tool for your breeding program! Hardly a month went by that we were not approached by someone wanting us to purchase, or better yet endorse, their new and improved product. But not one of them, so far as we could tell, paid enough attention to the type of information we wanted to know. We wanted an intense desire to pursue, investigate, and interact with anything out of context.

A sizeable chunk of what drove our certainty was episodes like a recent phone call about graduate Louisa. After 10 minutes of pacing, poking, and refusing to stop, she'd led a parent to her boy's bedroom and indicated a strong interest in exploring under the bed.

"She barked and dug at the carpet," the mom had told me, "and poked her nose under Philip's bed. Right about then I'd realized Philip had a little cut on his hand, a fresh one that was bleeding. So of course I got down and really looked under that bed." The mom had to stop to catch her breath. "Julie, he had somehow picked up a big hunting knife my brother-in-law uses for dressing out deer."

There had been a long pause while both of us thought about five-year-old Philip and a huge hunting knife.

"Now," the mom pressed on. "How, how in the world, would Louisa know the knife was dangerous? What made her try to alert and try to dig it out? For all she knows it could be a dog toy."

Scent, I knew, at least in part. The scent of deer, possibly of blood, the woods, the man who was not part of the regular family. And the knife was different. Just like motor oil to Miss Yellow collar, the knife was new to Louisa. I had a short flashback of a fat black and tan puppy persistently digging underneath a big towel to drag out an old sock filled with oregano. Yes, Louisa had shown us her tendency early.

I thought about Louisa and Philip while watching Mr. Green collar wandering the puppy pen. He stalked around, tail straight in the air, never so much as glancing at the humans. He took a casual sniff at the motor oil, but kept going, head down, focused elsewhere. He encountered the barrier at the far end–away from us, away from his momma–and yowled in protest. He pawed the wire and tried to stand up against it. Sherry scratched a few notes, and we exchanged glances. No words were needed. We were both thinking, *nope! Find that boy a different job.*

We knew this process worked, but it was abominably time consuming. It could take a couple hours to work carefully through a litter of nine pups on just this one experiment. And we would repeat it with multiple different objects and different contexts in the next few weeks. We had our own repertoire of checkpoints, developed and blended from copious trial and error over the years. It worked incredibly well, but carried a an expensive price tag measured in hours, not dollars. And it took half of forever to get even a skilled trainer adequately fluent in what to watch for. Today I observed pup after pup work through this specific test, repeatedly hauling my thoughts back from concern about tomorrow's full schedule that had two presentations to prospective donors.

At home, a sharp disagreement sprang up with Scott. He took one look at my haggard face and started pushing for me to take some time off. I couldn't and I knew it. He knew it, too, but neither of us had a workable solution. Over and over, our thoughts kept coming back to Lisa's decision, knowing that we, also, were rapidly approaching similar cuts. Too many things had changed, and we were going to have to change with them—one way or another.

Chapter 29

"Nothing in the world is more dangerous than sincere ignorance and conscientious stupidity."
—Martin Luther King, Jr.

The next day's grant presentations proved grueling, far beyond expectations. I missed both shifts of my training classes because of requests to extend the time for questions at the end of the presentations. One grant committee had come to the farm to hold the meeting right in the puppy room. The other required an hour's drive to the other side of town. By the time I pointed my van homeward, I wasn't even sure I should be driving. A growing pain in one eye and a general dizziness removed much of my sight and all my resolve. The creativity of my autoimmune condition had lately decided to center itself on some optic nerves. It wasn't adding up to anything good.

When I turned up the long driveway, despite the clock's stated time of nearly 11:00 pm, the puppy building shone bright with lights, inside and out. When I noticed, I did a last-minute swerve at the fork to the building by the front field. Pulling up next to the door, I could see Sherry's truck and Trent's small SUV.

A knot of apprehension rose. Odd hours and disrupted schedules with small puppies could mean trouble. This litter was still very young. Any illness or problem could be a big deal. But before I even made it to the deck, I was reassured by laughter from the open windows and door. It was April again, featuring mild weather and warm breezes. The sweetness of honeysuckle drifted on velvet darkness.

 Dipping my feet into the "shoe bath" of disinfectant by the front door, I stepped inside and took in the scene. Sherry and two other trainers were on the floor with the whole gamboling group of dog larvae.

"Hi." She looked up at me briefly before returning her attention to the pups. "What's up?"

"I was going to ask that myself," I said, moving to the sink to wash my hands before touching any pups. "I saw the lights on and thought I'd come over and see what was happening this late."

"Classes ran long," Trent said from his partially submerged position among the fur balls. "And I didn't get to see these guys all last week."

Sherry was flipping pages in the spiral logbook, our informal arrangement for all to leave notes on anything and everything: feeding progress, medical treatments, and behavior observations. Each trainer could check for what had been going on since they were last with the pups. "What's this nonsense in here about Green-collar boy and the consult this afternoon? Who is Janice Tellers? I missed something."

I sighed heavily, finding a seat. "She came in with the group from the Piedmont Foundation. I guess they decided they should bring their own dog expert to assess what we're doing."

"Hmmmm." Sherry's nose was still buried in the

notebook. "Who the heck is she?"

"Sounded to me like she is a breeder who promotes her own dogs. I wasn't sure what to make of it. Best guess: she knows somebody on the Piedmont board, or else she's working with another group who has a grant application in. It didn't go well. She was really critical of our setup, of the pups, of our evaluation methods. You name it, she didn't like it. I haven't been lectured that much since high school."

This got Sherry's attention. "You have to be kidding me. So that's what this note is about Green? He wouldn't go to her?"

I had to laugh. "It was almost feeding time, and none of the pups were very interested in her for that alone. But Green wouldn't interact, wouldn't lick tuna juice off her fingers, wouldn't engage in any of her games. He just turned his back on her and walked away. Big surprise, right? We already know he's a hardhead."

"Yeah, so how did we get from that to her wanting him?" Sherry was scowling. "What was her criticism?"

"About him specifically? That he was fearful and shy, and we should consider euthanizing him–or giving him to her to socialize."

The notebook dropped onto Sherry's lap with a muffled profanity. "Are you kidding me? Did she really?"

I looked over at Trent. Back to Sherry. I was too tired for this discussion. "Yes," I said. "I mean, no…. I'm not kidding, and yes, that was her official suggestion. All the foundation people looked at me expectantly, like they thought I would jump at the offer." I put my head down on the edge of the puppy fence. "Why are you so surprised? She isn't the first or the 20th breeder who's tried to do an end run around us."

"That's a little different from cutting into a grant application," Trent objected. "You said.... what?"

It felt like a 200-pound bench-press to pick up my head and answer. "I'm afraid I ran out of patience before we finished. I asked her what the odds were that a three-week-old pup would turn its back on something it was afraid of. Then pointed out he wasn't a dog we planned to keep, anyway, so it wasn't even pertinent." I slumped back down in my chair. "No courtesy points for me. Then I got a 10 or 15-minute additional lecture on how she tested pups, and therefore how she knew that pups from her own kennel were far better suited for this work, also for police patrol, search and rescue, mobility assistance, yada, yada."

"In other words, she's an egotistical fool." Trent was getting more irritated. "Her dogs are "ideal" for five different jobs, huh? That proves she's a functional illiterate about dogs."

"Pretty much." Rubbing my eyes, I thought I should definitely have gone on to my house, straight to sleep. "I believe I mentioned it didn't go well. Plus, I made the mistake of telling them about Chessie and the billiard balls."

Sherry closed her eyes. "Tell me you didn't. You know nobody ever believes that."

"No," I admitted, "They don't. But we were already losing them, so to heck with it. It was something else to try."

Chessie's case study had some examples we didn't normally attempt to explain. She was a young shepherd who'd gone to a family with three children, and had taken it upon herself to break up an autistic eight-year-old's use of the family pool balls as weapons against siblings. We knew the dog's behavior had its root in the "big" reactions from the parents when billiard balls became missiles. Chessie solved the problem by hiding all the balls. The parents were amused and proud. We were horrified. All we could imagine was the fatal spectacle of a graduate dog choking on a small, smooth ball. Once we insisted the balls be kept locked up unless under direct parent supervision, the issue faded. But we could never quite forget the mental picture of Chessie having stuffed all of them under a chair cushion and posting guard on top, oblivious to the shrieking demand of the eight-year-old to move so he could have the balls. The mercifully brief episode left us with a new appreciation of the dogs' ability to apply their own solutions to parental concerns. It was beyond bizarre, well into the category of chilling.

Stories like this—intense examples of extrapolated function—was a tough concept to explain to the average inquirer. The dogs were smart, perceptive, and incredibly bossy. And their behaviors could be quite off-putting to the skeptical. For someone already doubtful about our program, a story like Chesses usually convinced doubters we were exaggerating. That's exactly what had happened today.

Sherry sighed and stood up, rolling up soiled papers and prepping the puppy pen for overnight. "So, how were things left? What do you think will happen?"

"I think we're not going to get the grant. It's a lot easier to critique than to prove up. For whatever reason, the foundation appears to be listening to her, not us. I'm done spending time on it for nothing."

Sherry said nothing, but not surprisingly, Trent was the one to lash out. "It's crazy! Isn't there an appeal process? How can they just stuff a stranger in your face and say you're supposed to do it her way? Are you going to–"

"Trent," Sherry cut him off. "Cool it. It's their money and they can do anything with it they want, under any conditions they want. It just means we've wasted lots of time."

"That's for sure." I got up and started scooping up small, furry bodies for transport to their pen. Even their momma was pressed up against the door of the back porch, finished with her evening run in the large yard and ready to settle down. "I think the application alone, forget follow up, ate most of a week."

"But this is the best litter we've ever had!" Trent was not planning to give up. "All but one are great prospects."

"I know it." I said, ruffling the fur of little Miss Pink Collar, who was finely attuned to every human voice and interaction around her. Her beautiful baby eyes were following our every move throughout her still-rather-limited field of vision. "And you know it. But neither of us have the funds in our change jars to cover thirty grand per dog."

Trent slumped down in his chair, face planted in hands. It was a familiar pose. I'd spent plenty of time that way myself lately. I didn't have any words of wisdom. We represented one urgent need in a frothing sea of urgent needs. Competition for every donated dollar was fierce. It was becoming ever more obvious that funding competition was often won by those with the better advertising departments, not necessarily the better programs. Barely a month before, we'd watched with a mixture of pleasure and dismay when another school received a high-six-figure grant. Their companion dogs for kids with autism were lovely dogs and did very well with families. But we could also easily see our graduates worked a half dozen more specific functions at approximately half the cost. It was hard to figure, and harder yet not to let your spirits plummet.

When the building was closed up for the night, Sherry and I wandered to the end of the parking lot closest to my house. In the past, we would have ended this discussion with extended dissection and debate on the porch. Tonight, we were far too exhausted. It was time for home and sleep.

"The group is getting really discouraged again," Sherry said, one hand on the door of her truck.

"I know," I replied. "I am, too."

"We're missing Nori, big time. She was such a confidence booster."

"We need better administration, period, on several levels." I leaned back against the side of my vehicle. "We've needed that for years. But we don't have it. And we can't afford to hire it."

"Besides," Sherry pointed out dryly, "If we could afford to hire it, we'd get crucified again for excessive overhead and lose all our grants. It's heads they win, tails we lose."

I studied her for a few moments. Even in the dim light from the half-moon, I could see a flatness in her expression that was not normal. "Are you feeling okay?"

I'd caught myself wondering about this often recently.

"I'm pretty tired," she said, not looking up.

I'd spent a lot of years listening to this woman minimize her own struggles. "What's up?" I turned to face her. "What's bothering you?"

"I really don't know. I'm exhausted, which is understandable. I think I've mentioned several times lately that I don't seem to be getting younger." Sherry stifled a yawn. "But I'm not just tired, I'm wiped totally *out* most of the time and I can't make it go away."

"Check your iron lately?"

"Going in next Tuesday. Annual physical." Sherry shrugged. "I guess I'll see what they have to say."

Chapter 30

"That's it." Sherry strode through my door a few days later. She immediately helped herself to the nearest recliner. "We have to have more help, and I don't care how it happens. In case anyone's forgotten, I'm almost retirement age now, and this has to stop."

I was at the kitchen table, elbow deep in training reports and struggling to stay awake, let alone alert and careful with details. "I'd say you picked a lousy day to start this discussion again," I answered, rubbing my eyes. "Except it doesn't seem like there are many good days this month."

"Forget 'month,' " Sherry said with an enormous yawn. "Things have been going downhill even faster since we started trying to find raisers for these last two litters. It's time to face it, Julie. Reality has limits. Nobody can keep this up. We're going to start doing dumb stuff and screwing up dogs."

"I know." I capped my pen and started gathering up papers. "I'm already doing dumb stuff with admin. Not like that's so new, but still."

Sherry didn't answer, and my own frustrations rambled out in a flood. "I'm a truly crummy business manager.

I'm spending nearly all my time on things I'm terrible at. But getting a volunteer for admin is impossible. And we know the problems about hiring, even if we could. As is, we're barely treading water and I'm not doing half enough to stay on top of all the details that need monitoring." I finished returning each dog's stack of paper to the appropriate folder, then folders to the file drawer. I made a wild grab for control of my rant, then turned to see what Sherry had to say.

That would be nothing. In the 90 seconds she'd been still, she'd fallen asleep sitting up. I made a half-hearted attempt to rouse her. "Hey, do you want to talk about this now or wait for an admin meeting?"

"Hmmm," was her only response. She swung her legs over the arm of the chair, pulled a blanket off the back to cover herself. And she was gone.

I clicked off the lights, walked out my front door, and left for the barn, deep in thought. No matter how much we grew, the various disabilities, especially autism, were growing more. Days contained only 24 hours. Hard truth stalked us: our training tribe, especially our most experienced–and our oldest–could not maintain this pace. No longer a temporary fix, this pressured routine had become our norm. General exhaustion no longer made an adequate description. We were flat used up.

The clinical therapy program continued to keep us above water. Several extended research projects were underway in Applied Behavior Analysis, using our dogs and our staff trainers. Three peer-reviewed studies had already been published. The resulting demand for similar dogs never slowed. It was often the only thing keeping our trainers paid. The dog sales and the clinical work brought an amount they could live on and stayed far more stable than variable grants for regular service dogs. But often trainers still ended up donating hours to work with clients in homes. For years now, we'd been thinking we were in stopgap mode, and improvement would be just around the next corner.

But paid, unpaid, or lavishly paid, nobody could sustain 80-hour weeks indefinitely. That was just physics, not willpower. Nothing but more people—quite a lot more people—was going to ease anything. And society seemed mostly unwilling to fund the service dogs.

I'd told no lie to Sherry: I was drowning in administrative work, a sad state of affairs by any yardstick. I was a crummy business manager, and I knew it, poorly suited by talent or training. Business administration is an art and science all its own. Our school's process desperately needed more capable hands, but such hands didn't work for free. Every one of our trainers had started in some profession other than dog training, but nobody came from a background in business administration. Yet every piece of program growth demanded a corresponding amount of oversight. Short of full-time administration, that demand fell on the senior trainers, regardless of suitability.

I finished rounds of the various barns, then parked myself in a chair near a pasture fence, trying to make sense of the endless tug of war between need and realism. It hadn't changed in a decade. In truth, I thought, it's worse than before because the school is bigger and has many more commitments. No matter how much we grow, the needs grow more. After a few moments, I let myself say the rest, at least in my head: it's worse, too, because your key people are getting old.

I watched my horses cavort with Sherry's. None had been ridden in so long I could hardly remember. All looked healthy enough, but remarkably shaggy from lack of attention.

I thought about the 17 young pups currently in early training. Logistics fought for placement in my mind: new applications, re-certifications, grant proposals, paperwork, public relations. Responsibilities bore down on me like a physical weight, and I felt the weariness all the way to the bone. Sherry was right. The time had come. We had to expand our training leverage or reduce the numbers. And it had to be now. We couldn't eternally wait and hope while nothing changed.

My wandering thoughts returned to the idea of using professional fundraising. It had derailed before, but maybe we should look at it again? No matter what the trainers preferred, that was a board decision and highly complex, including the risk of public scorn for "overhead."

Supposedly, the road to hell is paved with good intentions. Because Sherry and I had started by volunteering our time and personal funds, part of our board still demanded a return to volunteer training. The conversation had started several times, but hit absolute refusal from our senior staff. That's the model we were trying to get away from, not expand.

But key members of the board continued to push. "Donated time has brought us a long, long way!" one had insisted at the last meeting. "Shoot, even I have learned to raise puppies. There have to be lots more people out there willing to help."

"We've made such a big deal out of using a volunteer administration and lots of volunteer trainers," another member said. "How can we possibly justify *not* building that concept?"

Sherry, Lisa, and I all did our best to explain that volunteer staffing has natural limitations, like any business would. Forget the dogs. No business can make certain requirements of volunteers the same way it could of employees, not even with part timers, who'd been our majority for most of the school's existence.

For those of us in the trenches, this seemed pretty basic. But it brought endless tension, endless disagreement. I had listened to this ongoing debate at a recent meeting, while also hearing Nori's long-ago comments echo from my trainer orientation: too many people think dog trainers do this job because they can't do better ones. The idea of dog training as a complex, professional skill just wasn't well recognized. Back then, I'd thought her position overly cynical, but I'd learned better. The prevailing belief was that we ought to be able to pull volunteers off the street, hand them dogs, and make it work on the strength of a few group classes.

What we were experiencing now was that the more success your program achieves, then the larger your program becomes—consequently the larger this problem becomes. Renee's statement from the previous year was directly on target: this was how nonprofits were penalized for growth.

The more delicate point Sherry and I couldn't raise was much more basic. We'd both spent huge amounts of personal funds on the project, and both of us had now also been full-time volunteers for longer than we wanted to think about. We'd run through all the personal assets we could liquidate, but most of the board still saw us as capable of operating full time on nothing. The expiration date on that arrangement had arrived.

Sherry finally showed up from her extended nap in my living room.

"Horses are already fed," I told her. "I thought maybe you'd just sleep through."

My long-suffering friend leaned on the fence, surveying the horses much as I'd done. I wondered if she was asking herself the same question: when would we ever have time to ride again? Her discouragement showed. I'd never seen this level of weariness and low spirit from her.

"Maybe let's take a day to think on things and then try a strategy meeting?" I suggested delicately. "You need to get to bed for real and so do I."

"Okay," Sherry finally agreed, not budging from the fence. "But I don't know what I might think of that hasn't already surfaced in the last decade of thinking."

I pushed myself wearily to my feet, glad to see her starting for her truck. "Do you have time to come watch the K2-B group tomorrow morning? If we're going to start dropping dogs, I think we should start there. Every one of them is way behind where they should be. Not one has a single valid skill marker for their age list."

I saw her immediately grimace in response. I was referring to a basic behavior shaping process through which we taught pups which actions from people they were supposed to pay attention to. Not that the dog necessarily needed to interrupt, but we were trying to teach them which behaviors to notice. It could be as simple as a door opening, because that action might precede a command. We had a whole checklist. Usually, the pups began learning these cues almost as soon as they left their siblings at seven weeks. By four or five months, they should be very alert to a dozen environmental cues.

"They're all good dogs," I hastened to explain. "Every one of them. The fosters are doing their best. But they don't have enough skill to keep the dogs where they belong. That's our fault, not theirs. I can't cancel training with clients to add training with fosters."

I double-checked to see that the barn door was latched, then continued. "It's just more of the same. You're right. It's either more people or fewer dogs. Otherwise we're going to run into deficits with advanced training that nobody will be able to fix."

"Full circle," Sherry said. "Too many dogs for the resources available. It seems so simple when you say it, but the details aren't simple at all."

We started down the hill, then paused by her truck where the trail to my house left the driveway.

"You're right about something else," I said, thinking of her words from last week. "The fosters are going to hate us, and the clients waiting will hate us more."

"I know." Sherry climbed into her truck. "But hell, some of them already do just because we're so far behind and so broke."

I trudged home in the company of my usual dilemma: where, exactly, was the ultimate dividing line between true dedication and just plain enough?

Chapter 31

"She knows herself to be at the mercy of events, and she knows by now that events have no mercy."
                    —Margaret Atwood, "The Blind Assassin"

Sherry never made it to class the next day. Early that morning, Barb found her midway across the parking lot, halfway between her car and the puppy building, leaning over, hands on knees. Her trainee puppy cavorted, ignored and unchecked, at the end of its leash.

Barb stopped to investigate. "What's up, girl?"

Sherry's voice was a gasp. "I can't seem to get my breath."

Barb leaned over, took one look at her gray face, and dialed 911. Barely two hours later, Sherry underwent an emergency open-heart surgery to repair an aortic aneurism. I sat, shocked and frozen, with several others in the waiting room of Cardiac-ICU, hardly daring to move or breathe. For the first few hours, we weren't given any hope that she would even survive.
Explanations blurred in my overstressed brain. It took me some time to understand that most aortic aneurisms were diagnosed post-mortem. Sherry's was a full six centimeters, and she was the only person in the history of this large hospital ever to survive one that size. It would be weeks before she left the hospital, and months before she picked up another training leash. We all wanted to

know what role stress and too-long working hours had played. Perhaps a major one? Maybe none at all? We would never know.

But the effect on the school, and especially the autism program, rocked our world worse than Nori's departure. We were shocked into drastic actions that might otherwise have taken weeks to decide. Now, such steps were just entries on a to-do list, no longer optional. Ultimately, we released all but four of our current puppies. It had been our best group yet, crammed with promise. The pups represented the payoff of many generations of careful selection.

We'd been correct about the response. Prospective clients were upset. Fosters were angry. Supporters were furious. My email box overflowed with lengthy epistles outlining frustration, disappointment, anger, accusations, and pleas to reconsider.

The board was divided and still arguing. Only among the trainers could 100% consensus be found. We all knew what reality was. Before Sherry left the hospital, we held another meeting, back in the pasture around a circle of dying coals, that ran into the wee hours. We compared notes, drew graphs, and mapped an exact timeline of hours needed. We found consensus on what we were absolutely sure we could cover with just our own hands and the funds already in the bank. We knew nobody was going to like the results. Not even us.

Several weeks later, I stood in the parking lot with Trent. We hovered over Sherry's seat on the puppy building deck, our attention divided between her and the family who'd come to pick up one of the released youngsters. Everyone was incredibly glad to have Sherry back.

Despite her weakness and atrophied muscles, her thoughts were as sharply pointed as ever. Even from an outdoor wicker chair, her opinions and evaluations guided much of our decision process.

Sherry kept smiling, but I could see she felt as sick as I did about the lovely little shepherd pup departing to be a pet. She casually sorted through the day's mail while we watched the family load up.

"We'll be good to her," said the woman, holding little Kira. "I promise we will. And we'll keep you updated." She kissed Kira's head and moved her front paw up and down to "wave" back at us.

None of us were worried about them being good to the puppy. We charged significant fees and had background-checked these people and verified references as though they were adopting a human child. No, our dejection wasn't about the dog. What drove our disappointment was that adorable, fuzzy face, with the bright eyes that watched every human move with such intensity. We didn't fear Kira's future, but we had plenty of grief for the loss of what otherwise could have been.

Trent said it best, as he brought Sherry a fresh glass of ice water and settled down in a chair beside her. "You know," he said, watching the family getting their car organized, "I used to think you guys were certifiably crazy. Then I switched to thinking maybe you were maybe just crazy enough. Now I think I'm the one who's totally nuts, because I cannot figure why people can't do math. I mean, I'm watching a dog vanish who could, say, for about 25 grand, pretty much eliminate, for about a decade, the chance of a $50K-per-hour 911 search."

"You left out the part about parents maybe getting five minutes of sleep now and then," Sherry said dryly. She was now dividing mail into stacks on the nearby table.

"Yeah, sure, but that's not my point." Trent always had his own take on things.

We understood. It was something we'd talked to death before now. These dogs were the proverbial dime of prevention against the dollar of cure. Now we just sat, watching a high-value prospect disappear down the road.

"Maybe some good old fashioned magic?" I asked. "Pity we can't freeze-dip these pups at this exact developmental point. Thaw them out sometime later when funding improves."

"Just talking about straight finances," Trent was a bulldog with a bone. "What part of this makes any sense at all? Most 501(c)3 contributions are driven by emotional appeal, right? Way too many programs are getting funded based on having the best PR department, not the best product."

"Isn't that true of just about any product, nonprofit or otherwise?" I asked.

"I guess," Trent grumbled. "But what is more dramatic, or emotional, or appealing than traumatized kids in danger? I can't get it figured out. What is missing that people won't help more?"

"Hey, where do parents' medical bills fit into your financial summary?" Sherry was reading from a handwritten letter. I could see her hands shaking even from the slight effort of holding the paper. "Can reduced primary care be a client benefit?"

"Huh?" Trent said, confused. "What do you mean?"

Sherry laughed. I think it might have been the first time I'd heard her laugh since well before her surgery, and it was a balm to everything. "This letter is from Nancy Delaney. Remember her? Their family got Jean last year."

"I remember," I said. "What's up with them? Didn't they move somewhere? Wisconsin?"

"Yes, they did." Sherry was still looking at the letter. Then she went back to the top and started reading out loud. "You'll be glad to know that Jean and Charlie are doing well. Looking back over last year, I've counted lots of milestones for Charlie. But last week I finally remembered to count one for me. You know we had a lot of trouble with Charlie's meltdowns and frustrations. Jean has been such a help redirecting those and giving us better options. When I went for my physical, the doctor was reviewing other years. As he brought up different things, I realized this is the first year since Charlie was two that he hasn't broken my nose at least once."

We sat in thoughtful silence until Trent wrapped up the conversation. "Nope, Sherry, in all those grant categories, I don't think there's a checkbox for that one, either. That goes in the category we better never tell anybody or they'll call us liars."

Chapter 32

"I suppose I'll have to add the force of gravity to my list of enemies." —*Lemony Snicket, "The Penultimate Peril"*

"What in the name of common sense is an Emotional Support Dog?" A door banged shut to punctuate Barb's question as she dragged her wheeled carry-on across the lobby. She was just now back from an overnight trip to Florida to check on some graduates.

"A who?" Carol was the first to respond. I heard their voices batting the topic back and forth as I sorted out my equipment in the back room.

"An Emotional Support Dog. Untrained, uncertified, privately owned. I just spent two and a half hours sitting next to one that wanted to eat my face for the entire flight."

"Never heard of that. What was it doing on the plane?"

"Being a security blanket for someone who was afraid to fly, I guess."

"Who authorizes that?" Theresa was passing by and wanted to know.

"The stewardess told me it was required by the FAA. It's nuts." Barb was not mincing words.

I couldn't stop the sigh as I listened. I knew that we— dealing solely in the world of task-trained service dogs— were behind the curve about Emotional Support Animals.

Years ago, Nori had made some vague mentions. I knew
the statute predated even the ADA. Around 1988, the
Department of Housing and Urban Development had
decided such dogs were reasonable accommodation for
someone with certain challenges, but the miscellaneous
regulations from the Fair Housing and Air Carrier Access
Act just didn't factor that much for us. It also had nothing
to do with service dog training, so none of us had paid
much attention. Not too many of our clients regularly
used commercial flights anyway, so the recent
proliferation had gone mostly unnoticed.

Usually, we stayed much more concerned about the
ever-present problem of poorly trained–or totally
untrained–dogs harassing our trainees and graduates.
That was plenty. But this was the second time just
recently I'd heard about a trouble on a flight. The
scenario Barb was describing did not cheer me.

"Are we really seeing a big increase?" I asked her a little
later. "Or do you think we are just more aware of it? I
don't remember anything about this until maybe four or
five years ago. Now it seems like it's in the news or
online constantly. I don't know if that's because there are
more of them or just more notice of them."

Barb continued unpacking the training gear from her bag.
She took her time about answering. "I really am not sure.
Way back, I agree, we were mostly a lot less aware of the
details. No help for that when you're new to the game.
But some of this stuff is getting pretty hard to ignore.
Having a dog trying to chew on you two solid hours is
tough to overlook."

I nodded, thinking hard. "But how much did we fly then?
I don't remember ever going on a plane with a dog until
around 1997ish. And I can't think of more than a dozen

of our clients who fly regularly."

"True," she said. "But now we're talking about some pretty pervasive stuff. We didn't get serious about the service dog fakers until Jax. But we didn't really have to. So I think the answer might be "both." More people skirting correct training and more people outright lying and abusing the system."

"So what's going to happen? This can't just go on and on."

"Hmmph." Barb clearly didn't agree with that. "It's already going on and on. You know my position. I think it's raving insanity not to go to some sort of national registration, at least."

Yes, I knew her positions. And her position echoed Sherry's. More and more trainers, however much they disliked the idea of any kind of larger, institutional oversight, were getting truly fed up with the abuse of the ADA. Some of the additional state laws helped, but some of them actually made things worse. We routinely fielded so many requests for "certifying pets" as service dogs we'd gone to straight canned replies, the board having forbidden us to discuss it with people beyond a few carefully phrased sentences. Emotional support animals were not our problem, but they sure were a symptom of the same disease.

Such questions lingered, maybe feeling larger than truth as we went about our daily work. It was not our business to mend the universe, but it sure was our business to protect our clients. That duty seemed to weigh more by the month. If we, as the seasoned pro trainers, were overrun with complications, whatever could we advise graduates?

My mind was still on the dilemma that night as I visited the puppy class. The reason for my visit was to watch the progress of one dog in a whole new classification for us: replacement dogs for families with autistic children. In recent years, our earliest graduates began aging out and passing away. Selecting a replacement–if a replacement was even warranted–was far more complex than replacing a mobility assistance dog. Families who'd originally come to us with a young child now had a rising adult with a very altered set of issues. Functions might be better or possibly way worse, but the entire scenario would surely be very different. The first dog adapted as the child grew, and the changes were readily absorbed. But often growth for the whole family was intensely affected by the dog's help. Losing one to old age or illness was a major life event.

When a service dog was too old to work well, or all the way gone, the one positive was that the parents were now far more experienced as handlers. We, the trainers, were the ones trying to catch up, and where we would have been without Lisa's guidance was anyone's guess, except for a single certainty: nowhere good.

The scene tonight was both reassuring and tension-inducing. Eleven pups bounced and wagged around the training room. Attentive handlers marched alongside. A maze of obstacles confronted the line of medium-sized babies: ladders lying flat, paving stones randomly dotting bunched-up blue plastic tarps. Orange traffic cones held numbered signs with a line or two of typed directions for the handlers to follow. Near the end of the obstacle course, a profuse stream of soap bubbles poured from our new machine. The pups were fascinated. We spotted only one that was rather worried about the bubbles.

In the middle of it all, one adult dog kept pace. He was the reason for my presence tonight. Small, lithe Kona, a beautiful black and tan boy, was the last pending graduate from the group of four we'd managed to salvage two years back. Two years now, since Sherry's surgery. The mental contradiction seemed like two days and two decades at once. If we hadn't exactly bounced back, we were crawling back. Sherry had resumed some work with clients. If not with the vigor and endless hours of the past, at least with enough to keep us moving forward. We were training and graduating fewer dogs now than just a few years ago, but we had a far more focused, determined staff. A collective mental toughness had taken hold among our very unified trainers, but we were still determined to do the most possible good with what we had.

Sherry's ruthless approach now allowed no exceptions. Every client screening, every home visit, had to serve at least two purposes: the original with the client/trainee, but it also had to serve as training for incoming new folks, either a younger trainer or a volunteer social worker. We could not afford to lose any more time developing additional capable staff.

We had three new trainers. None was working full time, but as contractors they filled enough hours to manage immediate needs. I watched from the corner, pleased with what I saw among this group of four-month-olds.

Kona, our upcoming graduate, was working well with his new family. The family's decade of dog experience sure didn't hurt. That major factor balanced our scramble to catch up with the far-different needs of their maturing son. Kona was attending puppy class tonight only to test his response–better to say his lack of response–to all the juvenile nonsense among his cousins. Kona was fine. He minded his own business, honored directions, and stayed focused on his family, so my purpose for the evening was fulfilled. After watching for about 15 minutes, I felt considerable relief and relaxed.

Glory, I'm tired, was all I could think. I leaned back against the wall behind my chair. Though I was doing fewer hours than before, constant fatigue still followed me everywhere. Even paying more attention to the progressive nature of RA wasn't making enough difference. More than the disease had progressed. Medication had also progressed to a point of needing weekly injections and bi-monthly infusions. I knew there would be some joint replacements out there somewhere, but so far I'd muddled along. But tonight I was beyond tired and achy. I could feel the impact of the last decade in every bone of my body. Face it, I lectured myself. It's been getting worse for weeks and you know it.

I heard a flurry of sharp barks on the training floor and reluctantly dragged myself back to the present. Nothing was wrong–Margie, our newest trainer, had quickly brought the puppy problem under control. I leaned my head back, plotting what words to add to my notes, and almost immediately felt myself drifting toward sleep again.

"Julie?" Kona's family stopped beside me. "Is it okay if we go on home?" The husband grinned proudly at his son and dog. The wife looked a little more worried. "I don't think Jon is feeling so well. You said Kona was doing fine with the pups, so...." Her voice trailed off.

"Yes, that's fine," I said. "Go ahead. Sorry. I should have come and let you know before now." I pushed myself up out of the chair. "All of you did very well tonight. I think we'll get your public access test scheduled. Are you comfortable with that?"

Huge smiles broke over both adult faces. "Yes!" They interrupted each other with enthusiasm for a good five minutes as I walked with them to their car.

Truly, I could hardly follow the conversation. I felt dizzy and lightheaded, borderline nauseated. I made it home as quickly as possible and crawled into bed with hardly a pat on the head for my own poor dogs who were frantic with joy to greet me after their day of waiting, waiting, waiting for me to finish with everyone else's dogs.

Chapter 33

"Black holes are where God divided by zero."
—Albert Einstein

By the next morning, general dizziness had progressed to a blinding headache centered in my left eye. I swallowed my limit of anti-inflammatories and Tylenol, and tried to get ready for the day. As I sat in the kitchen, slumped over my coffee, I became aware of Scott's voice drifting from his office. He was on the phone. The lilting cadence of his native French finally registered. I'd forgotten. He was headed out today. Again. This is no way to live, I thought, despairing of our lack of time together.

When he joined me in the kitchen, he knew my thoughts instantly, coming to sit down in the next chair. "Come with me," he pleaded quietly. "Please."

He waited. I couldn't even respond. I knew I couldn't go. How could I possibly? But oh, how I yearned just to climb on the plane with him. At this exact moment, the most compelling attraction might have been the potential for seven or eight hours sleep inflight.

"You've done your share, Julie. Both of you have. The rest of the world is still out there. You've earned some time off. Come with me."

I could not, and we both knew it. There was no realistic way, at least not today, not without ignoring every piece of my commitments. But our parting was highly stressed, highly depressing. Sherry and I had both reached the point where age, physical challenges, and enormous stress were combining to force a slowdown. In previous years, we'd longed for it by preference. Now we were coming to it by necessity. Every month that passed made me understand Nori's decision better.

"What if it means stopping everything?" I'd asked Sherry not long ago during a rare chance to sit in our former hay bale conference room.

"What if we delay that decision so long it gets made by default?" Sherry countered. "Neither of us is worth a third of what we used to be, at least in the practical sense. If we don't make some changes, it will all crash anyway when we do. What then?"

As usual, we had no answer. That one major issue had never been resolved for more than a year or three at a time: most large, successful training schools ran from endowments built half a century ago, in far different economic times, and long before the competing interests of John Q Public's access to GoFundMe.

Besides, we'd known for years we were up against a double standard of operation. Nonprofits were expected to run on business principles, but prohibited both by law and by public perception from using so many of the tools available to regular businesses. In our world, overhead–salaries, facilities, infrastructure, advertising–was evil and to be considered a waste of donor funds.

But substantial funding for overhead was the one and only thing that would rescue either of us–or the school itself–before the work of a lifetime crashed down around our ears.

I watched Scott depart for the airport with my heart dragging somewhere around my shoes. It would be weeks, if not months, before I saw him again. And I could not tell if the crushing fatigue was greater in my bones or my spirits.

I sat at my desk one morning the next week, staring at the large calendar on the wall, transferring notes to the computer. Mostly, I tried to ignore the persistent pain in my eye, and stayed seated as much as possible to combat the dizziness.

Our next litter of pups would arrive in barely a month. I thought ahead to the sleep deprivation, jammed schedules, extra work. We'd carefully maintained the tradition of the bonfire socials with the staff, finding increased recognition of purpose and cohesion among the trainers much improved. We all knew our roles. Inter-staff confidence was at an all-time high. My confidence, however, was taking a big beating: could I shoulder my load?

For me, the worst of the problems since Nori retired: the inexorable push that kept me away from the dogs and chained to administration. The endless responsibility of a function for which I was so inept was eating my morale. But as always, we had no other option.

We'd returned, briefly, to the idea of using professional fundraisers, even despite the looming criticisms of evil overhead. We'd brought in a few for consultation. One or two had volunteered their time to help. But without exception, every one of them wanted to make substantial changes to the function of the school or dogs–or at least changes as to how it was presented to the world. They immediately honed in on what was more marketable above what was real to our clients.

Repeatedly we halted the process, uncomfortable with what amounted to misrepresentation in favor of rainbows and dancing unicorns that might be more profitable. Was there such a thing as too much honesty? I wasn't sure, but I wasn't about to lie to the public for more funds.

Yet, the letters and pleas from parents went ever forward. I sat at my desk that day, trying to read through a few. In the regular mail, a photo of a child in a Cub Scout's meeting beside a small, black German Shepherd wearing a custom Cub Scout cape: *We never thought our son would be part of any group, anywhere, ever. Draga opened a whole new world for him. Her practical help has improved Chris's focus enough that he's taking part in the group well enough for us to be far away on the sidelines. Neither he nor the other members even know we're here. Other members no longer see Chris as an awkward misfit; they're in awe of him and how he can handle his dog. He never lacks for conversation, now, because he can always tell them about Draga....*

Then a heartbreaker: *I saw your training group on the morning news today. It was as though a huge lightbulb went off in my head. I can't send you much money, but my husband and I wanted you to have this small check. As I watched the show and the demonstration, we came to the firm belief that our son would be alive today if we'd had one of your dogs. Last year our boy slipped away from us, literally through a hole under our backyard fence, while I was distracted by an accident with my younger son. He drowned in the nearby river a few minutes later....*

Another plaintive plea: *We met one of your dogs at the*

*grocery store yesterday. It was beautiful to see, but it
made both of us cry. We've been on your waiting list for
almost two years now. Is there anything you can tell us
about when we might get a dog?*

Another letter surfaced... I made a face at it and set it
aside: a note from our attorney detailing the latest in his
struggle to protect us from a lawsuit. Our alleged crime?
Failing to agree to train some woman's poodle.
Reluctantly, I picked the letter back up, scanning his
explanation about the upcoming depositions. I thought
back to the day this woman had first called. Poor
Theresa, still trying to adjust, had fielded the call. "Hey,
Julie," she called to me from the lobby desk. "What's a
hypo-allergenic dog? And why don't we train any?"

"Well, if you want to get technical," I answered, "that
means a dog has been tested and verified not to contain
any substance, in hair, dander, saliva, etc., that a
particular person is allergic to. So it really doesn't apply
to very many."

"So all poodles aren't hypo-allergenic?"

Entering the room from the far side of the lobby, Sherry
heard this and laughed. "No! That goes right up there
with the nasty rumor that they don't shed. It's all a
vicious lie. Remind me to introduce you to Herbert
sometime" Sherry's ancient standard poodle was the bane
of her housekeeping efforts.

"She says she's going to sue us," Theresa announced.

"Because....?" I wasn't overly worried. Yet. We heard
this an average of once a week.

"Because we won't train a puppy she picks out. She says

we're discriminating against her medical condition."

Sherry plopped her stack of folders on the desk. "It won't fly, Theresa. Don't worry about it. That's like trying to sue your dentist for not doing surgery on your knee."

"But why won't we?" Theresa persisted. "I'm not saying we should. I just need to know how to answer better. I didn't know what to say."

I glanced at Sherry. This was her domain.

"You can't be oppositional." Sherry parked herself in a nearby chair and took the time, however scarce, to answer the young trainer fully. "Don't waste your time with rationale. Someone who's looking for a specific answer isn't going to hear the reason. She just wants to push back." Sherry paused and thought briefly. "What do you do with an excited pup who's acting out and bouncing around?"

Theresa answered promptly. "Give him a task to do that you can praise."

"Right," Sherry agreed. "You're not training this caller, so you can't give her a task. But take it in a direction she isn't expecting. Refocus and use a different measure, not what you're arguing about, but something else. Don't contradict. Use something related, but not oppositional. Maybe, for instance, something like "our grants for this year allow us to train 30 dogs, no more. Those are already chosen and in training, so let me give you a couple of other places to try."

"Well that's low," Theresa folded her arms. "Sic her on somebody else?"

"There are places that will consider it. Check your

resources notebook." Sherry pointed to the green binder on the shelf. "That's what it's there for, remember?"

"Yeah, yeah, sorry." Theresa subsided and turned back to her computer screen. "But what if she sues us?"

"Then we'll let the lawyers handle it." Sherry stood up and re-gathered her folders. "Don't burn up your time worrying about it. They won't."

Sherry was almost always right. Except when she was completely wrong. This lady would never convince a jury, but she'd managed to convince a lawyer. By now, we were cynical enough to realize the lawyer had his eye on the likelihood of a settlement from our insurance carrier. Scott was getting riled at the frequency of this technique, not just on our behalf, but for other schools. He was making noise about wanting to shake things up with a counter-suit. I agreed, but it wasn't my decision. Meanwhile, our insurance rates were more than triple what they'd been just five years earlier.

Setting the letter aside, I rubbed my eyes and wondered if I had more ibuprofen in my purse. Was it worth the effort of standing up to find out?

Glancing out the office door, I could see Sherry departing with a group of young trainers for work on public sidewalks downtown. I could literally feel the physical effort she was making to keep going. As though she sensed my gaze, she glanced over her shoulder as she herded the group out the door. She needed to be resting and doing her physical therapy, I thought. I needed to dial it back, way back, or I was going to be in substantial health trouble.

For all the years I'd worked this job, all the gurus, self-appointed and otherwise, had continually hit us over the head with the same advice: "Don't look unstable. Show them the product. Exude confidence. Prove the result. Make them believe you believe it."

Except we are, I thought. I could not summon the energy to be positive. We have been. For years. And the responses just are not there. Are we doomed to fail from burn-out because we volunteer-trained our first score of dogs? It really looked that way.

I dug into the pile of papers in front of me and resumed the endless internet searches for potential grant sources. But barely an hour elapsed when the pain in my eye took over the entire left side of my head. Swirling waves of dizziness hit me in black, disorienting waves. The pain pulsed and radiated until the screen before me blurred too badly to read.

Sometime later, Carol entered the office and found me sitting in the dark, computer monitor switched off. She flipped on the lights and stopped short.

"What's up with you?"

I cringed from the light, ducking my head farther down into my folded arms on the desktop. "Headache." I said. "I'm not feeling so well."

"That's the third time in a week," Carol said. "At least, that would be the third time I know about. Have you been back to the doctor?"

"Not yet."

"Because….?" Carol's voice was impatient.

I couldn't think of anything to say. It took most of a day to see a specialist. What should I neglect in order to pull that off? Sure, I knew it was stupid, yet here I was. Can't dare quit. Can't dare let yourself be accused of faltering effort or… looking unstable.

Yet this choice, too, was moving out of my hands. My vision receded, fever mounted. A full-blown auto-immune flare took me over. Grant hunting went by the wayside as I was fully occupied trying to get out of bed and care for my own basic needs. All I could think of for a positive spin was that this hadn't happened at the same time as Sherry's surgery. Living so close, we'd so far been able to backstop each other, at least enough to keep afloat. But the snarky jokes about "not being 25 anymore" were no longer funny. Neither of us was aging very well.

Chapter 34

"Even strength must bow to wisdom sometimes."
—Rick Riordan, "The Lightning Thief"

I was barely back on my feet enough to walk to the training room when the next litter of pups arrived. Unfortunately, a ruptured uterine horn meant the babies arrived via emergency C-section, and another several thousand dollars of our reserve vanished. In sheer desperation, we jammed a leather sofa into the whelping room. The smooth surface of the cushions and front were slick enough to be disinfected. I could stay there and complete my "recuperation" about 20 inches from the puppies. At least this served the purpose of monitoring pups and taking extensive notes on their varied and oh-so-important behaviors. We solicited help from volunteers several times each day to disinfect the room and do various routine tasks. With their hands and my notes, we got the pups to the seven-week mark.

Yet my dilemma did not resolve. Months passed before I had a full understanding of this latest flare-up. At the moment, all I knew is that the dizziness had broadened into a pervasive balance issue. I could manage only by hanging onto the nearest surface when walking.

Then one day I had the most amazing thought, which came to me right along with one of those infamous IQ self-checks. I was pretty sure I knew a trainer of service dogs. In fact, there were one or two very capable such

dogs residing right in my home. I stared at myself in the
mirror that night. "You are an absolute fool," I said out
loud.

Our school had decided years ago to complete full
service dog training on all the breeding stock we owned,
primarily to remove any possibility of tunnel-vision, and
to prove up, beyond doubt, which dogs were best at the
actual work. I looked away from the mirror to see Rio,
grandson of the long-gone Bear, lying near me, watching
attentively. He'd already worked for years as a demo and
evaluation dog for autistic children. Of all Bear's
progeny, this one had his spirit and character more than
any other. It had shown from his eyes since babyhood.
Noting my extended look, Rio rose to inquire. Then we
departed for the supply closet to find a suitable harness.

I knew I'd face an objection because Rio was the
successful sire of multiple litters, and I was not about to
neuter him. This spay/neuter topic was a hot-button
Catch-22 in the service dog industry Though our school
was only on the earliest cusp of understanding the
potential harm juvenile spay/neuter can do to dogs, we
were adamant that any dog who couldn't complete the
exacting training for service work had no business
becoming a parent. So we stood in (often lonely)
opposition to the common position of that day that all
dogs had to be parted from their hormones before starting
public training. Yes… it was definitely controversial, and
like most such topics, had half a dozen different facets to
consider.

Though the law is entirely silent, most programs of that
day said no intact dogs. Many had specific codes of
ethics prohibiting it. And they had plenty of reasons, the
first simply to standardize dogs to a reasonable common

denominator. Nearly all their clients come from among the general public and were not skilled professional handlers. Beyond that, the issue is not necessarily about *your* own dog. The responses of other dogs, less-well-trained, less stable, more reactive, might make your own dog's good behavior a moot point. The nasty factor of random dog encounters had only grown worse.

Here, however, we were considering a dog who had not only proved up as viable in two different working venues, but who'd done hundreds of hours of work at demonstrations, schools, and as a "tutor" dog for clients to learn from. Nor was I going to be caught by surprise at a strange dog's behavior. So… what, I thought. I can use him if I decide to. Technically speaking, Rio belonged to me, not to the school, but I wanted official approval before starting out.

The easiest route to stop criticism was for us to take the same test as all graduating clients, preferably publicly, so anyone curious could watch. It turned out to be quite fun to re-take the accountability hurdles. Barb, serving as our school's current training coordinator, set it all up with completely objective, third-party oversight. It was an interesting switch of perspective to be the evaluatee instead of the evaluator.

Rio, tall, solid black, statuesque, proficient, took just a few days to adjust to his new harness. I didn't need "heavy" support for walking, but only a touchpoint that would stay available and not move away. I needed to pull more than push. And I needed the function of retrieving anything I dropped. That was a big piece of my trouble; keys, phone, or wallet on the floor had already left me flat on my face more than once. But this was easy for Rio.

I asked myself the same questions I'd asked hundreds of
clients: can you solve this problem with a mechanical aid
or two? Why is a dog the only answer? A quad cane, for
instance, can be as effective–and considerably cheaper–
than a dog for walking support. For me, that really wasn't
true. How I countered my balance issue had more to do
with grabbing and pulling than with leaning down on any
surface. Nobody understood the exact neurological
details, but even my Physical Therapist thought I would
be better served by the dog than by any adaptive device
we could come up with. And if the program was going to
survive, somehow I simply had to get mobile again.

Rio utterly danced through his test, even if I didn't. It
was held at a hardware big box store. He was beyond
thrilled to be out and about with me, working through the
days instead of home waiting for me to return. The tasks
themselves were fantastically easy for him. He strutted
through the lumber section, tail a-wag, eyes flashing.
From housewares to checkout, he carefully positioned
himself exactly where I needed him and didn't let it
waver. He never even turned his head toward the intense
distractions placed in his path: extremely good food,
running children, other dogs. It made no difference. He
was already a pro.

I was glad for the solution, but not so as completely
enthralled as he. The necessity couldn't be more clear,
but I was concerned about the added time of keeping a
dog with me every step of every day. For the uninitiated,
it may seem like a grand, fun thing to "take your dog
everywhere." Reality is considerably less enticing. Most
trainers who hear these remarks sincerely wish to grant
the speaker a few days' education, preferably in really
bad weather.

Rio was now on a much more rigid feeding and elimination schedule to make sure we didn't have private trouble in public. I now had one more big task before leaving the house for anything: get the dog dressed, equipped for the weather, and make sure he was spotlessly clean from nose to tail-tip. Every day's schedule, every single stop, every chair chosen, every transaction undertaken had to be filtered through his needs as well as my own. Was he doing his job but being unobtrusive? Was anyone reacting poorly to his presence? Would he fit under my chair? Was his tail tucked out of the aisle? How many people would stop me to ask questions? Sure, sometimes it led to additional volunteers, perhaps, but it also contributed to a lot of lost time and, often, complete mental exhaustion.

Of course, all these issues had been standard for me for years now. In such issues of being out and about in public, training a dog isn't much different from relying on one. But the one very large change? It was no longer optional. I could no longer consider: "I have exactly 120 minutes to do these three things and make it to an appointment on time. I'm not taking the dog since I don't have time to spend 12 of those minutes brushing him and wiping off mud." No, in the current scenario, if I planned to do the trip safely, and get back minus injury, I had to take Rio. He loved it. The ham.

I, on the other hand, experienced all the normal ups and down of loving it and hating it. Nobody could deny, however, that it was keeping me functional. Daily, I set my teeth and waited for the flare to subside. I could do this. The proof was right here in the harness handle. I was maintaining an abbreviated schedule, filling my role. We were making it. Better days would come. Or so I thought.

My full realization had not yet arrived.

The call came from my rheumatologist while I was grocery shopping. Shelves at home had grown badly depleted while I made frantic rounds of catchup among fosters and clients. The familiar dizzy fatigue pulled at me, and I knew I had to wrap things up. I was supposed to be limiting myself to half days. Hah. Fat chance. It was time to get home. I hated taking calls in stores, and normally would not. But I'd been waiting for this one since mid-morning. I stepped out of the foot traffic, tucked Rio behind a display of dry cereal, and answered the phone.

"Hello?" I didn't bother identifying myself, since I recognized the number.

"May I speak with Julie, please? This is Samantha at Dr. Carter's office."

"This is she." I felt a slight sinking sensation. Not what I'd expected. Usually the receptionist, not the nurse, called to schedule next appointments.

"Very good. I needed to let you know a few things. We've adjusted the prescription drops for your eyes, pending a visit to an ophthalmic surgeon, which I've scheduled for next Thursday at 11:00. Does that time work for you?"

"Surgeon?" It was the only word I could get out.

"Yes, follow-up to Dr. Carter's assessment about the scar tissue and pressure on your optic nerve. We're going to need a long-term plan to blend the treatment with your other meds."

In that single moment, despite many far more specific

medical statements, her word finally penetrated: this wasn't going away. The realization broke over me with a crash that I actually heard somewhere inside my head. I held Rios's harness tightly, hearing his inquiring whimper, but my vision was spinning too violently to see his quizzical, upturned face.

When most people decide to retire, or make a major change in their line of work, it usually happens with much contemplation. Love it or hate it, most of us can best tackle such decisions from a distance–it's approaching you or you are approaching it. Not as many people talk themselves so completely into denial that they get the complete learning experience at once, in public, right beside the Cheerios.

I felt a physical impact from the knowledge. How could I not have seen it coming? Sheer dismay broke over me in waves of increased dizziness. Leaving the much-needed groceries in their cart, I gripped Rios's harness and walked carefully out of the store. I finally understood this was no longer stop-gap. No, I'd changed sides. No longer was I the determined trainer leading the effort and stacking up the analyses. Now I'd be the one with the disability, struggling to compensate, attempting to handle daily tasks taken so much for granted by most of the world's residents.

I sat in my car, too numb for tears. Rio broke the rules, climbing onto the next seat, pushing his head against me and licking my face. He realized my distress and wanted to help. I stroked his silky head, glad for his weight leaning against me.

How many times had I heard the truism that "Nobody really gets it until you get it?" I'd trained thousands of

dogs. Thousands of clients. I thought of all the lectures
I'd given to trainers about how each situation is
completely different, all the urging that they stay aware
of individual struggles, of the enormity of the life-
changing impact. I stared at myself in the side mirror. I'd
been listening without hearing. Watching without seeing.
Now, I told myself, you get to find out just how useful all
that lofty advice was that you've always given everyone
else.

Chapter 35

"No one ever told me that grief felt so like fear."
—*C.S. Lewis*

Knowledge is one thing. Acceptance another. I had years ahead to prove how little I'd ever understood about disability. But I hadn't been wrong that day in the cereal aisle. The changes were permanent. I never returned to full functionality the way I wanted, but I learned lots of coping strategies. In the best traditions of immune system disease, ebb and flow still happened. Better days, worse days, and medium days all came to visit. As months passed, I proved to myself the truth of what I'd glibly told many a client: you have to give yourself time to adjust. Time to adapt.

In tiny increments, I adjusted, at least some, and pushed my productivity upward again. Little by little. On some days I could manage without Rio. Other days I wasn't much good even with him. Hard as life is, it does go on. Normal will eventually find a new center. Much of the long term, however, depends on what other factors in your life also change. I thought I'd faced the biggest, but once again, time was about to prove me wrong.

My normal schedule still contained as much as I could handle of lessons, evaluations, training, and writing, even if my role was now far more supervisory than active. From dawn to dark, trainers rushed from building to building. Clients drove in and out. I was surely less help than I'd been previously, but some things you can't just quit. I'd lashed myself to this mast, and, come what may, the ship sailed on. We weren't growing, but with the new clampdown on matching numbers to dollars, we were holding our own. Every morning, as soon as I could stand on my reluctant limbs, I "rushed" also, even if it was most definitely a ghost of what "rushing" looked like in the past.

Despite dog demands, farm life also still went on, at least after a fashion. Some factors—equine projects, new horses, and long trail rides—were things of the past. We just couldn't. But Sherry and I both had a handful of remaining horses still serving as our personal therapy critters. This crew was mostly older, now due for annual vaccinations. Sherry was also selling a horse, a younger gelding, the last of the horses bred years before. His pre-purchase exam was on the checklist for the vet. She'd reluctantly decided he'd be better off with someone who could spend more time with him.

Today was the day, and I already felt the extra intrusion on a packed routine. But Sherry and I had set the vet appointment weeks before, agreeing to split the farm call fee to pinch pennies as much as possible. I flexed my aching hands as I set out for the barn. On the way, I stopped at the training arena, eyeing the current crop of adolescent dogs. Things looked pretty good today. I made a few mental notes, pulling out my phone long enough to send myself an email about young Pasha. I wanted to see him work around the younger pups soon. He was currently giving some of his classmates a rather hard-looking stare, and we'd need to see if that got worse around more rambunctious or less-known dogs.

I arrived at the barn ahead of everyone else. Sherry

wasn't there yet. I shut the horses into their stalls and decided I should go wake her up. It wasn't yet mid-morning, and I knew she'd been up late driving back from a client assessment. More than once recently, she'd slept through her alarm, wreaking havoc on the next day's appointments. I called, but got no answer.

The vet's truck pulled in as I put the last horse up. I stopped briefly and handed him a list of tasks. He and his tech would get started while I went to wake up Sherry. In any other circumstances, I would have let her sleep. But today, because of the documents for the pending sale, she had to be present. There was no help for it.

Sherry's dogs were in her yard, barking their announcement of my arrival. They're sure wound up, I thought, pulling my truck off the long, winding driveway near the front porch. Those woofs had an abnormal amount of energy. The first hint of real trouble didn't come until I reached the front door and realized the dogs–who had been in the yard moments before–were now leaping against the floor-length window up front. That's odd, I thought. If they'd just been let in, then Sherry was up. Why wasn't she coming to the door?

When two of the dogs reappeared in the backyard, still yelling their heads off, I stopped waiting. Doors were rarely locked here, because what stranger would walk into a house with four noisy German Shepherds? I slipped inside, careful not to let anyone escape. "Sherry?" I called, "Are you up?"

All the dogs went quiet as soon as I got inside. A strange cloud of fear and dread closed over me. Every dog stopped. An odd stillness gripped them. The oldest among them, Karaine, Rios's mom, crouched by my feet.

Then young Jett abruptly raced to the kitchen, raced back, and flung himself against me.

An icy hand gripped me deep in the gut. I believe I knew the truth before I walked the remaining few feet to the corner. Sherry lay on the floor near the door to the backyard. No movement. Rushing to her required a slow-motion, terrified effort that until now I'd encountered only in fiction. It seemed to take an hour to get there.

She must have hit her head. A dog knocked her over. Dozens of excuses crowded my brain in the space of one indrawn breath.

But I knew. I knew before I saw her face, rigid and fixed in death. I knew she was gone. A giant, ragged rip the size of life itself tore my world in two, forever dividing reality into all that had come before that moment and all that would come after. All history faded and all the future grayed out of focus. I dropped to the cold tile beside the best friend I'd ever had, and my world simply stopped. The staggering loss crushed every thought.

All that followed—CPR, frantic phone calls, ambulance, police—was all a blur, and all for nothing. I and the vet, a friend of many years who'd raced over from the barn, stood in stunned silence as events swirled around us. But Sherry was gone.

Family arrived. Arrangements began. Word spread. I was numb to it all, barely aware. When I finally left her house, I was vaguely surprised to see that dusk loomed. Had it been eight hours? Ten? The passage of time had no meaning that day. I stood on Sherry's front porch and looked away to the pasture and woods beyond. The first tinges of autumn gold showed in the tops of the trees.

From here, I could pick out the bend in the river where we'd so often ridden and walked. I noted the lights in the arena beyond the road, and some detached part of my brain realized trainers and volunteers were waiting for me. Waiting to hear…. what?? What can I possibly say? I didn't know what to tell them. I didn't know what would happen. I yearned for Scott's presence. He was surely the only person in the world who would understand the depth and breadth of my loss. But he was thousands of miles away, unable to return anytime soon. Other than that shapeless longing, I don't believe I had a single coherent thought that night. I have no memory of what words I spoke when I finally pushed myself down the steps, into my car, and back across the road.

A week, then another, passed in that same shocked fog. On a quiet night near the end of September, the trainers, staff, and board of our school gathered to wish Sherry goodbye and to celebrate all that she'd been to so many. I listened to Lisa speak to the group, recounting in very personal terms what Sherry's life and focus had been for her and Colby and to so many others. Another of Sherry's lifelong friends told long ago stories that few of this group had ever heard. The president of our board shared other recollections. We all sat together in the training pavilion, looked at photos, told stories, wept, laughed, and speculated.

When the last mourner departed, I once again sat alone under the bright smear of stars and felt no relief. My dogs pressed around me, beginning a few months of altered behavior that they never showed before nor since. With their hypersensitivity to human behavior and moods, they did not play. They did not ramble. Hardly any of them even barked for weeks. They lurked and watched me, so I suppose they knew me better than I knew myself.

In the months that followed, I made my own memorial to Sherry the way I knew she would prefer. When colorful autumn had passed to full winter, I dug up and moved dozens of tiny hickory saplings. I searched our acreages for any I could find that were located with poor chance of thriving, or alongside multiple others and in need of thinning. With help from some of the young trainers, I dug them up and moved them to "our" spots. I planted them along the riverbank. I planted them by the horse pastures. I planted them on top of the enormous hill in the center of my property. I planted a whole small grove near the porch where we used to sit in the evenings and watch dusk lower on the Blue Ridge. I planted so many I knew it would be impossible for all to survive. But they were hardy natives; some would grow tall and shed their golden autumn light for decades to come. I tried to envision that perhaps someday, someone else would enjoy their stunning beauty and, just perhaps, feel the spirit that had lived here. I knew Sherry would have agreed.

Two of her dogs stayed with me. One stayed at her home with her partner. Jett went to live with Trent, who planned a detailed and extensive career for him in the ever-blossoming field of clinical therapy. Jett would also make a fabulous dog for public education. Sherry's horses were more challenging, but within a few months, I'd managed to find homes for all but the one I kept. Others could care for them far better than I could.

Only a few weeks after Sherry's death, however, I could not be surprised to learn that ancient old Karaine, our most successful canine momma ever, had her own ideas about this new arrangement. Somewhere in this journey,

I'd stopped being surprised by how often dogs died shortly after their owners. Twelve-year-old Karaine, daughter of our foundation momma and half-sibling to now-departed Bear, began to decline. When she began refusing food, I hesitated only slightly. The old girl was making her position clear, and my only role was to agree. It was obvious her heart had gone on before. She missed Sherry, and she'd had enough. I stroked her head gently and told her I understood.

Fortunately for us, our dog vet, as well as our horse vet, made house calls. I released Karaine to permanent rest from a pile of pillows on my front porch, beneath the flickering orange and gold of the autumn trees where we'd raised more than 50 of her puppies, as well as many more grand-pups and their next generations. Karaine was never a "licker," but she repeatedly slurped on my hand and arm in those last minutes. I've always wished I could better understand whatever she wanted to say. Because at that horrible, grief-stricken time, I felt a substantial portion of her disillusionment with life.

When the news of Sherry's death first broke, Nori took the next flight from Phoenix and stayed for several weeks to help try to get us all back on track. It was straight volunteer work, and we loved her for it. But as surely as I'd known the hard fact of Sherry's passing, I also knew we were up against a problem for which there was no solution. Many lessons would become clear to me over time. So many pieces of knowledge happened later that I could have put to good work in the chaos of that one autumn. Unfortunately, life doesn't teach lessons that way, and in the shock and grief of the moment, we tried more than one solution that would better have been left alone.

A series of emergency meetings netted few solutions. We tried using less experienced social workers to assist. We tried cross-training the best of our trainers in psychology and human education. But it wasn't working. We'd never acquired a trainer who knew both specialties as well as Sherry had, nor who had her level of dedication. She'd led efforts several times to establish new cross-training, but with limited success. Now there was no more time to try. Not years, not months. We had weeks, or days. We located a single social worker with enough dog training experience to fill a short-term role. But the rate for her services exceeded the total available for all our trainers together for the rest of the year. Our only solution—a poor one, at that—was to double up, sending multiple people to each prospective client, and often to each current client. This was no longer a training exercise overseen by a volunteer Master Social Worker/psychotherapist. This was double and triple wages for every training visit, even during the thin selection of times those different schedules could match. The logistical nightmare taxed program resources beyond any reasonable level.

One by one, the school's beleaguered and overwhelmed board members dropped by the wayside. It was a jolting lesson to me that so many who'd flocked to us in better times were now awfully quick to assign blame for failure to cope. Only a handful of the board members who'd been personal friends to me or Sherry were sticking, many of them paying much of the extra expense out of pocket, just as Sherry and I had done in the far past. It was not sustainable now for them any more than it had been then for us.

We all hoped for better, while simultaneously beginning to understand that we were out of time. If we had both remained healthy, a different set of circumstances might have ruled. But we didn't. And they didn't. Even recognizing I was driving myself to another flare, I struggled to break the cycle. I spent an inordinate amount of time analyzing and reanalyzing myself, the situation, the future, until I knew even Sherry, the uber-psychoanalyst, would have told me to get over it.

I have forever wondered if the school's outcome might have been better if she and I had not been such close friends. Would less grieving have let me come up with better solutions? I didn't think so, but I couldn't rule it out. Everyone, at some time in life, experiences a first loss of another human that absolutely devastates their entire world. For many, it is a spouse. For some, it is a child. For others, it might be a parent. Or sometimes, like mine at that moment, simply a closest friend. The details can be any combination of individual factors assigning massive significance to one person. For me, Sherry's place in my life was absolutely unique, and nothing in my entire life had ever hit me so hard.

The more public portion of our friendship was that, together, backed up by an incredibly competent, dedicated group of trainers, we'd been able to create the proverbial total that was greater than the sum of its parts. We had pulled projects off together that neither of us could possibly have done alone.

The more personal part was much tied up with completely different factors, primarily that Sherry taught me more about life than any other human ever had. And had brought me more joy and contentment in her companionship than most of the rest put together. Losing her friendship and her presence was the greatest-ever blow to my world. Yet something else was dragging at me. I could feel it, but could not articulate the vague undefinable thing. I read. I brooded. I complained. I drove my dogs out of their poor, fuzzy minds.

When Scott finally returned to the states the next spring, a huge part of my mental weight lifted, and I reveled in his support. We spent days dissecting, analyzing, trying to plan. But even as summer passed, and another autumn loomed, I was still grasping for something. I was reaching, questing–and so out of sorts that it remains an amazement the poor man continued to put up with me.

As I'd learned not long ago, understanding the challenge of disability differed vastly from living it. Now I began to learn the life-changing impact of "highly significant death." This was a term I'd come across on a website. What an asinine phrase, I thought. I sat at my desk late one evening, coming to the bottom of the article on a page purporting great insight on grief and loss. In what perverted universe, I wondered, is any human's death not highly significant? I turned from the screen, scanning the tall pile in the special box I'd always reserved for critical issues that had to be solved the very next day. Except the crisis pile was now the largest pile on the desk.

The term from the article lingered and annoyed. Is there any such thing as an insignificant death? Yet there was truth there, and it pushed me hard against realities I wanted to avoid.

I thumbed through the Immediate Crisis Stack, scanning a veritable catalog of needs we had no way to meet. One stood out to me: beautiful little Presley, one of Bear's last sons, a talented, dedicated autism service dog, had died. The family was borderline hysterical. They needed another dog, and they needed it yesterday. And I was helpless. Late into the night, I sat in that chair, scribbling notes, making lists, and casting away one useless idea after another. I knew that for 90% of this paper pile of issues, no answer was available. No matter how much I wanted to, I could not alter that reality.

But I could not make myself stop trying. Sleep and rest, mental and physical, had substantially eluded me for weeks. Tonight would be no exception. I stayed in that dark room, lit only by the glow of a computer monitor. Through the open windows drifted the cool breeze of approaching autumn, welcome in its freshness. Gradually, the racketing chorus of summer crickets stilled. Sometime before dawn, I fell asleep on the pile of papers and awoke only when the dogs demanded to be let outside.

Chapter 36

That next morning, I'd managed a shower and coffee by the time Trent showed up on my doorstep with Jett trailing. He was the last person I expected to see. And the last person I would ever have thought would be the one finally to bring me to my senses.

"You look like hell," was his thoughtful greeting. "What you doing? Lying awake stressing about everything you can't do?"

I was too tired to think of a good answer. It didn't seem productive to tell him I hadn't even bothered to go to bed. Wordlessly, I held the door open and let them in.

Jett and Rio exchanged nose licks and departed for the yard to dig holes. Trent parked himself in my kitchen and started swilling coffee.

"I needed to give you an update," he said, "before I tell the rest of the trainers and the board."

Uh-oh was my only comprehensible thought.

Trent read my silence perfectly. "Yes," he said. "I'm going to take the job with the school in New York. I think it's the right move and I think it's time."

Among the thoughts swirling around my mind, none was

dominant. Barb had announced her retirement just a few days before. She, like Nori several years before, had decided it was time to focus on her new grandson. Carol had turned in her resignation last month, stating an inability to work cohesively with the new social worker. All the reasons were irrelevant, and we all knew it.

I nodded, knowing I had to answer, but still could not come up with anything.

"You haven't said a single word since I walked in here," Trent groused, moving himself from the kitchen table to a recliner, where he appeared to settle in for a lengthy discussion. "Since I'm going to be heading out by the end of the month, do I get to tell you what I think without you going off on me?"

That did it.

"I haven't gone off on anyone for months," I answered testily. "Can't say that I have the energy for it." I refilled my cup and decided on the other recliner. "Say your piece."

"Okay," he started, paused, and started again. "When I started training, you were maybe five or six years into this gig?"

I nodded. "Six or seven, I think."

"And it was another eight or nine before you and Sherry started the autism thing."

"Not really that long," I had to add. "That's just when you started hearing about it."

"So, fine. You were my next-up in the chain of command when I finished my internship. And again when I joined the ranks of the autism army."

"Right," I agreed. "Not my decision on hierarchy the first time, but the second time, I was all the choice you had."

"Yeah, yeah, I know." He waved a hand impatiently. With Trent, it was always hard to tell if he was irritated or just emphatic. "So, what's the main thing you used to tell us back when you were trying to get trainers to understand the autism dogs?"

This required some thinking. "Umm... probably the biggies were how effective we could see it was and how many people were calling."

"And...?" Trent prompted.

"Well, funding, of course. When was that ever off the top of the list?"

"Right. But what else? Broader than all three of those?"

I stared at him blankly, brain exhausted, fogged. I heard steps in the hallway and didn't need to look around to know Scott was listening.

Closing my eyes, I thought back. Opened them again, staring out over Trent's shoulder to the rolling blue-green hills still floating in the morning fog. I heard the shrill call of a Redtail, saw the dark shape diving over the pasture. Somehow, the cry and the streak of motion brought something into focus. I looked back at Trent. "Recognition. Awareness."

He pointed at me. "Bingo."

Relaxing against the overstuffed chair, I felt something loosen inside me for the first time in months.

"You and Sherry outlined all the problems. Showed us all the possibilities." He shifted in his seat and set down an empty cup. "And stressed that none of it would ever change until we could build better recognition, everywhere, that the dogs were a viable option."

I thought about the new trainers' instruction. Brochures. Websites. Media features. Endless preparation to teach them to represent our issues accurate, so we could build... yes... recognition. Because without that, we couldn't get anywhere.

"When you first started doing this, how many schools did anything at all with autism?"

I shrugged. "I really don't know. Hardly any. The internet as we know it now was barely a thing. Research was harder. Publicity was worse."

Trent pressed on. "So, all these dogs, all these years later, what's been our average monthly reach online?"

A light switch flicked on somewhere in the back of my brain. "Hmm. Around 300,000."

"And how many at-least-decent schools are cranking out dogs for autism?"

Another bulb struggled to life. "I haven't tried to count, but I'd guess at least a hundred."

"When was the last time a reporter, or a sponsor, hit you with that old line about "can the dogs really do that?"

I had to pause for thought. "It's been a while. Not sure."

Trent was relentless. "How many other trainers did you guys teach to do this stuff?"

"Forty-three." My reply was the automatic product of years, but the realizations swamping me were new. Dragging myself out of the chair, I crossed to the sink and splashed cold water on my face. Behind me, Trent stayed quiet. I looked at the coffeepot, then bypassed it for ice water. I held up my glass in silent query to both men. Two heads shook, but neither spoke, silence adding weight to Trent's words.

I stood there for another long minute, looking back at the younger man sprawled in my living room. He'd been one of our biggest skeptics. And now?

Is he really right? Were our most important goals already somewhere in the rearview mirror? I was thinking it, but could not make myself say the words.

Trent shot out his trademark challenging grin. "Can I ask the most dangerous question?"

"You probably better not," I said, crossing the room to the patio door. Two big, black dogs bounded onto the porch. I let them in, red dirt, dragging tongues, and all. Jett gave me a passing lick, but went straight to Trent. Rio straddled the water dish and stuck his entire head inside.

True to his nature, Trent forged ahead, despite my objection.

"I just have to wonder if you think you, yourself, or just this group, maybe, has to train every single dog on the planet for the remaining centuries that the world stands?"

I sat down on the floor beside my dog. This was stuff I would not debate.

Trent stood up. "You're the best trainer with a shepherd

I've ever watched operate, but you can't do it now, and
you know it. Or if you don't know it, you should.
Damned sure we all know it. Sherry was the best people
analyzer I ever met, but she's gone. It's time to call it,
Julie. And I mean call it a success: you guys pulled off
what you started. The forward surge is huge, and you had
a gigantic piece of that. You gotta let the rest go."

He was all the way to the door before I could make
myself say the words, muffled against the top of Rios's
head. "I know."

He looked back, donned his sunglasses, and nodded at
me. "Good," he said. "you need to know." He started out
the door. "I'll stop by before I leave." Jett bounded
behind him to their truck.

I waited only another moment before getting up and
walking into Scott's arms. He still held his silence after
months now of trying to make me see. But it took the
oppositional trainer with whom I'd so often clashed to
get through. Tears pushed out, but it wasn't exactly grief.
Was this relief I felt? It took some time to decide. Maybe
a little. But not entirely. It was subsiding tension, the first
true easing I'd felt in years of endless demands.

We'd set out to do something specific. Several
somethings. Had we just become so caught up in the
effort that we didn't bother to notice completed goals? So
we just kept setting new goal lines one after the other?
That's not always a bad thing, if you're honest about it.
But goals require realism, and that's where Trent was
right. The options no longer belonged to me.

A cold nose and furry body pushed between us. We
looked down to see Rio begging for attention. Behind

him, the other dogs lined up expectantly.

"I think," Scott said cautiously, "it's time for us to focus on here and now a little more than the past."

I looked from his hesitant expression to the bright eagerness of the five canine faces nearby. "You're right, of course," I answered, discovering an astounding ability to take a full, deep breath. "Let's take a walk?"

"After you." Scott reached for the door handle.

Before either of us completed the first step, all the dogs were through the dog door and waiting on the grass below the porch. One hand on the porch rail, the other on Scott's arm, I picked my way carefully down the steps. With my now-customary extra care about footing, we all started for the river.

Chapter 37

"Great is the art of beginning, but greater is the art of ending."

—*Henry Wadsworth Longfellow*

Winding down a program with thirty years of history is no simple matter. The calendar had turned and turned again, before we resolved all the logistics. Appropriately, the crisp air of autumn had returned to the foothills when the training room doors closed for the last time.

I sat on the porch alone one afternoon, surrounded by the furry companions that remained. Sherry's memorial saplings were growing taller, shimmering gold in the setting sun. Their sparkles shifted and rippled in the bright sunshine. I could not be in this place, among all its familiar sights and sounds, without thinking of Sherry. I knew I'd never stop yearning to discuss the issues with her.

Life moves on. Whether we like it or not, adjust or not, cope or not. What would she say? For quite a while, I'd had trouble moving beyond that question. The overall decisions about the school carried enormous weight, with life-changing implications for many. Yet, she and I had come to similar conclusions not so long before her death. Even then, we both knew we might have to stop. We just hadn't had a clue how close it was, or how totally the decision would be taken out of our hands. Yet I still spent a lot of time wondering what she would think. As each decision was made, each item clarified and set aside, I grew ever more sure of what her answer would have been.

I was pretty sure she'd say to stop lollygagging and get on with life.

All the trainers had shifted on to other work. Two of the most experienced were staying local and starting private training businesses. With them as the backbone, we arranged a network for graduate team support. We filed the dissolution paperwork with all the right places.

As hard as it might be on the ego, it had been easy to recognize that the clinical therapy components no longer needed me, anyway. Now a broad, far-reaching, diversified effort handled by professionals in private practice, many qualified people would continue the work. In truth, most of them were probably relieved I was going to leave them alone.

Theresa would be the last of the newer trainers to leave for a job with another school. She'd surprised me last month with this decision, having taken an instructor slot with a school in California. Of all the trainers, I'd thought she might have been one of the least likely to stick. But especially since the morning Trent mentally smacked me over the head, I'd deliberately ratcheted up my emphasis on encouraging and coaching the youngest–and most vulnerable. I hoped it had helped. As young as they were, it was the best final investment I could make, knowing they would carry the knowledge and experience forward to others.

Scott stuck his head out the front door. "Hey, what about the blue tub in the hall?"

I turned to him, not even trying to suppress a smile at his disheveled enthusiasm. His eyes had never lost the irrepressible, zesty spark I'd so long admired. "It goes in storage. Everything in blue tubs is for storage."

"Got it." He disappeared with enviable energy.

Just a few more days now, I thought, glancing around me at the farm. We were bound for the road, finally, after years of waiting for our chance to go together. New plans, new locations, new horizons. We would be back to visit, I knew, but never again to a farm, never again to such a beautiful acreage. Not unless we won a lottery and hired staff.

I was ready to follow him inside to help when I saw a mini-van turn into the long driveway. I paused, turned, frowned. Dogs woofed, but stayed put when I gestured. Scott rejoined me on the porch to see Theresa pull to a stop and wrestle a bulky but thin box from the vehicle.

"Hi, you guys!" She hurried up the steps. "Sorry I didn't call ahead. I know you're packing. I won't keep you, but I needed to leave something."

I was glad to see her. Despite my certainty of the decisions, aches of regret and nostalgia still hit hard. Watching Theresa's youthful enthusiasm eased it a little. We were sending Willa and Yancy with her to her new job in Santa Barba. The two young, healthy German Shepherd females had huge potential for future generations of similar dogs. The western school had written to me they were excited to meet them. I'd answered back as best I could, encouraging them to rely on Theresa's input about the dogs.

The two beautiful creatures, one reddish sable, one very
dark black and tan, now rode in regal pride, surveying the
world from elevated crates in the back of Theresa's van. I
couldn't look at them without seeing bits and pieces of 20
ancestors looking back. *It's okay,* distant whispers
seemed to say. *We're still here.*

Theresa pushed the oddly shaped rectangular package
into my hands. "Trent found this on an old video. It took
a while to get someone to lift the picture out and enhance
it well enough to print."

I lifted the top with considerable caution, just barely
peeking inside. I could think of quite a few videos from
the past I wasn't fussy about seeing again. As it turned
out, this was one I never known existed. I went still as I
heard Scott's breath catch.

The view was from the hill above where we now stood.
Sherry and I rode horses across the pasture, moving at a
canter up toward the barn. Scattered around the horses,
front, back, and side, raced several dogs of varied
colors—shepherds, retrievers, and mixes. My hands froze
on the box and my entire being seemed to condense down
into that one frame. There, encapsulated in a single
photo, was the very spirit of my former life: easy
camaraderie, full understanding, and beautiful rolling
hills covered in the orange-gold of autumn. Horses'
manes and tails streamed in bright color against the grass,
while smaller dark shapes ringed the riders like an honor
guard. Long moments passed before I could move. I
thought I might cry, but realized the emotion swelling in
me was bigger than grief. Something inside surged up
and forward as my eyes held on this peculiar treasure, the
photograph of a lifetime. Probably several minutes

passed in continued silence. Finally, I tore my eyes from the photo and looked up at Theresa in amazed silence.

"It's from all of us," she said simply. "Nobody knows quite what to say, but we all understand at least some of what you both put into everything that happened."

"Thank you." I said, quietly and carefully. It seemed horribly inadequate, but words just weren't especially useful at this moment. I couldn't make them work for the sunburst this picture brought to my heart. "I am... so glad to have this. I think you know how much."

"Yeah," Theresa answered. "I do. I think I really do." She shuffled her feet a little and jammed her hands into her pockets. "I had a pretty big argument with Valerie Anderson last week."

"Valerie...?" I thought about the former puppy foster and felt actual resentment that anything would jar this moment. "Why in the world? What's to argue about at this point?"

"Well, I went with Barb to the dog show, and Valerie happened by. I heard her talking to Barb. Val was going on about why you quit training, and why she thought it was a bad choice because you'd–and I quote– 'abused the effort' from people who'd volunteered so much time. Barb tried over and over to head her off, but she just wouldn't quit. I lasted until she said that all of us had always made bad choices about fundraising. Then we really got into it."

I waited, not being able to think of much constructive to say. These were things I did not want to hear, and no longer wanted to think about. I'd done my time with the frustrated and the vindictive, and had no desire to relive any part of it, even through a brief recollection. Scott's hand pressed against my back, out of casual view. He understood, totally, and, like me, wanted this part of the discussion just to go away.

Theresa was no longer scuffling her feet. She knelt on the porch and started petting Yelda, plush coated black daughter of Rio, who was leaning on her legs. "I told her she knows nothing about it. We didn't part on very good terms. I just thought maybe you should know about it, since I'm leaving and she's running her mouth a lot."

"You're right, Theresa. She doesn't know much about it. But she knows her own part, and that probably feels like neglect of her effort." My mind stayed only partly on the conversation, my eyes still riveted to the big photo, my hands gently caressing the frame. "It's impossible to give someone full context, even more so when they don't want context."

Silence.

I took hold of myself, looking over at the young woman, recognizing the frustrated disillusionment on her face, exactly as it had so often been on my own. "Theresa, they see and hear their own experience, and that's valid too. It can take some time to see the end of one thing as the start of another. Hopefully she'll get there on her own. Nobody can do it for her."

The young trainer's hands went motionless on Yelda's fur. "Do you regret it? Do you ever wish you hadn't pushed so hard?"

I heard the implied question behind the spoken one. I

understood her exact meaning. We'd all wondered what additional toll the stress and schedule demands had taken from Sherry. But I'd come to terms with that months ago. If I hadn't done my part, Sherry would have gone ahead on her own. Potential toll would have been the same, and any good would have been less. I looked up and met Theresa's eyes carefully. I wanted to be sure she was listening.

"No. I don't regret it. And I don't believe Sherry did–or would have–either. Whatever anyone says or thinks, I don't resent our choices. Things, us, the people, the program… I mean, every part of everything is completely different now. We have to deal in reality, not wishes. It's the same for you. Where you're going and what you'll be doing will be very different from here."

I stepped backwards, deliberately pushing into Scott's support, grateful for it. "But that's life, Theresa. Mine, yours, and Sherry's when she was still here. Even before she died, we both knew we might not be able to go on."

I paused, studying the young woman, who was obviously still struggling with resentment. It had been my job to teach her not just to train, but to cope with results of training. It seemed so important to communicate this one last lesson. Maybe she could understand sooner than I had.

"Theresa, do you remember what we talked about in your first trainer orientation meeting? That very often, maybe most often, we don't build programs according to a particular plan or ideal?"

"Yes," she answered slowly, clearly thinking and remembering. She fixed her gaze on the deck planks.

"You said that new efforts, new programs, tended to grow up around whatever resources were available, whether or not you–we–thought it was ideal."

"Exactly," I said. "That's what I hope you'll remember. None of us gets a magic wand. You do the best you can with what's in front of you. Then you take the results, and you do the best you can with those. Thirty or 40 years later, you'll be in a whole new place, and you'll realize that's what shaped your entire life. Everybody's seen the memes: "Life is what happens when you're making other plans?""

Theresa nodded slightly, but didn't look up.

I had to press a little more. "I can say all this now without the same frustration. But lots of times I've felt all the disappointment you're feeling." Reaching behind me, I grasped Scott's hand, wanting to be sure he heard me too. "But now the disappointments are way overshadowed by knowing about people who benefitted. That includes us, the people who did it. We all learned, grew. We didn't always choose how everything happened, but good things happened anyway because so many people chose to do their best with what we had."

I took a long breath, knowing I was hitting the limits of reasonable understanding for one so young. Time to be more direct.

"Theresa, for a long time we thought we'd build a big, permanent school to carry our ideas into the future. But as things turned out, we built you guys instead–the whole big group of you who knows how to train and reach others. And we built them." I gestured to the dogs. "We all built them, right?"

Theresa finally met my eyes. She stroked Yelda again and nodded. This much she could apparently agree with.

I strained to find a last few words, knowing that I also had to let this go, let her learn it on her own if she wouldn't hear me now. "It's different than we planned, but who knows that it might not be better in the long run. How can anybody ever regret that?"

"I guess not." Theresa slowly rose. "Maybe it's harder for me to see. I barely made it past my apprenticeship and here we are."

"But you did make it," Gently touching the canvas again, I faced her. "You've worked with dozens of people in the last few years, and you did very well. Spend some time on your drive thinking—and I mean with an open mind—about the people you've already helped. Please? I think part of your fun can be keeping them in your mind while you see where the new job takes you. You might find lots of benefits that never would have happened here."

I glanced sideways at the print. "You 'youngsters,' as we call you, and the young breeding stock dogs, are the ultimate legacy that Sherry, Nori, I, and the other old farts get to be proud of. Go get it done, and don't let regrets drag you down."

She finally smiled. "Okay. I promise I'll try. Is that good enough? I can't pretend I don't wish I still had this job."

"Yes, that's fair. Keep me updated, will you?"

We finished our goodbyes, and I watched her van, heavily loaded, ease down the long, curved driveway. The white vehicle glinted between the brightly colored trees, then was gone. The waving golden leaves of the hickories seemed to send their own farewell.

Scott patted my shoulder. "I'm going to walk down and check the mail," he said, departing without another word.

I spared a passing thought for how well he knew me, then returned my attention to the beautiful creation in my hands. Raising it up again, I turned it to the sunlight, watching flickers play across the stilled forms just as they had so many times in real life. Carefree relaxation and blended lives of varied creatures came to life on the canvas. The varied shapes and colors of the group against a stunning background of rolling foothills, golden hickories, and blueish mountain peaks. It was a perfect capture. An essence that defined an entire era.

A furry bulk pressed against my leg. I reached down to stroke Rio, feeling his gaze probe. Ever sensitive, he studied my unusual stillness. My hand stayed on his silky head, and I picked out his grandfather on the canvas. Caught in the long-ago moment, Bear raced along with the horses, just off my stirrup. This single frame portrayed so much of my life that was now history. I knew many a future hour would pass while I reveled in the photo and the era it represented. I didn't set it down again until I heard Scott's tread.

He inspected the piece again over my shoulder. Silence held for a long minute. Or two. Or three. Finally, he spoke. "We've been waiting for the right day. I think this might be it."

I hesitated, but only briefly. I nodded. A few minutes later, we set out for the familiar curve of the river where generations of dogs had frolicked and learned. We

carried canvas tote bags, his two huge, my one barely
medium. The entire contingent of shepherds followed.

Through long years of aging dogs and corresponding
losses, both expected and unexpected, we'd delayed the
inevitable with cremation rather than burial. Many, many
losses. Many, many unresolved circumstances. Triumph
and heartbreak, relief and regret. Our dogs. Clients' dogs.
Strays, puppies lost, retirees who finally came home.
Nothing had ever felt final enough. We were never sure
where or how to bury whom. But things were different
now.

We stopped along the high banks of red clay, above
smooth pools and churning whitewater, under flickering
golden light from tall autumn canopies. Here we had said
our final farewell to Sherry over three years before.
Today, we paused long. I closed my eyes in a brief, silent
word of thanks to each of the wonderful dogs we were
here to honor. Then we reached into our bags over and
over, bringing out each precious container, again and
again emptying clouds of ashes into the puffs of breeze.
Silver they sparkled, carried on the wind to the water, the
trees, the sky and mountains above. They drifted, rose,
fell, and only gradually flew from our sight with last
winks and dips. Scores of dogs, hundreds of affected
lives, each carrying a joy, a story, and accumulated
wisdom for the ages to remember. For a long time
afterward, we stood silently still, our own tribute to the
value we'd been gifted here.

Eventually, I felt Scott's arm on my shoulders. "You did
all you could, Julie. You did more than you really should
have tried. But Trent was right. What you and Sherry and
the rest did was a big pebble splashed into a big pond.

The ripples will go on forever."

"I know," I admitted, shifting my gaze to the gold canopy above. "I really do know it. And I know it's time to go. But it's still hard to leave. Especially this spot right here. It's so beautiful here. So peaceful."

"Of course you'll miss it. How weird would it be if you didn't? Everything you feel is a measure of what you put into it. That's why it hits you so hard."

As was so often true, he could summarize what I couldn't. Yes, you value most what you strive for most. But there was more. Everything this place represented to me was far greater in its totality than any one person's impact, especially my own. Like minds together almost always magnify their combined effects on others. To me, our combined legacy was rooted right here. Whatever the future held, far from the Blue Ridge, this knowledge would stay. And I knew it would always be intertwined with pride in a determined group who'd worked so hard to meet critical needs.

If I'd learned anything for sure in this place, in these years, it was a bone-deep certainty that the lives you touch, both people and their non-human companions, are what matter in the end. The fact that an era closes does nothing to change that significance. For the years we were able, an imperfect group gave their best effort to such a goal, and the influence would carry forward forever. In these last moments, gazing one last time at the astonishing beauty of this place, I knew it like never before.

"Come on, kid," Scott punched me lightly on the shoulder. "The world awaits."

Looking up at him, I suddenly knew it really did. Who knew what was out there? Any more than I had known what was right here when I first rode down this trail more than a quarter of a century ago. "All right." I returned the fake punch. "You're on. Let's go."

I looked around for one last moment, knowing it was my final view. But I would never forget. I left part of my soul in those peaceful woodlands that day, yet we walked away secure in the knowledge that the richness of life we'd known there could never truly end as long as it lived in memories.

~~~~~~

Acknowledgements & Clarifications

*"What we once enjoyed and deeply loved we can never lose,
for all that we love deeply becomes part of us."*
—Helen Keller

From earliest consideration, this story provoked so many assumptions, even among my closest friends, that I knew clarifications would have to happen. Using the phrase, "based on a true story" can prompt far too many projections for a novel that has some memoir qualities. The parallels of this book to my own past are plentiful. So, first, you can be sure every possible question has already been asked about exactly how much of the story is true. In order to answer that, we need to define some terms.

How much of the book is "true," meaning told as actually happened in real life? None. It is fully fiction, correct in historical context, but with fabricated details and people, deliberately steering away from actual events.

How much of the book is "true," meaning a faithful portrayal of life inside an average service dog school of that era? All. Despite being fiction, *Shepherds of Our Hearts* hopefully presents the reality and lifestyle faced by schools, clients, and service dogs roughly between the years of 1988-2018.

No doubt some of the story will sound familiar to almost any service dog volunteer or employee, but that's because of the commonality of factors. It's realistic fiction, not fantasy, and that means using typical scenarios, some of which play out scores of time in a single year.

Most novelists write from what they know and I'm no exception. The flow of events—albeit greatly simplified—does loosely follow the general idea of the training group with which I spent most of my adult life. But for this project, I gave myself a specific challenge: could I tell a made-up, "parallel universe" story well enough for readers to become immersed in such a multi-decade journey? I wanted to show how life happens for thousands who live in, work at, develop, and run service dog schools. I wanted readers vicariously to live the completely common highs, lows, struggles, and triumphs. Others will judge how well I managed, but some advance readers responded as though I'd written a memoir. No, I definitely didn't. The whole timeline and all details differ vastly different from real life—all of which would be quickly apparent to anyone who ever worked with me or Sherry.

As a tribute, a handful of canine characters in this book were given the names of real dogs who were my incredible four-footed instructors, notably Abby and Athos who taught me much, and Bear the Second, who belonged to me from the day of his birth to his death more than 14 years later. He was easily the most magnificent, talented, reliable dog for working with autistic children that I ever encountered. Another such dog is Tucker, who was a real-life prototype for clinical therapy, though the true saga was very different from this storyline.

All this book's staff, fosters, clients, and volunteers are products of my imagination, though they, also, are collectively typical of a plethora from my past. As with

the dogs, a few of the fictional humans were named—
with permission—in honor of their real-life counterparts,
and each deserves a word of acknowledgment.

First and foremost: the exceptionally intelligent,
compassionate persona of Sherry, who was my co-
conspirator in a quest to engineer wider use of service
dogs for autistic children. My original motive for this
book was a wish to give her at least a small portion of the
credit she never received in her too-short life. The beauty
of the setting where we lived was real enough. We did,
indeed, share our work, our dogs, our horses, our
bordering acreage, and our porches.

Lisa, also a friend from real life, does lead Project Hope
Foundation along with her co-founder, Susan. Lisa taught
us to broaden our perceptions of autism and of how dogs
could serve. She coached our long-ago entry to clinical
therapy, graciously and professionally not allowing us to
self-destruct. By teaching us to extrapolate, she
ultimately spread impact many times farther than would
ever have happened otherwise. Project Hope Foundation
now has nine separate campuses serving a broader
spectrum of needs than ever. They remain my go-to
referral for any family with challenges from autism. I
couldn't send this story into the world without
acknowledging the vast role Lisa and her son, Colby,
played.

Finally, Scott's fictional character was much like his
own, central to my life in every way. He deserves eternal
credit for his forbearance, his solid, unfailing support–
and for not selling me to the circus.

But what drives a theoretically sane author to attempt
such a blend? The idea for *Shepherds of Our Hearts*
came to me during the intense grief after Sherry's death. I

had so many regrets. Between losing her and my own declining health, frustration and anger were immense. Yet I knew other people in other schools struggled in ways that were extremely similar. Our situation was hardly unique. I believed a story like this one needed to be told. It wasn't possible for it to be a memoir, but I hoped to get it close enough to represent common truths.

If you are one of those involved with such schools, you already understand All The Things. If you're not one of those involved, here's a challenge: do you know someone who *is*? Find yourself a bonfire, a fireplace, a stack of hay bales, or even a good restaurant table. Ask your friends to tell you—with brutal honesty—their very worst and very best moments. I dare you. You might get some surprises.

As the time approaches to stop typing and call it finished, I am sitting in a room where the walls are covered with photos of dogs. Rows upon rows of sweet faces, splendid in their attention to their humans, all stilled now to eternal quiet. I am certain their presence lingers, and I feel their scrutiny like never before. Despite the fictional nature of this book, it's the collective spirit of these incredible creatures I yearned to portray. I hope I've presented their character and essence with justice. These dogs changed the world for many people, but most especially for me. We understand essentially nothing of what comes after death, but I dream of reunions, hoping that if their souls remain aware, they know how much good they did and how greatly I miss them.

By my feet lie a few remaining progenies. Many of the extended family are still out there serving around the globe. But for me, for "us," the old fellows near me now are the last of the line. Considering the surging rates of disabilities, my enduring regret remains the lack of resources to continue the impact those dogs made. Since they can no longer do so in person, I'm hoping now they can assist in a new way. A percentage of proceeds from this story they taught me to write will support Project Hope Foundation. After all, that adult housing still needs to be built.

Inside my mind I still take long walks along a faint trail in the Blue Ridge foothills, where a whitewater creek froths below, where quiet rules, nature surges, and rich woods still spice the autumn breeze. I linger there often in the halls of my memory, believing that even when I am gone, perhaps especially when I am gone, faint echoes of laughter, hoof beats, and barking dogs remain. I hope someone walks there still. I hope silent beauty still seeps into souls. Far above, I know blue mountains still stand guard over remnants of a lane where many a delighted child ran free with a watchful dog. I will always remember. I will always treasure.

For each reader, I hope this story can spread the peace from that remarkable place outward to you.

—Julie Nye, December, 2020

Cover

A special word of thanks to multiple gracious cover models, two- and four-footed! All books need good cover art and who could be better than a few of those who helped inspire this story? Here are black and white representations from the covers, with labels.

Below/front cover: real-life dogs from my past.

Opposite/back cover: people and dogs with identifying information—or not—according to their individual preferences. Each is from my (non-fiction) former work among service dogs.

Photos

Back cover photos counter-clockwise

Lyric Rogers and Sherry Brown with "Leo" in 2008.

Kaelynn Partlow, autistic therapist and best-selling author of *Life on the Bridge*, as a service dog trainer with "Hotshot," *c.* 2013.

Liz Kreiser, LCSW and psychotherapist who uses Animal Assisted Therapy in her practice, as a service dog trainer with "Paddy," *c.* 2011.

.

Steven Bunn with "Liam" in 2018.

(continued)

Sherry Brown and Julie Nye with some of their horses and dogs, *c*. 2001.

Colby Lane with "Cleo," *c*. 2007.

Bryant with "Imme," *c*. 2008.

Suggested Resources

<u>Dog Training</u> *All* working dogs must have an excellent, *reliable* foundation. If you are looking for high-quality advice, I suggest starting with Connie Cleveland's online materials, many of which are free. *obedienceroad.com*

<u>Autism</u> If you'd like to learn more about autism, I suggest starting with these two options:

- Project Hope Foundation, led by co-founders Lisa Lane and Susan Sachs. *projecthopesc.org*

- Kaelynn Partlow's book *Life on the Bridge*, which can be ordered from any bookstore with its ISBN number (979-8991035507) or it can be purchased on Amazon.

(continued)

- **Nonprofits** If you're interested in my general opinion on the state of USA 501(c)3s, I completely agree with Dan Pallotta's superlative overview in this 2013 TED talk: "The way we think about charity is dead wrong."

  youtube.com/watch?v=bfAzi6D5FpM&t=23s

About the Author

Julie Nye established a life-long interest in dogs, horses, and storytelling before she started kindergarten. After college, she converted her growing dog expertise into volunteer involvement with multiple service dog organizations, eventually becoming a trainer, a board member, and the co-founder of a specialty program for training dogs to work with autistic children. She has been a freelance writer since 1986, with a variety of books through different publishers.

Nye, who makes her home in Michigan, is pictured above with her two German Shepherds: Voelker, a retired service dog, and Ajo, a young upstart with absurd amounts of energy.

www.ingramcontent.com/pod-product-compliance
Lightning Source LLC
Chambersburg PA
CBHW060817120726
47909CB00006B/1956